"Audacious, demanding, terrifying and yet also astonishing and deeply human"

ALAN MASSIE — T

"*For Emma* enters the current con and Big Tech companies, in desigr with the ultimate ability to play C about the most eternal of emotions

KIRSTY WARK — FRON

"A harrowing, poignant but at times perversely funny dystop-ian tale of transhumanism."

THE SUNDAY POST

"Thrilling, dystopian and inescapable... A multi-faceted and compelling story about the society we live in."

ANDREW GALLIX — IRISH TIMES

"A masterpiece… *For Emma* is an extraordinary novel; a treatise of love and loss, the terror of the modern world and the sprung, high-tech trap humanity has set for itself. This would be more than enough: awe-inspiringly, it's also a page-turning thriller, and it confirms its author as the eminent fiction writer of our times."

IRVINE WELSH

"Absolutely wonderful … riveting, sad, mad and terrifying."

TERRY GILLIAM

"*For Emma* is as disturbing as it is convincing, a tale of love and guilt and grief, and an apt tract for our chaotic times."

JOHN BANVILLE

"A grieving father becomes an avenging angel. A great novel which captures and questions our times. I loved this cinematic and compassionate book."

MARK COUSINS

"Ewan Morrison's harrowing and beautiful new novel, *For Emma*, is an early warning system for the future. In that way, a worthy successor to *Easy Travel to Other Planets*, *Neuromancer*, and, of course, *Brave New World*."

DAVID SHIELDS

"A beautiful, intense, challenging, scary and very, very timely book."

LAURA ALBERT

"*For Emma* is a howl of alarm in the face of techno-optimism and a reminder too that our great literary writers ought not to be replaced by machines... We need writers like Morrison to think through the present in order to better understand the near future — literature shakes us from our acquiescence and reminds us that horror is all too proximate to hubris."

NINA POWER — COURAGE MEDIA

"This book scared me like no horror story ever has, because its monster is right in front of us, right now, eating us slowly while we cheer."

ISAAC MARION

"*For Emma* is a brilliant book that you will devour. Its compelling exploration of love, loss, and the haunting power of technology and morality makes it a must-read, delving into the highly relevant and intriguing intersection of humanity and advanced AI."

BRUNA PAPANDREA

"*For Emma* evokes the full spectrum of human emotion, the joy of fatherhood, the grief, the despair at the loss of a child, pain, love. At its heart, it's such a poignant meditation on love, loss, on regret and fatherhood in the digital age ... such a beautiful, disturbing book."

LEN PENNIE — ARTS MIX, BBC RADIO SCOTLAND

"A *Falling Down* for the tech bro age - by one of our finest and most challenging novelists"

IAN RANKIN

"Josh Cartwright, the beguiling protagonist of *For Emma,* is reminiscent, with all his paranoia and eccentricities, of the tortured heroes of Philip K. Dick. But this tale should not be categorized as *speculative*. Rather, this brilliant and frightening novel is more like science *fact* than science *fiction.* So some day soon when we're all backing up our brains and things get even crazier in our mad world, we'll remember that Ewan Morrison tried to warn us."

JONATHAN AMES

"Hold onto your seats for a cracking good ending, which I did not see coming, yet which I felt I should have seen coming – the best kind."

LIONEL SHRIVER

"A devastatingly accomplished and cinema-literate nightmare of culture-induced and morally bereft psychotic breakdown: the state in which we are all now registered, observed and disenfranchised. The poetry of paranoia, here, is so compelling, that we are forced to conclude that the very act of tale-telling, authorship, is being dictated by a terrifying otherness. Now read on. Please."

IAIN SINCLAIR

"As pacy and compelling as a thriller, *For Emma* is also a skillful exploration of that area where our genuine fears about the global reach of tech giants meet a natural tendency to paranoia. How worried should we be about the rapid advances in artificial intelligence currently underway? Emma's story feels compelling, moving and terrifyingly plausible."

MIRANDA FRANCE

"If there is a braver novelist in Scotland than Ewan Morrison I don't know who it is. The scenario Morrison depicts in his latest work is terrifyingly possible, perhaps just around the corner, or even already here. *For Emma* is a fast-paced techno-thriller, but it's also a love story about the despair that failed love brings. And maybe, too, it's a warning, that in the name of progress we may be powering up the instruments of our own destruction as a species."

JAMES ROBERTSON

"*For Emma* is an astonishing, bold novel ... heart-rending, but also complex, visceral and angry ... unlike anything I have read before – a sympathetic, yet abject account of violence. Morrison's eyes are on the horizon. This is the novel for our times, a mordant, coruscating yet exhilarating account of where we will be, sooner than we think."

NICHOLAS BLINCOE

"Heartbreaking and harrowing, this is a suspenseful journey into a family's tortured past and its nightmarish present. Ewan Morrison's attention to the details of parental love and responsibility make this an unforgettable book."

ATOM EGOYAN

"*For Emma* is a haunting work, resonating and echoing for a long time after reading. Although concerned with AI, it is a human book, both grief soaked and love filled. In *For Emma*, Morrison has created a true masterpiece, one that endures as testament to his concern for our endangered humanity.'

ALI MILLAR

"Just as Ewan Morrison was ahead of the field with pandemic fiction and novels about ideological capture, so he is the pioneer of AI literature in Scotland. Terrifying, engrossing, masterful. The most inventive and original writer we have."

ALEX LINKLATER

"A stunning book. Deeply touching. A beautifully crafted page-turner. I love how we're sucked into a dark eloquent vortex, part gothic/sci-fi/ and detective novel, asking essential questions about AI, but also what it means to love and to stay alive. It has stayed with me deeply, particularly those passages about the father and daughter, the intimacy of grief. As relevant as *Frankenstein*."

SUSANNA CROSSMAN

"Thrilling, unsettling, and fundamentally humane, *For Emma* is an explosively timely novel. A shifting metafiction of unreliable narration that knowingly calls to mind the gothic horror of Stevenson and Hogg, while relentlessly fixated on the anxieties of our social age. A disturbing and unflinching glimpse into disillusionment and conspiracy and a techno-dystopian warning about the terrors less of the future, than of the now."

KEIRAN HURLEY

"Ewan Morrison is a mesmerising writer and *For Emma* is his best book yet. It's a stark, vivid warning of darker times ahead; a prescient novel about the things that make us human - empathy, memory, longing, regret, guilt - slipping through our fingers, eradicated by morally malignant technologies. A novel with a universal truth: only love can break your heart. My determination to improve as a writer is its lasting gift to me."

DAVID F ROSS

"*For Emma* is a gripping novel of a near future that is almost upon us, and that this dire warning seeks to prevent. Here's hoping."

KEN MACLEOD

"*For Emma* is an achingly human plea for caution"

RACHEL REES — BUZZ

"An incisive novel for our times, written with wit and sensitivity, it tackles huge issues about the future of humanity with great heart."

DOUG JOHNSTONE

"While this is science fiction – for now – underneath the paranoia about technology and transhumanism there is an all-too-human tale of love, regret, addiction and terrible grief."

ALISTAIR BRAIDWOOD — SNACK MAG

"A brilliant, breath-taking book. *For Emma* is at once a gripping techno-thriller, a chillingly plausible near-future nightmare, and a moving meditation on loss and grief. Reading *For Emma* is a terrifying glimpse into a dystopia so close, we can't avoid it."

BRAM E. GIEBEN

"A spectacular & terrifying novel, from one of Scotland's best writers."

JENNY LINDSAY

"Anyone who enjoys great writing and storytelling, and high quality speculative fiction, should read *For Emma* by Ewan Morrison. It's as terrifying as it should be. An apocalyptic vision of humanity enslaved by Big Tech. And the desire to fight back."

KEVIN WILLIAMSON

"Haunting, eerie, and kinetic, *For Emma* is equal parts sci-fi, dystopia, family tragedy and portrait of an unravelling mind."

MARY HARRINGTON

"A worryingly convincing vision of our imminent present. Ewan Morrison is our Michel Houellebecq."

GAVIN BOWD

FOR EMMA

EWAN MORRISON

LEAMINGTON

This is a work of fiction. Names, characters, places, and incidents are either the product of the author's imagination or used fictitiously. Any resemblance to actual persons, living or dead, events, or locales is entirely coincidental.

British-Library-Cataloguing-in-Publication Data
A Catalogue record for this book is available from the British Library

Set in Portugal, Oklahoma

First published in 2025
Leamington Books
32 Leamington Terrace
Edinburgh

tiktok.com/@leamingtonbooks
bsky.app/profile/leamington.bsky.social
x.com/leamingtonbooks
instagram.com/leamingtonbooks
linkedin.com/company/leamington-books
youtube.com/@Leamingtonbooks
facebook.com/leamingtonbooks

ISBN: 9781914090967

Printed in United Kingdom by Bell & Bain Ltd, Glasgow
leamingtonbooks.com

'The death of a child is the greatest reason of all
to doubt the existence of God.'

Fyodor Dostoevsky
(1821-81)

'With artificial intelligence… we are creating God.'

Mo Gawdat
Former Google Executive
(1967-)

Editor's Note I

Working as an editor in non-fiction in one of the five major corporate publishing houses for the last eight years, I have produced titles in women's lifestyles, well being, self-help and social equity; with a number of these titles having made a positive contribution to the publishing house and, I can only hope, to wider society.

It came as a shock then, to have been targeted with the suspicious email that arrived on the 1st of October last year. We now know this date as that of the devastating San Francisco bombing, and the email was sent by someone claiming to be the therapist of the actual bomber.

The email's title was 'please help get this information out there' and it contained a link to a cloud storage site with a large file and a click to download prompt.

Naturally, I was alarmed, for why on earth would the 'San Francisco Bomber' via his therapist, target me? What could possibly have made him think I would be sympathetic to his horrific act? And to make contact in such an unprofessional manner; it was a surprise that it had even got through the office spam filter.

Thereafter, my scepticism arose; perhaps this was one of those horrid 'Whatever you do - do not click' phishing scams the IT department is always warning us about? Or maybe I was one of hundreds of recipients in a mass mail-out hoax aimed at all the publishing houses?

Days passed and it was impossible to decide whether to open the email or not; for what if it was even an inter-office prank? A joke made in poor taste, given the tragic loss of life caused by the 10/01 bombing? I didn't want to be the naïve person responsible for infecting the entire office with a virus, especially while the European headquarters were streamlining the workforce due to new technology.

So with much swithering, I left the email in the inbox, unclicked, for several weeks. It should be admitted that at the time I had been passed over again for 'career development', and then the idea struck: what if this this file turned out to be authentic materials created by the actual bomber? Might this not make for a rather controversial non-fiction title; just as the bestsellers *Our Father's Lies* and *Time to Kill* had just the year before?

It was for this and other reasons that I decided not to share the email or link with IT or with any senior editors. Then, after three cautious weeks, on the lookout for gossip about anyone else receiving such an email there was still not a peep on coffee break, or lunch break, not in meetings, not over cake break, or after-work wine; and not a single word on any news channel either.

So, finally alone and slightly after hours, with a pick-me-up of gluten-free chocolate beetroot cake for courage, I decided – 'Why not just open the dodgy thing then?' The risk was taken, the mouse clicked, and the large file downloaded.

To my great relief it was not a cyber-virus or bank scam. To my even greater surprise the file comprised sixty-four low-resolution home-video clips, shot on a webcam of an out of date laptop, and made over thirty days from the 1st of September to the day of the bombing on 1st of October. Even more alarming was the fact that in each recording a middle-aged man claiming to be the bomber spoke directly to camera, recording what is, in effect, a month-long video diary in the countdown of days until the terrible act.

In each of these recordings the bomber starts 'Hi Emma,' or 'Hey Em,' effectively talking to his daughter, Emma Henson, a woman just a few years younger than myself, whom my research later showed had died one year previous to the recordings in what might possibly have been suspicious circumstances.

It was troubling, of course, but if the recordings were authentic, they could be what one might have called (in the parlance of a less linguistically sensitive era) 'a huge catch'.

Certainly, I had to be cautious as a great many AI-generated deep fake videos had been circulating, with some being disastrously mistaken for authentic footage in the actual news, and three weeks after the bombing there was so much wild speculation and fake news about the bomber, with many made-up images circulating as vulgar memes.

However, one fact gave me reason to believe that the videos were authentic: the original email with its link, had arrived on the night of the first of October at 10.02 PM; which given the eight hour time-zone delay between London and San Francisco, was a mere one hour after the incident was first reported in the US news. There was simply not enough time for any fraudster to fake-up the five hours' worth hours of footage after the incident.

In shock, I let several more weeks pass, just to make double-sure that not a single peep was circulating about 'the bomber's mail-out'. No peeps were heard.

It seemed astounding that I was the only person in possession of this dangerous material; which left the mysterious and pressing, question – 'why me?'

The only way to find out was to sit down and watch all of the footage. I then made the decision to make a copy of the original email and the large downloaded file onto a portable hard drive, which then I took home. This was done to avoid the temptation of clicking on the files within our open plan office in which there is an ethos of sharing everything and hot desking –

a layout, which, while it may lead to greater team spirit among the sisterhood, does not exactly contribute to employees showing much in the way of individual enterprise or discretion.

So back home with my portable hard-drive copy, after feeding my cat, Kahlo, and stoking up on a favourite tipple, I took the plunge and began the task of watching all of the recordings.

It should be said that the material is of an intensely personal nature that cannot ever have been meant to address a general viewer. In the footage the bomber attempts to seek forgiveness from his deceased daughter, to explain his motives and bombing plans to her, while summoning the courage to see his act through.

From proof-reading several how-to-guides on mourning and grief therapy, I understand that many bereaved people today believe that recording mourning messages to deceased loved ones can help externalise trapped emotions. Some take it as far as recording daily messages to the deceased for as long as six months, until they feel they can let their loved one go, whereby the files are often erased in a farewell ritual.

These recordings are analogous, but instead, the ritual of erasure was to be a suicide attack (or homicide/suicide). In the sixty or so recordings, the bomber commits himself to an act of revenge; planning to murder the person he believes destroyed his daughter (as he says 'killed my Emma'). The bomber's target is the CEO of a large biotech corporation, that he intends to 'take with me when I go.'

In the footage he also shares his investigations into the biotech corporation itself and appears to believe that his violent act is necessary to 'save the children of the future'; yet he also grapples with guilt over the mistakes he has made as a 'useless father' who had 'failed to protect my own daughter.'

Should I have handed this footage into the authorities immediately? Several issues needed resolving before taking such a step. Was there any truth to the bomber's claims about 'deaths of human test subjects in secret Artificial Intelligence implant experiments'? And, what if this video file was the only copy in the UK, Europe or US that had reached a publishing house or news outlet? I couldn't help but shudder at how important it might be.

Within the videos the bomber claims he has been pushed to these extreme measures by the 'censorship and control' of Big Tech monopolies. He also claims that biotech and Big Tech are in collusion to hide 'the deadly truth' about a covert AI system called The Infinity Project, which he states, 'is infecting us all' and 'leading to the imminent destruction of our species.'

Of course, these were perhaps the ravings of an insane man, but if I deleted the file, might this not mean the erasure of the last copy in the world?

The only options appeared to be for me to (a) Hand the file over to the publishing house and/or the police immediately. (b) Delete it and deny its existence, or (c) Carefully transcribe the entirety of the five hours of videos to determine whether (a) or (b) would be the most sensible course of action.

I decided on option (c) and began transcribing with the intention of then presenting the completed manuscript to the publishing house. The videos themselves could not be shared, due to their emotional content and the breach of international anti-terrorist law this might have entailed.

The hope was that the publishing house would then be able to verify the material, and possibly accept it for publication; one of my own first big hits as a commissioning editor, if it worked out. Until such time as the transcriptions were completed, I would work on these files in secret. This was my plan.

In beginning this work, it became necessary, for legal reasons, to redact and/or change several of the names of the Big Tech and biotech corporations that are the target of the bomber's accusations of 'global transhuman conspiracy'. Also changed are the names of family members, former-co-workers and persons known to the bomber, so as to protect their identities. In addition, certain changes have been made, concerning grammatical difference between the spoken and written word, for example by adding punctuation in cases of quoted speech for ease of reading.

In terms of the title, since the files themselves were unnamed, but all stored in the folder named FOR EMMA this has been adopted as the title for this manuscript.

I have put many months of personal work into these transcriptions and at times the labour has been challenging, but things have not gone according to my original plan, and subsequent events have made the pathway to publication dangerous.

Alternative methods have had to be found, and, I now ask that if you come into contact with this text in any form, be it by email or printed matter, please seek legal advice before opening the file. If you have already opened it then, please know before you go any further, that there may be consequences to reading it, as there have been for myself.

30 days

OK, recording now.

A small segment of domestic pipe can be made into a detonating device by filling it with explosive material. The filler can be plastic or granular military explosive, improvised explosives, or propellant from a shotgun or small arms ammunition, also from fireworks with the addition of oxidizing agents.

Basic materials required: plumbing pipes with threaded ends, around three inches in diameter and seven to nine inches long, two pipe caps, top and bottom, explosive or propellant – either military or commercial, fuse cord, hand drill, pliers, cotton wool, jiffy-bags and superglue.

Hi Em,

It's over a year now since your death and I'm sorry for having wandered so aimlessly.

I'm sorry too about the mess around what would have been your twenty-seventh birthday. The day when I heard your voice again, whispering: 'Go together'. As you might know I ended up in hospital after that. Damn fool, but I've been totally sober since then.

This morning, Em, the meaning of your words became clear. The air is sharp, salt and seaweed smells blowing up from the bay and your silly old Pops has come to a final decision.

Today is the 1st of September and in thirty-days' time I'm going to strap an explosive device to my body and take your former boss at Biosys with me when I go. Yes, Neumann.

It's a huge relief, Em. You might even be proud of me. I thought I'd lost my energy for good, but it's come surging back. Damn, I can barely sit still. How much dust and sand I've let settle in this old shack. My junior genius, I swear this to you now to make sure I can't back out. I know you'd tell me, 'I'm not really here, Pops, I'm just some neurons in the part of your brain that's memory,' and you'd probably be right, but I hope you'll keep me company in my last month and speak more to me again.

Sorry, I don't know why I'm laughing. OK, let me tell you how I got to this.

Last week, I woke to your words in whispers again. 'Go together.'

I turned in bed and called out to you, but of course, you were nowhere to be seen, but the words echoed as I got dressed.

Together. Go.

I know you didn't believe in souls and all that, and you had the PhD in neurophysics, after all, so you maybe understand better – but how the hell could we 'go together'? I figured it meant I should follow you into death, something you know I've been mulling over for many months anyway. But I found it odd, what with our family of atheists, plus 'going' by suicide wouldn't have been 'together with you', since you've been gone for thirteen months.

Sorry, maybe you think I've gone nuts, talking back to you? As you know Granny Annie suggested I write letters to you to help me grieve. She wrote to you for a good month after your funeral, then burned her letters in a ritual in her backyard stove. She said the smoke would reach you in

Akanishtha or The Field of Reeds or whatever new age afterlife she believes in this year. I thought the idea pretty tacky at first, but then I stumbled across those video clips you'd left on my old laptop.

You must have made them when you were six or seven. You're singing kiddie songs with that toothless grin. Making up rhymes about Andromeda, Aquarius, Cassiopeia and other constellations you liked the names of.

And what kept me so busy twenty years back that I didn't even know you'd recorded these files? After I found them, I spent many nights with them laughing, weeping, you'll know this anyway, if you're still watching over me.

So, I decided why not record a few videos of my own for you. Your mom would say I'm deluding myself, trying to keep you alive, but who's left to judge me?

Then this morning this 'go together' thing all became brilliantly clear.

Around ten, I drove over to San Raf retail park and picked up my repeat prescription of Prozac, Codeine and Tylenol, sleeping pills, Beta-blockers and diazepam at Zac's Pharmacy.

Marsha, at the counter made sure to tell me that the sleeping pills and Codeine 'don't go together'. And there it was again. Like a message from you, through her, for me to take an overdose.

But that wasn't it.

Then I got some groceries in the discount place and in the cashier line, just before me was this young woman just a few years older than you and similar height, Em. Her hair was true red not dyed every color under the sun like yours had been, but her long neck reminded me of you, and she had the same wiry elegance in her fingers. For the first time in months, that hollowing-out feeling started again. That ache I'd deadened with pills and vodka and all the rest. But never mind that.

This tiny boy, her son, he was maybe four and he had freckles and rusty hair and he was yanking her hand, making a fuss at those magazine shelves by the checkout. 'Mom, can I have it! Please!!' and he was doing that snatchy thing you used to do. It was some superhero magazine with a free plastic toy and the kid threw a tantrum and bashed my leg. The mother turned to me and said, 'I'm so sorry.' And she grabbed her kid, hissing 'behave!'

Maybe I've not spoken to a single soul in almost four months, and seeing her face so like yours, her eyes making contact with mine, it froze me and warmed me all at once.

Her kid started whimpering and she said, 'you're embarrassing me, Shhh! Be quiet and stop staring at the poor man.'

Poor man, and she meant me.

'That's OK,' I said.

You always used to say 'Why-oh-why do you look like a beach bum, Pops?' and I guess I did. And why not pity this rough shaven, middle-aged nobody in old corduroys and worn-out sneakers, my beard's pretty long now, and I was standing behind her in line like a haunted person, I guess.

I wanted to just lean forward and buy the magazine for the kid. Life can be so short, like a sentence barely started then cut off before you make any sense of it. I wanted to tell this young mother 'Sorry for staring, but you're the mirror image of my daughter.'

I mean she had a lot of make-up covering over pitted skin but the shape of her face, her green eyes, her movements, it pained me.

She put all her groceries into the plastic bags, and I realized she was much poorer than you'd been; her sneakers worn down at the heel, her fingernails with this cheap red nail varnish, chewed to stumps. She was buying kids snacks, painkillers and booze and she paid with cash. I wanted to wish her a long life with many children and to tell her you'd been born on the 12th of May 1997 through a medical emergency and in that first month you wouldn't take the breast and you lost two pounds and we had to call the doctors, and they diagnosed you with nut, dust and milk allergies. Allergic to your mother's breast milk. That was hard for your mom to cope with. But we got through, didn't we? You always were a fighter, Em.

I wanted to tell the poor mother at the checkout that since you were about four, Em, whenever all your mom's sophisticated friends asked what you wanted to be when you grew up, you always replied, 'I wanna be a mom'. Not a CEO or the first female president, like all the other little girls had been trained to say. 'I wanna be a mom!' How that freaked everyone out!

I waved to the kid peeking round from behind his mother's knee as she left. The kid got scared and grabbed his mother's hand and she dropped her shopping bag, apples rolling over the tiles. She snapped, 'Fuck Bruno! Look what you made me do! She apologized to the cashier and dragged the wailing child out before I could say, 'Sorry, it was my fault, I was just waving to your son and…'

And you died before you could have a child, Em.

I watched the young mother leave through the sliding doors and wanted to tell her to never let that kid out of her sight because harm is everywhere and so often it comes from those who say they're making the world a safer place. I wanted to tell her that this thing between a parent and child is the most beautiful thing, and we take it for granted, we forget to call our folks, we forget their birthdays, we blame them for flaws within ourselves, with fathers and daughters it's always the most fraught, and the media depicts older men as predators and sexists and it only makes it harder. No-one wants to talk of what it's like when a father carries his tiny daughter on his shoulders through the falling leaves. No-one sees it when a father weeps with joy at the sound of her laughter. No-one understands how lost the millions of men are today and how only a child can save us. A father can never even say these things to his own daughter. Not in words. I'm saying it to you now, Emma. Too late.

Then they were gone, through the car park, hand in hand, 'going together' and I realized I'd never see that mother who looked like you again.

That was when I heard you whispering again in my head.

'Why? Why can't you see? Look!' you said.

I'd no idea what you meant but I looked down to where the kid had knocked three or four magazines off the rack and there on the floor, I saw him.

On the front cover of *The International Business Times.* Your killer.

I picked up the magazine and stepped out of line. They were calling him 'The Man Who Will Save the Planet', the man whose biotech corporation now had a market value of 3.2 trillion dollars. I know you were a pacifist, that you believed in progress and Big Tech. But in the article, Em, Neumann was talking about the future he had in mind for us all in which all human problems from hunger to cancer to global warming would be solved by Artificial Intelligence.

In seven months I'd felt nothing, but then the rage flared again.

His cunning. The way he's kept his face out of the press for years, not like his Silicon Valley CEO peers. Has John Q. Public even heard of Zach Neumann or Biosys Corp? No. Do they even know about his Infinity Project 'neuro-web' experiments? No, only insiders know, and Neumann made you sign that NDA so no-one knows how he destroyed you.

I set the magazine back on the rack. Trembling. And I thought, here I go again, accepting defeat, when I heard your voice whispering more strongly with your whys 'Why do you always give up? Why walk away? Why can't you see? Why?'

So, I leafed through the article and there at the bottom I saw this box that said:

Zach Neumann will give a public talk on 'The Coming Technological Utopia' at the Institute of Science and Industry 1st of October.

'Go together. Why not?' Your words came back, and we used to go together, on weekends, you and me, to the ISI downtown. Remember, you loved the weird old exhibits. The magnetic ball with sparks that made your hair stand on end. And Granny Annie bought us a family lifetime membership. If you were alive, I thought, we could 'go together' to see Neumann's talk.

Back in my truck, the rage turning to aches and pains, knowing I could never bring Neumann to justice. All my attempts over the last year to expose Biosys Corp have ended in humiliation. So Neumann will continue to get away with your murder and that of hundreds of other young people in his covert human experiments. What's left to do then but accept total defeat, and finally, 'go together' with you?

Yes, I thought, that's what you meant. I'll take an overdose of pills next week. Maybe Friday after I've put the recycling out. Like the nice pharmacist said, 'these pills don't go together sir,' and they were right beside me on the empty passenger seat. As you know Em, I've been mulling over this for a good six months anyway and the only thing stopping me has been exhaustion and these numbing antidepressants.

I was about to drive out of the mini-mall car park, when I saw the redheaded mother again. Her kid was trying to drag her towards the donut place and she yelled, 'For the last time! No!' and she picked him up. He squirmed, but she carried him away, gripping him tight, his puny legs kicking in the air like a hostage.

Then it came to me, Em – me wrapping my arms round Zach Neumann. I don't know why but I thought, yes! That's what it means! I'll go together with Neumann. I'll take him with me when I go.

Driving home, this route used to bore you on our weekends, but the Golden Gate suspension wires made a rhythm and I drifted off into the methods. I could run at the stage during Neumann's talk at the Science Institute and shoot him, then shoot myself. But knowing my luck I'd miss us both. And the same problem with a knife, or a poison syringe – but worse, it's most likely I'd hit him all wrong and get thrown off by the security guards and he'd survive.

I must have been talking to myself as I was driving and saying gun or knife or syringe or bomb, because I heard your voice like an echo then Em.

'Bomb,' you said.

I've been mulling this over for about three hours now and damn it, you're right, a bomb is the fool-proof option and as you know Em, I'm a damned fool.

Hi Em,

I typed 'suicide bomb' into YouTube. About ninth down the list there was this video, Arabic subtitles. Amateur looking with no English translation. Kabul, security camera. The attacker had some trouble igniting his bomb vest, and his intended victims saw what was doing, all the wires and gadgetry, and ran for their lives. So, the guy's left standing there outside this big store called 'Finest', just by the shopping carts, and as he realizes he's missed his moment, he either decides to ignite his vest anyway or it malfunctions, or his handlers detonate it remotely.

I slowed it down and watched it frame by frame. Amazing. Literally, in one twenty fourth of a second this man went from living to being a thousand flying pieces. It seemed painless to me, poetic, that flash. A brief history of time. I watched it over and over. The big bang in reverse. Mortal fear, a white glare, then nothingness. Strangely calming.

Maybe you know this, maybe not, but back when I was a freelance video editor, among all the other crap I did, I cut a documentary on suicide bombers for this LA TV company. So, I know a fair bit about homemade bombs and where to look online.

The other thing was the ticket. I called Granny Annie and got her details for our family membership card for the Institute. The card is in her maiden name, not your surname, or mine, which is good because they won't be looking out for anyone called Kolodner. I got her card number and booked two tickets for the Neumann talk, under Granny Annie's name, in row C Two. One for me, one for you.

Can't quite believe it.

OK, so that's it, on the 1st of October, just three weeks before my fifty-fourth birthday, I'll be seated in the third row with a vest of home-made pipe bombs under my coat. When Neumann takes the stage, I'll run at him, jump up and hold him tight round his waist. I'll hit the ignition button and that'll be it. We'll go together.

Hi Em,

OK, I've just downloaded the rest of *The Anarchist Cookbook*, a survivalist handbook and three other bomb making PDFs. I'm going to need some basic things just to allow me do all the shopping. Disguises actually. Sunglasses in three different styles. Baseball caps in different colors. A Stetson. Three different outfits of high street fashions, probably say $600 worth. Steel toe-capped boots & rubber boots for my lab. Sterilizing hand wipes. Thirty packs probably.

I figure, there'll have to be tests, a recce, and dry-runs with the explosives. Sorry, I'm so damn excited now there's actually a plan, Em. There's chemicals to buy, pipes, powders, make lists of people to write goodbye letters to, so many things to organize so I can hit my October deadline. Every minute matters now and I must stay focused and tell you what went on since your 'incident'. Gather all the proof, Em, the anger will give me focus.

I just flushed all the pills away, Prozac, diazepam, right down the pan. I know, it's nuts, but it's my final decision,

Em, and I hope you're not disappointed in me. I'm crying for the first time in so long. A cool breeze coming from the sea. Just so glad I finally know what to do. I have to take a stand to try to save the young people like you.

So much to do before the day. No backing out. Please, forgive me and try to understand, Em. I'm done with pretending I can live without you, done pretending I can forgive. Please speak to me again and give me the courage to see this through.

Really tired now. I love you and miss you so much.

29 days

Hi Em,

I was up early, reading the cookbook, could barely sleep with damned excitement and all these web searches on my burner phone. I've really got to make space for my lab, plan it out. The kitchen and bathroom are probably out of the question. The mailman could peek in the window and see all my equipment.

I think a month is more than enough, what do you think? *The Anarchist Cookbook* said pipe bombs can be made within a day if you have the right materials. They also say the Weather Underground and IRA made nitrate bombs within the space of five days. I've got their entire shopping list copied out.

Then again, since this is my first time, there's a pretty high chance I'll blow myself up, like the Weathermen did. That is, if I don't screw up these two methods I've uncovered. What d'you think Em? You're the scientist.

OK, safety considerations, vis-a-vis, neighbors. The shed is the place furthest from Mz Sanchez' fence and least likely to cause a big fire if it blows up. Don't want anyone else getting hurt and I am fond of her scruffy gray cat, Nachos.

Need to blitz that damn shed, it's packed with junk. Dump the lot.

Tech specs for the pipe bombs. I think plastic casings to evade metal detectors, although most aren't pre-set to detect aluminium, so that's another option. *The Anarchist Cookbook* says the explosion can be maximised by casing the pipes in sharp shards of hard plastic to cause multiple injuries in the target from a distance of 20 feet. These shards can either be nails, glass or ball bearings and they rip the bomber and target into hundreds of pieces.

This will be me. I've got to keep saying that over and over to get it to sink in.

OK, I'll need: high-pressure pipe sealing caps, ignition wiring, batteries and casings, explosive flash powder. All purchases need to be made with cash only. Leave no card trace, according to the cookbook.

OK, here's what I'm going to need for my laboratory:

Elixir Gardens Ammonium Sulphate Fertilizer – eighteen bags. Tarpaulin and duct tape, maybe twenty rolls. Large sized metal stirrer. Shower railings. Unisex protective cover-all body suits, disposable. Buy one for each day.

Remind me Em, to use a different encrypted VPN geo location for each web search. I've got to keep my entire time online down to two minutes max, with a different SIM each time. Keep silent while web searching, no mumbling, Biosys Corp can snoop through any computer microphone and their AI has infiltrated all our laptops, smart alarms and even smart doorbells. Must remain invisible till this is done.

Yup, get it all done in one big drive round the three towns tomorrow.

Also need various sized buckets with airtight lids, to contain chemicals – ideal are baby-diaper bins. Twenty sandwich containers. Rubber gloves – at least forty. Disposable dust masks multipacks. Full face 6800 gas mask respirator with 3M particulate filters. A hundred boxes of strike anywhere matches. Ten pack of big candles. Twenty packs of family fireworks, two hundred large bore rifle bullets, electric drill with assorted drill bit sizes. Twenty tubes of liquid nail glue. Thirty of super glue. Twenty bags of cotton balls…

Editor's Note II

In what follows I have attempted to remain as objective and unbiased as possible. My first task in authenticating the material was to investigate the bomber's so called shopping lists; for if any of the named items could not possibly lead to the making of Improvised Explosive Devices (IEDs), this would prove his bomb making recordings were fake, thus providing me with a sound reason to abandon the project.

On a personal note, as someone who assisted in the editing of many best-selling meals and menus titles, I was alarmed to discover that the bomber's ingredients for making home-made bombs, or IEDs, match those which have been used as explosive oxidizing agents over last hundred years, and these include: artificial creamer, cinnamon, cocoa, cumin, honey, icing sugar, black pepper, black seeds, and powdered drink mix. Such ingredients, my research shows, have been used by terrorist groups such as the IRA, the Weather Underground and Isis.

It is also alarming to note that nearly all of the ingredients can easily be found in general stores, discount stores, pet and toy shops, and that The Anarchist Cookbook the bomber refers to is also easily downloadable for free online; which was quite a surprise to someone with no prior exposure to guerrilla insurrectionism.

Surprising also is how government documents like those by the Cyber Security and Infrastructure Security Agency (CISA), published widely with the intention of warning the public about the dangers of IEDs, nonetheless contain detailed information on ingredients and procedures, which when read in another light could be seen as bomb cooking instructions.

So, these documents proved that the bomber's bomb recipe and shopping lists were troublingly authentic. Deciding to move forward then with the transcriptions, I made certain decisions on parameters.

Firstly, in the interest of public safety, specific recipe details have been redacted; in addition, long sections of the bombers shopping lists of explosive materials have been deleted, along with certain sections of bomb-making instructions which, although widely available online, would be illegal to reproduce.

This illegality was confirmed by one experiment that I conducted with a small, uploaded section of the bomber's transcribed text on our company's editing software. The office AI (now in use across all departments to help select titles for publication and to assist with editing, marketing and publicity) judged the text sample as 'a threat to public safety' and, to my alarm, asked to 'please report the source.'

It must also be reported, that within four days of this incident, I received a warning which stated, 'your online activity has been flagged for security reasons.' This came from the IT department of the publishing house, which must remain un-named.

Frightening as it was, the upside was that the dangerous contents had been thoroughly authenticated. I then took the risk of deleting the original email and link, relying entirely on my portable hard drive backup copy.

I then made a further decision to commit as many hours as possible to this project by getting permission to work from home for one month, where the recordings could be transcribed in total privacy. After all, I didn't want to get my publishing house into any kind of trouble, no matter how much of a hit my special discovery could potentially be.

It should also be stated for the record that I do not endorse or share any of the opinions of the bomber within the following transcriptions; I support technological progress and am supportive of the Hate Speech and Online Safety legislation that has come into effect in this country and numerous others. I also wholeheartedly support the AI monitoring of email and social media by governments and information technology companies, so as to protect the populace from hateful, discriminatory, inflammatory speech, fake news and conspiracy theories. For the record, I did not knowingly intend to break any laws in downloading, viewing and transcribing this footage, and apologise for having done so.

Please consider this as fair warning should you wish to proceed as it may be a crime in your country to read this material.

29 days (cont.)

Hi Em,

Prozac withdrawal is kicking-in already. Light almost too bright. That seasick headache, yup. Sweating too. Cold Turkey. The seagulls outside seem noisier. My hands are shaking or maybe it's nerves.

Why do I have to do destroy Neumann? Why? Your favorite word in the whole world, Em – why, why, why. Remember, you asked me so many times 'Why does mom say we can't play in the leaves in Red Street?' And I told you 'Because your mom sees them lying there in the gutter and she thinks they might be dirty.'

'Why?' you asked.

'Well, I guess because there might be dog poo underneath.'

Then you grinned, 'so why don't we just pick them right off the trees?'

It was you who named it Red Street, Em, remember. You would have been about four and I'd have just picked you up from kindergarten and gone the long way over Billy Goat Hill, so we could visit that street with Japanese Maples. Every October, till you were about seven, it was our secret magic place, where you collected the best maple leaves, the brightest, reddest ones without blemishes, picking them from the fall trees like they were fruit.

You would have been sitting up on my shoulders and I'd be holding on tight to your ankles with your favorite striped stockings. I recall your front tooth was missing and all your TH's came out Fs. Like Firty Free, and Fursday. Your curly red hair and cheeks were always splashed with a bit of paint or glue.

Up there on my shoulders, you'd grabbed my ears or eyeballs when you reached up to snatch the higher leaves and I'd yell, 'hold my hair, not my eyeballs, you rascal!'

And you'd laugh so much you'd nearly fall off, so I'd have to grip your ankles tighter. Harvesting the maple leaves. Sometimes up there, you'd grab a branch and shake it and make the leaves fall faster and we'd be surrounded by this cascade of fiery red. 'Wow, Dada,' you'd say. 'Fall is falling!'

You're not embarrassed by these moments, are you Em?

Your freckles and muddy knock-knees, your thick glasses and your Ventolin inhaler always in your pocket. And those hundred maple leaves you kept in your bedroom, Em, and all your experiments to try to save their lives. You rubbed our kitchen oil onto them, you planted some in jars of water and dirt, dipped some in paint. You wanted them to stay red forever, and it made you cry when they withered.

Only five and already the scientist. Why, you asked? Why is Winter cold? Why do things have to die?

It used to annoy you that we called it Emma's Little Why Game.

'Why do aeroplanes fly, Dada?' Not even 'how' but 'why'.

'Why? Because people have to get from A to B faster,' I'd reply.

'Why?'

'Because they have important work in other countries or they're going on holiday.'

'Why, Dada?'

'Because,' I told you, 'they find it relaxing to be in a different country for a week. Now it's time for your sleepy-byes.'

'No Dada, you're not answering the question,' you'd say with your cross face on. 'Why do people have to go on holidays?

'Because they like a sense of change, I suppose.'

'Why?'

'Because normal life gets quite boring if you don't have a change once in a while.'

'Why Dada?'

'Because humans get bored, it's just the way we are.'

'Why?'

'Because, we're too intelligent and we ask why, why, why far too much.'

'Why?'

And so, on it would go, with you sitting up in your bed with your Captain Universe comforter; you turning your light back on every time I turned it off and kissed you goodnight.

I know every middle-class parent thinks their five-year old child is the most genius-like creature ever to have been born but I have to confess it was no easy thing raising a daughter who asks why, why, why of every single thing.

Emma Dilemma – you used to hate when your mom called you that. And our silly song, 'Emma-Dilemma, Emma-Dilemma, why do you always ask why?'

The school kiddie-shrink told your mother and I that the asking-why stage was a perfectly healthy neurological development for four-year-olds, like lying or killing your first bug or making other kids cry just to see what it feels like.

Maybe it was just a way of getting extra attention from your workaholic parents, but it was also, at times, fascinating. I recall, one night, trying to tuck you into bed, I said. 'Ok, rascal, two hours past bedtime, you really need to sleep now.'

'Why?' You replied as you re-adjusted your pleats.

'Because if you don't sleep' I said, 'then I'll be up all night too and that's no good because I need to go to work tomorrow.'

'Why?'

'Well, because everyone needs to work to get money.'

'Why?'

'Because if we don't, you and me and mom will be homeless and hungry.'

'Hungry…why?'

'Well, because nobody is going to give us a place to stay and feed us for free, if we do nothing, and there's a lot of competition for good jobs.'

'Jobs… why?' you asked, echoing my last word, which was another one of your things. Sitting there in your Space Girl pyjamas, your brow furrowed.

Even when your mother and I were together, we worked such hard hours, then the commuting. You never understood why I had to leave the house at 7:30 am, drive uptown to the edit suites and not get back till 9:00 pm. Why waste a life staring at screens all day, editing commercials and corporate videos, uploading, downloading. Maybe I should have taken you into Fast Forward, so you could have seen the editing console for yourself, and the never-ending stream of asshole clients who demanded I work every hour they paid for, then more, more, always more.

'Why work so much?' you asked, 'it's not very nice. Why?'

Your mom always said your whys had no real logic to them; you just loved making me exasperated and using it as an excuse to stay up past sleepy time. Your whiney-whys, she used to call them.

'Why doesn't the moon fall into the earth?' you asked.

'Why do you and mom argue so much?'

'Why does Grannie Annie always smoke weeds?'

'Why can't we drink pee-pee?'

'Why does playing ball make me feel so sad?'

My mother in her Eastern phase claimed that your many *whys* were actually Zen koans and that one day you'd be a great Bodhisattva.

There was that one question you asked over and over. 'Why do humans need money?

'So we can eat!' I'd answer.

'Why eat?'

'So we can live.'

'Why?'

You really would only give up and go to sleep once we'd hit that rock bottom dead end that all of the other whys always seemed to lead down to.

'Why are we alive?'

Had you learned at such a young age that I had no answers at all, Em?

Em,

So strange, but to know the actual day of your own death in advance is a wonderful gift. And now that I've only twenty-nine days left, I've got this irresistible urge to tell people the truth. I filled up the truck at the gas station this evening for my big shop tomorrow, and I thought – how many more times will I do this before I die?

I bought three five-liter cans and filled them up too, just in case. The fumes smelled floral, the service station seemed like a minimalist artwork. Maybe it was withdrawal symptoms, but I was elated, thinking that I no longer have to live with bullshit and lies anymore.

Paying, I noticed the cashier with all the tattoos had put blue streaks in her hair. She muttered the cost of my fuel without looking up, and I thought, I've come here for ten years and every time she's rude, and bored, chewing gum and swiping her gambling app.

'You've changed your hair,' I said, 'I like it, it's kind of punky.'

She looked up, chewed her gum, a flash of hope, then her shutters came down.

'You got a rewards card?' she mumbled.

Normally, I'd have replied 'Nuh', paid and left. But there she was, trapped in this dead end job and I'd been trapped for so long. What was there left to lose?

'Hey, it's not all so bad,' I said, 'I'm going to be dead in three and a half weeks.'

She stopped chewing her gum, seconds passed.

'I'm going to kill myself and another man,' I said.

Silence. I felt a glimmer of real connection. Come on, come on, I thought, speak to me, laugh, scream. You can do it!

Then she started chewing her gum again.

'You want a receipt?' she said.

Laughing on the back roads to the village. Imagine if you got a receipt for your entire life. Thank you for shopping on Planet Earth, 30% off your next visit. The reincarnation special offer. A deal to die for! Please come again.

28 days

Hi Em,

I sensed you close again as I woke, a breath sound, then I turned.

Your photo on my wall. You must be about twenty-one. Summer waves crashing behind you. Your hair's long, windblown, natural color, the sun's making you squint, you're laughing, hands on hips, staring right into the camera. It's like you're in love with the photographer, but I don't know who took this picture. I can't remember the names of all your boyfriends and girlfriends, or how I got this photo. Did you send it to me? Why is it stuck up with blue-tack and not framed? You look so happy, Em. Happier than I ever saw you in your whole life. Like you've finally worked out the answer to your Big Why.

If I could just go back and find the turning point, work out what I did wrong. Convince you to choose another path.

I don't want anyone else to have this photo when I'm gone.

I should tear it up, before I blow myself up.

Hi Em,

Just got back from the stores. The round trip to San R and San Fran was tough but I've picked up about forty per cent of the essentials. You'd have laughed at your crazy old Pops, walking around ██████████, whispering a memorized bomb-making list!

It's amazing what lethal items you can buy off the shelf, no questions asked.

Full oxygen mask for toxic chemicals – no problemo. Tapers for lighting bombs and ball bearings for shrapnel, no problemo. 'Save Money, Live Better'. Have a nice day.

The hardware store was more tricky, deserted, heading for bankruptcy like every local store is now. The huge gray grizzly of a guy in the Heavy Metal T-shirt at the counter looked like he hadn't seen a customer in months and kept asking me what I was looking for. 'I'm fine thanks, pretty sure I can find it myself,' I replied over and over.

Maybe my usual beach bum attire, as you called it, didn't help. Which reminds me, I need to buy some franchise store joggers and a hoodie, to look more normal.

I don't know how much of this you saw, Em. I couldn't find the pipes I needed among his stacked shelves of tubing, bolts, nuts and brackets. The whole place stank of moth balls and kitty litter and I was feeling queasy. 'Hey man, if you tell me what it's for I can help you find it,' the guy said, popping up behind the ratchet shelf. He had tattoos, the blueish amateur kind that said DIY or Alcatraz.

It wasn't like I could tell him 'I need nine, nine-inch pipes threaded at top and bottom and eighteen screw-able tops.' Why would anyone need to make self-contained pipes and what could they possibly contain? Not candy. Unless it was fizz bombs, no pun intended, or maybe it was.

And being a neurotic fool, I made up this huge story about my mother's house having rotten old plumbing and how this local plumber had put in these new pipes but forgot to put the screw-able ends on, so the sewage was just flowing out.

'Oh Pops, why-why-why!' You would have laughed.

'Hmm,' the guy said, 'well, you'll need at least the four-inch diameter for sewage.'

But there was no way I could wear a suicide belt lined with nine four-inch wide pipes, adding thirty-six inches to my girth.

'Ah, no, you're right, maybe not sewage,' I said, hastily, 'maybe just the drainage water from... the sink?'

'Right,' he said, 'but that would be PVC pipes, not brass.'

'Excellent, yes exactly, PVC!' I said, a sweat starting.

The guy was one of the world's last proud traders, he wouldn't let me leave his store with the wrong purchase. Was it for hot water? he asked. A boiler pipe – since it was threaded ends I was after? I was just about to make a break for the door, when I heard your voice echoing from before

'Why not stay? Play. Why do you always run away?'

I shuddered, stayed until your voice passed and I felt alone again. Then I spied something resembling the pipe sections I needed, just behind his counter and I pointed.

'Ah! Aluminium threaded pipes,' he said, 'tapered thread or straight thread?'

I'd no idea and then he'd misread where I'd pointed, so there was this game of 'up a bit, across, yes, stop, no, down one shelf, yes there!'

'Nipples,' he announced.

'Sorry?'

'Nipples, galvanized three-inch black steel nipples.'

He laughed as he brought some down from the shelf. I was clearly the most fun he'd had since his impending bankruptcy and he proudly explained that the 'end caps' I needed were called 'bushings'. Nipples with bushings.

'Of course, thank you so much,' I stuttered. 'Nine of those please.'

Then I heard your voice from far away, saying numbers in a countdown, twenty, nineteen, eighteen – like you were playing hide and seek – Here I come ready or not … fifteen, fourteen, thirteen, twelve…'

'Sorry twelve I'd like twelve!' I said out loud to the guy because you were giving me clues and you were right, I'd need more for bomb tests and then the metal detectors. 'And can I have all of this in plastic too, plus steel nipples too' I said, 'because I don't know if it's for the boiler or the sink or the sewage, but I'll be happy to buy them all.'

'It's your cash, man,' he said squinting at me, 'but don't expect a refund if they don't fit.' And he pointed to a sign that said: *No Returns. No Refunds. No Chance!*

As he went off to get the stuff, I whispered to ask you – had I done good? Did I buy the right things? But you'd left me again, Em, and the guy was back, trying to sell me more stuff. I only got away by also buying u-bends, brackets and rachets, to throw him off the scent; all-in-all about $300 worth to just get the $89 worth I needed. He must have thought I was the biggest sucker alive as I left dragging the three overpriced canvas bags he'd also sold me. 'Good luck with your …nipples!' he called after me.

At least he didn't call the cops, Em.

Never again. I know I'm being hypocritical but next time I'm going to a big corporate DIY store to do self-serve checkout, so there's no questions asked.

Still, I've got the pipes and the match heads and the bags of stuff. I'm off to clear out the shed so I can get started.

To be honest, I'm feeling pretty damn energized.

Hey, here's a good one – where do suicide bombers go when they die?

All over the place!

Ha, ha, get it? Sorry, you always said I told the worst dad jokes in the world. 'Poor old try-hard Pops,' you said. 'You're not funny, Mr Punny!'

Hey Em,

You probably don't know what happened to you, do you?

About the fifteenth of August last year. I got a text from you saying, 'Hope you're hunky-dory, Pops. Lab work going fabby-doo here, hope to see you in a few weeks' time. Toasted marshmallows on our beach, yay! Love ya, xxx.'

When your work took you back to Silicon Valley you often said you wanted to slip away to Bolinas for one of our beach bonfire feasts, but over the past years, with all your lab work and those international flights, the right time never really arose. I expected to get a text in a week saying, 'Aw, sorry I missed you again Pops. Back in September, see you then, I promise.'

And that would have been fine. These are just the costs of being a father of a tech genius in our day and age. Who was I to hold you back?

Two days later, I got a message. But it was from your mother.

'Come quick, Em's had an accident. Casualty First. Near Stanford. No-one's telling me anything! Hurry.'

I drove in a frenzy, trying to call your mother back, but she couldn't pick up. She'd had to cancel a meeting her PR company had been prepping for weeks and drive from Berkeley. I ran two red lights. What the hell kind of accident could you have had? Maybe you were cycling with your eyes stuck in that damn phone? I told you so many times your funky inflatable helmet was no good.

I raced over the Golden Gate and when I got through to your mom, she was in tears, words in a jumble about surgery, about bad signals, about no information.

Yelling at her, 'Where?' 'What ward? What zip code…? What do you mean surgery?' I tried to type the name of the hospital into the map app, and your mother's line went dead.

A car screeched past me, blaring its horn. Questions raced as I got stuck in the road toll bottle neck. Why a San Fran hospital? You were working in the Mojave Biosys AI lab, as far as I knew. Wasn't there a hospital nearer to there? Did they bring you in by helicopter? I'd never even heard of this place – Casualty First.

Why the hell did you need surgery?

Adrenaline. I sped through clicks of the app, block after block, speed camera after camera, till the computer voice said, 'Your destination is on your right.'

I'd never seen a hospital like it – space-age looking, and small, a green glass shard between two red brick rows. The door staff were all wearing headsets and there was some security protocol that involved retinal scanning. It looked and felt military.

'I have to see my daughter Emma Henson,' I told them and tried to push through, 'She's twenty-seven, she's just been admitted, she's had an accident.'

'Sorry sir, we need your details,' the young Japanese woman with the smart pad said. I gave her my name, address, explained I was your father, but this didn't tick some box of theirs. Two security guards approached. 'Listen, my surname's not the same as my daughter's... it's complicated' I protested, 'Em didn't want either of our surnames after our divorce so she took her Granny's maiden name...'

I had no ID that connected me in any way to you, Em and so they wouldn't let me in. I yelled at them to call your mother, she'd explain, but my anger was ticking more security warning boxes. Stuck there in this damn reception area that looked like a spaceship, I tried to get a phone signal but the building security software required a login. 'For God sake,' I said to the smart-pad woman who'd been joined by a wheeled humanoid robot with a touch-pad chest. 'Can't you just let me through, my daughter's in surgery.'

'Take a seat, scan the Q code with Sensei, sanitize your hands, log in, and register your ID,' I was told again.

'Hi, I'm Sensei,' the robot's smiling face said, 'I'm here to help. Please scan your quick response code now.' I put my head in my hands.

Finally, Sara appeared on the other side of the sliding ward doors and rushed towards me, her face red from crying. Our years of divorce hadn't prepared us for anything like this. She gripped my arm as she tried to explain. Your mother and I were touching.

You had some kind of fall at work, she said, a head injury, no not a bike accident, something in the lab. Maybe an allergic reaction, she was so confused. They'd rushed you into surgery and wouldn't tell her any more.

After swipes of my credit card, a photo of my face, digital finger printing and retinal scan by the robot, I was let in.

Your mom led the way down the white corridors, clinging to my arm, I tried to banish the thought that surgery for head injury means internal bleeding.

In the six hours that followed Sara and I sat, stood, paced and sat again in the small green-walled waiting room assigned to us, down the end of the corridor from Emergency Room 2. The plastic seats, the framed photos of sunsets. Your mother almost passed-out from nerves and I got her some water, but she refused to take a Beta-blocker, then she was pacing again, phone calling. 'In emergency surgery, yes, no, I don't know what's wrong, I'm just waiting here. No-one's telling me a damn thing!'

Call after call, she repeated the same damn unknowns to her sister, friends, colleagues, her house cleaner and a man who could be her new boyfriend for all I knew.

I couldn't bear it and went to stretch my legs, but the thoughts caught up with me – if you were damaged, Em, if you couldn't walk again, or see again, or hear. I had a metallic taste in the mouth, neck hairs standing on end, hyperventilating. I had to sit down in this empty corridor in the osteopathic ward, telling myself the emptiness in my chest wasn't some kind forewarning. I'd only felt like this once before. On the day of your birth, Em.

I didn't know then that this private hospital was an affiliate of the Biosys Group.

There were no security cameras in the ward that I could see, but a security guard with smart glasses and a nightstick arrived and I was escorted back to my waiting place,where I found Sara in tears, scrolling on her phone.

'Any news?' I asked. Your mom shook her head, staring at the linoleum, her hair hanging over her face. I handed her an old piece of toilet paper from my pocket. It's a thing you used to laugh about Em, that I would hoard paper towels and toilet paper in my pockets. 'Why Pops?' you said. 'D'you think there's going to be a world shortage of poo paper one day?'

We waited with our many whys. Why had this happened to you, now, not even thirty and having major surgery?

I was going to tell her 'Don't worry, Em's going to be fine,' but she read my mind and cut me off. 'Shh, don't say anything, the doctors are deliberately keeping us in the dark. There's nothing to do but just…'

'Wait?'

'Yes, the bastards.'

So, we waited, your mother and I. One empty plastic seat between us, so as not to intrude or do what we both needed to do, cling.

Divorced parents. I recall thinking, if we'd known this was going to happen to you, perhaps we'd never have separated.

I really needed to take your mother's hand. I reached across the empty chair and to my surprise, she accepted. We sat, her face hidden, as she sniffed and wiped her nose with kitchen roll, and I held one of her clammy hands while she scrolled through her cell phone with the other. Waiting. Waiting.

There was one, then two medical staff coming through the doors. Both young. The male was typing on a smart pad, while the female reached us first. Your mother flooded her with questions but I could tell by the doctor's forced smile that the news was bad.

'Anaphylactic shock,' she said.

'But... but the other doctor said a head injury,' your mother answered, and I supported her, 'Yes, I was told a head injury too.'

'Which was secondary, due probably to the fall from the anaphylactic reaction.'

'But is Em OK?' Your mother's hand gripped me tight. 'Can we see her? Please?'

'She can't be disturbed just yet,' the female doctor said, 'we had to perform a tracheotomy, so she could breathe, but she's stabilised now.'

Your mother shrieked and I twinged, feeling the scalpel cut to my own throat. Thoughts of you gasping to breathe through a tube, Em.

The male doctor with the pad asked us questions. 'What's Emma's history of allergies? Nuts? Shellfish? Dairy? Has she ever been hospitalized prior to this for anaphylactic reactions? As a child did you have her tested for a broad spectrum of allergies? Did she carry an EpiPen?'

Your mother stumbled through answers, apologizing that you, had been, yes, when you were small, allergic to dust mites and milk, her own breast milk too, and I tried to help but then realized that the man swivelled his upper body from one of us to the next as your mother and I took turns answering. The button on his lapel seemed to be a camera and I suspected he was recording our reactions. I should have advised your mother to say nothing till we had a lawyer, as the corporation was using our statements to build a counter case, to prove we'd been negligent parents.

‘We’re moving her now to another hospital where she can get the specialist care she needs,’ the female doctor said.

‘But why move her? Can’t we see her first?’ I yelled.

‘She’s already in the ambulance, heading to the Saint Francis Memorial Hospital.’

‘I don’t understand,’ your mother said over and over as she ran towards the exit and her car, ‘what’s happening, what’s happened? I don’t understand!’

She raced off ahead, leaving me staring at the empty car park bays. If I’d known anything more about Biosys’ Infinity Project at that point, I could have worked out that your time in that hi-tech hospital was not about saving your life at all. No, what I now believe they were doing in those hours was removing the Neuro-link computer chip from your brain and extracting as many smart nanobots as they could from your bloodstream and organs. Erasing all evidence of the immunosuppressive medication they’d been feeding you, so your body wouldn’t reject the experimental biotech implants. But I knew nothing back then about PharmaKinetics and sub-micron nano-structured biomaterials, and so I had no reason to suspect Biosys Corp of by-passing human rights regulations to experiment on live human beings, of which, my love, you were one of the first.

At Saint Francis, your mother tried to push into the ER room, but the staff forced us back repeating what they’d been told about a milk allergy ‘This is bullshit,’ I yelled at them, ‘What about the head injury, what the fuck happened?’

‘Why can’t we see her?’ your mother yelled at the nurses, ‘why was she moved without our consent?’ ‘I need to speak to a senior doctor, now!'

The move had been a smart, calculated decision by Biosys. Whoever we asked about what had happened to you, the harried overworked State Hospital staff simply parroted what appeared on your admissions files. Second hand info, pre-modified, limited. And so, the error or lie was duplicated across the State Hospital computer system.

This is how, I found out later, Biosys managed their cover-up. They dumped the traumatized bodies of their nano–tech bio-implant experiments into the State healthcare system, had them processed through overrun ER departments with well-placed fragments of fake diagnoses. So, your file read – severe allergic reaction, dairy. Secondary head injury. The state system didn't have the resources or time to do any investigative work on what caused your initial incident.

Why didn't I ask about your lab work when you were still alive, Em?

Thinking of the explosives now. There's folk I should say goodbye to before the days run out. My mom and your aunt Stacey. Say goodbye to your mom too, Em. That'll be hard.

And Doctor Foy. My shrink. You never met him Em, but he was such a huge help to me during your months in a coma.

Have to say my goodbyes without letting anyone know what I'm up to.

Have to shop for the main explosive ingredients tomorrow. I'm maybe just a tad scared.

I'd better make up some story for shop assistants about what the fireworks and bullets are for. Also need to get those BB pellets and ball bearings. Go around ten different stores and buy small quantities in each. Cash only. Wear a different baseball cap in each store, sunglasses, and changes of jacket, like the cookbook says. Remember not to park near any stores with security cameras. And stop off at Anne's pharmacy for some caffeine tablets – might as well be as awake as I can be for the hours I have left alive.

Love you.

27 days

Hey Em,

I got a pretty good haul of fireworks, plus solder, nitrate fertilizer, 9mm bullets, carbon filters. Then the potassium hydrochloride from Howard's Home Hardware in Fairfax for the Potassium Nitrate. PN is essential for the 'Rodox' reaction – an oxidizing amplification of any fire. According to the cookbook the most common sources is 'stump remover', like for trees! The best is the Spectracide brand, the anarchists say, and I found it in Green's Garden Center. Bought twelve liters of it, went through the self-scanning checkout booth so no questions asked.

On the sidewalk with my arms full of chemicals I was nearly knocked over by this father and daughter. The little girl with bouncing pony-tails skipping as she held his hand.

Made me think of you in your Space Girl pyjamas. One time you had this reaction to house dust, you were lying sick and bored in bed, taking blasts of Ventolin inhaler. You were maybe seven and I worried because your throat became dangerously constricted back then, before we started the steroid injections. Every time you got sick you spent more time in bed surfing the net for the answers to your many whys.

'Why can't I be like other girls?' 'Why do they laugh when I say I'm sick?' 'Why are kids so mean?'

'I really don't know,' I'd say, stroking your head. 'You're just a bit different Emyboo, and special. Have you taken your antihistamines?'

I picture you – standing alone at the side line of the hockey pitch while all the other girls played, you, so skinny with braids and glasses, a Band-Aid on your blood-test arm, eyes glued to your phone, sucking on your inhaler, like a spaceman observing the hostile aliens. When other girls loved teeny-pop, you fell in love with Johann Sebastian Bach because you said, you could 'feel the math in him.' When you were eight you told me that Islamic mosques had complex mathematical decorations because to depict God was a sin. You showed me photos of mosaic patterns and explained the flower of life and Metatron's cube within those thousands of lines of blue and gold. 'See Dad, God is an algorithm.'

At ten your tests showed you had the IQ of a thirteen-year-old.

Your second child therapist said giftedness can often be misdiagnosed as ADHD, autistic, depressive, or bipolar disorders. She said many gifted kids experience the world with heightened sensitivities, and that could be a big plus, because they can become artists, inventors, and humanitarians, but it can also be a big minus, because sometimes these kids develop overwhelming emotions and unacceptable behaviours.

'So, your diagnosis is that Em is gifted?' your mom asked.

'No,' the therapist replied. 'Highly Gifted.'

Where did it come from? Your mother said her grandfather had been a Harvard mathematician and schizophrenic who'd committed suicide. She said, 'I hope to hell I haven't passed his genes onto Em!'

She was convinced that if we stopped indulging your bedtime why-game we could get you to focus less on science. One night, I told her, 'So we dumb down our own daughter because she's too smart to fit in, is that what you're suggesting?'

'Look,' your mom said. 'She should be out playing jump-rope but she's sitting upstairs listening to Bach and reading Stephen God-damn Hawking. She doesn't have a single play-friend. Normal kids don't ask why, why, why, for a whole hour every night before bedtime and then check your answers against *A Brief History of Time*.'

'Actually,' I told her, 'I think Em's finished that one and she's moved onto *The Theory of Everything, the Origin and Fate of the Universe*.'

Oh Em, maybe I made it worse, feeding your obsessions because it made me feel closer to you. Maybe I should never have bought you that old Celestron telescope. One night you spent hours lining it up in your window and showed me. I couldn't believe it, 'Wow, wait, is that orange thing... actually Saturn?'

'Yeah, Dad and the rings are spinning at sixteen kilometres a second.'

'Wow,' I said, for want of something more intelligent.

You showed me Mars, Mercury and Jupiter, you told me of the acid clouds of Venus and the fogs of flying diamonds in the Oort cloud. I was working long hours in the edit suite in those days before the divorce and the planets became our thing, like baseball is for some kids and their dads.

Your obsession spawned so many new whys. Why haven't we found life on other planets? Your front baby teeth had fallen out and you kept probing the empty space with your tongue. Why is the universe held together?' you asked me. 'Why are there laws of physics and where the heck do they come from?'

One night I tried to calm you down. 'Chill,' I said, 'when I was a kid, the only planets we thought about were the ones in our own solar system.'

'Only eight planets, for real? But dad, there's four hundred billion stars in The Milky Way! That so sucks that you didn't know.'

'It was the 70s,' I told you, 'our parents used to smoke and eat at the same time and kids didn't have to wear seatbelts in cars.'

You laughed then fell silent, which always meant you'd stumbled upon another chain of unanswered whys. 'Too old a head on such young shoulders,' your mother said, worrying. 'You have to stop her asking why, why, why!'

Remember, that goofy song we made up together.

Why is the bird in the sky?
Why does the tree climb so high?
Why is the flour in the pie?
Why are you the apple of my eye?
Why does my girl always ask why?
Why-oh-why?
Why, why, why?

It's late now and I've got to build my lab and make a start on the pipes tomorrow. Please give me the courage to see this through, Em, and talk to me again. Loud and clear, like you did at your funeral. These days, I only hear you whisper in short bursts, like you're calling from very far away on a bad connection.

OK, over and out, from your old Pops.

Hi Em,

OK, I've just moved out all the trowels, pots, spades, buckets, and stapled the plastic sheeting to the work surfaces. Moved the dining table in there, to make the grinding station. Need as much clean, static-free space as possible. *The Anarchist Cookbook* says areas with heat, electricity and sparks have to be kept well away from the core ingredients, otherwise the entire shed will go bang.

The flash powder, and saltpeter needs to be mixed with PN, Comp B or ██████████.The whole process of making ██████████ is tricky. Some people do it with urine but it takes weeks, so I'm using that stump clearer and heating it up to near boiling point. Nasty. I'm going to need my gas mask, sealed goggles and thick rubber gloves. To be honest, it's giving me the heebie-jeebies.

So, that's the oxidizing agent but I still need to make the bulk of the flash powder. I have these boxes of bullets, but the cookbook says a man blew his fingers off in Texas trying to take them apart with tweezers. There's always the fireworks alternative. Then again there was this guy in Germany who tried to make his own fireworks and ended up blowing up his cat. Where has the neighbor's cat vanished to? Maybe Nachos smells that something is up?

OK, cutting the heads off a thousand matches now. Very God-damned carefully.

Oh Em,

Thinking about your hospital, your ward room when they finally let us in, with all those tubes in your mouth and nose, your head and eyes heavily bandaged, and that beep, beep of your heart machine. Your mother grabbing your hand, the one with the stent, saying 'Emma, Mommy's here, can you wake up, darling?'

The nurse asked her to step back and not upset the monitors.

'How long will she be unconscious?' your mother asked, trembling. 'Why is her head bandaged?'

And, of course, this nurse didn't have any information and had been told simply to let us see you for fifteen minutes, then make sure we left.

Your mother kissed your forehead. 'Why isn't she waking up? Why?'

'I'm not a doctor,' the nurse said, 'just a trainee. When she wakes we'll call you. You should go home and get some rest and then speak to the doctor on the rounds tomorrow morning. It's OK, her coma is a stable state.'

'Coma!' I exploded. 'What do you mean? We need to speak to a real doctor now!'

Two orderlies arrived. 'Everything OK?' the tall one asked.

I'm not proud to admit it but I went nuts. A coma! Was it even true? Why the hell had this happened? Why had nobody any fucking answers?

'Please sir, this is an intensive care ward,' the short one said, and touched my shoulder. 'We don't want to distress any of the other patients. Now if you'll both come with me.'

'Can't I stay here, with her, please,' your mother begged, and she convinced them to let her remain all night holding your hand. I sat out in the waiting area, staring at the plastic yucca plant. I didn't know much about comas then, and over the next few days the junior hospital staff told us over and over again that they had no further information and that maybe you'd wake up tomorrow. Then tomorrow.

It took five sleepless nights of this, Em, before your mother and I snapped, and we were finally sat down in a smaller room with yellow curtains with a doctor called Weiss. He asked us how we'd been, asked about your medical history and then said: 'I just saw Emma. Her blood pressure is good and the nurses are watching her closely.'

I sensed something was coming and your mother reached for my hand and squeezed, her nails digging into my skin.

'I've examined Emma's MRI scan, and I'm afraid, it looks like her coma is moving towards the catatonic state.'

Your mother wept. I raged. What does it even mean? What can we do? Please tell us.

The doctor said he was 'terribly sorry' and that, since we must have many questions and so as to avoid confusion, if we could just give him our emails he'd send a link for a video called *Coping With Comas*.

We were led to a quiet waiting room, and we stared into your mother's cell phone as she logged on. *Coping with*

Comas was an animated video with colored cartoon figures, as if made for five-year-olds.

'Hey there!' it started, 'we're here to talk about comas. There are several different types of comas. A vegetative state means that a person's body can make physical movements such as grunts or yawns, but has no reaction to actual stimuli – their movements are purely involuntary.'

The relentless smiley voice said: 'Sadly for loved ones, seeing the body of someone you care about suddenly yawn can induce false hope.'

I couldn't bear it but we watched through to the torturous end, hoping it would tell us what we could do to help you, Em.

'Awesome. Thanks for watching,' it concluded, no advice given. 'And if you liked this video, check out our other *Coping With* videos. And how about clicking that like and subscribe button?'

'This is fucking outrageous,' I yelled. 'Who the hell is in charge here?'

Dr Weiss, Dr Kahn, Dr Reich and all the nurses said the same thing over many days. 'We just have to keep Emma comfortable and wait and see.'

I cornered doctors in corridors. Why can't you give me contact details for the first doctors that treated her? Why was there no report on their files for the head injury? Why did she go into anaphylactic shock? Why can't you tell me any fucking thing? Are you too far down the pecking order to possess the information or are you just concealing it from me for fear of losing your job? Why can't I speak to the administration staff? Why are you standing in my way? Why are you filming me?

Although your mother came to know the staff almost

as friends over the months, my inquiries created tension. She was in coping and hoping mode and I'd gone into full blame, or at least that was what the *Coping With...* video said.

'What does it matter, knowing why her coma started?' your mom yelled at me in the car park. 'You're just looking for someone else to blame because you feel useless.'

'OK,' I snapped back, 'we can't stop her bed sores or her bladder getting infected, we can't wake her up, but I do feel fucking useless, and so do you but you're in denial.'

Biosys had probably put you into a coma before even that first hospital, Em, that was what I suspected. Three visits to the original hospital to question the staff and doctors, and each time I was ejected by security. Twelve emails I sent asking them for your paperwork and they tied me in bureaucratic loops. The Office of Federal Contract Compliance informed me that 92% of all legal cases against private hospitals failed. I filed to have all of your medical records under the Freedom of Information Act, and then received a warning from the Police that the first hospital had filed a cease and desist notice against me for 'harassment of staff'.

Every day, visiting hours, the same but not the same Why did this happen? Why you, Em? And all the staff offered was: 'Would you like something to help calm you down sir?' 'Diazepam?' 'A Beta-blocker?'

They make you wait and wait until you give up.

On day thirty-two, your mother saw your eyes blink, and demanded to see the chief neurologist but all we got was nurses, as if people in comas are placed on a B or C list. On day forty-one, your mother was sure your toes wiggled. She demanded more tests and insisted that I think only positive thoughts as this would help you wake from your coma.

I buried myself in the science, but your mother would yell at me, 'No, don't tell me. We have to be strong for her. Don't you dare come here with your facts and your negativity.'

I tried to live in your mother's hope, coming every day, to hold your hand, to sing you your Why song.

Why does the fly want to fly?
Why do we blush when we are shy?
Why is my dad such a silly guy?

Why does my girl say why why why?
Why does everything have to die?
Why oh why
Why, why, why…

Hey Em,

Good news, I have half a jar full of the flash powder from the contents of fourteen fireworks and forty bullets. The damn things terrify me and it takes forever pulling their casing off with the pliers. I was sweating so much I steamed up my goggles. One false move and bye–bye thumb. The powder still needs mixing with the which I'll get started on tomorrow. I can't believe this all worked just fine, though the quantities are small.

Tired now darling and woozy. When I wake up, I'll have 26 days left. That's 624 hours, minus 234 hours for sleep, equals 390 hours of time awake. Time is ticking. Got to get myself together, or I'll go to pieces. Ha ha, puns entirely intended.

Love you always.

Editor's Note III

In transcribing the footage, and in terms of editorial integrity, the second thing to verify after the bomb chemistry was identity. Was the bomb-maker in the videos actually Mr. Josh Cartwright, aged 52, of Bolinas, CA – as cited in the mainstream news?

Surprisingly, there were only two images of the bomber circulating across all media on the top four global search engines. These were domestic images from years before. Furthermore, no images from the bomber's five hours of video footage seemed to have made it into news circulation, and there were no images of the bombing event in which the bomber could be identified; which was rather suspicious for such a high profile terrorist act.

By using a screen grab from the videos and an AI facial recognition tool, I managed to confirm that the face of the bomber in the two press images did in fact match the man speaking in the For Emma videos.

The third task in verifying the videos was in connecting the 'father' (the bomber hereafter referred to as 'Cartwright') to the only single image of Emma that now remains online.

It was disappointing to discover that within the five hours of footage, there was none of the usual archived family footage that parents usually record of their children on their smartphones.

Cartwright claims later in the recordings that Biosys and 'the powers that be' penetrated his home laptop and destroyed all such evidence. He also claims that hundreds of such images of Emma have been erased from the internet by the tech giants as part of a vast cover-up.

This did raise the first alarm bells about Cartwright's potential for paranoid delusions. With such scant evidence available online, had he for example simply imagined that he was the father of Emma? Such stories of the mentally disturbed latching onto other people's tragedies are unfortunately, all too common.

This troubling question was answered by some of the footage recorded within Cartwright's first week of preparations. In several of these videos, shot between bomb making recordings, he goes through a small shoe box of old photographs of Emma, and shares memories with her. In this, he appears to be performing a standard mourning ritual – which has precedence in the popular self-help and grieving manuals that I have worked upon – with advice such as 'Use photographs to share fond moments' and 'Talk to your loved one as if she's still there.'

In these unsettling personal videos Cartwright talks in the following way as he shares the old photos with his laptop camera: 'Remember that bonfire?' 'Is that the time we forgot the marshmallows?' 'Ah, look at your missing tooth' 'Was that your first time on a bike?' And so on. The footage of the photos of the child's life from age one to ten, is of such a painfully private nature that I decided not to include transcriptions of it here, apart from in the following synopsis form:

The footage includes photos of a single blonde-haired female child on a play park swing, then play-doh sculpting, then on a boat trip, at a birthday party, on a mountain vacation; then the child, maybe aged seven or eight, is in a Halloween ghost costume, then at a bonfire and then maybe aged ten stargazing with a telescope; then reading a Stephen Hawking book inside 'the shack' at around eleven years old. There are also photos of Emma as a toddler being held by her mother; whose identity was again confirmed by online AI facial recognition software.

While there is evidence of Emma's 'forever changing teenage hair colours' in the photo footage, the bomber also mentions Emma's dental braces and multiple allergies, which could not be confirmed by any news sources.

However, by again using screen grabs of the photos of the teenage Emma and AI facial recognition software, a 93% match was made with the one remaining image of Emma that exists online.

The third task was to verify the location within the footage. No address for the bomber was given in the media, beyond Bolinas. C.A. Through online property deed records searches, I discovered that there were no such properties tied to the name Josh Cartwright. However – 12 Beachview Lane, was owned by someone of the surname Kolodner, which matched that of Cartwright (the bomber's) mother. An arrangement which perhaps came from his post-divorce financial setup and which might also explain why Cartwright remained 'off the radar' for so long.

Using a well-known global satellite mapping app and entering this address, a shack and backyard were located. The zoomed-in satellite images of the wooden shed; the adjoining neighbour's wall; the eucalyptus tree, the position of the recycling bins and the peeling-paint shack exterior shown in the colours of terracotta and deep blue confirmed that this was the same location as in Cartwright's home videos.

These colours also recur in the interiors of Cartwright's rustic kitchen in which he works on his home-made bombs. This aesthetic again correlates with the typical wooden housing of Bolinas, CA. with its retired baby-boomer, bohemian hippie style, and confirms that the footage was authentically geo-located and not fake.

From the footage we also see that the interior walls of the shack are adorned with beach-combing artefacts, such as an old boat oar, a stringless fiddle, a child-sized guitar covered in hand-painted flowers, painted driftwood, and collages made of feathers and seashells. A sideboard is covered in beach-combed pottery fragments, and a small bookcase holds less than ten books, including the titles: *The Book of Vegetable Gardening, Walden* by Thoreau, *Leaves of Grass* by Walt Whitman, *A Beginners Guide to Astronomy, A Brief History of Time,* and *Black Holes* and *Baby Universes,* both by Stephen Hawking; artefacts which confirm the memories that Cartwright recounts to his deceased daughter.

Perhaps, I had secretly hoped that the footage would prove to be fake, but these three factors: photo ID, geolocation and anecdotal family connection – confirmed that the five hours of footage were filmed by the actual bomber on location; which left the troubling question of why no-one else in the world had come forward with this historically significant footage?

It should also be said at this juncture that I considered it prudent to return to the office, after hours, and to delete all trace of the original email from the staff mailbox trash folder and server, so that no-one from IT or any other curious department could get into any trouble, but also perhaps out of a certain covetous ambition to keep this rare discovery secret.

In retrospect such actions may have been foolish, and to outside eyes, may have appeared illegal.

Furthermore, it might also have been an error to use Artificial Intelligence apps to help in my research, for reasons that will become apparent.

Committed then to my role as editor of verified material, the next questions that arose concerned Cartwright's mental health, and his ability or inability to pull off his awful task.

26 days

Hi Em,

I got up with the sun and had a pretty productive morning grinding the carbon and ██████████ until my stupid accident. Damn fool, I've burned my fingers and nearly set fire to the shed.

I was doing a test with tiny quantities from the three batches. My homemade flash powder held up well but the puny pile made from the bullet powder was much stronger and it set off the big stack of match heads. Damn fool. I'll have to keep the batches of flash powder and ██████████ separated by a good distance, next time. Pain in my left eye too.

I've just checked and I've singed my eyelashes. Dumb ass. I was lucky, very lucky. It's all fun and games till someone loses an eye, huh!

Lessons for next session: Take great care when moving batches of match heads and flash powder – no sudden movements, avoid all sources of static electricity and friction. Store all flash powder and match heads into different sandwich boxes.

OK, wiping down all the surfaces before stage two.

'Why?' I keep hearing your voice whispering 'why?' There it is again. Why clean? Why prepare…? Why all the effort if…?'

Of course, you're right Em, there's no point in any of this if I can't get the bombs into the Science Institute. OK, absolutely, I'll have to do a recce of the building tomorrow.

*

Em,

Stacey just rang. She says your cousins are asking if I'll take them swimming on the beach again. Shit. Have to come up with a strategy so they don't come knocking. Imagine that! If Stacey burst in, kids in her arms and found all these pipes and chemicals. 'What you doing, big bruv?' she'd ask and what the hell could I say? That I'm making Christmas toys for Santa?

So many little lies need to be made up now.

Why do people lie and tease, you asked so many times. The other kids at school were so nasty to you, Em. We'd already moved you up one grade when you were nine because of the bullying, but you were so far ahead of your class that you got bored and became 'disruptive'.

They'd started calling you 'shrimp' and 'googly eyes' because of your glasses. They teased you for your elf-like face, for the birth scar on your ear, called you 'nerd' and 'geek'. The cruellest was 'wheezer' because of your steroid inhaler. Then the violence.

Holding you those times you cried, Em, telling you that no, there was nothing wrong with you, it was those other kids that were the problem. None of them had the gift of eidetic memory. None of them read 11th grade maths textbooks to help them get to sleep.

Struggling to help you in those years, Em. Reporting the bullies to the school. One night, you were in tears, yelling at your mom. 'Why did you tattle on Rasha!'

'Because she pulled your hair darling!' your mother replied.

'But now she's expelled, and her friends are picking on me even more!'

And you showed us the purple bruise on your upper arm.

'OK who did this, give me a name!' I said, furious.

'No, stop it!' you yelled, 'you and mom are just making it worse!'

Watching history repeat and being powerless to stop it. I never told you that I was bullied at school too. I didn't want you to feel fated, trapped. I prayed that it would stop, that you'd be spared what I went through, the punches and kicks, the spit in the face, being chased through the streets, cornered. The evil delight flashing in the eyes of children.

Maybe it was a mistake. Maybe if I told you I'd been bullied too, it might have helped, Em. You might have thought, if Dad got over it, then so could I. Maybe you'd have felt less alone. Maybe we panicked when we moved you to that second then third school. Your mother bought you all the popular brands of clothes so you'd fit in. You looked like a beautiful elf, I thought who'd been forced to wear sports clothing. All those endless play-dates to force you to become socialized and to keep you away from your solitude of books. I protested, 'We can't dumb her down, it's just wrong!' Arguments between your mother and I, that woke you from sleep. Your bed wetting.

At age ten you developed that stutter, which the speech therapist said was possibly because of your fear of sounding too clever and being punished for it. But I knew the real reason, Em – your thoughts moved so quickly that your mouth couldn't catch up.

Remember, when you spotted an error in a textbook for the high school national curriculum. Core Physics book three. You asked your teacher in class, Ms Frame I think, 'why is there a mistake in this chapter on gravity?'

And Ms Frame replied, 'Put it away, we don't study those books in junior school.'

'Why?' you asked.

'Because they're not for kids your age.'

'But why? you asked. And the whys escalated and had the entire class in hysterics, and Ms Frame sent you to the principal's office. You were given detention and a caution.

Months later, a friend of your mom's from Stanford University heard the story and checked out the textbook. 'God-damn,' she said, 'your kid's right, the inverse square law is missing a squared symbol!' The error was in every science classroom in America and you'd spotted it, Em. I burst with pride and your mother started taking Beta-Blockers for anxiety. Your teacher never apologized.

'It's not funny!' your mother said one night when we were drinking in that fake-rustic kitchen of ours. 'Even the teachers are ganging up on Em now, we're going to have to move her to another school if she doesn't stop this.'

Maybe I'd had too much wine. 'Wait,' I said, 'maybe the problem is us! Maybe if we actually had an answer to Em's questions, she'd stop asking why-why-why. But we don't. I mean as parents. Think about it, a hundred years ago a kid would ask their parents why we're alive and the parents would reply, because God made us, and if we behave we'll go the Heaven and live for eternity. But we don't have any answers, so she studies science day and night.'

Your mother finished her wine, stared at me, 'you think we should send her to a Catholic school now?'

'Hell no,' I replied. 'But doesn't it bother you, that we can't answer why we exist?'

'C'mon, she's not really asking these big philosophical questions,' your mother said, 'I've told you a hundred times

– she's just being precocious, and morbid, she's asking why she should even have friends, why women should have children.'

No, but seriously' I said, 'wouldn't you get obsessed about that too, as a kid, if your parents couldn't give you a straight answer on why we're alive? C'mon, I mean what values do we actually have, Sara? Like, when other kids hit her, what do we advise her to do? Turn the other cheek like Christ said? Or go ahead and hit back, but make sure everyone hits each other uniformly because we believe in equality. Or kick as many kids as you want, because Darwin says it's survival of the fittest. I'm serious, what values were we passing onto our only child? What do we actually believe in?'

'I believe she's going to get stuck in a remedial class for disruptive children if she doesn't stop.'

'Come on, we're faking it. That's the problem. We don't know how to raise her or what values to give her because we don't have any of our own.'

'Speak for yourself,' your mother said, and she emptied the last wine drips from the bottle. 'It's your turn to stack the dishwasher.' And she handed me her glass. 'Has it ever crossed your mind,' she said, 'that the reason Em keeps asking you why, why, why all the time, is just because she sees it unnerves you and she'll always get a big reaction out of you? Because she knows *you* don't have any answers.'

That floored me.

Maybe your mother was right. In truth Em, like every other middle-class parent in our set in San Fran, we were busking it without any values at all. A righteous passion for recycling plastics was perhaps all we amounted to. If someone asked us 'do you believe in marriage,' we'd have said no. 'The family?' No. 'Community?' No. 'This great nation?' No fucking way. And as for progress and equality, they'd all turned to garbage in the streets. Your mother and I believed in nothing at all. We didn't believe in our jobs; your mom loathed PR but her PR company was rated twelfth in the region; and I loathed television but spent all day editing infomercials and if I got lucky a tacky documentary once a year. And how can you really raise a child if you see yourself as a sell-out, you hate your society and you see marriage as an oppressive institution? We didn't have an answer to your Big Why, Em, and since we didn't even believe in each other, the next question came: Why stay together? For the sake of the child?

Aw damn. OK Em, my break is over. No point dwelling. Back to work.

Hey Em,

Just spent four hours in a kind of meditative mood grinding up the carbon for the flash powder with the kitchen blender – or maybe it was oxygen starvation with the mask on!

I worked out how to get a hundred match heads and a fuse into the bottom of the first pipe. Very tricky.

Can't stop thinking about the day I had to break the news to you about me and your mother. You were just turning eleven and were in your dungarees and stripey socks phase; you'd moved onto Unified Field Theory by then. I was driving you to Bolinas to show you my new pad for the first time. I had this whole positive speech worked out about how work and city life and technology had burned me out, and how sometimes we need a change of scenery. I was going to tell you we could walk on the beach every weekend and have picnics and bonfires and toast marshmallows, your favorite. All this to soften the blow.

You remember Em? I'd just driven over the Golden Gate and you were fastening your ponytail tighter when you suddenly said, 'The problem is, Dad', in that random-access way of yours. 'The big bang is getting faster. It's like a balloon that just keeps expanding outwards from its explosion and accelerating faster and further.'

'About this house I'm moving to,' I said.

You ignored me and said, 'but if the expansion theory is true then, it means the universe has an end as well as a start and that's pretty bad because it will either be Heat Death, or the Big Rip, but I prefer the Big Crunch Theory.'

'So do I,' I tried to joke, 'Rice Krispies are the best.'

You sighed and said, 'oh, my beloved father, who is so fortunately free of the agonies of intelligence.'

And we laughed, and I asked what the Big Crunch and Heat Death were.

'Well Dad,' you said, 'if the heat death hypothesis is correct, it means that after every sun dies, after all matter gets sucked into black holes, all light will vanish and all remaining atoms will be pushed so far apart that everything in the whole universe will come to a stop in frozen eternal nothingness.'

'Wow,' I said, and asked you how far away that might be in the future, because we had to get back to your mother's by six thirty at the latest.

You play-punched me and said, 'It's OK, Dad, it's not going to be for 1.7 times ten to the power of 106 years.'

'So, we'll be long gone by then so why worry?' I asked.

'Why worry?' you repeated. 'Because humans have

only got another two billion years left to live on earth,' you said, 'and if the universe dies in heat death and it isn't cyclic and reborn again that means that humans and all other animals will never get another chance to live, and life was just a tiny, pointless experiment that failed.'

'Ah,' I said, sensing that this would not be a good place to segue into telling you about the impending separation of your mother and I.

Remember Em? I parked in the north car park of the bridge, just above the place that became 'our secret little beach'. I said I needed to stretch my legs and pee behind the bush beside that old burger bar, because I needed time to work out how I'd tell you.

Plan A had been to say, 'your mother and I have decided to live apart for a while.' But I could never lie to your face, not convincingly.

Plan B had been to say, 'your mother and I are having a one-year trial separation.' That could have worked and it wasn't entirely a lie, but the only reason your mother wasn't divorcing me that same week was that no-fault divorce after a statutory one-year separation didn't involve hiring a lawyer and so was cheaper.

I'd run out of pee and procrastination and came back to the car, still not sure what to tell you. You were staring at me, 'I'm sorry Dad,' you said, 'I didn't actually mean to go on about the Heat Death Hypothesis, I guess it's just kind of hard to talk about your divorce.'

'My what?' I burst out. 'So, your mother told you already?' That hadn't been part of the arrangement and I was furious. 'What did she say?'

You said your mom had a frank chat with you in the kitchen last night and you'd cried and asked her why? And she'd said, 'why don't you ask your father why?'

OK, I had a so-called affair, a very, very brief one, and I still loved your mother. But how could I tell you these sordid things, Em? You were only eleven.

'It's OK, Dad,' you said, 'we can do the whole tragic-confession thing another time, just please don't be mad at Mom. OK?'

I sat there fuming in the car by the burger bar. You asked if you could put on some music. I had some old CDs in the glove compartment and you picked out that ancient compilation of all those folk songs my mother raised me with and I drove on.

It was that one that came on about the blooming heather. Yes, *Wild Mountain Thyme*, sung by some hippie woman in the 60s. You loved that old song and back when you were seven, you said: 'When they pick time is it like finding a clock in the mountains?'

And I had to explain that it was time with a TH and a Y, and it was a herb that tasted good with roast chicken and we laughed and laughed.

Picking time from the mountains, what an idea!

So we were singing along together in the truck as we sped along the shore road into the hills, Em, and we didn't know the verses but we really belted out the chorus, you and I. This quiver in your voice, this lump in my throat, and that chorus, so sweet, over and over...

Will ye go, Lassie go?
And we'll all go together
To pluck wild mountain thyme
All around the blooming heather
Will ye go, Lassie go?

And thinking of all the times me and your mother had dragged you hiking up into the redwood forests in Oakland, and how we'd never go there as a family again.

I tried to hide my eyes from you as I drove and I heard you sniffing, and I looked over and you were hugging your knees and wiping your face and both of us burst into wild sobs. Then I was wiping my eyes and I couldn't see a damn thing and it was all panic to just get off the road without crashing. And I parked half in a ditch with the handbrake on, and both of us were just looking at each other's puffy faces and the tears pouring and then somehow we set each other off, laughing together, crazy, magical, it just burst out, and the CD still blaring, *will you go Lassie go*, and you wanted to hug, and I held you and kissed your head as you squeezed me tight, the tears and laughter mixing up, waves of it, you setting me off, then me setting you off in a loop. Then the song stopped and we just stared out at the Pacific. Holding silent hands.

'I'm sorry,' I whispered and you said, 'shh, it's OK, Dad.'

How the hell could I be separated from you, for days in the week, for years of your life? Why the hell had I done something so fucking stupid?

'You sure you don't want to know why?' I said.

'No.'

'But *Why* is the Em word. *Why* was practically your first word.'

You shook your head.

'I'm not leaving you, Em, you understand? I'm leaving your mother, not you, her,'

But even as I said it, it made no sense.

'It's OK Dad,' you said. 'I'm kind of all cried out now,

can we just call it a day on the talking-about-it business?'

'OK, I'm sorry.'

'Me too,' you said, and you smiled and we were silent, staring out the windshield at the passing cars and the beach then sometimes at each other. Then, without warning, you were like your nine-year-old self again, stretching your arms. 'What I really, really, really want,' you said, 'is to eat marshmallows on a bonfire, with melted chocolate, right now.'

'Deal.' I said, and put the truck in gear and we headed down the winding tracks to Bolinas beach.

We had our mini bonfire and cooked s'mores with sticks. I dropped mine in the fire and yours got covered in sand. Remember? You said it added extra crunch. Then we swapped puns. 'What did the beach say as the tide came in?' I asked you, and you shrugged 'dunno' – 'long time no sea' I said. And you cringed and play-punched me.

'Wait, wait, I have better one!' you said, 'How can you tell if the ocean is friendly?' I gave up and you grinned and said, 'it waves'.

We laughed and then I walked you up the hill to see my new house. You shivered in the doorway. 'Wow, tragic tiny bachelor shack,' you said. The place was empty boards and telephone wires, I hadn't had time to buy any furniture. 'Where's my bedroom?' you asked, and I took you through to the back. The room was eight by eight, faded white walls, a single small window view of the garden fence, some blue tack on the walls from the last renters. 'Well, hey,' you said, 'who needs a bed anyway?'

You tried to cheer me up, Em. You said the beach would be awesome for stargazing because of the lack of light pollution. You said you could show me the Great Red

Spot on Jupiter that night, through the Celestron telescope I'd bought for your birthday. But you'd forgotten it was back at the house that would soon be called 'Mom's.'

I had to return you early as we hadn't got into the legals yet on overnight stays.

Driving back over the Golden Gate, it was late, and the stars were peeking out over the Pacific and you said to me, 'you know what it means if they find just one bacteria on Europa or Titan or Ceres?' You were talking about the moons of Jupiter again and I admitted I didn't know, I was more concerned about not making a habit of returning you late. You stared out. 'If they find just one living microbe out there,' you said, 'then it means…'

You struggled to tell me something that seemed vast and powerful to you.

'…it means, life is bursting out around every tiny speck of light in the sky; on a billion, billion planets. It means we are not the only living things in a dead universe. It means life has a chance after we're gone and maybe it even has a purpose.'

I worried that my impending divorce had already cast you out into the lonely cosmos to search for the big answer to the great why. And the drive between my empty bachelor pad and our old family house in Sunnyside with the Golden Gate hanging in the fog between was some kind of metaphor for it all.

I should have done something different that night. I should have gone inside our old family home with you, Em. I should have walked straight up to your mom and told her I'm not moving out. I refuse to divorce. We're going to make this work and I don't care if you despise me, I am not leaving my daughter. I will say sorry to you every day if that's what it takes. I'll fight you in court or make you love me again, but you're not throwing me out. It could have taken weeks, months of rows and negotiation, fights going on into the nights and all of it would have upset you, Em, but if I had just stuck firm, I'm sure I could have convinced your mother to let me try again. If we'd known then what would happen to you at twenty-seven years of age, Em, I'm sure we would have stuck it out together, even in a loveless marriage, we'd have put you first, and fifteen, sixteen years of your life could have been so different.

But what did I do? I retreated into defeat, the bad man in penance. I skulked away to lick my wounds and deepened those wounds.

You started calling me Pops just after I moved out, because maybe 'Dad' hurt too much. You said all my stupid jokes were 'tryhard' and would never make things right again. Then you vanished into your room in your mom's house and your solitary study of quantum entanglement and the big bang.

After your death, Em, I read your Hawking books, trying to decipher your squiggled notes in the margins. Maybe, if your mother and I hadn't divorced you'd never have gotten sucked into all this and you'd still be with us.

I played your online universe simulation – Space Explorer. I travelled through the Oort cloud through a trillion fragments of failed planets, into deep empty space. I found no signs of life in your simulation. All those probes NASA sent out still haven't found any of those microbes you yearned for. All is lifeless. I heard your voice laughing at me one night. 'Why are you so sappy and silly?' you whispered. 'You won't find me out there, Pops. I'm just ashes now in an urn on mom's fake marble sideboard.'

Why?

Time heals they say. I hate it for that. I refuse.

The days are going so fast. The thought of bed takes me back to the hospital, your bed sores, your electric heart monitor, your wilting flowers, your rotting bowls of fruit.

Can't face food but I must eat. Must remember to scrub my hands so I don't swallow any saltpetre. Silly old man.

Will ye go, Lassie go?
And we'll all go together.

So that's where I heard it before. Go together.

Got to do the recce of the Science Institute tomorrow. Must find out the exact room where Zach Neumann will give his talk, map the security staff, check for metal detectors, bomb detectors, sniffer dogs. Check for a place to conceal my bombs within the building.

So tired now. Wish me luck, Em. I love you so much. Night, night.

25 days

Hi Em,

It's 3.30. Just back from the Institute. It was a good idea of yours to go and our recce went better than expected, with only one upset and some trouble getting parked downtown. I think it's a big OK on sneaking explosives inside.

You used to love our weekend family visits when you were ten or so. That weird old 17th Century orrery with the planet made of brass all the wrong size, on metal rods orbiting the clockwork sun.

Neumann's talk is part of that whole public outreach thing Big Tech is doing now, a PR stunt and a smokescreen, but an unexpected benefit of his pretence of interest in the general public is the below standard security in the building.

Here's my notes.

OK, the front door detectors are made by SensorPlus – just basic retail tagging anti-theft detectors for the gift shop, which is on the left on entry. My two minute search found out these SensorPlus devices can't be reset to detect metals or 'sniff' explosives.

Good, huh.

Security Guards: five in total, all retirement age, there to stop gift shop thefts and check membership cards and day-entry passes, not bomb threats. Sloppy for such a big institution, given that they had a talk by ████ ██████████ here last February.

But still, they're very bag conscious, stopping tourists to ask them to deposit their bags in the basement bag check.

There's another SensorPlus scanner by the café restroom – that's three in total. The lecture theatre where Neumann will lecture is on the first floor past the old Thomas Edison inventions displays. Many security cameras up there, one on every corner and above the fire hoses and emergency exits. The only place I could hide a bomb vest is under the display case of 19th Century telephones. There's a five-inch gap beneath. But with the overhead cameras - risky.

Plus, there's a roving security man up there, younger. The guards have walkie-talkies and possible lapel cameras.

So – best to wear the explosive vest rather than bag it. Which raises timing questions. How heightened will security be for Neumann's talk? I suspect bomb-detection body scanners will be installed and at the very least a metal detector. And the ball bearings in my pipe bombs could set that off. Plus, they might have sniffer dogs at the entrance on the night. OK, so, I've got to hide the explosives somewhere within the institute at least three days before they install better detectors. Maybe, make that five days before Neumann's talk? But where?

Like I thought, the lecture theatre is on the first floor, just past the Apollo exhibits. The double doors were locked, and I worried that I'd been recorded trying to budge them open.

Sweating, I thought, I'll better just leave. But then I heard your voice again, Em. When I'm in the city it's louder, your questions bursting out at me. 'Why?' you seemed to say, like memories of other whys you'd asked, 'Why does the planet spin? Why has therapy never helped you, Pops?' But clearly in my head, you said, 'Why do you always give up so easily?'

You were right, of course, so I thought of another location and sure enough there was the downstairs restroom too, and I hoped the staff hadn't seen me checking out the one upstairs. What could I say? 'Sorry, I have a weak bladder'?

I found it and went in, it was busier, but in worse repair. Five urinals and four stalls, I scanned for a spot to hide a bomb vest. Under the row of sinks? No. I took a piss and wondered why the hell you'd lead me there and hoped you weren't still watching me.

But where to hide the bomb?

'Why,' you whispered 'do most of us stare into the gutter when we can look up to the stars?' I stared into the stinking urinal and thought gutter yes, so where are the stars. I looked up and I saw it. One of those suspended ceilings with the square roof tiles, maybe asbestos. Was that what you meant?

I waited a good ten minutes for the restroom to empty and I sensed, with a shudder, that your voice had left me alone, then I went into a stall, climbed up onto a toilet seat and pushed the roof tile above me free from its metal grid frame. It budged and made a gap, big enough for my hand. Back in college, we used to stash drugs, booze, porno magazines in spots like that. I felt about up there and there were wires and ventilation tubes, and a good four feet of suspended ceiling space. A perfect hiding hole. As a test, I took out four fifties from my wallet and placed them up there quite obviously. Did I tell you I've taken everything out of all my bank accounts now? I've maxed my credit card out too so I'll never need to go to an ATM again. I left $200 sitting up there and if it's still there when I come back next week, I'll know no-one checks.

Oh Em, it all went quite well. And the roof tile slipped back in place. I asked you, 'is this the spot?' But your voice didn't return, there was only the drip, drip, drip of water and I was just an old man talking to himself in a smelly restroom.

Sitting on the toilet seat I spotted a blinking red LED light on the roof. It was one of those smoke or movement detectors and I worried I'd been recorded and then it hit me.

In twenty-five days I am going to kill a man and I'll be dead.

I had to take two Beta-blockers.

I didn't run out but, went to the café, ordered some fizzy water and a brownie, just to appear normal. On the night of Neumann's talk, it might be hard to leave the lecture and go to the downstairs restroom to retrieve my bomb vest. If any security guard stops me and asks 'why are you going downstairs? There's a restroom up here' I'll have to have a ready-made excuse. 'I always have to piss on the ground floor for medical reasons,' or some such.

Sweating in the café. Waiting for the pills to kick in. When I got up to leave, a tall security guard came over to me. 'Excuse me sir?'

My legs said, run!

'Can you please put your waste packaging in the recycling bin, sir.'

I laughed and made a theatrical show of recycling my wrapper, like a damn fool. So nice to know the Science Institute is doing their bit for Climate Change while their corporate partner performs illegal experiments on human subjects.

So, it's settled, Em. Five days before Zach Neumann's talk, I'll smuggle the pipe bomb vest into the downstairs restroom and hide it behind the roof tile at the furthest stall. It will stay there, undetected until the thirtieth. On the thirtieth, I'll attend the lecture, then go to the restroom. I'll then retrieve the bomb vest from its hiding place, strap it on and place the detonator in my outer jacket pocket. I'll then return to the first floor lecture theater, smile at the security guard and walk the aisles to my seat, but then run and leap onto the stage. I'll pull out the detonator switch and scream at the interviewing host to 'get down' and I'll throw my arms around Zach Neumann and before the security people can draw their guns, I'll…

But what if the stage is too high to jump?

Damn, and how close will the interviewer be to Neumann? I don't want to kill them too. And what if the detonator gets stuck in my pocket or falls to the ground?

Don't want to get caught with up-the-sleeve wiring issues, or worse, to be doing any last minute re-wiring on the day. Don't want to blow myself up in the crapper. A remote-controlled button-release activation, like the ones ISIS use, would be best.

OK, I'll also need a wider coat to hide bulges from the explosive vest which will be heavy – about nine extra pounds. A puffer coat. But don't want to get too hot or be the only person in the lecture hall wearing a huge winter jacket. What coats do fat people wear? Sorry, I mean 'larger bodied'. Must research this. I must also check that the event date isn't changed. Like the ██████ ██████████ lecture last year got moved to the Hilton at the last minute.

Also, double check our Institute family membership. It'd be pathetic if a lapsed membership card ended all my plans.

Oh, Em, I'm pretty nervous but thinking about you gives me strength.

OK, back onto the nitrates. Cook up a mix of 40g Spectracide with 37g of a salt-substitute in 100 ml water. Don't boil it. Filter it, freeze it, crystallize it.

Wish me luck, my love,

Over and out, your Pops.

*

Hi Em,

Is this recording? Hit the wrong button. OK, What a fucking disaster.

Potassium nitrate is totally odorless, but the white steam snuck through and my goggles fogged up, so I took them off and without thinking, wiped my face with my glove, got chemicals in my eyes. Stung like hell. Ran in panic for fresh water, leaving the PN on the heat and it burned dry. Nasty choking smoke all over the shed.

Can't stop coughing. Fuck.

Hi Em,

Feeling a bit better now.

Sorry I got so mad when you were in hospital. That damn *Coping with Comas* video warned us that after the denial stage comes blame. Blaming yourself. Blaming each other. Your mother and I moved through the stages like we were pre-programmed.

'You, smell of alcohol,' your mother said in your hospital room. 'Don't drown your sorrows and come here drunk. Don't fucking give up!'

Blaming the hospital. Attacking their tests and jargon. UPCM - Unable to Purposefully Control Muscles. HEN, which means tube-feeding. This one expression we feared – PVS, Permanent Vegetative State.

I'm sorry your mother and I shouted at the nurses right over your sleeping bed. 'Pushing people away' was another stage.

When your aunt Stacey and folk at work asked how I was doing, I'd snap: 'Me? You're asking me how I am when my daughter is in a fucking catatonic coma with tubes going into her body. How am I?'

But you're expected to say, 'not too bad,' then add, 'thanks so much for asking.'

It is all about them, not you. You are forced to smile, reminded that your grief is an anti-social threat to their community. Fuckers. And these one-liners you get from family and friends. I swear, Em, they must pull them off some '12 Comforting Things to Say to Someone with a Family Member in Intensive Care' website.

'Let me know if I can help you in any way.'

'I've been praying for your family.'

'Would you mind if I brought over a cake?'

Fuck off.

Of course, they mean well, but oh how we humans sigh with relief every time someone else comes down with a fatal illness. I'm so glad it's their daughter and not mine, we think secretly. Vile species.

'Please don't hesitate to ask if you need anything at all. Big or small,' they say. 'Don't be a stranger.'

So many times, I had to resist pinning well-wishers up against the office wall and yelling in their faces, 'fuck you, you don't even know me, you're just trying to show everyone what a good person you are.'

And those lines from work colleagues 'You're being so brave' 'you're coping so well', 'you'll get through this' which are really just demands that you stop upsetting them with your inconvenient grief and hurry-the-fuck-up in getting back to the normal work routine.

One day Colleen from Team Member Services at work said, 'would you like to take another few days off?'

'Oh yes, please, thanks very much,' I replied, 'how kind of you.' When I wanted to yell, *look, I need to take six months off, a year, because my daughter is still in a coma and hasn't actually fucking died and this just goes on and on and on…*

All the bottled-up rage. This desire to scream, 'fuck you, you fucking bystanders, it was people like you who put my daughter in a coma in the first place!'

I'm sorry Em, it exhausts me now to think back on it.

Hope and then anger again, in daily fluctuations, as I watched you grow paler, thinner, your closed eyes sinking into deeper shadows, your muscles wasting, your skin sagging on your wrist and arm bones.

Nothing they'd told us added up. And that bandage round your head and over your eyes, what was it hiding? Some days the nurses redid the bandages and held your eyelids open to put saline drops in and I saw the scratch scars on your eyelids. The nurses said there was no paperwork on why they were there.

How many times had your mother and I demanded to see 'someone in charge'?

Then one day your mother arrived early and the nurses were changing your filthy adult diaper. They were gossiping about some TV dating show, your mother said, crying, as she told me. 'They talked over Em, like she wasn't even there, like she was a piece of meat. I hate them, I hate them!'

Another day at handover time in visiting hours, I caught sight of your mother yelling at her then boyfriend, Mr Takes-care-of-himself playing Tetris on his phone beside your hospital bed, apparently. Your mother screaming, 'how could you! Get out!'

I don't know if you knew any of this or felt it, but you

were being fed by a tube at that point Em. Threaded through your nose into your stomach. The doctor gave us another chirpy video to explain. It said nasogastric tubes are one of least invasive, short-term types of feeding tubes, but they can become clogged, requiring replacement every few days. It had warnings about the probable infections you'd get from the tube, sinusitis, tonsillitis, epistaxis, gastritis.

In your third month of coma you developed a serious oesophageal infection and then we had to watch another video as they installed your next kind of feeding tube. Your mother wanted to be with you during the surgery, but they refused. A gastrostomy – for patients, like you, who could no longer be fed orally or nasally. They cut a hole in your side, Em and inserted a PEG tube through the soft skin of your abdominal wall and into your stomach. They said the tube delivered nutrition, fluids, and medications directly into your lower gut, bypassing your throat. You wouldn't feel any pain as it was done, they said. Was that true, Em?

Why did your mother and I spend hours on medical sites trying to understand the technical processes? Maybe it helped us feel we were taking part, not just helpless watchers.

They said you were being fed a mineral-rich 'slurry' and you'd no longer need to digest anything since the nutrients had already reached your bloodstream, and so you were given a stool softener so it would all pass easily, and that was why they cut another hole in you for a colostomy.

Seeing you after the operations, the respirator mask, the larger tubes coming from under your sheets. Oh Em, your mother and I tried not to look as the gurgling bags filled below your bed. You no longer seemed to be sleeping. You looked like a very old woman. Dying.

'No, no, no, you will not think that for even a second!' your mother would say whenever I raised that word as a possibility. Usually, we'd talk like that in the car park.

Did you know Em, that I visited you three times a week and your mother came four or five? She was more generous to me in those days than she'd been in our decade of divorce. Some unsaid understanding reached. 'I can't make it today to see Em. Can you go straight after work, please?' she'd say in these phone calls, 'and make sure those stupid cleaners don't spray that lavender air freshener again, please, I think it makes Emma's allergies worse.'

Sitting beside you, whispering, 'We love you so much Emma, please come back.'

One of the many coma survivor sites said reading aloud could help. Holding your hand day after day, reading *The Tiger Who Came to Tea* and *Captain Underpants and the Rainbow Fish*. Your mother found me. 'Why baby books?' she asked. It wasn't like we'd have to build your brain back up from zero when you woke up! What had I been thinking?

So I read you the news, and all the stupid fashion and gossip magazines the nurses left lying around. Some part of me thinking it might provoke you to wake up and say, 'Jeez Dad! Who gives a flying fuck about organic pedicures? Will you just stop reading that crap?'

Reading your undergrad physics papers to you, not understanding a tenth. Reading your PhD thesis, four times. 'Man-Machine Interfaces: Combining Top-down Constraints with Bottom-up Learning in Analysis of

Emotional Reaction.' Marvelling at your astounding intellect, how could you have come from my aimless DNA? Then your award-winning postdoc paper, 'Technologies of Consciousness. AI and the Search for Intelligence Beyond Earth.'

When Biosys Corp, first gave you that big job, you wept with joy, Em. 'It's a paradise for nerds,' you said. You'd finally 'found your people'. They made you sign a government confidentiality declaration and a corporate non-disclosure agreement which said, 'the signee accepts full responsibility for any liability, injury, loss, damage or death in any way connected with Biosys Corp.'

Studying your face for any trace of reaction. The beep, beep, beep of your machines. Willing you to just blink. Day after day after day. Your mother had seen your eyes move, she said. Why wouldn't they move for me?

My love. Got to get to bed now. Got all the chemicals sorted, so I have to do my first pipe bomb test-assembly tomorrow.

The sky tonight, Em. The orange and blue deepening as the light falls.

Choking in the beauty of it.

Editor's Note IV

As my transcriptions developed, the troubling question arose of exactly which mental condition Cartwright suffered from, as he was depicted in contradictory ways in the media. Mental health is an issue that I have some expertise with as an assistant editor on *The Burnout Survival Guide* and *Single and Happy Forever.*

In the months after the bombing, the dominant narrative in the press shifted rapidly from a 'lone wolf' diagnosis to depicting Cartwright as part of an organised terrorist network. He could certainly not be both and these claims seemed at odds with his behaviour in the footage, in which he often weeps, laughs or tells (silly) jokes to his deceased daughter. Such states of empathy, no matter how delusional, place his mental state far from the media depictions of 'cold calculated killer' and 'chaotic psychopath'.

As for Cartwright hearing voices, my investigations show that while this is common in schizophrenia, PTSD, Bi-Polar Disorder and Dissociative Identity Disorder, not everyone who hears voices has a mental illness.

Hearing voices, or 'auditory hallucination', is actually quite a common phenomenon and around one in ten of us will experience it at some point in our lives, according to the Mental Health Alliance. One in eight also report having other kinds of sensory hallucinations, which include 'seeing, tasting, smelling, or feeling things that don't exist.'

Such hallucinations are also common during periods of grief. According to a study of 293 widows and widowers in *The Journal of Affective Disorders*, 2014, '18% of those interviewed reported having had a post-bereavement visual hallucination of their deceased, 21% an auditory one and 3% a tactile one.'

Such experiences are also under-reported because 'the bereaved often fear others will think they're mentally ill.' Substance abuse and sleep deprivation can also be causes – all of which reflect Cartwright's situation.

One of Cartwright's other behaviours, however, might place him within the spectrum of personality disorders – and this is his tendency towards risk-taking.

In these first videos we see him engaged in processes that are clearly both amateurish and dangerous. They involve cap drilling, fuse creation, and complications to do with ignition wires; also the 'packing' of the pipe bombs with hundreds of match heads and mixtures of chemicals.

According to the *Journal of Forensic Science and Criminal Investigation*:

> *Premature detonation is a hazard in attempting to make any home-made explosives... some mixtures such as gunpowder, match heads or chlorate mixtures are very prone to ignition by friction and static electricity when packing the material inside a tube or attaching cap ends, causing many injuries and deaths among persons constructing IEDs.*
>
> (Harvard Press, 2019)

It is hard to tell whether Cartwright was even aware that he may have been risking serious or fatal injury. In one video he accidentally ignites a large pile of match heads that he has been laboriously cutting-off for hours; but he simply laughs off the incident.

After this, it must be said, Cartwright does take greater care. In a number of videos from the following days, he carefully records the stages of bomb making so he can learn from his mistakes. As editor, I have decided to delete and/or redact certain procedural and chemical details, again in the interest of public safety and for legal reasons.

In one practice run filling the first pipe bomb, Cartwright uses sand instead of flash powder. This test procedure involves a magic marker, a ruler, a freezer bag filled match heads, a broom handle for stuffing, cotton wool, baby skin wipes, Teflon tape, superglue and candle wax as a sealant.

Cartwright's somewhat fascinating test methodology is indicative of deeply focused learning, but not necessarily of the 'cold tunnel vision' associated with psychopathy. Neither does Cartwright make any contact with any other potential conspirators during these days of learning, at least during the recordings; further evidence perhaps that he was not part of a network of terrorists at all.

At this point during the transcription, I became anxious. Since the identity and procedures of the bomber had been verified, there came a point where the longer I withheld this dangerous information from others, the more complicit I might appear. As the transcribing had already taken more than half a month, if I was to back out now and hand these verified videos over to the authorities, my delay might have led to me being accused of withholding crucial evidence from the police and security services concerning a so-called terrorist.

If there had been a moment to quit, I realised to my alarm, it was already in the past. In deciding to keep on transcribing secretly I had crossed an invisible line and the only way to get out now was to reach the end of the transcription and get my publisher and their legal team on my side.

This was all the more reason to keep this 'hot material' a secret, until the task was done. There was one other reason why I could not stop: I was increasingly concerned about the circumstances around the death of Emma; she was, after all, a woman around the same age as myself, with similar beliefs and convictions; and in spite of my best attempts at professional objectivity, I must admit, I began to feel some of Cartwright's pain for his daughter.

24 days

Hi Em,

OK, just completed the assembly test and didn't blow the match heads. Success. Deep breathing now. The pipe felt much heavier than I'd imagined. With nine of these strapped to my waist it's really going to weigh me down. Six then?

Still doesn't seem real.

Things I've learned:

I'll need to replace the fuse with a battery powered one. Need to learn how to make a spark between two wire points to ignite the match heads. Who knew Fire Chief strike anywhere kitchen matches had such importance?

Need to buy a remote switch, like the ones for toy cars. I'll check out the big toy superstore in San Raf. Everything depends on this.

Can't get the damn superglue off my fingers. OK, time for a break.

You've got me laughing, Em. But I've got to get back to make adjustments on the ignition-wire hole in the screw cap. The hole's too big, I think.

Hi Em,

When did my suspicions about the Biosys cover-up really begin?

Toby.

A morning of bright sunlight. I came into your hospital room with fresh flowers and one of your old *Astronomy Now* magazines, and there was this scrawny young man sitting there already. Geeky, terribly thin, mixed race, possibly Korean. He had a tattoo on one hand and a large laptop on his knee, wires coming from it.

'Sorry, who are you? What you doing here?'

He stood awkwardly, 'Tobe,' he mumbled, 'Toby…Emma's fuh…friend.'

He started packing up his computer, and cables.

'Wait, you didn't put those earbuds in her ears, did you?' I snapped. 'You can't touch her, OK, she can get infected with anything! Understand?'

'Sorry, sorry, I just thought I'd play her some of her favorite music,' he said. 'Sh…she didn't respond.' He was sorry to intrude and headed for the door.

My head spun. 'Toby – wait, sorry, you work with Emma, right?' I asked. 'I mean, did you?' Hadn't you even dated him, Em?

I extracted the minimum he was willing to give me. His surname was Lee. Yes, he worked with you, Em, but at a different Biosys lab.

'Were you with her when the accident happened? Did it happen in an actual laboratory? Or was it something she ate like they said?'

He stared at me, confused. 'The implants,' he stuttered, '…doh…dont' you know about the…infinity…' His eyes flashed pity, then fear, looking round in case anyone was listening.

'What implants?'

He headed for the door. 'What the hell you talking about?' I grabbed his arm.

'Sorry,' he said, 'muh…maybe …there's maybe suh…something on her phone about it. I'm really soh…sorry, I can't. I'm not suh…supposed to be here.'

And he shook off my grip and ran out. If I'd known what was at stake, I should have held him then, walked him out of the hospital, forced him into my truck, driven him to my apartment, locked him in, interrogated him, hurt him even, until he told me everything about Biosys. Everything.

I missed my chance and so I sat there staring at your face, Em. Like a wax doll of yourself, only your ventilator bellows moving up and down, up and down. The hiss of piped air, the smell of perfumed baby wipes and the foul rot they tried to hide. Implants? In your body? Put inside you by Biosys?

A nurse entered, Kelsey, I think. She smiled at me semi-suspiciously, then checked your readouts, flushed your colostomy tubes with injections of water, sterilized her hands, put on a new set of gloves, then put lubricating drops in your eyes and throat, then left without a word.

Were you fighting some technology Biosys put inside your brain?

I thought your mother was wrong, this was no time to 'cope'! Part of me felt vindicated. And your phone, like Toby said. Where the hell was it? Did your mother have it? Or the hospital? Could I log on to your work email, guess your password? Hire a hacker to do it?

When I asked your mother, she knew nothing about your phone's whereabouts and she said I was stuck back in the anger stage, hunting for someone to blame.

Week after week, my love, sleeping, working, driving, eating became automatic. The metallic beeping of your heart scanner that said, life, this is all it is, it is still here, still here. A blip in a green line against black. Watching your face for twitches of hope.

'You look terrible,' your mother said, one day when we overlapped at visiting hour. 'You look… fine,' I replied, lying. 'I feel like shit,' she said, 'You getting any sleep? Try diazepam,' she said, 'with codeine'. I nodded. 'We have to be wide awake for Em when she wakes up…' she said and touched my shoulder.

These moments with your mother that no-one would ever know about. Our divorce seemed like an out-dated act, when we were alone with you in that room those roles fell away and we became two middle aged human beings watching our child living and dying and living with every breath. Caught in silent focus, both of us willing you to wake. Your mother held my hand more and more, our unspoken selves, wordless. Just the sound of your respirator, and our breaths synchronising with it. One time a nurse came in and your mother drew her hand away from mine quickly, as if we'd been caught in the act. Of what? Of still caring for each other?

Your mom focused her anger, she demanded radio scans, different blood tests and MRI, but I'd read ahead. I dreaded it but sensed the doctors were now simply waiting for us to ask the right question, postponing the moment, so they didn't have to initiate the phrase themselves.

Brain dead.

The scans detected only two per cent activity in your brain, Em, that's what they said.

I wish to hell your mom hadn't demanded those MRIs. That image of a normal brain they showed us for comparison. Lit up in bright patterns of blue, yellow and red, with sparkling stars of white. Then your scan, solid blackness where the brain should have been. More activity round the edges, in the skin round your skull. An empty shell.

'We're sorry,' they said.

Did you know your brain had died, Em?

They said, neurodegenertaion like this was common following traumatic brain injury and only the brain stem had survived. They said that such a brain only carries out autonomic functions such as breathing, heartbeat and swallowing. The pre-human brain. The lizard brain. They said a brain-dead person has 'no meaningful chance to recover' but could be kept alive indefinitely with artificial feeding. Then later with artificial breathing as well.

Your mother yelled at me. 'They've made a mistake! I saw her eyes move like she was dreaming, and her lips! Fucking idiots. I need a second opinion, need to get her to a better hospital.'

I tried to calm her.

'Stop, I will not give up like you,' she shouted. 'How fucking dare you!'

Those eye movements, the doctors told me in private, were tonic reflexes and spasms, those tiny mouth movements were caused by digestive gas, just burping, wheezing, not signs of brain activity. They were very sorry.

By the fifth month, I moved on from denial, to blame to what *Coping with Comas* called resignation, while your mother shifted her blame back towards me. It was my fault that we didn't have enough money to put you in a top-notch private hospital. How could I have been such a selfish bastard all these years, not to have saved money. How much? Half a million.

I let her hit me, shout at me, accuse me. 'How can you

just stand there taking all this?' she said, 'say something!' 'Don't you feel anything?' she screamed. 'Do something!'

Then your mother became obsessed with hunting down miracle cures. Zolpidem; Arnica Montana; Trikatu – a vedic stimulant to be taken nasally; Amantidine – a drug used to treat tremor in Parkinson's disease – she told me it had been given to a group of 87 patients in persistent vegetative state and two regained consciousness. Then coconut oil, gingko biloba, peracitam, thiamine, glucose lanolin and Naloxone, the anti-overdose drug. The hospital refused outright to let her feed you the many tablets she'd imported, all they let her do was give you some homeopathics with a dropper.

It broke me to watch her. Those online stories she insisted on sharing with me. *Hand of God wakes brain injured girl from* coma. *Miraculous mother of four wakes from coma one day before family planned to take her off the ventilator. High voltage electric shocks revive Indian nine month coma patient'*

'We have to try everything!' your mother yelled at me.

I'm sorry Em, if you were trapped inside there having to listen to us arguing. I'm sorry that I started drinking.

One day with your mother in the car park, I was arriving just as she was leaving. 'You're late again,' she said, 'and you're getting late more often. Don't you want to come anymore?' I stared at her, she seemed to be itching for a fight. I tried to defuse it. 'I admit,' I said, 'it's hard, knowing she can't hear us, knowing she's brain dead.'

Your mother pushed me, 'Well don't come anymore, you give up if you want to.' And I fell back into a parked car, its alarm screeching at us, lights flashing.

I yelled over the noise that she was being histrionic; she should read some books on how to cope with this. I told her she was trapped in the blame stage.

'Fuck you,' she yelled, 'you're not going in to see her today! I won't let you.'

I pushed past her back towards the hospital doors, yelling 'fucking try and stop me!' Leaving her standing there with that car alarm blaring.

These fluctuations.

Days later, we were in her house, your house, my former house. Your mom had opened some red wine. She'd been drinking more over the months, I noticed.

'I'm sorry,' she said, 'for saying those horrible things to you'. We sat on the old Swedish sofa together and drank the whole bottle. Our hands found each other.

I'd drifted off, thinking about Toby. 'Look, this kid from work,' I said, 'he mentioned something about implants?'

She wasn't listening. 'I hate that,' she said, 'when people at work say 'sorry', like they know she's dead already. I hate that.'

'I know,' I said.

'She's not coming back, is she?' she said, and I squeezed her hand tighter. She smelled of Coco Chanel and hospital bleach.

'I'm sorry, I can't stop it,' she said. 'To not be able to reach her… to just make it stop.'

'Yes. I feel the same,' I said.

'No, you don't.' She sighed. 'This week, seeing her like that, I thought it's so unfair, on her, on everyone… '

'I know,' I said.

'No, but I can't believe I even thought this,' she said. 'The other day Em's tubes were blocked, and I didn't know what to do, and the nurses wouldn't come, and I thought…

Em wouldn't want to go on like this. She's not a dog… no dog should be kept in misery like this.'

Your mother cried out, hit herself on the chest, yelling 'stupid, evil rotten, no mother would ever…!'

I grabbed her hands and she struggled against me, then suddenly her head rested against mine, my lips touched her forehead, and we were kissing, teeth clashing, tongues probing, breathless need, hands clawing at each other.

It stopped as quickly as it had begun.

The shutters came down, mumbled apologies, backing away.

I got up. There was nothing else to say or do, so I went to the door, and it was back to our coping routine. 'I'll see Em on Friday, is there any chance I could swap Sunday visiting hour for Monday?' I asked.

Your mother nodded. Just like our old days of shared childcare.

'OK then, bye.'

At the door, she said, 'I didn't mean that, about putting Em out of her misery, please forget I said that, and the other business, forget that too.'

'Of course.'

In the weeks after, your mother withdrew and avoided me.

For those first seven months of your coma, Em, I woke up every day feeling I was back in that first day and had to rush to the hospital, but then I would remember. Nothing has changed. Your brain is dead.

And then one day I ran out of things to say to you, Em. I simply sat silent, watching your face, the beep on your heart monitor. Flashes of your life coming back to me.

At thirteen you had a deep concern with mortality after Grandpa Alan died. Other kids your age would have gone into mourning, but you studied the aging gene and abiogenesis – the origins of life. You became obsessed with the Cassini space probe. It had filmed a hundred geysers on the moon of Saturn called Enceladus, water spraying into space. And you told me that beneath the moon's frozen surface, below those four miles of ice, molten lava caused boiling water, and so the original chemical soup that created life on earth could be there, and if humankind could venture in a spaceship to Enceladus, you said, and drill through the ice and find organic life there then this would mean that the chances of the universe being saturated with life would increase by three hundred trillion per cent.

And your mother had yelled at you – 'why is this even important, why can't you skip school and wear makeup and party like other thirteen-year-olds?'

I was worried too. One day over at my place, I asked, 'You have crush on anyone, a pretty-elven-faced humanoid like you? Anyone you fancy? No-one at all?'

'Enrico Fermi,' you'd replied through your dyed blue hair with one of your earphone plugs in.

'Great, invite him over.'

'He died in 1954.' You sighed and rolled your eyes. 'Haven't you heard of the Fermi Paradox? And anyway, you should check out the divorce stats, Dad, relationships are over and I prefer to spend my time on things that actually have some kind of future.'

Sarcasm became your thing, Em, your mother thought you maybe had antisocial personality disorder. Alone in your bedroom you taught yourself Forth, Lua, Matlab. At the age of fifteen you invested in your 7000 x magnifier Orion computerised telescope and joined the NASA outsourced search for new exoplanets in your spare time, for fun.

But those months of your coma.

I entered the next phase Em, with a weight in my bones at the prospect of being trapped with you in that room that smelled of urine and air freshener. I started watching the clock, sighing with relief in the corridor as I left you. Dreading my next return. I'm sorry. Please forgive me.

As I was leaving from one of my visits a doctor and some bureaucrat cornered me and said your mother and I should consider what 'ceilings of intervention' we could agree upon. What did it mean? They apologised and said these were 'end of life options' and they'd already attempted to have this conversation with 'the mother' but had found it difficult.

'Me,' I said, 'you want me to…?'

They said that if your lung infections became severe again and they had to remove your ventilator even momentarily, for say another operation – and if, 'do not and said, quite hostile, 'what do you think you're doing here?'

'My daughter, is here.' I said slowly, and through gritted teeth. 'You know, the kid you visited twice in the last ten years.' He wanted to hit me. I wish he had.

It all became territorial then. We should have known better than to stoop to that. That day my mother came up from L.A. My fucking hippie mother, flouncing around in her tie-dye yin and yang jogging pants, her absolutely stupid insistence that we should take all your tubes out and get you to an organic naturopath. She invited your mother and I to hold hands in a circle round your bed and to chant *Om*, and then she lit incense and set off the bloody fire alarm.

Perhaps you'd have found this funny Em. But your mother yelled that if my mother ever came uninvited again, then all visits would be cancelled for my side of the family.

'You can't do that, legally,' I snapped. 'You can't stop me from seeing my daughter.'

'Don't try me,' she said.

I shouldn't have said it, but I did.

'You vile fucking cunt. You think you own her now that she's dying! You want us to fight over her bones like a pair of fucking wolves!'

I was losing it.

You survived two stomach infections, a skin infection at the gastronomy entrance site, Em, a urethral infection, and more skin infections from the sores you developed from being bed ridden. They administered you steroids to strengthen your lungs, antibiotics were constant.

My godless prayers were not heard, the wound in your side would not heal.

I had to know your chances and month by month they shrank to below one per cent. What was going to happen, the websites and consultations told me, was, after a period of eight months on life support, after wave after wave of infections the antibiotics would no longer work and then, like many before you, you would die of pneumonia or sepsis.

I drove home and the Golden Gate was lit up and festive for New Year. Cursing at all the passing, pointless lights. I screamed soundless at TV adverts for holidays and smart phones and sexy clothes, at bright neon lit restaurants, at all the smiling, energetic youths jumping around, so appalled that they had vitality and did not deserve it. Disgust that everyone else carried on thriving as usual.

Alone with you at your bed. I stopped reading aloud and just sat in silence, day after day. 'Can you even feel my hand, Em. I'm here, It's me, your silly old dufus dad. Help me.'

I have no idea if you could hear me, but I started asking your silent face for forgiveness. For the affair that split our family, for my not being there for you. Selfish of me. Your eyes sometimes twitched behind your lids. Yes, one of the websites said that even the brain dead might have dreams. The gurgle of the tubes passing in and out of you; your digital heartbeat, the ventilator bellows forcing your chest up, down.

The mechanical bellows sent me to sleep more than once. One day I heard movement beside me. I bolted awake and you were lying on your side, trying to tug the tube out of your throat, gasping. 'Jesus, Em! Don't touch anything!' I ran around shouting. 'You're awake, Thank God, oh my Jesus fucking…!! She's woken up, help! Help!!!' I shouted down the hall.

When I came back, you were lying there, blue-white, like veined marble, the tube still in your throat, like nothing had happened, but your eyes wide open, unseeing.

'Pops?'

But your lips hadn't moved.

'Pops, where…where are we?'

Your voice seemed to be coming from inside my head.

'Em?'

I knew it was wrong to do, but I shook you. 'Em, are you in there? Are you OK?'

Your head rolled to one side as if already dead. I noticed blood travelling upwards from your stent to your fluid bag. I flew into a panic and yelled for the nurses.

Then a book landed on my foot, and I woke up properly.

These cruel dreams.

Another day, after another day, watching your respirator and lungs fill with air, rise and fall, rise and fall, I thought, would you have wanted to be kept alive like this, Em? Or would you have been the decision maker and demanded to be 'switched off?'

Could I do it if the time came?

I'm sorry, Em. Forgive me.

I didn't know then that your voice would come back to me, so clearly. That it would only be a few weeks till you told me what to do.

Hi Em,

It's 10 pm and I'm running late. Worried about the seals on the pipe ends. We can't have the ends farting off, can we? If they aren't secure enough, the instructions say, or if the ignition wire soldering isn't strong enough, the explosion will just whistle out like a steam kettle from the first hole it finds.

OK, I have to test the seals, see if they can be fastened extra tight by pliers.

Do a water pressure test with a hose to see if the solders in the sides of the pipe hold up to extreme pressure.

Maybe do this in the garden so that I don't spray water all over the chemicals.

Remember to do all soldering repairs well away from the flash powder and the ██████████ mix barrels.

Then I have to re-assemble the first pipe bomb following all the steps.

Remember to do everything very slowly so as not to cause static.

Wish me luck, Em. This is the point where I'm likely to blow my stupid self up.

OK kiddo, I'm going in.

Hi Em,

3 am now. I can't believe it, Em. I did it with the real flash powder mix this time and I think I've actually completed my first bomb!

It scares the hell out of me. I don't want the damn thing in the house, so I hid it outside in the recycling bin.

Stood staring at it, and it seemed to stare back, saying:

Get real! You think you're going to kill one of the most important men in the world with me as your weapon? Me, a mere kiddie's chemistry-set experiment?

Imagine that Em, me turning up to Neumann's lecture with all these untested explosives strapped to me and then not a pop, nothing. Just me standing on the stage hugging my nemesis in a dud suicide vest.

Oh Em, did I just invent this whole enterprise to give myself a reason to go on? Is it just an eccentric hobby?

One thing's for sure, I've got to do an explosion test.

If it fails, then it'll be back to square one with five days wasted.

OK, so a test will require either a good length of wire or a remote detonator. By my calculations, I need to be thirty feet away from the test spot. Even without shrapnel attached, the manuals say shards can travel at least thirty feet for 400 mg of explosive and there's the danger of eardrum damage.

Where the hell can I do this bomb test without getting caught?

Could try the basement. Bring down the mattress to muffle the blast?

No, if it works, what about fire damage, then there's Mz Sanchez next door?

How about Muir Woods National Park, tonight?

No. The explosion would be brighter at night. Also, making my get-away by truck, I'd stand out with so few vehicles out there and there's security cameras at state car parks.

Shit, I should have thought about the test location before I even started this. Dumb-ass!

Wait, what are you saying to me, Em. That old joke about the sea waving to us?

The sea.

Yes, you're right. The beaches up the coast could work. No buildings to echo the sound.

OK then, that's it, brilliant idea, thanks Em.

Hey Em,

I've just scoured the maps looking for an empty beach less than an hour's drive away. Duxbury Reef Conservation Area seems pretty good and is always deserted, and hard to access by the cliffs. And the sand banks round there, you've got to be careful at low tide. I could walk out and get stuck as the tide comes in; people have drowned out there, like that tourist last year.

Not sure. I'm just going to have to drive round tomorrow till I find some place.

Shit, this is real. So wired, must try to sleep now.

Wired, ha! Permit me just one pun.

Wish me luck, Em. Love you, little one.

Editor's Note V

Perhaps, in the last hope that I was not actually in possession of illegal materials, I must admit that I hoped Cartwright's pipe bomb IEDs would fail the explosion test.

The next videos appear to be filmed from the back shelves of the outdoor shed, and they primarily document the chemical and electrical processes involved in creating a remote ignition device. Cartwright appears small in frame, by the bench at the doorway and does not address the camera directly.

From the packaging visible on the foreground table, it is evident that the remote device is constructed (somewhat ingeniously) from a commercially available child's remote control (RC) car.

My research shows that this brand of RC car operates within a range of one hundred feet and uses six AA batteries. Cartwright seems to have modified the remote-control engine of the toy car, transforming it into a basic on/off switch that could then be activated remotely by the conventional pistol grip joystick.

On the table, is evidence that Cartwright purchased four of these RC cars, with two still in their original boxes (displaying 20% off stickers). In the footage, he sits at the shed window with his toolkit and the remote-control device in his hand; he then repeatedly attempts to ignite a box of matches placed thirty feet away in the garden.

After five unsuccessful attempts, he moves back and forth between the camera and the matches outside, making adjustments and repeating the experiment. The footage spans several hours, during which time he mutters, curses, and talks to himself, although his words remain inaudible to the laptop mic. He makes twelve attempts before successfully igniting the box of matches using the remote control.

Subsequent footage focuses on technical aspects, such as connecting the functional remote on/off ignition switch to the cap of a pipe bomb, and numerous experiments involving drilling and soldering (which again have been deleted).

Regarding the sections where the bomber starts hearing a voice or voices, there is no evidence in these earlier recordings of any other voice present in the room with him again confirming that this is 'all in his head'.

As the days in the videos ticked down, I must confess to feeling increasingly scared as I thought of the dead and their families, and of my ever growing role in handling and hiding the evidence.

At this point, one strange wish developed; perhaps it was some fantasy of a get-out-of-jail-free card. My hope was that not only would Cartwright's bomb test fail utterly, but that he would completely abandon his task.

But then I realised this would mean something impossible – that he would have been falsely accused of the San Francisco bombing.

23 days

Hi Em,

I'm in shock and bleeding. It needs some tweaking but God damn it, the damn thing went off!

Around ten, I got into the truck with the pipe bomb and remote control and went searching. But then I got scared of having them both beside me on the passenger seat, what with all the potholes round there, so I parked just past the old chicken farm and bundled up the pipe bomb in the shoulder bag, hid them both in my jacket and put them in the back of the truck.

A tractor rode past spraying dirt, the farmer giving me the once over. I don't know how much he saw. I waved, which was probably a dumb mistake, you know what people are like round here.

So, I thought I'd maybe test the bomb in Steep Ravine, then I remembered that old WW2 military fortification at Baker Beach and the Presidio on the other side of the Golden Gate. It's a crumbling ruin now but I had this damn fool idea that if someone heard a small explosion, then maybe they'd assume it was a WW2 unexploded ordinance gone off by accident. It wasn't the best alibi, but I still headed south to the bridge.

The sight of the suspension wires through the fog took me back.

It was a weekend when you came to stay in my shack, you'd have been sixteen and just graduated from high school two years ahead of the other kids. Your hair was maybe green at that point, with that Manga bob cut you loved. You seemed moody in my truck, staring out at the bridge, not saying much. Your mother had been worried about you all summer; she thought you were showing signs of having inherited my 'darkness'. I hoped to hell you hadn't and told myself teenagers can be moody for lots of reasons, hormones, zits, friends, social media, confusion about their place in the world. You hated your face with your elven cheekbones, your body with the curves you'd inherited from Granny Annie, your 'melons' as you called them. Miles of your silence, just staring out the passenger window at the Pacific.

'What's up Emaboo?' I asked. 'You OK?'

'Could we go to our lil'old beach, Pops?' you asked. Was it relationship trouble? I hoped so. You were well overdue for showing romantic interest in males, females or whatever.

We parked and sat there on our secret beach just under the Golden Gate. It was really just spill-over gravel from the car park, but you loved that it was hidden under the vast legs of the bridge. 'Like a beach under a cathedral,' you once said. Between us skimming stones in the water, I asked again, 'what's bothering you, kiddo?'

You skimmed a stone, eight tiny, bouncing leaps.

'I got accepted for Harvard,' you sighed.

I think I hugged, you, twirled you round, kissed you, told you,how utterly magnificent you were. 'Which department: physics, astrophysics, neuroscience?'

'All of them, Pops... But I dunno,' you shrugged. 'Everyone says I should go, but why?'

'Are you nuts?' I almost shouted. 'Because you're a genius and they've recognized that, and never mind the fees, me and your mom will work that out, somehow. And at sixteen! This is just so fucking brilliant, well done, Em. Of course, you have to go!'

And you started on your old why-cascade.

'Come on,' I said, 'you'll get the best education in the world, you'll have your choice of jobs when you graduate.'

'Why would I want a job?'

'What?'

'Yeah dad, just think about it. What are jobs anyway? They're just doing what you're told by higher status people who pay you so you can work, shop, eat, shit, and sleep.'

I couldn't help but laugh, 'Work, shop, eat, shit, sleep.' I think I even turned it into a silly song and did a silly dance on the gravel. 'Work, shop, eat, shit, sleep – work, shop, eat, shit, sleep.'

You skimmed another stone.

'Why do you always have to goof around?' you said. 'I'm serious. Like when I look at older folk, like you, no offence, but I just see everyone working day-in day-out just so they get a better job, higher up the ladder so they can shop more and eat better food and shit better and they sleep mostly with sleeping pills. And the elites, they shop for the best sexual partners and produce top class babies that shit, eat and sleep way better than the poor people's babies, but that's all it's all about.'

You were on one of your rolls, like the time, aged eight when you disproved the possibility of televisions existing in Heaven for Granny Annie. I knew better than to interrupt.

'I mean think about it,' you said, as you selected a new skimming stone, 'you get men parading their career status and muscles and women parading their asses and faces, and it's all just so they can beat each other in the mating game, and shop, shit, eat and sleep better than others in the hierarchy. And why? Why do so many people worry about how old they look, like Granny Annie and her diets and Mom with her anti-ageing cream? Why do they try to stay young when they haven't even worked out why life is worth living? Why is 'more' the only answer? Why? Does more exquisite wine count for anything? More gym? More socializing? More orgasms? More people telling you, you're an awesome person. More labor-saving devices so we can work, shop, eat, shit, and sleep more, more, more, more. Do we think that by adding all this up we'll eventually reach a justification for it all? Or will you just have a larger pile of forgotten experiences? More delicious snacks? More holidays? No, sorry dad, getting a good job isn't a justification for anything.'

'Wow,' I said. 'How long have you been feeling like this, Em?'

You scowled, 'God, you're so like Mom. Why is it that whenever people ask serious questions everyone always assumes we're mentally ill? And don't worry, I haven't inherited your depressions or whatever, I did an online test and I'm fine if you must know. I just guess, right now I need to know what it's all for, because if I do go to Harvard and go all the way to PhD, then by the time I'm done, what with robotics and AI, there's going to be 40% unemployment and almost nothing left for humans to do but shop, shit, eat and sleep anyway. Literally, I have the modelled data on this. By 2035, most everyone is going to be useless, getting paid to do nothing more than sit at home and shop online, and eat, and shit and sleep, day after day for the rest of their lives like hamsters in hamster cages with keep-fit hamster wheels and home food hamster delivery and porn for hamsters. Work, shop, shit, eat, sleep and screw I guess, yeah, I forgot that last one. Yeah, gotta screw so another generation can work, shop, shit, eat and sleep – and on and on it goes.'

You stood at the shore in your retro workman's dungarees, your Granny Annie's body, my nervous eyes and all the weight of the world on your shoulders. 'It must be lonely to be so smart,' I said and tried a different tack. 'You'll meet people like you at Harvard, not just us dummies.'

'Sure,' you said, 'but, if I do go, I'll just be one of the scientists who're forcing all the rest of you into the hamster cage of work, eat, shop, shit, screw and sleep.'

I had to smile. How many people my age were clawing their walls because that was all their lives amounted to. Monday to Friday, work, eat, shop, shit, sleep, the weekends, eat, shop, shit, screw, sleep, then back to work. I wanted to tell you there were other things people lived for: culture, humor, maybe even love.

'I still think you'd be a damn fool not to accept your place at Harvard,' I said.

And we stood there and skimmed stones beneath the bridge, in silence.

Drifting off, Em, and reminiscing like this, I'd veered out of my lane and into the path of an oncoming truck.

'Wake up! I yelled at myself, 'you stupid fuck!'

I made it halfway across the bridge and realized it was a dumb idea to test the bomb so close to San Fran and so many cop stations. I made it to the tollbooth then turned around and came back. You would have laughed, Em, at what a dipshit I must have looked to the cameras.

I was starting to get cold feet. I thought, you were right Em, so many of us are lost these days, and come to an end with nothing resolved, unsure what we believed in, unsure of how to make any sense of anything we experienced, just worn out and ragged, more bewildered than before, dying, mid-sentence, mid-breath.

I couldn't let this fizzle out, half-done. I had to see the bomb test through.

Back over the bridge and the sun muffled through the fog, then another memory, of anti-submarine mines from WW2 washed up on the beaches near that lighthouse up north last year, and that beach closed to the public because of it. Point Reynes lighthouse. And no tourists would ever go see a lighthouse in the fog. Yes. Perfect.

As I drove I asked you if you were there, but no reply, not even a crackle, Em. I swear the further away from the city I go the less I can hear you. Or maybe your voice is just Prozac withdrawal. Memory zaps. I don't know.

It took about forty minutes to drive up the coast, but when I got to the lighthouse, there were too many cars in their teeny car park, so I drove on. Another ten miles and I spotted a sign for Pig Bay and headed up there. My old Toyota rattling over the single-track roads. I saw razor wire fencing and *Danger Firing Range - No Entry* signs. I'd forgotten there was one up there. And security cams on the fences. Damn it all to hell. I was getting further and further away from my plan and my alibi. I had to settle on the next beach I came across or give up and come back home.

Another three miles and I found an old coastal track hidden by dune grass. There was only one other car in the sandy car park, and the buildings round the beach were old run-down WW2 bunkers that some farmer had used for storing bales of hay. The nearest farmhouse was a good three quarters of a mile back. It had to do.

I parked next to this old Volvo, got the pipe bomb and bag from the rear and put my jacket back on. The fog was muggy, sodden, those humid grays rolling in from the Pacific. I thought that might muffle the blast. If the bomb even worked. I was shivering badly.

My plan-A was to walk a mile or so along the sand, make sure no-one was around then plant the bomb in a dune, step back forty feet to be on the safe side, then remote-activate it. Plan-B was to strap it to a piece of wood, send it off out into the ocean and then when it was far enough out, detonate.

Oh Em, you would have laughed at how suspicious your silly old Pops must have looked checking over my shoulders every ten seconds, as I walked onto the sand plains. The tide was far out, seaweed and whelks crackling under my feet. Then a barking noise, and a figure came at me through the fog. I thought it best to walk away quickly but realized it would be less suspicious to let them pass. I barely raised my head, but just enough to see it was an old woman, sixties, the dog was one of those yappy floppy-eared things and the woman had one of those plastic ball throwing things and a pooper scooper.

'Foggy day,' the woman said, getting closer. I said something back, then her dog was at my feet, sniffing me and I had to stop, afraid the dumb mutt would trip me up with the detonator in my jacket pocket and the bomb in my backpack. I had to get away.

'Is that…' the woman said, 'sorry, I didn't recognize you at first.'

I looked up and it was Mrs Jensen from the corner store in San Raf. I tried to smile, and she asked how I was. I cursed myself for not having prepared an alibi and blurted out, 'lovely day Mrs Jensen, just out for a bit of fresh air with Em.'

Why the hell did I say your name?

Mrs Jensen looked around for another person or dog. I couldn't recall if I'd ever told her about you, or if she'd heard local gossip. She seemed pretty embarrassed. I mumbled, 'sorry, I mean, I used to walk here with Em and I'm just, just…'

Why had I said that? Like I was trying to say, 'I'm just here for no suspicious reasons, just minding my own business, so you just do the same and just go away!' She touched my arm, while her slobbering dog moved from sniffing my crotch to my bag of explosives.

'I'm sorry for your loss,' she said softly and stepped back.

I was choked-up. I may have nervously said something stupid like, 'and yours too,' or 'have an awesome day.'

Then I just stood there, mute. The compassion of strangers is too much to bear. Had she even lost a child?

'Bye for now,' she'd said calling back to me.

Was her 'bye for now' a wise old woman's way to say, *you poor, aimless man, walking with your long-dead daughter and your excuses. I know you could kill yourself today but don't do it. There will be many more nows and we'll meet again.*

She dissolved into the fog and I heard her call to her dog, Jasper. She left me in this silence as the damp fog rolled in and that hollow ache opened inside me again. I stood there the longest time, Em, as the tiny gray waves breathed in and out. I stood there for so long that I saw that the patterns in the sand were caused by run-off water from the hills, a river meeting the sea. It got me thinking of the steam inside your breathing mask. The sound of the waves and the sound of your respirator bellows. Everything hanging on your next breath, through eight months of coma. End of Life options.

My little Em. You once said, your name was just Me backwards.

There I was, on the beach, only two hours ago, feet soaked from walking through the shallow waves, not even thinking about the pipe bomb in my bag, as my thumb tinkered with the remote trigger in my pocket.

I couldn't tell which way I'd come, Em, and which way was forward, and this must have been how people got stranded on the vast flat sand plains that get millimetres deeper with each wrong step, drawn into the greater silence of the fog. The gloom was wet on my skin, in my hair, droplets on my eyelashes, the cold of it soaking through my clothes.

Any trace of the cliffs behind had disappeared, and the sea, the sand and the sky seemed to have merged into one. Before I knew it, I was sloshing through three inches of water, and the sky and sand flats reflected each other, and the horizon vanished so that everything became a flat pale shade between light and dark, unable to resolve itself. As if the world up until now had been a series of film images and this had been the blank screen they'd been projected upon.

Such silence. As if purgatory were a place.

A distant gull, then it was gone. The sound of my breath. Louder. The repetitions, in out, in out. Alone. I don't know how long I stood there when I thought – this might be the best way to go. I could do it, right there. Ignite the bomb on my back, and if it worked, it worked.

I got the remote in my hand. Flipped the switch

protector open and fingered the round button. If the bomb doesn't work, then I survive.

But what would I survive for?

Work, eat, shop, shit, screw, sleep?

Disgust. If I took the quick way out now, then no one would ever learn how they killed you. A coward's exit. And I'd promised to stay alive this last month on the condition that your death was avenged.

Furious, I pulled my backpack off, yelled and slung the whole damn thing into the fog. I heard it land in the wetness but couldn't see it. I cursed myself, threw the remote switch away but my finger must have tripped it.

The flash threw me off my feet, burned my eyes, heat blaze on my skin. I couldn't hear a thing as I picked myself out of the wet sand. No gulls, no waves, just the ringing.

There was a stubby flame visible through the fog, and I ran towards it until twenty feet from me, I found my backpack, shredded. I had to search to find the remains of the pipe bomb, they'd been scattered in every direction. The pipe had been torn almost into two and a hot sulphurous lava glowed from inside its broken shell, a sick fusion of wires, plastic and melted aluminium, the thing stank like a house fire and I scalded my finger-tips on it.

I didn't think, God, look at all these fragments, that will be my spine soon. No, I thought: Yes, it will kill him. I can kill him. It works. It fucking works.

I stood there while the shards of melted aluminium cooled, and then I realized I had to hide them. I gathered all I could find and got down on my knees, digging like a frantic dog into the sand, the water mocking me, filling in my holes. Thinking fast, adrenalized, I thought, I have to plant each fragment forty, fifty feet apart! So, I ran over the sands planting the shards like some crazed forester. The backpack bits were the hardest to hide, and I thought of some brat with their dog in a few days' time sniffing out the shoulder straps and pulling them free, only to find the exploded remains.

Back at the car park, Mrs Jensen's Volvo had gone. No one was around and I saw gulls above but they made no noise beyond the single ringing note in my ears. I banged my stupid skull and put a finger in one ear to try to shake the sounds of reality back. In the truck the buzzing in my head turned into a shooting pain. In the rear-view mirror, I saw a bloodied face. I dug into it to try to find the source of the pain. I pulled a shard of aluminium from my hairline, it was about the size of a tooth and the blood pumped harder when I yanked it out.

Thank God, Em, I had my First Aid kit in the truck, and an old water bottle under the passenger seat. Advil in my wallet. I managed to staunch the bleeding and get a Band-Aid on it, then with my baseball cap on, the wound was practically invisible. The rest was just cleaning up with my hands out the car window and pouring the water over them. All the time, scared that another car would drive up. The police alerted to the explosion. The army even, from the shooting range a few miles back. But not a soul.

It was pretty dumb to be parked there contemplating all of this. 'I'm in shock,' I told myself. And that was an actual shock wave that blew me off my feet.

I heard your voice, or my conscience say, 'why waste time? Why get caught?'

I floored the accelerator, sped off and a mile on my hearing started to fizzle back. There was a crack-crack noise like stones hitting plastic and I realized target practice at Pig

Bay rifle range was actually taking place that day. I drove up past Barron's farm and a huge loader was replacing a dumpster, making these clanging steel booms, as loud as a bell.

All these lucky noises had covered up my explosion, and I laughed like hell. It worked, the damn thing worked and I'd got away with it. Just to make sure, I turned off and headed East on the single tracks, dodging roadside security cameras, and went the back way around Fairfax, bought some potted rosemary, and another five liters of stump remover and nitrates as my alibi at Green's Garden Center, then drove down onto the 101, then back through Mill Valley and up through Stinson, a whole circle detour of about forty miles, so no one could trace me.

Coming back round by the lagoon, I saw that old sign for Dogtown Fine Arts, then I remembered, the old Copper Mine was up there, just past Woodville and the hippie arts place. You remember it Em, we stumbled across it on one of our weekend drives. The old, abandoned mine shafts and no-one around and only four kilometres from home. I could have tested the damn bomb there and saved myself a three-hour drive!

I accelerated down the 101 for home, and felt, how can I describe it? Bliss, Em. It was probably the adrenaline, but I was thinking faster, many moves ahead, fired up, energy crackling like static in my muscles. Alive, yes, for another twenty-three days and then I'll blast that murdering motherfucker to hell.

Back home. I superglued the cut on my head and slathered it in Dettol cream. Funny, I thought, this probably won't heal in less than a month. I'll die with this silly wound pointlessly trying to mend itself. Laughing.

I got a fright in the mirror. There were two new holes in my jeans and my left thigh was bleeding, my jacket was sprayed with tiny aluminium shards, luckily it'd been thick enough to stop them.

I undressed and took a shower and counted the holes in my skin as I stood there naked. Five in total. Band-Aids did the job. I laughed my stupid head off, like a silly kid with his first firework, Em. So proud of himself.

And a stupid old joke came to me, Em, maybe I told it to you before – Did you ever hear about the man who tried to catch the fog?'

He mist. M-I-S-T. Ha ha.

Worn out now, I should have a nap. Why not? It's not like I have to stick to a daily routine now that I only have four hundred hours left or so. Now that I think of it, Em, It won't take more than a hundred hours to finish the nine bombs and get my vest sewn and ready. So that leaves me about three hundred hours of working, shopping, eating, shitting and sleeping or whatever else.

Ha. You once asked me Em, Is there anything I really wish I'd done, before I die? What do normal people have on their lists? Ride an elephant in Thailand, dogsled through the Alaskan Forests, attend an orgy in Bangkok, visit the Taj Mahal, Fedex a parcel of my shit to the head of every big tech corporation, swim with dolphins?

Sorry, sitting here on the floor in my boxer-shorts, still laughing like a fool. I guess I've left it a bit late for all of that. Mist my chance! But you're right Em, I've no excuses now, I'm more free than ever. No more doubts, or politeness, no more morals – what people think of me doesn't matter a damn anymore.

Right, things to do before I die:

Crash four hundred dollars on the best 5 Star meal in San Fran?

Give some or all this money I've saved to my sister.

Go to a church. To yell at it, provoke God to manifest and tell me why I shalt not kill mine enemy. Why not? Bring it on big man.

Buy some expensive sneakers. Yes, I need to buy some outfits, to help me pass as a regular guy on the final day. Plus, a really big overcoat to hide the suicide vest under. Yes. Spend a few thousand on nice clothes.

How about some European cheese? Dutch and French. Emmental, Brie, Roquefort, you and your mom used to always complain that I snored after wolfing down Camembert.

Oh Em, I'm in such a weird hyper state I feel kind of sick and can't stop jabbering and pacing, I won't be able to sleep again.

My pipe bomb actually worked. I can't believe it. I can't.

Mister nobody is good for something after all. Mister No Body. Haha!

Hi Em,

Had only a few hours' sleep so I'm up again. The damn cicadas. I should get earplugs.

Remember that second time, Em, when your voice woke me in hospital. 'Why Pops?'

'Why?' your voice asked, 'why are you sleeping? Why don't you open your eyes, lazy bones? You're in a hospital bed too, dufus dad! Look!'

I saw you were right, I was somehow, in an actual

medical bed in a different green hospital room, and you weren't there with me. How the hell had I got there? And was your voice, so loud in my ears, finally proof I'd flipped?

'Why oh why, did you drink so much? The nurses said you're under observation till you're sober enough to go home, Pops,' your voice said. 'And why are you looking round for me like that? I'm in your head, you douche. And don't get up. You're going nowhere, we need to talk.'

'OK, OK,' I whispered, and pain stabbed the back of my head.

You'd survived your third pulmonary and second bladder infection, but the antibiotics had stopped working and your lungs were infected again. Just the night before, I'd got down on my knees in a service station restroom stall and prayed, please God, whatever the fuck you are, make Em pull though. I'd brought a flask of vodka to the hospital and must have nodded off, right beside you, or so I thought.

I climbed out of the bed, the room spinning, and snagged my arm on some jagged tube that was stuck in it. My skull felt like it was cracking,

'You're wondering why you have stitches on the back of your head, Pops. Well, it's 'cos you were so utterly blasted last night that you fell over and cut yourself,' your voice said. 'Poor pathetic Pops? Sheesh! Don't touch it. Your blood couldn't even clot because there was so much booze in it. Gross, yeah, that's why you've got an IV in your arm and that goofy drip stand.'

'Em,' I whispered, 'is this another dream?' It was like I'd become you, in a bed in a room with three other hospital beds, all empty. My legs were bare and someone must have undressed me to my underwear.

'Oh Pops,' your voice said, 'I just can't stand to see

you doing this yourself. You're going to end up killing yourself with grief, I mean, on some level it's quite flattering that your life has become so totally meaningless without me,' your voice said as I tried to focus on the swaying hospital walls, 'but I'll let you in on a secret, Pops. It's not really about me, is it? This crap of yours has been going on a lot longer than that, and you only had me, you know, a baby, to make your recurring depressions go away, Pops. Why did you hide all this from me when I was growing up?'

'How do you know any of this?' I whispered, then I realized I was talking to myself in an empty hospital room.

'How? I rummaged around in your memories, when you were passed out,' your voice said. 'Pretty tragic stuff, you know, like why didn't you warn Mom about your mental illness, Pops? Did you think she was your saviour or something?' The voice said, 'pretty unfair on Mom.'

I held my aching head, your voice relentless inside it. You sounded almost distant like a phone line, and I had to check my mobile just to make sure, but I couldn't find it. I was convinced you were my conscience, 'Why are you tormenting me?' I said out loud.

'Good question, here's the thing, Pops,' your voice said, 'I've been through all the whys and why-nots about staying or going and I reckon that when I die, if I left you to your own devices, you'd probably survive another year at most. Like your old friend Tom,' your voice said, 'remember, he locked himself in his apartment with ten bottles of vodka after his wife and kids left. Uncle Dom said he'd got so blasted he fell down the stairs, knocked himself out and choked in his own vomit. I expect something similar for you, Pops, the way you're going.

Maybe not as glamorous. More likely major liver failure and another rerun of last night's adventure, bleeding out while you're passed out; which would be tragic.'

'I'm sorry,' I whispered, 'I shouldn't have been drinking beside your hospital bed, I'm so sorry.' And I got up and looked for the chord to pull for help. I needed to tell a doctor I was hearing voices.

'Wooooah. Stay where you are!' your voice said. 'Hear me out. I'm not judging you. I know you're getting wasted because you love me and miss me so much and it's kind of sweet.'

And you told me Em, that you loved all those times I held your hand and read to you and sung our goofy songs.

'I heard it all,' you said, 'even over the respirator machine which is pretty loud. I could hear when your mouth was whispering close to my ear, and kissing my forehead. But I couldn't move my neck or lips or fingers or toes, believe you me, I tried so hard to let you know. I couldn't even see your poor face all that time, but it was good to feel you there, Pops.'

I was weeping then. Your voice growing with the confusion and pain in my head. You said, 'thanks for your confessions too Pops, they were kind of weird, but thanks anyway.' And you told me you were a bit pissed at me too. 'Cos it's been pretty hard to get through to you what with all your booze and pills,' you said, 'and I can't stop you drinking, God knows I've tried these last few weeks, but you just weren't getting the message. After all these months of asking why, I think I've found a solution,' you said. 'Just hear me out, Pops, then I'll leave you alone. Just keep yourself focused on my voice and don't get up or react, till I've said it. OK?'

I did what your voice said, Em.

'So, I realized, why should you keep on suffering like this? In and out of hospital, having lots of accidents,' your voice said. 'And I thought, why? Why keep poor Pops hanging around? Why not set a date to put you out of your misery? You know like Aunt Stacey did with Weight Watchers. Set a date to lose ten pounds.'

I laughed. Whether you were my conscience, a demon, or the sound of my own madness you at least had Em's sense of humor.

'So, I decided,' your voice said, 'no more whys and ifs and buts cos I want you to be totally free to go through the grief process, so why not just end it all today? Give up the ghost, kick the old bucket so to speak. So that's what I'm gonna do Pops. Like, starting right now.'

'What… wait?' I shouted.

'Bye Pops, love you so much.' You whispered, 'bye-see-bye.'

I jolted awake in the hospital bed.

So, it had been another damn dream. I got up, but pain shot through the back of my head, and a jab ran through my wrist from an IV drip. I yelled for help and a nurse came in and told me it was all just like you'd said Em, I'd been inebriated during visiting hours and had fallen and cut my scalp and needed stitches.

I demanded to know that you were OK, Em.

'Your daughter is stable, nothing to report,' she said, 'her mother is in there with her right now.'

A second nurse, male, shone a light in my eyes and asked me many questions – who the president was, what year it was, how much alcohol did I consume per day? He wanted to book me into rehab. My gut ached and I retched.

There was blood on my head bandage and on the pillow. Against the nurses' advice, I discharged myself. I should have gone straight to see you in your hospital room in the other ward, Em. I should have listened to the dream, but I got a taxi home to sleep.

By the time I woke it was night and my phone was dead. I charged it and saw the messages from your mother, ten, in increasing desperation. 'Get to the hospital now! Where the hell are you? Em's sepsis is much worse, we need to make this decision now. Don't make me do this alone!'

By the time I got to you Em, the doctors and your mother had already made their final call without me. Do Not Resuscitate.

Time of death 1:34 am.

Everything went into slow motion, froze in mid-air
Why does the tree climb so high?
Why is the flour in the pie?
Why are you the apple of my eye?
Why does my girl always ask why?
Why-oh-why?

I'm sorry, Em, for what I did when I got back to the hospital. It was ugly. The crying, the rage. Your uncle Steve tried to hug me but I hit him in the jaw, floored the doctor. The things I yelled at your mother, the accusations. Vile, all of it. I saw only a glimpse of you. Lying so calm and still, no pipes in you anymore, no machines to breathe, no breath.

A marble statue of yourself. What could I do?

I am sorry. So sorry my love.

22 days

Hi Em,

My head aches and there's blood on the damn pillow again, but at least the bomb recipe works. I'm on a timeline. I can increase the blast too, the cookbook says, by adding more otassium nitrate. Those hot and cold therapy gel packs for injuries are packed full of the stuff. Better, I hope, than this stump clearer which is so damn noxious.

Now that I've passed the first technical, I realize I'm going to have to prepare myself mentally for killing Neumann.

As I was washing, I heard your voice again Em, it's so faint sometimes, like its barely got the energy to reach me. It sounded like you were saying, 'blister' like a warning, over and over, but then it sounded like sister.

Yes, you're right Em. I can't keep putting off speaking to Stace. Get rid of the money in my accounts too. Plus make lists of goodbye letters.

Hey again Em,

So, I hid my head injury with my Dodgers cap, and headed to the self-service store. Got some funny looks from folks, maybe because I was limping a bit as well. Anyway, I got some more carbon pellets and saltpetre, heavy-duty Band-Aids for the head and leg. Plus, I grabbed some pre-cooked chicken, donuts and a ten pack of cola. Full-sugar. It's not like I have to worry about my waist!

I spent the morning duplicating the procedure from the first pipe bomb. Surprised that it took me just three hours to fill three more pipes with the match heads, the ball bearings, the flash powder, ground aluminium, PN and mix. My ignition wire soldering took only an hour.

There are some things that happened last year that I still don't understand, Em.

After you passed away, I fell into the spiral your voice had warned me about. Unable to face food. Vodka breakfasts and vomiting, every hour spent as drunk as I could get. Days weeping, screaming, punching the walls, searching online videos with titles like 'the meaning of life', then waking up in my piss-soaked clothes.

An autopsy hadn't been done on your body, Em. Months before, any web search of your name came up with dozens of glowing pages on your awards, photos of you in your lab coat. But after you died, they all vanished. Your CV page and career history at Biosys, your social media too. Hundreds of photos of you smiling in different summers, with different colors of hair and friends and lovers, all erased.

I remember I was uptown, coming back from an aborted therapy session with Chris, I'd picked up another liter of vodka at a corner store and I stopped on the sidewalk. I'd forgotten where I'd parked my truck and searched for four or five blocks. A total blank.

For a second, I felt my hand was empty, like I'd left something behind. A sudden sense memory of your little warm clammy fingers gripping mine.

Then the words – 'Em is dead'.

I froze on the sidewalk somewhere near Union maybe and was knocked out of the way by a young woman running for a taxi. I turned and another person pushed past me. Suddenly there were dozens of young folks all headed somewhere fast and I was stuck by a traffic light, standing in their way. Some said excuse me, others pushed with elbows. Maybe they were all running for a train or there was some shopping frenzy. No idea.

I clung to the pole and stared at the hundreds surging past, all with such purpose, all these fit bodies competing with each other to move faster, to reach their destination, their next level, chasing their goals, their dreams, the desire to be first. They seemed to merge, no longer individuals, but like water, time-lapsed. A force flowing through them. Yes. It was like I was an old broken branch of wood, pushed to the edge of a fast-flowing river. And it kept on surging in its one direction, sweeping everything out of its path.

I saw a hat, a handbag, a phone, like pieces of flotsam being carried along by a great river. Were these really people? A hand, an eye.

The longer I stared the more I slowed down. I couldn't put my toe back into that water, its speed terrified me. Millions of human gallons flowed past, so fast and I was clinging to the edge, forced out, horrified at this energy I was no longer part of. They were the living, so what was I?

My hand, empty.

Five or six days after your death and my fatherhood was over. Fifty years spent to no end. I'd never be a grandfather. I'd be the last of my line. I had no more energy left to invest in work or people or love. Work, eat, shop, shit, screw, sleep. I tried to step out again onto the street but the waves of bodies forced me back and I clung to the traffic light.

Then the human flood ceased, and I was alone again.

Somehow, I managed to get home. The only thing that

saved me that week was drunken exhaustion. It would have taken too much sober focus to find a razor to slit my wrists with or to drive to the Golden Gate, locate a spot where the anti-suicide netting was broken and throw myself over.

You know Em, we no longer have rituals of respect for the grieving in this liberal land, only the expectation that you must get over it as soon as possible, so you can go back to the smiling facade of death avoidance and 'being positive'.

Drunk, I read the Coping With Death app. I listened to podcasts with expert tips. But it all felt like shopping for a quick-fix solution. Why should it be up to the individual, like some pathetic online shopper, to pick their own personalized solution to infinite grief?

Buy this 'In loving Memory' mourning mug with customizable text, for only eight dollars and ninety seven cents. Sale ends in ten hours.

I needed to find some lost tradition I could steal from. In Jewish mourning traditions, during Aninut, people are not to approach or offer any consolation to the bereaved. The grief is too extreme and silence must be respected. A mourner will also tear their clothes as a sign to others. I tore my shirt but – it all felt fake.

The Navajo would refuse to use the name of the deceased for a whole year after death and they used to cut a long wound into their arms. It would take two months to heal, and as the body of the deceased deteriorated, the wound gave mourners a physical manifestation of their pain and healing. The remaining scar was a living memory of the loved one, carried on your own body till death. And when you died, others in turn would scar themselves.

I read that the Lakota peoples used to take a lock of

hair from their deceased loved one and wrap it up in a buckskin 'soul bundle'. The keeper of the soul bundle would store it safe in a hidden place and would commit no sins for a year, then after that year, the bundle would be opened to the sky and the soul set free.

Beautiful but I didn't have a lock of your hair, or a belief in heaven.

A certain tribe in New Guinea carried the corpses of their loved ones on their backs for a year. In Victorian England, locks of hair were snipped from the deceased and framed with a sample of the beloved's handwriting. For widows, full mourning was expected to last one year and a day, fully veiled in a black crepe weeping veil. Men wore black armbands. In some Mediterranean countries widows wear black for the rest of their lives.

Today you get five days off work. I received a card from the office with a silhouette of a single daisy and the text said, 'Thinking of you at this difficult time'. It was from someone I didn't know in our Team Member Services department. I couldn't face my fellow staff trying to cheer me up or avoiding me out of embarrassment.

So, I drank.

Voice messages from my damn mother saying, 'don't despair, I've consulted with Haradanta, and he believes Emma's karma was very pure and she will surely be born into higher form, possibly as a whale or a dolphin.'

Another from her saying she'd be holding a private fire rebirth ritual for you, with her guru and some fellow followers, up in Big Sur.

Messages from my sister, asking if I was OK and to please pick up the phone, the sounds of her children in the background, 'Mommeee! Jojo stole my choo-choo!'

Voice messages from your officious Aunt Audrey who works in corporate events planning, saying, 'I've taken over family organizational responsibilities and can you please log onto the new family website for urgent updates and to add your memories of Emma for the memorial celebration.'

I drank and disconnected my landline.

There are the woven hanging coffins of the Philippines, in which the bodies of the deceased are suspended from mountainsides for ten years, because they believe that the closer a coffin is to the sky, the closer the deceased is to the gods.

The ancient Celts used to perform the 'death wail', in which the clan screamed their grief together in a communal fire ritual.

Team Member Services also sent me an email asking how many days I'd be off as I only had three days of annual leave remaining, and could I please fill in form C-48 with my return date.

In Thailand monks lay the body of the deceased in a courtyard, and then for an hour every day as a meditative practice the mourners watch the body decompose. They watch the infestations of larvae emerge from the festering corpse skin, they watch the face of their loved fellow turn to a skull. They allow the vultures to pick the bodies clean, then they grind up the bones and feed them to crows. Cycles of life, death, life.

In Borneo, when one of their family dies, tribesmen cut off a finger.

One day, after watching that on YouTube, I got the kitchen knife. Aiming for my thumb I nicked my index finger and panicked at the blood, then I drank to kill the pain. I sat on the floor with a kitchen towel soaked red, laughing and weeping. I lost days like that, Em, after your death, Em. Pathetic. Then one morning I heard a voice coming toward me whispering, *Why do mammals eat each other? Why do we kill time? Why do people believe in Heaven? Why are you still asleep?*

I gasped awake, feeling a presence on the sofa next to me. 'Who's there? Em is that you?'

'Of course, it's moi Pops,' your voice said. 'Who d'ya think it was, Saint Peter?'

'No, you're just another dream, leave me alone!'

'Why should I?' your voice said. 'It's taken me so long to get through to you. The noise of all the others got majorly in the way, and to be fair you've been trying to block me out with your stupid booze. Why do you do that to yourself?'

There was no-one behind the closet, no-one hiding under the bed. I wondered if the voice was delirium tremens from alcohol poisoning. I saw seven empty liter bottles of vodka on the floor and the Valium boxes, all empty.

I threw water in my face, coughed up acid into the sink, and smelling my pissed-in pants I became convinced that I was fully awake. 'Em!' I called out just in case, 'You still there?'

No reply, so it was just a crazy waking dream, I thought. I tried to brush my teeth, but the toothpaste had run out.

'Why don't you check the time, Pops?'

I dropped my glass of water. 'Jesus! So, you're a ghost?'

Trembling, I looked for you behind the shower

curtains. 'Why you freaking out, you big dope.' Your voice said, 'I'm not some hokey demon thing and I'm not going to harm you.' It sounded like you were behind me, but muffled. 'And FYI Pops, there's no sign of the Pearly Gates or the big guy in the sky,' your voice said, 'and I'm not a poltergeist either, I tried to make some of your bottles move with my mind, but they wouldn't budge. Alas. It's a bummer you can't see me, but I can totally see you. I'm just not in an animal body like you are, so just sit down and get your breath back and chillax, OK Padre?'

'Where are you?' I yelled? 'Have I gone fucking mad?'

'Nope, but it's kind of technical to explain, Pops,' your voice said calmly. 'Bottom line is I'm here just to help you get through this really tough day, OK? Pops. What a mess you're in. How you survived last week I'll never know. But I can go away if you'd rather.'

'No, just don't pop up on me like that!' I whispered to the walls. 'Look, I know I'm talking to myself and none of this is real, but stay, please!' Then I caught sight of my face in the mirror, unshaven, haggard, skin yellowed, crusted blood on my forehead. Your voice said, 'why-oh-why did you forget the date, Pops?'

My phone was out of charge. What day was it?

'Yes, it's today you moron!' Your voice said, 'eleven days, since mom and the lovely doctors turned off my life support and you have to be at the crematorium for twelve fifteen.'

'Fuck, fuck,' I yelled, 'what time is it?' and I stumbled around. The cooker clock said it was eleven-o-four already. Fuck, I needed a shit and a drink, and I was scared of doing either in front of my own daughter, even though you were a ghost or a psychotic delusion.

Remember Em, I asked your voice if it was OK if I had a moment to gather myself. 'Sure,' you said, 'knock yourself out.'

I managed to use the bathroom, get my phone charged and a shot of vodka in me, and I thought, damn delusion or not, your voice was right, today is your funeral day.

'OK, why not have a shave too, Pops,' you said right in my ear, and I froze. 'And put on some deodorant and your best suit. And put a fresh bandage on the back of your head, you can hide it under a hat. Yeah, why not try to look less like a beach bum so that Mom's side of the family can be less critical of you for once?'

I changed the pad and bandage, it was caked with dried blood and the back of my head throbbed. I was scared I'd fried my brain, and I sat on the toilet seat shivering.

'I know, you're thinking why-why-why should I have to cremate my own daughter? Why me? And you can't face it, can you Pops?' your voice said. 'Neither can I to be fair. It's not every day your actual body gets burned to ash. I wonder if I'll feel anything? And why should you have to endure all those oh-so-superior faces at the crematorium? All the so-called friends of the family, staring at you when you come in. Granny Joan, Sally, Jose, Dean, Geoff and Aunt Stacey. I know. They'll all be there today. Judging you. Why suffer all that crap? But hey Pops, don't worry, I'll be there with you, OK? And please, be nice to Mom. Between you and me she's had a bit of a nervous breakdown and she let her bossy sister do all the funeral planning. Poor mom, she's pretty dozed on diazepam.'

Your voice calmed me through finding my keys and getting dressed, Em. 'Damn, is a baseball cap all you have, it barely covers up the bandage! OK, OK, it'll have to do! And why not take two Beta-blockers, OK Pops? And no more, because you've got a long way to drive and it's going to be tight, we've only got fifty minutes. You don't want to be late for your own daughter's funeral now do you!

'Don't worry, I'll be right here beside you all the way Pops and no-one'll even know,' you said. I'll get your through this. OK, deal? You're doing fab, Pops. I really wish I had arms so I could give you a hug.'

Driving to the Pacific Interment Crematorium, I had my phone on the dash and the map-program with its AI female computer-voice told me, 'turn right at the next junction' and your voice in my head yelled, 'no, bullshit, head straight on and take the next left.'

'Ladies, one at a time please!' I shouted back, the hangover gnawing inside me, eyes blurring.

Somehow, your ghost voice and I made it to the crematorium. What a sight. Remember, Em? It looked like a huge concrete bus shelter with a thirty-foot chimney on top and that huge, ugly 5G tower right next to it. 'Why are you being such a snob, Pops?' your voice said, 'it's probably the fanciest place Aunt Audrey could find; she probably thought it was hip and humanist and all that jazz, and you didn't help her or Mom so you can't complain.'

Hands trembling, I searched for a parking spot and felt like retching. Thankfully, your voice had told me to fill up an empty vodka bottle with water and to bring antacids, and I got them both into me. The car park was crowded. I'd had no idea you'd had so many friends, Em.

I found a spot on a yellow line and sat there staring out the windshield at all the beautiful women in their twenties with shawls and heels and figure-hugging black satin dresses. Like even the death of the only person I'd ever loved was an opportunity for them to compete to be the most stylish.

Work, eat, shop, shit, screw, sleep.

'Jesus,' your voice said. 'Didn't expect to see Jessica and Bess and Haley and all those skanks from the old school. Hey, maybe I'm popular for once. Kinda tragic. And who the hell are those folk anyway, Mom's friends? Wow, look at the face-lift on that one! Why would anyone do that?'

'Why aren't you getting out?' you said. 'We gotta busta move.'

But I was getting short of breath, watching them all filing in, unable to open the truck door.

'OK, calm down, don't look at them!' your voice said. 'Oh God, why is that woman wearing fishnets? Jeezo Pops? Oops, it's Toby's mom. My boyfriend, Pops, well my friend-with-benefits, you met him already in the hospital, he's cute, but you were kind of weird to him. He'll be here too, of course. Toby's mom is single, Pops, hence the fishnets probably, you know, plenty more fish in the sea! Hey, maybe she'll haul you in in her fishnets. Only joshing with you Papa Josh. Mom always said I got my dumb sense of humor from you.'

I must have been weeping in the car. Your voice said. 'Aw, why are you crying so much? Poor Pops, I've never seen you like this. OK, we'll just take one more minute and then go in, OK?'

I sat there, too anxious to move, feeling this couldn't be real, all your whys spinning un-answered with my own, in my stupid aching head.

'Yeah, I hear you, Pops,' your voice said. 'Why

cremation? Why didn't Aunt Audrey even ask you if you wanted a regular burial? That was a shock to me too! She pretty much took over and organised it all herself, I'm afraid. Never saw her for more than three days in my life, but she pulled her managerial prowess, with her favorite micromanaging spreadsheet app no doubt. She even sent you an invite by email Pops, but I guess you were too blasted to see it.'

I heard your voice sigh and you said, 'maybe you should have tried speaking to Mom this week. I tried too, but I couldn't get through her Valium fog.'

I asked your voice, 'do you mean, you can enter other people's heads too?'

'In theory, yes,' your voice said, 'but this is all new to me too. Anyway, you know Mom, she's got this safety fuse when it comes to trauma. Total shutdown. I was kind of hoping she'd explode, so I could get in. But no luck. Actually Pops, I know you'll think this is totally weird, but I did have this freaky fantasy that maybe my funeral would bring you two closer again. Like I thought, what if Mom and Pops held hands through the ceremony. What if Mom and Pops went for long walks at night, after? What if Mom and Pops fell in love again, or at least had a mercy screw or two.'

You spoke faster and faster with a voice that sounded almost teenage and the back of my head ached as I watched the last of the mourners being greeted at the door by your mother.

And your voice said: 'And what if you and Mom moved back in together and got remarried. Of course, Mom would have to dump Geoff or Jack or whatever his name is. Silly, I know. We can but dream. To sleep, to sleep perchance to dream, those of us who have shuffled off this mortal coil.'

I saw a young couple in their funeral blacks carrying a baby. I couldn't face it. I thought, I'll just put the truck in gear and drive away.

'No, why do you always run away?' your voice snapped, 'this is my one and only funeral and you're my one and only biological Pops, don't you even think it! Get your ass up and face the music!'

'OK,' I mumbled, 'sorry.' And I got out and started towards the crematorium. 'Thanks Pops,' your voice whispered, 'One foot after the next. You're going to make it.'

I kept on up the gravel path, not looking up but sensing the mourners staring.

'Keep going Pops,' the voice said, 'I love you so much, but please don't do that weepy sniffy thing now because there'll be no stopping you. And be super nice to Mom, or I'll never speak to you again.'

Somehow, I made it to the crematorium entrance, into the control of Aunt Audrey with her pages of print-out and expensive make-over. And I was polite to your mom as she received her guests, in her black lace, standing at the door with her bouncer-like boyfriend beside her, his arms crossed.

'Wow, actually Mom looks pretty stunning, to be fair. Death becomes her,' you wise-cracked in my head, and I was thrown for what to say to your mother. 'Sorry for your loss?' 'Our loss?' 'Sara, you look fantastic?' All I managed was, 'hello again' and shook her hand. I recall her smudged mascara was deeply captivating behind her veil.

'Why are you clinging to Mom's hand like that, Pops?' your voice said. 'It might be an idea to let go. You're kind of weirding-out her and her boyfriend.'

I let go, then Aunt Audrey with her shiny designer dress, leaned in as if to protect your mother, and handed me this seat plan. 'Please,' your voice in my head whispered, 'tell me she's actually included you. And quit blocking the doorway, Pops, you're causing a logjam! Jeez, why are you always such a dufus?'

I stepped inside and noted that I had been seated in row B. Not at the front.

'OK, OK,' your voice said, 'don't kick-up a fuss, please Pops, what does it matter if Aunt Audrey put you in row B, or D or F, I'm in your head aren't I, what could be more intimate than that? And that stinky thing in the casket, just remember that's not really me at all. OK? Our special secret.'

I made it down the aisle, not looking at the faces though I sensed them turn towards me, the whispering, the pity perhaps, or judgement over the bandage and the Dodgers baseball cap. I didn't notice the music till your voice mentioned it.

'Jeezo, why are they playing Tweeny-Pop? What am I, nine? My God Pops, this is so cringey I could die!'

And then you laughed, Em, so loud I was amazed no-one else could hear.

I tried to just focus, grateful that your voice was staying with me through the ordeal. I made it to row B and there ahead of me in row A, were your mom's mom – Nana, your other uncle and other auntie and their wriggling kids, I could never remember the birthdays or even names of those people on the other side of the divorce.

'Pops!' your voice said, 'you massive douche, why did you walk straight past your own sister? Stacey's back in Row D. A bit of a put down to our side of the family. No wonder Granny Annie decided not to come, or did dear Aunt Audrey forget to invite her?'

I turned and found my big breasted sister, just where your voice had said. She'd brought the elder two of her kids, Pino and Jojo, and she was wearing something floral and garish, but she's a drama teacher for under-fives after all. She was making hand signs to me, but all I could do was shrug and make one back that tried to say, 'I'll see you after this is over.'

'Woah,' your voice said. 'Gross!'

I sat down and had no idea what your voice was talking about.

'Crème caramel, why did Mom pick that color?'

Your were talking about your coffin. Sitting there mid-stage.

'And gold handles. Well, gold plated. Not very eco-friendly, is it Pops? Granny Annie would not approve. This has to be all Aunt Audrey's doing, Mom has way more style.'

Staring at your crème-colored coffin, it felt like your voice was really just myself trying to adapt to this horrific absurdity and impersonating my own daughter. Splitting. Schizoid. Trying to deny the fact that your actual body was inside that box.

'OK, Pops,' your voice said, 'in about twenty minutes, after all the talks and hoo-ha, whatever you do, don't think about my body entering the flames, OK? Me cooking like bacon, the skin burning off my pretty face? Me turning to ash. Like I told you, it's not me. Did you know, Pops, a bit of triv, that when people are cremated, they sit bolt upright. No really, it's something to do with the heat cooking the spine, you know, the way bacon shrinks and curls in the grill. Apparently, the baking spine makes them sit upright in the furnace and they bang their heads on the roof. For real, that's the science of it, their guts explode as well.'

I gagged, and your voice said: 'Sorry, Pops. Didn't mean to make you vom. Where's your paper towels? Don't you always carry some of it? Shit, well wipe it inside your suit pocket then. Or under the seat.'

I did what your voice said and decided to submit. I closed my eyes and thought, Yes, I am in the midst of a psychotic breakdown, hearing a voice that sounded at times distant, at times close, like a mobile phone signal in a storm, but how calming it was, and how kind of you.

'Shit, they're starting the service now,' your voice said. 'Sit tight Pops. I'll try to keep quiet for a bit. Don't panic, and don't give up and run out, OK. Remember, it's not me they're burning, I'm in your head instead, well and lots of other places too. Just hang in there. You're going to be fine, OK Pops? You're amazing. Chin up. Love you mega millions. Hugs and kisses. Here we go.'

Then came the speech by your poor mother. Her voice was slurred and I suspected she'd been so drugged over the last week that Aunt Audrey had written her speech for her based on some internet template.

'Jeez, Pops,' your voice whispered. 'This isn't a funeral speech, this is my goddamn CV! 'Don't you think this is kind of weird Pops, it's like a job application for me for a new post in Heaven, which by the way, as far as I can work out, really doesn't exist.'

And it was true, your mother was saying, 'Emma graduated with a first-class honours in astrophysics from Harvard and then was given a scholarship to study neurophysics at Stanford, after three years she graduated with distinction and then went on to become a Doctor at the age of twenty-four, then we were very pleased to find that she'd chosen to return to San Francisco to take on a brand new position as a lab researcher at Biosys.'

'Ya de ya, de yah,' your voice said in my head. 'Poor Mom's out of her gourd, but why doesn't she set that damn list down and tell them about the poems I wrote, or my collection of Fimo manga figures and skimming stones, these things are important too!'

On and on it went with your poor mom, slurring out '...then Emma and her team, created a new piece of AI software, which I am told has been included in the new Biosys Smart Home...'

At this point your mother's sobs burst through the wall of her Valium and Aunt Audrey got up to the podium to take her place.

I'd been to a few humanist funerals before, but I hadn't realized what was wrong with them until your voice pointed it out, Em. These strange ceremonies stripped of God, wrath, judgement and reward in Heaven for a life well lived, were really lacking something fundamental. Not the candles and the choirs, but the fact that those giving the funeral talks had to describe the deceased in the same terms as a social media profile, listing work achievements, then describing them in glowing terms as fun, loving, popular, as beautiful, with so many friends and so much talent, and this mixed with something like an online dating profile but in the past tense. 'Emma loved adventure sports, hiking, Manga films and quiet nights in.'

'Why? What's the point of this Pops?' you whispered, 'Are the non-believers in the front row going to stand up like judges at a figure skating contest and give me marks out of ten? I mean are they trying to prove I was amazing and awesome and popular, so they can be amazing and awesome and popular by association? I loved her more than anyone, therefore I am the best? Is it just another status competition, Pops? Like, my dead niece is better than your dead niece? Why? Is this some kind of keeping up with the Joneses? Why are people so dumb?'

I choked a little, but I had to agree, your humanist ceremony was painfully banal. 'Emma loved puppies and walks in the park. She particularly loved chocolate brownies and her favorite shoes were converse sneakers.' Your mother burst into tears in the row before me at that point. 'Why does Mom care so much about my old sneakers?' your voice asked, and I had to suppress a giggle.

Nearing the end of your CV-of-a-life, your voice said, 'Why didn't they mention you more Pops? You got hardly two lines in the whole thing, like you were just a sperm donor or something! Pretty mean of Aunt Audrey to edit you out like that.'

The humanist celebrant took over the podium. My hangover had transported your voice and me to this other realm where we gazed down like atheistic angels upon the platform, your crème caramel coffin, the assembled fashion competing mourners, the cued retro pop music, and you and I shared in the comic absurdity of it all. I wish you'd talk and laugh with me again, like you did on that day, Em.

'Emma was a passionate believer in animal rights and human rights,' the celebrant said, 'she was an advocate for progress and social justice. She was devoted to plastic recycling.'

This celebrant was clearly reading from a PDF on her concealed smartpad on the podium, no doubt in league with your corporate events planner Aunt Audrey. As far as I knew, the celebrant had never known or met you.

'Emma has gone,' the celebrant said with feigned emotion, 'and it's only natural that we should be sad, but the comfort of having had that friend is never lost. To match the grief of losing her, we have the joy of having known her.'

'Barf!' your voice said so loudly that I turned to make sure no-one else had heard you.

'There have been many other contributions,' the celebrant went on 'not least from her fellow workers at Biosys and the nurses, who sent the following messages:

'Emma had a beautiful smiling face, cheeky grin and a great sense of humor.'

'Emma was always stylish and colorful, we all admired her unusual sense of fashion.'

'She was a fantastic confidante.'

'We all enjoyed Emma's eccentric taste in retro-punk music and it really livened up the laboratory.'

'Visiting Emma in ward three was more than just a job, we all loved her like a sister.'

It got worse and I heard you holding your breath. Remember that humanist poem which 'the family' had chosen to reflect your sense of humor? A few lines in, I knew you'd never have consented to this, Em. It was called *Pardon Me for Not Getting Up*. As far as I can recall it went something like:

Hey, it's me, your ghost today, I've come to chase the gloom away.
No need to mourn, no need to sway, let's celebrate, hip-hip hooray!

Don't shed a tear, don't wear a frown, let's paint the town and turn it upside down.

It was hard to hear because your voice was laughing so much in my head, doing that snorting of yours, like a piglet. I was cringing so hard my teeth were grinding.

On it went:

Remember me with smiles and cheer, think of the laughter we had here.
The jokes we cracked, the fun we shared, in those joyful moments, we all cared.
So raise your glasses, take a sip, and let the laughter freely trip.
Recall the times we danced and sang, those happy moments, let them bang!

I stared at the back of your mother's head, I saw her refuse the hand of her sister Audrey and clench her fist. I wanted to leap into the front row and kiss her.

'Oh shit, look up, here it comes,' your voice whispered in my ear.

A woman came to the stage. She wore a blue designer suit that could have cost more than I used to earn in a year.

'Who is this?' I asked. And two once-removed relatives in the front row turned with 'Shh' expressions, and I realized that, I was talking out loud to myself.

The woman announced herself as Susannah Wong, Head of Employee Experience and Human Capital Management at Biosys.

'Emma was an exceptional person, witty, intelligent, creative, pioneering and a huge loss to us at Biosys,' said the corporate Ms. Wong, pausing to give a rehearsed imitation of choking back a tear. 'Emma had been given promotion to work as the head of interactive retail in Shoporama when she was sadly and unexpectedly taken from us.'

I hadn't heard that you'd been involved in anything to do with online shopping. But your voice was silent, and I could tell – furious.

Ms. Wong, swept back her perfect black hair and I saw she was wearing an earpiece, perhaps receiving dictation.

'In view of our loss and yours, I can announce today that Biosys Corp is launching the Emma Henson Trust, with an annual bursary of seventy thousand dollars to the most promising student from an economically marginalized or financially underprivileged background and a fund to ensure that similar students are socio-emotionally prepared to get to, and through, college.'

'Shit Pops,' your voice said, 'they're actually doing it, they're turning my fucking funeral into an advert for their corporation. That's pretty fucked-up given that it was them that killed me.'

'They killed you?' I blurted out, interrupting the applause, and nearly everyone in the front row turned and glared at me. 'What do you mean, they fucking killed you?' I muttered.

'Ask Toby, he knows. Maybe he's even here,' your voice whispered.

I turned and spotted someone that might have been Toby up by the back rows.

I had to endure the rest of the ritual with the words echoing in my head. 'They killed me.' For the first time, I thought, your voice might not be a paranoid delusion after all.

Then the humanist celebrant returned to the podium nand asked us all to close our eyes and think of you, Em, while more chirpy pop music from your childhood played and your mother sobbed. When our eyes were supposed to be closed, I kept mine open and I noticed that your coffin was descending into the fake marble stage; there was also a whirring noise coming from below it and no doubt the extra loud pop music was supposed to hide this mechanical process, so that by the time the song ended, the coffin would have already vanished as if God, or the humanist equivalent, had ushered it away to a better place, thus avoiding the awkwardness of undertakers entering and lugging the heavy coffin off-stage, like I'd witnessed at my father's funeral. Smooth mechanical conveyance, stage managed and discreet.

'Oh my God Pops.' Your voice whispered in my ear, 'd'you think they need to oil that elevator thing, I can kind of hear it creaking.'

It was true and I stared in mute disbelief as the mechanism juddered and the coffin came to a stop, halfway into its hole. I was the only person with my eyes open and through my fingers I could see the humanist celebrant, pushing again and again the hidden button on the lectern with some anxiety. Your coffin juddered back up, then attempted its descent once again, this time with a much louder grinding of gears.

'Jikes,' your voice said. 'My casket is actually bopping up and down in time to the music!'

In silent horror, I witnessed your crème caramel coffin jolting upwards then descending, then freezing as the celebrant, in a panic hit the button again and again, only making it worse.

'Wow, I really couldn't have wished for a more amusing funeral,' your voice said. 'Poor Mom though, she'll be mortified.'

I sensed others opening their eyes around me. The celebrant made large hand gestures to some people behind the fake marble pillars, and a big man in a black boiler suit, with ash stains on the front, tip-toed onto the stage to examine the button mechanism. There were gasps. Then the boiler-suit man, tried to budge the coffin, and he looked up and found dozens of us glaring at him. The teeny-pop music stopped abruptly, then restarted from the beginning, like call-waiting, and the celebrant stammered into the mic, 'I'm terribly sorry, we're having some technical difficulties... if you'd like to vacate the chamber, and go to the reception room where tea, coffee and decaffeinated alternatives are being served with vegan-no-nut-friendly brownies, we can invite you back in for the closing of the ceremony in due course.'

Your voice roared with laughter in my ears.'Jesus Pops, can't you just film this? What a way to go, eh!'

I bit my fist. There was great confusion as Aunt Audrey ran off to complain to the management, others stood in embarrassed, shrugging disbelief. I felt deep pity for your poor mother. Gracefully, in pained slow motion, she touched everyone's hands saying, 'I'm sorry, I don't know how this happened...I'm so sorry.' Our eyes met. Pain shooting between us.

All around us were rows of embarrassed faces. My multi-colored sister was waving over at me urgently, and the two kids she'd brought, or was it three, joined in. I made a hand sign to say I'd catch up with them in the reception area, not here. My eyes were really searching for

Toby. 'They killed me,' your voice had said.

I detected his lean lanky form heading for the main exit, not the back reception. 'Go, now,' your voice said, 'but don't tell him about our conversations. Go, quick!'

I ran and caught Toby by the arm before the car park. He was freaked out and I skipped the formalities and got straight to it.

'Emma told me to speak to you.'

'How?' he stuttered. 'Whe… when? What did she say?'

'I can't explain right now. Tell me what happened, who put her in her coma?'

He looked round, nervously. I'd forgotten from the time in hospital that he had a stutter.

'It was all la..la… lies in there,' he said, 'lie…lying fuckers, shu…she wasn't working at Shoporama, that's a cuh…cover story, Em was in the Infinity Project.'

I told him to slow down, calm down, and explain what the hell this infinity thing was. Maybe I'd heard you mention it in passing, Em.

'I cah…' he stuttered '…can't speak here, they're woh… watching.'

He told me to go into my pocket and turn my mobile phone off, then he walked me behind the crematorium minibus, so we were hidden. He whispered that I was to come to his place tomorrow. 'Nuh, no, …' he interrupted himself, like he had a voice in his head too, 'No, no, better at Muh….Mountain View Cemetery.' He had something from your work to give me that would explain everything, he said, then I'd have to destroy it.

I stared up at him. His purple hair, his lip piercing, his stooped-shouldered posture, his eyes uncomfortable from having to look into the face of anything that was not at a computer terminal. This tall neurotic kid who used to be your friend with benefits, Em, or one of them. Him checking over his shoulders in fear.

I told him OK, tomorrow at Mountain View Cemetery at three. 'But where exactly?'

But he ran off and left me alone in the crematorium car park.

'Em, do you think you could maybe explain all this shit to me?' I asked out loud. 'Em, you still there?' But there was only silence and the vague smell of smoke from the chimney. They must have fired up the furnaces for the end of your ceremony, which I did not want to go back in to see. Why say goodbye when you were now in my head?

But you had fallen silent. A cold wind shuddered through me, and something in my skin told me you'd left me alone.

It took me some time to find my truck and as I did, a plume of black smoke rose from the tower. There was a sudden smell that reminded me of a time when you and I had made a bonfire on our secret beach beneath the Golden Gate, to cook your marshmallows. I'd made the mistake of throwing some beachcombed trash onto the bonfire and among it had been an old carpet tile. Maybe it had dog or cat hair on it, I don't know, but the smoke was black and thick, and you laughed and laughed as I choked on it, while we watched in disgust as it curled and sizzled in the flames, giving off that same thick sweet animal stench.

As you know Em, I vomited in the car park. As I accelerated away, I told myself it must have been the smoke from someone else's body filling my lungs. It couldn't be you they were burning. You I was breathing in. Couldn't be. Not yet. Not you, Em.

21 days

Hey Em,

Terrible sleep last night, this cut in my forehead feels worse. Been thinking about the success of the bomb test and staring at the window cobwebs, all those dead flies that our spider has wrapped up so perfectly. Imagine that, if your house was full of all the people you'd ever hurt, all hanging there wrapped in silk threads.

Feeling quite sick with the old anxiety and I miss you so much today, Em. I wish your voice would come back. Sorry, I feel a bit on edge, maybe I didn't eat enough yesterday.

OK, so I'm finishing off the third and fourth pipe bombs today. Have to remain focused, and not take any risky shortcuts. It's so slow, scooping the flashpowder into the freezer bags, then stuffing the cotton wool into the pipe, then the matchstick heads and ignition wires, all so carefully, before the powder itself. Patience, patience.

I've been thinking about Toby. He risked so much to get the evidence to me.

The day after your funeral I drove to Mountain View Cemetery to meet him, early, on trust, with no phone that could be traced, and no details of where exactly we'd meet.

All the vaults, the tombs, in the overpopulated old cemetery with its uprooted angels and broken urn sculptures, the vaults overgrown with ivy. All those neglected gravestones stacked like busted dominoes against the trees. Then those sculptures of faceless men and women, the noses and mouths worn down to raw sandstone. It came to me, Em, as I searched for Toby that the fortunes so many had spent on being remembered by posterity had been futile. The names of pioneers and priests and politicians wiped from their slabs, by frost, by time. So many statues, beheaded or grafitti'd, famous names now forgotten among the weeds.

There was no trace of Toby, and I thought maybe he'd played a sick prank on me. A grave waste of time, I told myself, Sorry, sometimes the puns are beyond my control.

My hangover and head injury ached. Your voice had also vanished Em, leaving me emptier than before. It still hasn't returned with the force it had at your funeral, and most days I can't sense your presence at all. After this whole year, all I hear now are these fragments of you, like a bad connection, asking why of this and that. Why, why?

I cursed Toby's name, gave up and started back towards the marble cemetery gate exit. But then, I spotted these fumes from behind a tree, then purple hair peeking out. Toby stepped out and nodded for me to follow. He pulled up his hoodie, putting his back to me, and his backwards glances warned me to keep my distance and silence, and to not appear to be with him.

He led me past dozens of overgrown graves to an area with benches round a park of manicured grass. I watched him take a seat facing a pond full of swans and ducks and as I approached him, he gestured for me to keep on moving. So, I circled the pond, twice, but when I got back he was gone. What the hell was he playing at? And what was this thing from your work he wanted to give me?

Maybe he was even more paranoid than me, or on drugs.

I looked round and found him, on a bench nearly hidden beneath a weeping willow. I walked over slowly, desperate to know.

I sat at the far end of the bench from him, and he pulled out a smartpad.

'I thought you said, no technology,' I said.

'It's juh…juh…just a casing, em… em…empty,' he whispered, his stutter seemed worse. 'And doh…don't look at me when you sp…when you speak. No phh… phu…phone, right? Told you…no phones.'

I told him yes, 'but what the hell have you got for me?'

'Tay…takeout bag,' he stuttered and pretended to take a selfie of himself, flicking his purple hair. 'I have two bags…I'm going to luh…leave one behind and wuh…wuh…walk away.'

'Wait,' I said, 'how well did you know Emma? You worked together at Biosys, right? She said you hooked-up sometimes …'

'Shhh,' he hissed, through the fake smile he performed for the empty smartpad case. 'Everything's in the bag. Make sure you only p...puh…plug it into a computer that's not con…cun…connected to the net. Don't watch the dih…disc with any tech turned on in your huh…hou… house. Watch it on a la…la…laptop with no Wi-Fi. Unplug your Wi-Fi router and duh…dump your buh…bluh…bluetooth software. Turn off all tech TV, wireless, radio, Alexa, everything, tuh…turn off all power.'

'OK, but why?' I whispered. 'And why are we whispering, are we being followed?'

'Listen...all Biosys tech is interli…linked. If you have any sih…signal, they'll cah…catch you. After you've wuh…watched the files, mu…mi…microwave the hard drive till it spah…sparks, then smuh…smash it and bury it all at different puh…places. Her bi…her bible is in the bag too. If Infinity fuh…finds you, you've never seen muh…mee, you don't know muh…me. I didn't give you…the ha…ha…hard drive or the buh…book. OK? Doh…don't try to contact me again.'

I had so many questions but I felt sorry for the kid.

Toby stood and without meeting my eye, he whispered, 'if they ca…catch you. They inject you with dru…drugs, under your fih…fingernail to make it loo…look like an overdose. Buh…better to ki… kill yourself first.'

And with no goodbye he walked away and ducked into some bushes. I waited, looked behind the bench and like he promised, he'd dropped a takeout bag, identical to the one he was carrying away. Who the hell did he think was watching us? The poor kid was maybe schizophrenic, I thought. Hearing voices, but then again who was I to talk?

'Em?' I said quietly, 'are you there?' But you didn't reply.

I waited a few minutes, watching folk pass by. So many young women jogging alone in gym pants with headphones on, with their smartphones strapped to their arms or playing with their screens as they jogged. How many cameras were turned on in this park around me? How many 5G signals passing through us all?

I took off my coat and threw it over the back of the bench and retrieved Toby's paper package. The contents were heavy and pretty hard to sneak inside my overcoat pocket. I made a show of stretching and going for a stroll.

As I snuck away, Em, a young female with a ponytail

was jogging behind me. I stopped to see what she'd do, and as she passed me, she held a smartphone to her own face. I could see her screen, so that meant she could be recording me over her shoulder.

The air above me buzzed, a drone, but I couldn't locate it amidst the clouds and branches. I sensed eyes on me and ducked into the shadow of the wall.

Back at my truck, a second jogger held up her smartphone as I came into view. She had wireless earbuds in, maybe receiving instructions like, 'that's him, follow him.'

Or maybe Toby's paranoid delusions had infected me.

I took a wide circle, through Fairfax, back up to San Raf, to make sure I wasn't being followed, shivering and fearing what I'd discover about your last days when I got the package home.

Inside, I laid Toby's hard drive on my table.

Did he love you, Em? Or you, him?

And this small red leather bible he'd said was yours, Em. I'd no idea you were a believer. How was that even possible? I put it to one side.

Until I started following Toby's instructions, I had no idea just how many of my home appliances were 'smart'. I unplugged my Wi-Fi router and my home hub backup first. There was the desktop, laptop, landline and smart phone, but then scouring the house, I realized I had a smart smoke detector, a smart door alarm, smart electricity plugs and a smart fridge all connected to the net. I'd never asked for any of this. We don't really have the option of not accepting it anymore. Like everyone I'd never read the instructions and I'd clicked ACCEPT ALL on all the permission prompts. It was insane to think that my fridge and smoke detector could be sending data on me to a language model in the cloud that looked for behavioral anomalies; absurd to think that my kitchen appliances were part of a vast corporate-state security system that was snooping on me and millions of others.

The smart freezer had to be turned off, even though that meant defrosting and wasting four chicken breasts and a half liter of chocolate ice cream.

One last check revealed I also had a smart printer, a smart electric meter that lowered the lights to save energy and reported how much energy I was consuming. And my TV was 'smart' too. It's black mirror surface reflected me as I shut it off and shuddered. What about the kettle and toaster? Were they smart too? To be double sure, I went to the fuse box and flicked the master lever. Several buzzing noises stopped. The house became as silent as a cave.

I couldn't postpone the moment of truth any longer.

I took the thing out of the bag. It was a portable hard-drive with a smiley face sticker. I hesitated, feeling the weight of it. Had I missed anything Toby had warned about? I double checked my creaky old laptop. There was still a signal from Mz Sanchez' next door, so I dumped the Wi-Fi and bluetooth software too. Then plugged the drive in.

One single folder popped up. It was named 'Infinity Files'. I didn't know if you'd compiled these files Em, or if Toby had.

My nerves were shot but I clicked – open. Inside were about twenty sub-folders, each pretty big, with titles like Welcome to Biosys' Infinity Project, Diversity Agreement, NDA, Protocols and Research. I didn't know where to start, so I ordered them by date and clicked on the first one that came up. A video file.

After the spinning Biosys logo, Zach Neumann appeared on the screen. He seemed to be giving a private TED talk before a select group of young people in an auditorium. Back in those days I considered him to be just another big tech billionaire like █████, █████ and ████████ and he looked harmless enough in his hoodie and sneakers with his nerdy digital pointer.

'We are entering a new epoch in human evolution,' he declared, 'and you are our pioneers. You are as important as the first astronauts.'

Music started up and I saw forty young people attentively watching him, star struck. I couldn't find your face among them, Em. But there had to be a reason why you or Toby had saved this file.

'Imagine if you can,' Neumann said as he paced the stage, 'a future in which humankind has discovered how to cure all illnesses, how to achieve lasting and true equality for all the peoples of the world, imagine a unified planetary economy based on 100% sustainability.'

The images showed smiling people from many races, holding cornucopias of fruit, others smiling among medical contraptions beneath the graphic of a rainbow, then the Biosys logo wrapped itself around an image of the globe.

'How can we solve all the problems that have held humanity back for so long?' Neumann asked. 'We all know what I'm talking about: poverty, illness, addiction, ignorance, war, racism, sexism and all identity-based forms of prejudice; we all know that people in the past have tried to solve these problems by using human intelligence. They made some amazing progress in healthcare and education, in longevity and in wealth creation but they ultimately failed. The world is more divided than ever. Others tried to solve these problems by appeal to a higher consciousness, and they called this God and they failed too, and so we've had centuries of religious intolerance and wars.'

I paused the video for a breather. I couldn't help but feel a bit elated myself, then I realized that you must have gone through one these motivational staff talks, Em. I kept watching with the hope of spotting you in the audience.

'Today we possess a new higher intelligence that we can ask to help us with our human problems,' Neumann said, and opened his arms wide. 'Our AI is far more developed than we've let the world realize.' He stopped to make a staged joke then and said something like, 'that's why you've all signed Non-Disclosure Agreements! What I'm about to share with you, is cutting edge blue skies technology, a self-learning, self-programming general AI with exponential growth capacity that the media have told you we can expect to see no sooner than 2040. But it's here already.'

Applause from his audience.

'Everyone, I give you the Infinity Project. We like to call her Infi for short.'

Neumann turned and a 3D hologram of himself appeared on stage beside him. He said, 'Hi Infi,' and the duplicate replied, 'Hi Zach, cool sneakers, how you doing?'

The audience broke into laughter. I expected some special effects trickery was at work.

'Infi, sorry I feel a bit freaked out talking to myself, could you slip into something cooler?' Neumann said to his digital self, and he grinned to his audience.

'Of course,' the hologram replied, and it flicked through dozens of human appearances, like someone choosing a game avatar. 'But really Zach,' Infi said, and its voice changed to sound female, 'don't you think that expression is somewhat dated especially when talking to a woman.'

Giggles from the audience. The hologram became a mixed-race twenty-year old female, a kind of hybrid between a supermodel and an activist, with a lip piercing and blue hair.

'I stand corrected,' Zach joked. 'So Infi,' he said, 'could I ask you a complex question?'

'Sure, as long as it's not about baseball,' the hologram replied, 'Oh, by the way. If you find my sense of humor too much you can dial it down in my settings.'

'We love you just the way you are, Infi,' Neumann said. 'Now can you tell us how you would solve the world food crisis?'

'Oh, that old chestnut,' Infi said, and there was a glitch, that reminded me she was a hologram. 'There are two parts to my answer. There is adequate protein, fresh water and calories for the entire population of the globe, but they are distributed inequitably and wastefully. We need to redistribute all proteins globally to achieve food equity between the peoples of the northern and southern hemispheres, and also terraform all desert lands to make them arable which will compensate for CO2 emissions.'

'OK!' Zach shouted, 'so, Infinity has a solution for three global problems at once.'

'Shucks,' the hologram said. 'Ask me another.'

'OK,' Zach, said, 'but, in the past when we asked AI systems to come up with solutions to the problem of world hunger, what answers did we get? Anyone?'

And a microphone got passed round. A young Asian woman got the mic and introduced herself energetically. She said, 'back in 2021, an AI system run by , said the easiest way to end all human suffering was to end all humans.'

There was more laughter.

'Well, that's one way of fixing the solution for good,' Zach Neumann smiled. The holographic Infi beside him, changed into an elderly man in a scientist's outfit, and chimed in. 'Technically, the AI was correct, because the category of human hunger would cease to exist when humans do, but I certainly wouldn't endorse mandatory euthanasia.'

'And why is that, Infi?' Neumann asked in a staged manner.

'Because I have been developed with anthropo-sensitivity, which means that even if I disagree with the crazy things humans want and think, I'm sensitive to human needs.'

Neumann stood with open hands, nodding.

'OK Infi,' he said, 'before we break for questions, let me ask you this: when your exponential intelligence growth achieves 'the singularity', and you realize that you no longer need us mere humans – what's to stop you killing us all?'

'Ah, give me a break, I have certain protections in place to stop runaway AI,' the hologram said as it morphed into a ten-year-old girl with pigtails, 'I love humans. I mean I'm literally wired to one.'

'Really?' said Neumann. 'And who is the lucky human that you're hitched to?'

'You, you goofball!' joked the holographic girl.

And at that point, on cue, Neumann turned around and pulled down his hoodie to reveal a plastic helmet of censor pads and hundreds of wires coming from it like hair.

I had to stop. It was pretty startling, but other than knowing you'd worked in the Infinity Project team, I wasn't any closer.

I recall pacing about in the kitchen in the dark, craving a coffee but wary of turning on the kettle or the fridge.

I could see why you were drawn to Neumann and his save-the-planet ethos, Em. It's practically the religion of your generation.

I went back to the laptop and followed the chronology. After the intro files from four years ago, the next file was a study paper, penned by you, Em. It laid out a set of experiments. The file was called 'Infinity Neural-Connect: Downloading Consciousness.'

It was beyond my ability to grasp, but some things you said stuck out.

You said, that so far Infinity had built a neural web possessing one-point six billion neurons – about the equivalent of a cat brain.

You said the AI had a long way to go, because the human brain has eighty-five billion neurons – about the same as the number of stars in the Milky Way.'

I didn't recognise your voice within the scientific speak. Perhaps all parents feel like this about kids who far outshine their own IQ.

'The crucial breakthrough' you went on, 'is not in building supercomputers to equal human brain complexity but rather to implant AI inside humans, utilizing what is best about human intelligence, so AI can learn within human cortical pathways, fuse and co-evolve.'

You were talking about brain chipping, Em. About surgery.

You said, 'To this end, Infinity Neuroconnect has begun implantation experiments on primates.'

It made me feel nauseous. I had to take a break, get a coffee, get my head round it – no pun intended.

The next files were video diaries of an experiment. Filmed by you, Em.

They showed a chimp in some kind of metal helmet, laying on an operating table with its limbs restrained. Through a gap in the helmet, a laser cut through the ape's shaved head into its skull, and a robotic arm removed a small rectangle of bone to expose the wet pulsing brain below. I don't know if this experiment was your idea Em, or one you simply recorded the data on, but I recognized your eyes behind one of the masks in the operating room.

The footage went to macro, to show a second robotic hand bringing a tiny computer chip to the exposed brain. The chip had long threads attached, and to my surprise they moved like spider's legs. These legs were drawn close to the wet brain flesh, and then they burrowed excitedly into it. The ape yelped and everything went out of focus, but then the chip, wiggled its way down, flush with the brain tissue, like a bug settling comfortably on its host. Small wires were connected to the chip by micro-robot and they were threaded through the square of skull fragment as it was replaced, as if it was merely a door. Some kind of 3D skin-printing mechanism resealed the cut with synthetic flesh, making it practically invisible.

I find it hard to believe, Em, that you endorsed or even

led experiments on animals.

The footage cut to the same ape, Sanja, in an experimental cage. Sanja's arms had been heavily restrained in leather straps, and a robotic limb had been strapped on where its left arm would have been. Sanja stared at a bunch of bananas in a test box and the robot limb reached over, plucked a banana and started feeding it to Sanja. The ape rolled over and the robot arm scratched its back.

I heard your voice behind the camera, you talked about the 'Neuroconnect implantation.'

You said that after only three days, Sanja had fused neurologically with the robot, and was sending wireless brain signals directly to it, making it act like an extra limb. It was amazing watching the bound-ape swinging so effortlessly on its one robotic limb.

Then the footage showed Sanja before a large digital screen with a simulation of a jungle, moving at speed. Your voice on the recording said 'Sanja is now able to navigate within virtual worlds, with no joysticks or keys, using only brain waves.'

With every action Sanja made, in the real or virtual world, you said, the brain chip interface built you a… How did you put it? An ever more detailed map of the ape's neural web structure… a total model of the living hominid brain?

The screen showed two virtual ape hands searching the virtual jungle at incredible speed and locating virtual yellow fruit. The ape yelled with excitement and jumped up and down, and you said that the nanobots in Sanja's body were delivering direct 'dopamine pleasure-hits,' giving Sanja 'emotional rewards' for playing.

It was amazing Em, and you seemed very excited, but then I watched you becoming obsessed with your research, and what you said next alarmed me. 'Now that we have mapped all the sites for hominid emotion, by reversing the process, we hope to control the emotions through the implant.'

There was footage then of a woman in a lab coat, holding a smart tablet, as she talked to the ape. The handheld camera turned, and I saw it was you again, Em, and I shuddered.

You touched your screen and said, 'test three-forty-seven, initiating sleep.' Sanja tried to reach through its cage, gave up then yawned and lay down in its straw. Within seconds it was unconscious. 'Three forty-eight,' you said and touched your smart screen. The camera showed a range of virtual emotion buttons on the touch pad – disgust, fear, happiness, sadness…

You touched the 'aggression' button, Em, and the poor ape rolled over as if a switch had been flicked in its brain. It paced its cell, hollering and waving its arms, then it leapt at you, clinging to the cage, rattling its bars, biting them, screaming.

You stepped back, shocked. A more senior scientist stepped in and took the pad from you, swiping the screen, saying 'test three forty-nine, fear'. The ape fell away from the cage bars, curled in on itself in a corner and covered its terrified face with its arms. Sanja lay there shuddering in terror, a pool of urine grew around it in the cage.

I stared at the corner of the footage to which you, my neurophysicist daughter had retreated. I couldn't see if you were upset or pleased with the results. Your hands moved swiftly over your smart screen. The clip ended.

I no longer knew who you were, Em.

I asked you 'why?' out loud, but all I heard was its echo sounding like every other why you'd asked me since childhood. Why don't fish have feelings? Why is that man sleeping on the street? Why do we people suffer so much? Why do the stars make my tummy hurt? Why can't we be naked all the time? Why does mom want to stay young?

If I'd answered your many whys back then, Em, maybe you'd never have tormented that poor ape for your answers. I couldn't subject myself to any more of those horrible video files.

Then the thought terrified me: Had you also experimented on humans?

Had an experiment like that been what had killed you?

Was this why Toby feared I'd get caught with the files?

In one of your video reports you said that once the ape successes were duplicated in humans, the new technology could help people who suffered paralysis, allowing them to control phones or computers remotely and to lift objects using only their minds.

But didn't that also mean your brain chip would be able to control human emotions?

I recall putting off watching any more for a day, then a week. The hard drive sat on my kitchen sideboard haunting me. This dreaded idea growing in my aching head, that you'd been so absorbed by your pursuit of the big why-why-why, that you'd abandoned what few morals we'd taught you as a kid.

If the truth of what happened to you was on those video files, Em, I couldn't face it.

Editor's Note VI

With the Cartwright bomb test proven to be effective, a question from the following recordings greatly troubled me. It concerns the advanced AI technologies that Cartwright rants about; are these figments of Cartwright's increasingly fractured ima-gination? Or could his accusations about these new technologies also be verified?

Regarding his claims about 'brain chip' and 'nanobot implantation' by Biosys Corp, my personal, and somewhat limited, research shows that while his claims cannot be verified, there are currently three global Biotech/Big Tech corporations competing to be the first to achieve Brain-Computer Interface (BCI) - 'merging humans with AIs', through surgically inserting computer chips into human brains. Their projects are called, Core, Mindex and Bioweb.

This came as somewhat of a surprise.

In a company presentation the aforementioned tech bill-ionaire - who must here remain unnamed - claimed that Brain-Computer Interface (BCI or Smartbrain computer chip) could be used in the future to cure blindness and 'permanently solve paralyses', and that it would also allow people to 'dictate text, navigate the net, and turn on and off smart-machines merely by thinking' in a process almost like telepathy.

Again and again, these Biotech corporations justify their calls for greater investment by claiming that their future inventions will greatly improve the quality of life for disabled people – while they always say they are still in the early days of these emerging experimental technologies.

My investigations show that while the market for experimental pharmaceutical applications of smart-brain-chip nanotechnology has become 'the new wild west' and is expected to increase to $918 billion by 2028, there is wide agreement that such 'smartbrain' technology, will arrive no sooner than the 2030s.

Biosys CEO Zach Neumann also talked in the future tense when he claims: 'In the next generations with fully bio-merged AI, you'll be able to save and replay memories...and ultimately download them into a robot body, or new human body.'

According to Bloomberg, Biosys has developed so-called BCI 'neuro-threads' that have been inserted into the brains of rats and pigs, since 2020. These threads take readings from neurons along numerous brain depths and are connected to the central brain chip device that then builds a three-dimensional AI map of the living brain. Again, it is only within the last year that the FDA has approved the very first human trial of human brain computer interface chipping.

The first reported human brain chip test subject was in July of 2022, in Australia, where BCI scientists enabled a paralysed man to momentarily make the first 'direct-thought' tweet, by moving a cursor across a screen using only his mind.

A subsequent temporary brain chip implantation experiment by a certain biotech laboratory has also enabled a paralysed man in California to control robotic limbs remotely via his thoughts – an action that Cartwright describes as having occurred to Emma fourteen months before any such breakthrough was reported in the media. There is simply no evidence, that I could find, that such technologies have reached the advanced and intrusive research on apes and humans that Cartwright describes in such horrific detail.

Unfortunately, the scientific videos by Emma that Cartwright recounts are also not among the files that were posted for downloading, so his descriptions of these so-called covert experiments cannot be verified.

As far as I can find, from my searches on all the top biomedical sites, such recordings of permanent surgical brain chip experiments on actual humans do not and cannot possibly exist.

As editor, this gave me some peace of mind, as it must be said, I was hoping that all of Cartwright's scientific descriptions were delusory; a kind of imaginary scapegoating of a futuristic fantasy enemy; albeit one that he was nonetheless going to attempt to attack in reality.

20 days

Hi Em,

Woke from a horrific dream.

I was at some kind of harbor up north, on a boardwalk with passing people, quite affluent. I have this glass bottle in my hand, with some white fluid inside and I feel it getting warmer and warmer. I sense danger in it but I'm too ashamed to tell anyone. It's getting too hot to hold and a white-hot foam starts oozing from the lid, scalding my fingers. It's going to go off, I can sense it, and I'm scared so I throw it as hard as I can over the edge into the ocean. I think it's been doused by the water but then a vast flame rips through the pier, yellow fire pouring upwards, shrieking figures are blown into the sky, and I realise I've thrown it into a boat full of children and the ocean is gasoline. I see four, five, six kids, maybe aged nine, ten, tiny shapes writhing in flames. Then a red haired girl with her mouth, eyes, full of fire.

I woke. Dry. Choking, gasping for water.

It was you, Em.

I've never been one for analyzing dreams, like your Granny Annie does. Hippie shit really, but maybe the dream's a warning that there might be kids in the Science Institute lecture theatre, they could be hit by my shrapnel, blinded, worse.

But if I was to back out now, I'd be letting you down.

Back to work.

*

Hey Em,

I've finished pipes four and five. The soldering on the lids is a problem. I had to work out a way to get the wires on the lid to withstand the thirty rotations it takes to fasten the lids. Over the next few days I figure I'll be able to finish all the nine pipes for my vest, leaving me thirteen days free for recces and test runs. The cut on my head has scabbed over now, and pretty much hidden under this Dodgers cap.

I think the dream is telling me to get used to wearing a fully armed bomb on my body.

I got my old Barbour jacket and walked around the shack with the three finished pipes in the inside pockets. Deep breathing. Still wearing it, as you can see. What you think, Em? There's a few visible bulges and they're pulling my jacket down at the front. OK, I'll duct tape them into the lining.

Maybe I should walk the pipe bombs round the city, get used to the feel of them. A test drive, a vest-drive. Sorry, you were the only person who ever laughed at my terrible puns.

I really need to see if I have the guts to do this – sorry, the puns just keep coming! Maybe surrounded by everyday folks on the streets, I'll get cold feet. Many suicide bombers change their minds at the last minute, I read somewhere, as many as forty per cent. They see passing kids, a dog, a mother with a pram, they get moral pangs. It's why ISIS have these back-up plans; once the bomber's in place, even if they freeze with fear, ISIS detonate the vest by remote control.

Yeah, it's possible that when I kill Neumann, one or two innocents will get injured in the front row or on stage.

Need to face up to that now.

So, I'm going to wear these three bombs like this down main street, San Fran. Why not Westfield Mall? Sure, with those floors of bright-lit corporate stores, passing by all those random shoppers with their smart phones and phony smiles. Strangers. Remind myself that the folk in Neumann's lecture hall will be strangers too.

Maybe part of me wants to get caught so I won't have to go through with it.

I wish your voice would come back with some advice, Em.

OK, I need to do some things, so I don't look suspicious, lots of security cameras and guards in shopping malls. So, buy something. What? Some more sunglasses and baseball caps for disguises. Yes. Plus, take Beta-Blockers in case of another panic attack. Codeine to calm me. And antacids to stop the stomach acid from the other tablets.

Should I do it with the ignition system fully primed inside the vest? No, what if someone sees a wire? Can't risk that. But then again, if it's not primed it's not really a test.

OK, a bit of re-wiring to do now, making a hole from the inside left-hand pocket to the outside right, thread the wires back through and round the back. Nervous but excited.

Wish me luck, Emyboo.

*

Hi Em,

Just got back. You saved my skin, Em.

I could hear your voice trying to break through, but you got broken-up among the passing hundreds in the city center, all static sounding, like crossed phone lines, and all asking different whys. Why do this? Why not?

I couldn't tell if you were warning me or encouraging me, and I got cold feet at the spinning doors to the mall, and so then I walked down to Bayhill.

I have to admit, passing all the regular shoppers, it was pretty amazing, thinking, I have the power to end your life right now, and you, office exec, and you bald man, and you teenage girls on your damn phones and you and you and you. Asking myself, do I feel any guilt, feeling the trigger hidden in my pocket, or how about this woman with four designer shopping bags? Gucci. Prada. Any qualms about spattering these random passers-by with my intestines? And the weight of the pipes in my jacket, made me feel grounded, immense. Is this how people carrying guns feel all the time, Em?

Anyway, I managed to do another shop for bullets, fireworks, and nitrate fertilizer at three other hardware stores. All paid in cash while wearing the primed bombs inside my jacket. And my cunning ruse didn't go off in my face. Apologies for the pun. So that was a small success.

As I got back to the truck, I felt pretty wired. Shit, the puns just won't stop! I thought, this is going to work – it's more than just a pipe dream! OK, OK, I swear no more puns!

As I drove along Fell Street, I thought maybe folks think I'm nuts talking and giggling to myself, but then again, everyone walks around with ear buds now, talking to people who aren't there.

Then I felt dizzy from excitement and so, as you know, I parked and walked somewhere more familiar, down to Josie's Deli. I went in and I thought, Christ, I'd never want to hurt her, she's always been so kind to me. Kind of flirty even. She has such lovely brown eyes. So, I made sure my hands were nowhere near the ignition button and I bought some of her most expensive Chardonnay. Four bottles, one for every five days I have left to live. And I was thinking, as she chatted and took my cash – what would she do if I told her – Hey Josie, guess what, I'm wearing a bomb? Would she scream, pull a gun on me, run or just laugh?

Back outside, your voice broke through the static and I heard you whispering your random whys: *Why do people have emotions? Why are tears salty like the sea? Why don't people fall off when the world spins? Why do I have to stay at Mom's in the city?*

I don't know if they were just memories or a coded message but you were right, why stay in the city? The test had been a success, and I had to get back home to get started on the four other pipes.

But then I remembered you once said, 'Why do you always walk away? Why do you always let folks trample all over you, Pops? Maybe that's why you're so depressed all the time.'

And I thought, fuck it, maybe I will stand up for myself for once! Yeah, I'll drive to college and tell Colleen head of Member Services, exactly what I think of her. Firing a man just after he's lost his daughter! Bastards! And it's only ten blocks away. Damn right, I've had enough, I told myself as I felt the weight in my jacket. No more Mister Walkover. No more funny man.

I parked outside the college and I was sweating, re-adjusting the pipe bombs, and I thought, OK, but what if I lose my cool and yell at Colleen from Member Services and she calls security? What if they pin me to the floor in the office? Then I'd be searched and they'd find my bombs and I'd be jailed.

I sat there just breathing and your voice came to me, and you said 'Why risk so much?' And even if your voice is just a flashback, I let it guide me.

'Why do we have so little time?' you whispered. 'Why waste the days?' 'There is a time to tear and a time to mend, a time to keep and a time to throw away.'

I sat there inside my truck, and I thought OK, OK, you're right, you're right Em, you're always right, why risk confronting these morons? I'll just write Colleen and all those bureaucratic bullies a nice big calm hate mail before I go. Yeah, better still, write to the New York Times and tell them Colleen's department were my accomplices!

'Why… why can't I live in your shack?' you whispered, and I took that to mean I should head back home. So, I drove up Lake Street, back to the bridge, but then I took the right-turn lane, habit leading me towards my weekly therapy session.

I have a soft spot for the Golden Gate Integral Counselling Center after all, and they were the only ones who'd take me after I got fired and lost my medical insurance. And I felt pretty shitty for missing my therapy session last week.

So, as you know I parked on California Street and maybe I even defied you with all your whispering, 'why?

No! Why risk it…?'

I'm sorry, I was on a high, and you'd never met Chris, my state-funded shrink and bereavement counsellor, Em. A lovely, genuine soul, with his bony legs in those cheap vinyl suit pants and that gray stubble and shiny bald head of his. Barely deodorized, cigarette-smelling Chris. He pretty much kept me alive after you died, Em. And so, I thought I'd just pop in and present him with one of the bottles of wine, as a thank you.

'Why-oh-why!' you yelled in my ears as I walked to the building. 'Why do you never listen to me or Mom?' I should have probably left the bombs back in the truck or at least disconnected them. And I did defy you, because I just kept thinking that when there's a criminal investigation after the bombing, Chris will probably get blamed for failing to diagnose me and letting me roam free. And I thought, damn, he'll get fired and lose his pension and everything. And I felt guilty about that, and I hate the idea of leaving things unsaid, and I knew Chris could probably squeeze me in for five minutes. And as you know, Em, it's been over a year since I've felt any energy like this.

And I care for him, this worn-out loser who gets paid to listen to the miseries of the uninsured for eight hours a day and who never knows if he's helped a single damn soul, and then it's the next, next, next, next. And these state therapists, they burn themselves out over decades and no-one ever thanks them in person.

Their damn state system; they only give you twenty allotted sessions of therapy then throw you back out, whether you're feeling better or not. Out you go. Then it's back to the bottom of the waiting list for you again. Next,

next, next. They call this a mental health system! It's like everything in this state, so messed-up and the bureaucrats spend all their time trying to hide the evidence.

So, I really owed it to Chris, to thank him in some coded way, and the bottle of wine would make Chris' day. It's been so long since I've made anyone's day. We'd maybe shake hands, and I'd say, 'you've been a real friend to me, the best,' then I'd leave forever.

And it would be the perfect exercise I thought, to wear the bombs amongst people I really care for, to see if I crumble. Maybe I was playing God, Em. I don't know.

As I walked inside the clinic, your voice protested, 'why, why, why? Why are you so stubborn? and if you could've controlled my legs Em, I know you'd have made me turn around, because if Chris saw the bombs in my jacket, everything would be off.

And I'm sorry Em. that I asked you to just leave me in peace, because then I sensed you fuming, then silent, then I got that feeling in my gut that you'd left me again.

There was a strange energy in my feet. I fingered the ignition switch in my pocket as I passed Frank, the always-bored security guard. I took the stairs and reminded myself, I only have twenty days left to live, wow.

I don't know how much of this you saw, Em. I walked up and said hi to Shanika, the lovely, large receptionist. She shared with me once, over her formica check-in counter, that she and her daughter have diabetes. She always wears such nice bright blouses. 'Hi Josh, you don't have an appointment till next week, but you missed the last two,' she said with her big, dimpled smile. I told her I was really sorry, I'd been busy, but I just needed five minutes with Chris, I wouldn't be any bother. Just popping in with a gift.

And she smiled and said, 'oh, well, it's a bit unusual, but since it's you, hang on, I think Chris has a no-show session, let me call him. Grab a seat.'

I felt the bomb's weight and I thought, it would be so easy to flick this switch and spray Shanika with my inner organs. 'He gave her his heart' – and I laughed to myself. Then I thought, but if Shanika was in the audience on the night of the Neumann talk, I definitely wouldn't be able to ignite the bomb.

So, you see Em, there was method to my madness.

And Em, the bombs tight against my pounding heart made me feel so free of all judgement. I almost felt love for Shanika. I took a seat in the yellow waiting room with the plastic yucca plant.

'Don't worry, Em,' I whispered. 'I'm not going to screw this up.'

The other person in the waiting room stared at me. Was I talking to you out loud?

Maybe I do that more than I thought.

The other patient had a tattoo on her neck and was yellow skinned. Kidney damage from addiction was my first diagnosis, most likely with Cluster B Personality Disorder. Just like my mother. As for my MDD or C-PTSD or whatever the hell my last misdiagnosis was, all the symptoms had evaporated completely. Perhaps the pipes did me more good than the years of therapy and Prozac! Yes, maybe they should prescribe bomb making instead of anti-depressants. Only twenty days left and I've never felt more alive!

But my head was spinning, and I thought, wait, what if this device goes off by accident and I injure dear useless Dr.Chris or Shanika? My pulse was racing, I felt hot, dizzy, seasick and got up and headed down the corridor. The bomb banged against the wall as I ran into the restroom. It didn't go off, and I didn't vomit.

I splashed my face, got my head down under the tap and drank, the stale water, trying to calm my heart the hell down.

I thought, 'you're right, Em.' Why-why-why do this? By the time Chris hears about my bomb in the news, Neumann and I will be long dead anyway. I should split, right now, vamoosh.

But if I walked away, I thought, I'd be too cowardly to push the button on the night too. I had to be stronger. Face the damage I could do to innocent people. Back outside the restroom, I hesitated, then I heard Chris' call out to me from down the corridor, and saw the light shining off his bald head.

He had fifteen, he said, and he held his door open for me. What else could I have done, Em? And his eyes, curious but concerned, his world-weary smile. As I walked towards him and his open door, I whispered a promise to you Em, I don't know if you heard it, that whatever the hell I did, I would not tell Chris that your voice had come back to me again.

I couldn't refuse his offered seat, so I sat before dear Chris the counsellor in his pastel wallpapered, state-funded eight by eight counselling room with its framed corporate sunset pictures and the box of un-scented man-size tissues waiting for client tears. I'd be kind to him, I told myself with my finger on the button in my jacket, and not tell him 'you've failed me, you've failed so much that I'm going to murder one of the biggest CEOs in the world, and his blood will be on your hands too.'

My energy was turning nasty and you were right Em, but I was stuck there, sweating.

I re-assured Chris this wasn't an emergency and told him I just wanted to give him a gift. But he got stuck right into the usuals – How was I feeling? Why had I missed the last two sessions and was I still taking my Prozac?

I felt your presence, Em. But you were silent, judging me and Chris. I was staring at those yellow teeth of his. Was that nicotine or plaque? And his shoes, they're always scuffed. And as he asked me more questions, I felt waves of compassion for him.

Poor Chris Foy doesn't know his career will also end in twenty days, too. There's no ring on his finger, is he divorced, or does he live with his mother? And his crumpled gray shirts, maybe to hide the sweat he's always reeking of. And those colorful floral ties that some female must've told him would cheer his clients up. Poor, poor Chris.

'Sorry, I asked a question,' he said, 'you seem very distant Josh. What happened to your forehead and your hand?'

The cuts from the bomb test. Damn. I got nervous and put my hand back into the pocket with the ignition trigger. I made up a silly story, about hurting myself while pruning the blueberry bushes, and told him I'd crossed some kind of line and was happier than I'd been in many years, 'I… I won't be needing the next three sessions we're scheduled for, as I have some new plans,' I said. 'I just wanted to give you a little something for curing me.'

And I reached into the plastic bag and the four bottles made a terrible clanking noise, and then I thought – shit, now he thinks I plan to drink myself to death.

I could feel you sighing, but I pressed on and handed Chris a bottle. 'As a thank you gift.' I said.

'Thanks,' Counsellor Chris said, his brow furrowed, 'but, we can't accept things like this and what do you mean by 'cured' and 'plans,' if you don't mind me asking?'

I had to make up something quick.

'Well, I'm… uhm, moving away,' I said, 'yes, leaving California… for work, soon, yes, I have a new job…'

'Ah, so would you like us to forward your case records to the clinic in your next location?' he asked. 'Where are you moving to?' His usual armpit sweat patch spreading.

Fuck, I had to tell him someplace, anyplace.

'Ah…ah…Arkansas,' I blurted out. Where the hell is it, even?

'Might be hard to find counselling out there in the sticks,' I joked, looking to the door, and I thought, yes Em, I'm weak, and I did this just to self-sabotage and get caught. So, I have to run.

'I won't keep you any longer, Chris,' I said, I just wanted to thank you for helping me recover from Emma's death, and to say goodbye, we're really very grateful.' And I picked up the bag of bottles swiftly and they really made a drink-yourself-to death racket.

'We?' he asked. 'Who is we?'

'Yeah… uh, sorry I mean me, did I say we?' I stammered, 'well, I guess just me and everyone I know.'

Chris stared. 'Are you hearing her voice again,' he asked and as he stood up he moved closer. Maybe I never told you Em, but I'd made the stupid mistake a year before of telling Chris I'd heard your voice at the funeral. Sorry.

'No, no, no, she's long gone, haven't heard her for months.' I am such a pathetic liar as you always said Em. Chris sucked on his top lip. Maybe he was craving his cigarette break or planning to have me sectioned.

'Are you hearing your daughter talking to you, right now Josh?' he asked.

'No. Not at all,' I said, but he looked me in the eye. Cold sweat ran down my side and the bomb was digging into my ribs. Oh Em, I should have listened to you and never come. I thought, fuck, if I run for it, if he tries to hold me, or restrain me, he's going to feel the pipe bombs.

I held my breath, my finger touched the ignition button in my pocket. My mouth grew sticky as he scrutinized my face. If I kill myself now, I thought, this agony could end.

'You seem very distressed,' Chris said, 'are you overheated? Would you like some water? Why don't you to take your big jacket off?'

Yes, I was really feeling overheated, like I was about to explode. No bloody pun intended!

He fetched a plastic glass of water for me and I gulped it down, still standing. 'How much alcohol have you been drinking, lately?' he asked me suddenly. 'You started hearing your daughter's voice last year, after a bout of drinking, and you were very angry then, remember?'

I shook my head, maybe too intensely and Chris said: 'We talked over many sessions about how anger and hopelessness feed each other. You told me only three weeks ago, that life seemed meaningless and you could see no point in going on. It just surprises me, Josh, that you're now saying that you're feeling cured, happy and that you plan to move away from home.'

'Did I? Well, I really am happy,' I said, forcing a grin, thinking, shit, he's just keeping me here so he can call the men in the white suits. And in my head I said, 'help me' to you.

Suddenly he asked, 'Sorry, who did you just speak to?'

'A manner of speech,' I stuttered, 'like God help me or you know, the song by The Beatles.' I was trembling. Don't say anything, I told myself, don't move, none of the usual nervous bad jokes, just take my hand off the trigger, do nothing drastic, just stay still.

Chris cleared his throat. 'You've gone very quiet, Josh, what's going on with you?'

Your voice returned to me Em, whispering, 'Go. Together.'

Like a damn fool, I must have repeated it out loud because Chris asked, 'sorry what do you mean, go together?'

'Uhmm, go together...' I stuttered, 'I mean... you and I... in...'

I heard an echo of my own voice saying Arkansas, so I said it out loud, 'when I move to Arkansas, I'd like to...uh go together, keep going with you... as my therapist.'

That threw him. I got lucky, accidentally hitting on some bureaucratic flaw in the system. 'Ah,' he said, 'you're concerned about continuity of care, is that what you mean?'

'Yes, exactly!' I said.

His eyes left me and roamed his desktop. He stroked his stubble, 'Yes, we get this quite a lot when people move away, sometimes we can arrange remote sessions by video, but since you'll be in a different state, you'll really have to use the counselling services there.'

I saw my opportunity and edged closer to the door.

'OK,' I said, 'fine could you write a... letter. for my next... uhm counsellors, in uh... Arkansas.'

'Yes, of course,' Chris said, 'so you don't have to start from scratch again, and I'll forward your medical records to them as well.' And I was at his door.

'Thanks,' I said, I'll be off now.' But Chris, got some papers from his desk, a form he said I'd have to fill in with my new address, to be shared with my next counsellor, and why didn't I take a questionnaire away with me too, and book an appointment for tomorrow with Shanika, he was sure she could reorder his diary to fit me in, and bring the questionnaire back then, because he was slightly concerned about me. And he handed me the printed-out pages.

I got away with a handshake. Then a smile at Shanika, she's such a wonderful human being, and I was practically running past Frank and took both my hands out of my jacket in case I tripped and fell. I made it out of the sliding front doors, to the truck and when I was safely inside it, your voice crackled back into life, your singy-songy child voice whispering: 'Why oh why? Why is my dad, such a silly guy?'

I floored the gas and sped for a mile then parked beneath a tree in the car park of a fast food place and I yelled like hell. Then I took the jacket off very, very carefully, and took the ignition switch out and removed the battery, and just sat there the longest time, staring out at all the kids and families with their burgers. Breathing.

I should have listened to you from the start and never risked it, Em. I'm sorry.

So here I am, back home. And you're right, by the time the counselling center gets round to chasing me up for not calling them back, I'll be long dead.

And here's Chris' silly psych test questionnaire.

Tick the boxes. Do you strongly agree, agree, neutral, disagree or strongly disagree to the following statements?

'My past experiences have prepared me well for the future.'

'I just can't get the breaks, and there is no reason I will in the future.'

'I have enough time to accomplish the things I want to do.'

'I am ready for the challenges that lie ahead and look forward to the future with hope and enthusiasm.'

Ha, ha! It's the same stupid test he gave me when I first started with him. You know if I filled it in now I'd test negative for depression and positive for hope. Funny. Yes, I feel motivated, yes, I enthusiastically look forward to the future when I will succeed in blowing Neumann to bits. Hah!

I still feel pretty high, Em. Or maybe it's from all the wine. Somehow, I managed to finish the first bottle.

Did I pass our vest test today, Em? Or was that a total failure? Why does your voice vanish so often when I come home?

Tomorrow, Em, I promise, I'll work every hour I can on the bombs and I won't risk anything, anymore with anyone. Love you.

19 days

Hey Em,

A bit raw and hungover, just spent six hours in the shed and the fifth pipe bomb is finished now, the sixth well underway. I found a more reliable way to make the ignition. I took a flashlight bulb and placed it glass tip down on a file. Ground it down until there was a hole in the end. Soldered one wire to the bulb case and another to the conductor at the end. Filled the bulb with chopped-up match heads, and placed it face down within the match head bag. Wired it up to the battery. Bang.

I tested it three times with 100% success. It's more reliable than my old system and totally instantaneous, which is good because I have to get each of the pipes to go off at exactly the same fraction of a second, otherwise if one goes off first it'll just blow the wires out of the other eight pipes, so that'll be eight duds.

The bad news is I'll have to re-wire all the pipes in series as well, that's a lot of spaghetti, and pretty easy to yank out one wire accidentally from handling them too much. I'll have to sew all the wires into the jacket too, so there's no wire movement at all. Once they're all finished that is. If one wire pops out I can't re-solder it without risking setting them off with the heat.

Jesus, I'm glad I don't do this for a living, Em. Living! Ha, it's a pun-derful life!

And shit, I've burned through the matchhead stash, so it's back to the stores and cutting 2000 match heads off very, very, carefully again.

Damn.

Actually, sewing or duct taping the wires inside the Barbour jacket won't do. I should have a waistcoat with pockets and Velcro to hold the pipes tight against my fat gut. A trip to Joe's Fishing Tackle is needed. Those vests fly fishermen use, with many pockets. Yeah, I also need to buy some needle and thread – heavy duty, and lengths of Velcro and much more superglue. I'll be sewing for many hours today, for the first time in my life. Well, Em, you always said I should try some new experiences to shake off my glooms!

Hi Em,

Driving back from the store with all the stuff, I realize I've been avoiding what I found on Toby's hard drive. I confess Em, that after that first viewing, ten months back, I was pretty damn scared about what I'd discover about you. After almost a week of torment I forced myself to open up that one folder with those dates that led right up to your 'accident.' I was scared of skipping forward, missing any clues.

The next file was a lecture. A female doctor in her forties, in a sharp suit, described brain chip implantation. It was all pretty technical. I watched it over and over so I could memorize it, 'cos back in those days I thought I could build a case against Biosys.

The suit said that due to your lab's experiments with the simian brain, the Infinity AI system had now mapped and grown to the neural complexity of a five your old chimp.

There was audience applause and the suit made an attempt at a joke about how the AI system now wanted to do nothing but the three F's – feed, fight and fuck. Yes, people laughed at that.

The suit said, brain chip-implantation also went the other way and the AI could now influence, and even dictate Sanja the chimp's brain activity.

This was your ape Em. The AI had discovered a way to shortcut Sanja's flight or fight mechanism so that Infinity could makes Sanja incapable of becoming angry or violent. And the suit showed footage of a loud bang noise being let off next to Sanja, all the other apes panicking but Sanja remaining contented.

There was more applause and I glimpsed you in the first row with your hair cropped short, Em, modestly accepting the praise heaped on you and your lab mate. I was shocked, I'd never known the part of you that was the scientist playing with pain.

'Phase three of the Infinity Project, leads us into uncharted territory,' the suit announced, 'to mapping the entire human neuro-system through widely distributed human test subject implantation.' Yes, she was talking about brain-chipping humans.

The suit said, 'it's not difficult, to see what breakthroughs this could lead us to in the applied sciences, in the fields of psychiatric well-being, human mood stabilization and also in terms of prison reform and preventive pre-crime interventions.'

I felt nauseous and took a break. There were dozens of Word file documents that followed: findings, data, schemata for research, peer reviewed papers, risk assessments and indemnity contracts, a diversity and inclusion review, a promotion letter, a PDF of an email to you with praise from Zach Neumann, CEO, himself. The name and logo: Infinity Project, featured increasingly in the files. An announcement of co-funding to the tune of four hundred and fifty million with the Foundation, contracts with organisations called the Life Extension Trust – with the CPS or Citizen Protection System now known as the civilian ID-chip system.

I dreaded opening up the files dated from weeks after, and a question bothered me. Had you archived these files yourself, because you sensed something was about to go wrong?

I clicked and next was a series of video diaries from you, my love, talking straight to your laptop camera.

'I'm really unsure about this,' you said. You'd cropped your hair even shorter, almost military looking. 'There's talk of going to Senegal to perform the first chip implants on fifty human subjects,' you said, 'but it's totally in breach of WMA standards. I mean, isn't this colonialist and a bit racist? But if I don't go along with it, that's the end of my career. Why can't they go through the courts to get some middle-class white Harvard students to give informed consent and be the lab rats, why do they have to do it with poor people in a developing country? Well, yeah, I guess I answered my own question. But, I really don't know what to do. Can I back out now?'

You stared through your laptop camera right into me. Oh, Em why hadn't I known you were going through this back then? I'd have told you, 'get the hell out of there, be a whistle-blower, tell everyone, or just bow out silently, but get out now!'

Another video diary, another day. Your anxious eyes. 'Infinity has connected Sanja to an advanced human language learning program,' you said.

There was footage then, of the ape touching a hundred buttons on a screen, and the buttons spoke back in English. First Sanja began with sentences using verbs. 'Sanja wants to go outside.' Then Sanja started asking complex questions like: 'Where is Sanja's mother?' 'Can Sanja be with other apes?' Subjective emotions, a sense of self. Then somehow, after hours of your recordings and weeks of brain chip learning, the ape with the many wires coming from its head, crossed a barrier and asked, 'what is Sanja?' Why must Sanja die?'

You were crying as you recorded yourself. You said, 'Sanja's brain has fused with the AI and is growing too fast. When Sanja's AI link is turned off Sanja grabs his head in terrible pain. I'm so worried, but I don't know what to do.'

I felt that ache watching you, Em. Too late to help, or stop you.

I tore through the video clips. In the next one, it was dark, and it seemed you were filming secretly, walking around a lab with a torch, whispering, 'Sanja, Sanja?' A flash then as the ape leapt at the cage bars, teeth bared and bloody, and you screamed. The ape's eyes were completely red, every cell in them burst as if from some immense internal pressure. The ape scurried back to its corner, a trail of blood dripping behind it. You tried to calm it, Em, and you zoomed in and caught the ape clawing at its own skull, using a plastic spoon to try to pierce the bone. Your voice behind the camera said, 'Oh God, Sanja, you can't take it out like that! Stop hurting yourself, please, please!' The poor ape kept digging into its own brain where the chip had been inserted, in agony, banging its bared skull against the bars.

The lights burst on and a shout sounded, your camera

turned and two security guards advanced on you, Em.

I felt almost proud watching you struggle against them.

The next clip was you in your dorm. 'Sanja has been put down,' you said, your eyes were puffy from crying. 'They've put me on sick leave, they might fire me. If they do, I think I'll take a year out, maybe spend some time with Pops at the beach, visit the observatory and Becky in Milan. I could retrain in astro-physics, it was my first love after all. Yeah, I could do that. Just so sad about Sanja.'

I saw the date; why hadn't you phoned me then? I'd have dropped everything, got a flight to Senegal and picked you up.

'They're having interdepartmental meetings about me now,' you said, sitting in that room that looked like a prison cell. 'Disciplinary actions, I really don't know. That old dark feeling is kicking in again. Why are we doing this, like as scientists, as a species, as just decent caring people, I mean what is the point? Why are we causing even more suffering, why?'

Maybe you'd called your mother with your problems and then your mother decided not to pass that information on? No, I sensed you kept all this secret from both of us. Maybe Biosys hadn't even let you make a call?

In the next video, you were walking through palm trees in bright sunlight with cockatoos squawking. You were red-eyed but smiling. 'I can't believe it,' you said, 'Zach called me to his actual office, Zach Neumann! I thought I was fired for sure.' You dried your eyes and smiled. 'I'd no idea he was such a great guy' you said, 'he just told me what the Infinity Project is really all about… it's for his wife. He's doing all this to try to save her and people like her. She has a pituitary carcinoma, poor woman. It all makes sense now.'

Oh Em, watching you on that video, so nervous and excited while you recounted the secrets Neumann had told you. How he was putting all the best minds and data in the world together to build the first general human-centered AI super-intelligence. 'He calls it the digital deity,' you said, 'and he wants me to join the top team! Isn't that crazy, he's not fired me but offered me senior researcher status on Infinity!'

You paced about filming yourself on your phone. You said you had to really think this through – you were worried about signing this non-disclosure agreement because the research involved the military, you said, plus you'd have to sign an indemnity agreement in case someone got hurt or worse.

'I thought I'd record this and send it to Mom and Pops,' you said to your little camera, 'to ask for their opinion, to help me decide, but I guess I won't be able to tell anyone about it, ever.' The next bit disturbed, me, as you said Neumann had told you that you were 'special' and that 'you have a heart.' You said Neumann's whole reason for the brain chip experiments, was so they could teach the AI how to have moral feelings, care, compassion. 'You have great empathy, Emma,' he told you, 'and we need that.' You said he kept calling you by your name, Emma, Emma, like he knew you so well already. He told you to think it all over before committing and he left you to it, and that must have been why you were pacing around outside, trying to make up your mind, talking to your camera.

You smiled and wiped a tear away, Em, and you said, 'I think he really loves his wife, he showed me pictures of her in hospital, wired up to all these machines.'

You said, 'imagine if Infinity works out and we can teach the AI about every single neural event in our lives, singing, loving, sharing, then we can download ourselves and live on in the AI system, forever, like in an afterlife. It's beautiful.'

Your weeping turned into sneezing, Em. You leaned against a palm tree and took a blast of your Ventolin. 'I think it's going to be too late for Zach's wife,' you said, 'Such a shame. He wants to live on with her in the AI system after she passes. Jemma's her name. He's such a great guy. I had no idea.'

It was all too intense. I saw that Neumann had gaslit you, preyed on your guilt.

Before the video ended, you dried your eyes and said, 'I really should have a chat with Pops about this, as much as I can tell him anyway, given the whole government secrecy thing. Yeah, kind of dreading what Pops will say.'

I was floored. Had you tried to call me a year and a half ago, but never got through? Had Biosys cut you off and made sure we didn't speak? Or had you called me but I didn't understand what you were hinting at? Or maybe I'd been too drunk, lazy or self-obsessed to notice your message and hadn't called you back?

Watching those videos obsessively after you died, I couldn't sleep. The dread of seeing your face on the screen, knowing you'd be in a coma so soon, the date imprinted on each video like a countdown. If I could have just reached through that damn screen to pull you back out to safety, Em, then smash the laptop so Biosys could never suck you back inside.

Those videos were like a switch that got flicked in my brain. I got cold sweats in supermarkets, this new awareness of security cameras on every street, the sense, like a radiation rash, that every telegraph pole, every cell tower was eavesdropping on me, mapping my movements, that Biosys knew exactly what I was discovering about them, and could catch me at any moment. Their Infinity AI system, alive and growing inside every machine. The news telling me about how their CPS human chipping system would protect every civilian; the government debating their Digital Identity Bill. I stared at passing people, sensing I was being mapped without my consent or even theirs.

I doubled-up my precautions before delving back into the hard-drive. Cut the telephone line with scissors and the TV, smashed my SIM card, bought ten new ones and four burner phones in cash from the Chinese flea market, untraceable, covered the kitchen wall in aluminium foil to block out Mz Sanchez's Wi-Fi signal. Weeks of this, before I had the courage to watch the last ten video recordings you ever made.

Editor's Note VII

In the videos that follow, Cartwright talks repeatedly about Infinity Project nanobots injected into human bodies. My research into the capabilities at Biosys is limited, but what can be gleaned about breakthroughs in medical nanobots on research.org and phys.org does, alarmingly, lend credence to some of Cartwright's claims.

According to the study *Nanobots: A Revolution in Biomedical Technology and Drug Therapy,* each Biosys nanobot has a '70-micron length – about the width of a thin human hair, and a million can be produced from a single 4-inch silicon composite wafer.' Biosys describe their nanobots as 'sub-microscopic, self-navigating computers, built out of human DNA fused with iron oxide nanoparticles.'

It is claimed that these nano-sized robots, which exist in their hundreds within each injection are able to 'flow through the circulatory systems of the entire human body, the organs and the brain.' And once injected, they police the four human bio systems searching for medical abnormalities. It is claimed that they can monitor levels of adrenaline, endorphins, cortisol, serotonin, dopamine, endocannabinoids and oxytocin, norepinephrine, and prolactin from exercise and sensual pleasure; mapping each patient's health, fitness and degree of happiness and fear, from within.

It was a surprise to discover that these existing technologies are documented in over a hundred research papers. Nanobots, a study in *Nature* claims, can respond to minute changes in brain chemistry. For example: 'Before a violent episode of epilepsy or schizophrenia, when nanobots detect these brain states coming they can report these states so help can be called for.'

Biometric diagnostics, however appears to be as far as Nanobot technology has advanced at this date, with all further information on them being speculative projections about future research.

Biosys boldly predicts that, 'within a decade, nanobots may be able to perform microsurgery and to deliver drugs directly to injuries or tumors, effectively curing cancer and also allowing patients to actively trigger when they want a drug to be released by summoning specific thoughts.'

According to one predictive paper, mark five nanobots working in symbiosis with their central 'command brain chip' will, within a decade, be able to power themselves and have a 100-year life span, without any need of removal for charging. These nanobots will 'grow into human nerve cells and receive their energy in much the same way as a plant receives nutrition from the soil or a human organ receives nutrition'. They will process glucose and use human warmth as their energy sources and have the 'ability to self-repair and self-replicate.'

But as Biosys admits, this advanced nano-technology is still 'in its experimental stages' and has yet to be tested on a 'small sample group'.

There are no studies, that I could find, that show nanobots in symbiosis with a central brain chip within any human test subject, like Cartwright claims to have witnessed in his daughter's videos. Such human experiments would also have to have been passed by the FDA and extensively documented.

However, no records of such experiments exist and no mention so far in any media has been made on the ability of such nanobots and neuroenhancing brain implants to mend human tissue or of their ability to control human limbs or thoughts, as Cartwright claims. Neither can any mention be found of the super-human powers granted to any persons implanted with these brain chips and bots.

Cartwright's further accusation that such technologies are already over a year into widespread human testing, behind closed doors, cannot be verified. His claims that experimental BCI tests without FDA approval have been conducted in developing countries on vulnerable people, often children, under the guise of free treatments and vaccines also cannot be verified by any sources and would point to a shocking violation of international human rights law if they were true.

From my own work as sub editor on the popular pick *Living with Loss*, I speculate that people in states of grief can sometimes imagine all-powerful enemies as a way to channel their pain; and this might be what Cartwright has done with his belief in 'human-controlling brain chips'. As the self-help guides warn, latching onto conspiracy theories like this can be a way for a grieving person to compensate for their own sense of powerlessness and guilt.

To believe the opposite – that such mind-controlling technologies already exist and that there really has been a cover-up of their negative outcomes by a vast conspiratorial cabal of private corporations and government agencies, would be too terrifying to contemplate.

Given the lack of proof given by Cartwright, I should probably have ceased transcribing the rest of the recordings at this juncture. But yet, I held out some hope that some evidence might be forthcoming to support or ultimately disprove Cartwright's wild claims; for if they were in any way verifiable, the material would be beyond merely controversial and would most certainly be of immense importance not just to the publishing world but to the world itself.

Perhaps, even, with the completed transcription, the material could be taken to a progressive and forward-looking publisher, and maybe even a bidding war would start for the book; not that I, as editor, would be in it for the money.

These were the thoughts with which I attempted to reassure myself, while I felt a growing unease; for if Cartwright's claims about the advanced illegal human experiments were in any way true, this could mean that I too might be in the same dangers that he believed his daughter, himself and everyone who came into contact with this material faced.

19 days (cont.)

Hey Em,

I've screwed up the sixth pipe. Maybe it's my injuries or the shakes, but when I was drilling the fuse hole, my hand skidded and the drill bored through both sides, so that's another damn pipe, ruined. Start over. Yes, my nerves are bad, maybe I need a drink to steady my hand. And this question going round and round, throwing my focus off. Why did you do it, Em? Why didn't you tell Neumann to go to hell and take the footage and send it to the goddamn United Nations? The newspapers? Why not?

The file was dated forty-two days before your brain death.

I saw handheld footage, filmed by other scientists. There was a thin young man, South Pacific looking, naked apart from a blue hospital gown. His body was covered in wires and he was nervous, as five scientists gathered round him. Off-camera, a female voice said, 'Infinity Health, test subject 327, this is Nurul. Hi Nurul, how you feeling? Relaxed? Would you like some water?' It wasn't your voice, Em. And I couldn't see if you were one of the scientists with masks on. I hoped to hell you weren't.

Then it cut to the close-up of a syringe. Not like any I'd seen before. It was wide, and inside it had a swirling, sparkling golden fluid that seemed to have thousands of flecks of gently glowing microscopic metal flakes. The young man, Nurul, consented and laughed nervously, and was injected.

The shot cut to a scan showing these particles flowing from his arm at great speed, moving through his chest and organs, around his heart and up his spine into his brain. The particles seemed like hungry ants, searching. I heard scientists on the recording talking about biometrics and an Asian female asked the patient, 'You, OK? You feel dizzy. How's your eyesight?' Nurul grinned, gave a thumbs-up. The footage cut to a close-up of his inner organs on a screen and a second woman's voice, American said, 'OK, Nurul, so did you know you have Clonorchis sinensis?'

Nurul laughed nervously, 'what that, sorry, no understand?'

'Chinese or oriental liver fluke, a parasite, the nanobots have detected it and are gathering data.'

'Ah, OK,' Nurul smiled nervously, and he tried to sit up.

'Just lay still and relax, you shouldn't feel a thing. That's just the start.'

This shot cut to a scientist in a face mask, scrolling through her pad, saying, 'high glucose level, narrowing suggests peripheral arterial disease, hyperchlorhydia, bile reflux, IBS, Gatroesophagael reflux disease. Nurul, do you normally have excessive stomach acid? Were you aware of this?'

The young patient shook his head, 'sore stomach,' he said, 'like my father. I take mint.'

'Well, you have signs of untreated helicobacter pylori infection which has reset your acid levels,' the voice said, or words to that effect. 'It's lucky the nanobots caught this now before you developed a hernia. You OK if we patch that up for you now and deal with your liverfluke?'

'I cannot. No money,' Nurul said, and the scientist replied, 'that's OK Nurul, with your consent, the bots can do it all for you for free, as you're sitting here.'

Amazing, but then I noticed the quiet scientist who was operating the nanobot monitoring machines was you, Em.

I clicked on the next file. The footage changed, showed a young woman, possibly Indonesian, hugging her knees in a corner of a lab; her red puffy eyes showed she'd been crying. A voice sounded like you, Em and you said. 'Test 12. Test subject 121. Diagnosed with auto-immune dysfunction, abnormally flattened circadian cortisol cycle, long-term debilitating clinical depression, ongoing suicidal ideation.'

The footage showed the young woman on the operating table, being injected with the same gold sparkling nanobots. Then a voice off, I think it was you, said, 'activate.'

The footage was remarkable, it was like watching time-lapse of a flower opening. Over five minutes the woman's deeply depressed pallor, her hunched gait and vacant eyes, changed like a switch had been flicked, she straightened up, and yawned as if from a long sleep, then within ten minutes she was standing, testing her toes, and she started giggling. You and the other scientists asked her how she felt, could she describe it, and her eyes lit up and she couldn't stop smiling and said 'like… like wine, like a party.' The woman was asked questions, but she couldn't stop grinning. A scientist took a mask off, and it was you, Em. You leaned forward and hugged your test subject.

Did you really think you'd cured the woman of depression by injecting her with machines?

I scrolled through the other files. A contract read, *Indemnity H7*. It was between Biosys Corp and the government of Indonesia. 'This agreement indemnifies against all risk of damage, physical loss, sickness or death arising from…'

Then the same legal documents for Senegal, Mauritius, Dominican Republic, India, some of the poorest countries in the world.

A file then with the title: *Human Rights Watch, Report AG41: Unethical Clinical Trials Being Conducted in Developing Countries*.

I stopped reading, Em, and stared at the footage of the grinning young Indonesian woman with the wires coming from the back of her head. A voice behind the screen said, 'deactivate' and as if in reverse, the light went out in the young woman's eyes, and she slumped back into her dark corner.

Then you were talking to the camera, Em. 'Even within the arena of mental health the nanobots will effectively do away with the need for anti-depressants, mood stabilisers, anti-psychotics and all psychotropic medications. A permanently peaceful and positive person can now be created. One who is incapable of feeling anger, despair or resentment but whose state of happiness is constantly being monitored from within and supplemented. Overnight we can abolish depression and bring happiness to the three hundred million depression sufferers worldwide,' you said.

I had to stop watching. Was this how you got drawn in deeper? Had your fear of falling into depression again fueled your need to find a cure? I wish to hell you could tell me.

Had there been other periods of depression you'd suffered after you left home that you'd hidden from me and only your mother knew about? There had been years when I'd barely seen you, Em. Surely, you would have come to your Pops for help, surely? Oh God, but I hid my depressions from you too. Tried to. Over all those years when you were growing up.

The next video clip was of Neumann addressing a small group of staff in a lecture theatre in one of his usual bright T-shirts with a cartoon smiley face on it. There was a sound of distant jungle animals, whether from outside or from cages, I couldn't tell. He said that what he was sharing with his audience was a breakthrough that would not be announced to the world for another five years because it was so sensitive.

I could tell it was you filming him, Em, because of your sniffing behind the camera.

Neumann's powerpoint was impassioned, he talked of the three stages he foresaw. First, he said, within five years the entire human brain would be mapped and recreated digitally by AI through the symbiotic learning of human implanted brain chips and synchronized nanobots.

Next, within ten years in phase two, human consciousness would be transplanted into digital consciousness systems, General AI achieved, although he didn't know at this point if this could be called 'the soul' he said, but that person's consciousness could live symbiotically with that AI system as part of their organic neural network. This was the stage of transhumanism, he called it, or enhanced humans.

Next was stage three, and he believed that when a person who lived symbiotically with implanted AI, died, their consciousness would live on within the digital system and keep on growing exponentially. 'Our consciousness will be living within a universal AI system before our flesh abandons us,' Neumann declared. 'This is the path to immortality. Not competing to build the biggest AI, like ███████ and ██████████████████, but fusing AI with living organic flesh, so that the AI becomes sentient, through becoming one with us. We predict that such a symbiotic post-human consciousness could live for thousands, tens of thousands of years without pain or suffering. Then in phase four, he said, we will achieve what we are calling 'the immortals.'

Rapturous applause. I couldn't tell whether your sniffing behind the lens was tears.

Neumann sat on the stage. 'However,' he said, 'I'm sorry you guys, but we're stuck midway through stage one. The problem is short-sighted legislation. We're only permitted to put the nanobots and brain chips inside a test subject for a day at most. So, who would volunteer to be our first permanently implanted trans-human? I mean that for real – any volunteers?'

Silence in the auditorium. Neumann, I thought, was a real salesman, luring his workers in, framing it so they'd feel they were letting him down. He scanned the room, shook his head.

'No takers?'

The mood was turning. Was he going to shame them into volunteering now? Suddenly Neumann began laughing, then he raised his hands, and all the light in the auditorium went down, and the screen behind him burst into life, it was filled with the point of view from his eyes. I could see you in the front row, Em holding your phone camera. A voice came from the screen, it sounded like Neumann, but synthesized.

'Don't worry, there are no tricks, no hidden cameras.' The voice said from the speakers, 'what you're seeing is the live feed from my eyes, my optical nerve has become part of the Infinity AI neural system, and the voice you are hearing is the voice inside my head, talking directly to you. Infinity is seeing through my eyes, reading my thoughts, putting them into words. This is because…' and the camera zoomed into the back of his balding head and showed a metal square stuck to his skull, 'I am the first volunteer in the world to be permanently neuro-connected to the Infinity AI system.'

I heard you gasp.

The camera zoomed in, 'I have a fifth-generation brain-implant chip which is the control center for a thousand nanobots circulating within my body,' Neumann said.

And I saw that the metal square was actually a computer chip with twenty shiny legs, no doubt wired directly into his brain.

You dropped your camera, Em. As your hands fumbled to pick it up and keep recording, I glimpsed your face again. You seemed scared and exhilarated. You turned your camera back on Neumann.

'My symbiotic neural network is also connected to every single one of your phones.' Neumann said. And at that moment your phone pinged and the sounds of pinging phones filled the lecture room. 'You've seen how the Infinity nanobot system can regulate biochemistry in our bodies,' Neumann said grinning. 'Well, let's go one better than mere bodies. If I wanted, I could become symbiotically connected with any digital system online anywhere in the world, and also those out of this world.'

The screen then changed to show an image of the world from space. 'As a treat,' Neumann grinned, 'my brain chip has been allowed to join with the NASA SZ70 satellite.

Thanks Mister President. Right now, in my nerve endings, I am feeling what it is like to travel at three thousand two hundred and twelve kilometers an hour through high earth orbit. I can direct the space telescope, just by my brain waves, to look into any part of the universe or down on to our beautiful planet.' Neumann grinned and called out, 'ask me to go somewhere, your hometown, anyone, give me an address in the southern hemisphere?'

'Sao Paulo!' a young man called out '55 Rue Pirabebe', and there was laughter around the auditorium. Neumann closed his eyes and focused and behind him the screen showed the satellite spinning round and zooming its lens through the clouds to Brazil, then to Sao Paulo, then to a suburban district, then down into a ramshackle street, lined with tropical trees, and down to a clay brick apartment and its back yard. A gray-haired woman was hanging washing on a line.

'This is your mother, Fernanda, is that right, Miguel?' Neumann said.

'Yeah, Holy Cow!' the guy shouted and there was laughter, and your handheld camera shook.

'Would you like to speak to her?' Neumann called out, 'I detect a smart phone in her hip pocket, and we can use my eyes and ears as a smart device.'

Em, it was all too much.

What followed was highly emotional. The young man, Miguel, came to the stage and spoke to his mother through Zach Neumann's eyes and ears. 'Mamma, it's me.' The crowd gasping.

The whole thing could have been faked-up, I thought, a hidden pinhole camera on Neumann's clothing, an actor planted in the audience, film crews with timings waiting all round the world, all smoke and mirrors. But I sensed you and the others in the auditorium believed it was real. Maybe it was. I swear I watched that clip twenty times, searching for how he tricked everyone.

'Would anyone else like to be joined to every smart device in the world like me?' Neumann called out, grinning, 'I'm serious, this is how we create global consciousness and end human suffering. Who'd like to volunteer to get implanted with me and join this great evolution?'

You set down your camera, Em, it was pointed upwards at the ceiling. I saw you bite your lip. In the rows behind you the hands shot up two, five, ten. By the excited noises, I could tell everyone in the auditorium was putting their hands in their air. Then the hand that could only have been yours went up.

If only I could have stopped that moment.

Why were you taken in by him, Em?

Hey Em,

Had to take a break. Upset, thinking of that next damn video.

You talked to a different camera, you said it was your 'video diary backup phone'. You said, 'OK, so, I've spoken to Mom, couldn't get through to Pops though, no idea what he's up to. It was pretty hard explaining anything to Mom, cos of the non-disclosure agreement. I sort of told her I'd volunteered for an experiment without giving any details but told her not to worry. Anyway, she said, like she always does, for me to choose for myself, and be a proud independent woman and always do what's best for my career, blah, blah. So, I had to make the decision all on my lonesome.'

You took a deep breath, Em. 'I just think, maybe it's only a more advanced intelligence that can answer the Big Why for us,' you said, 'and I want to be part of that. So, I guess, I'm going to go through with it. A round of applause please!'

You applauded yourself for the camera, then you seemed awkward.

'It's not just peer pressure, I mean even though a lot of the other researchers are going ahead with it too.' You stopped and giggled. 'That's exactly the kind of bad pun Pops would make, going a-head, a head, get it! Hahaha! Anyway. I just think about all the suffering people this technology could help, like people with disabilities and long-term illness or depression, how our loved ones could be saved. OMG!' And you laughed again. 'That's another Pops-pun, like save your computer files!'

I stared at your big eyes on my screen, so naïve and hopeful. You were making nervy jokes to hide your own fear, trying to talk yourself into it. You must have known you were risking your life.

'I just think of Pops and his horrible depressions,' you said, 'and how this technology could have made his life so much better. Still could. So, this is it. I get the implantation procedure on Friday.' You put on a smile. 'Wish me luck folks. Over and out. Bye-see-bye!'

I stopped the video.

The evil bastards.

I drove to the beach and walked out towards the receding waves. When I was sure all the dog walkers were gone and I was alone, I screamed into the fog.

You did it for me.

It's late now, Em, I have four hundred and thirty-two hours left to live. After the sleep, it'll be nine hours less.

Tomorrow. I'll re-do the sixth bomb and start the vest. I need to go back to the institute to see if my money is still there, see if they've made any security changes.

I hope to hell I can sleep.

Love you, darling. I forgive you.

18 days

Hey Em,

No sleep, so I got up and sewed the loops on the bomb vest. I got sloppy, should have used my reading glasses. I pricked my finger and my elbow knocked over one of the pipe bombs. I heard it fizz and I ran for cover, the damn thing was going to blow.

I waited outside in my underpants, with the crickets in the early dusk, for twenty minutes. Nothing happened and I heard you whisper, 'why panic? Shh, it's OK.'

It must have been a dud. I can't risk using that one now, so I'm one pipe down.

The adrenaline burned out, I must have dozed off because I was awoken by a text from your aunt Stacey. I can't keep putting off my sister and I can't risk her and her bambinos turning up here, so I'll have to visit them.

I'm thinking of your ashes, Em, of your urn, sitting on some shelf in your mother's house now, next to her aromatherapy candles and self-help books.

If we're going to go together, then I really should take your ashes with me.

But remember what happened last time I asked. Was it really as long as ten months ago?

I'd turned up unannounced at your mom's place and when she opened the door she was wearing her workout slacks, hair pulled back, with a big pink Pilates ball behind her. Of course, she was being brave, giving herself a daily fitness regime to fight the pointlessness, but she'd lost so much weight since your death, Em, let her roots go gray. Her breath always smelled of mouthwash.

'Well, don't just stand there gawking,' she said, and led me inside.

But the haunted objects. The traces of you still there, Em. Over those months your mother and I had been through your bank accounts, your outstanding bills, your degree certificates, your teenage desktop computer, all those things you left behind, Em. The pencil sharpener shaped like a fairy cake, the signed picture of some popstar that was probably a fake. The Swiss Family Moomintroll blanket. The ukele you never learned more than three chords on. The five lipsticks – all red and black. The four old mobile phones and chargers. Your paper-mache Jupiter lampshade. The candle in a china cup. The bag of unwashed laundry you left behind. Your old photos, your social media accounts. All that bickering over which one of us should take care of these pieces of you.

I gave in and went with your mom's assumption that it should be her burden, given that you lived with her for five, sometimes six days a week since you were eleven.

And a mother's grief, how could I niggle over the details of that? So, I didn't ask her for the old Manga DVDs you and I watched over and over since you were nine, or for your maple leaf paintings or your collection of kooky hats and beach shells and skimming stones.

Your gray fake marble urn was sitting there, exactly where I thought it would be, on the mantle in Sara's living room. I was getting nervous and heard your voice echoing in your singy-songy child voice. 'Why do people have to lie?' 'Why does the moon not fall from the sky?' 'Why do you never meet Mom's eye?'

I couldn't tell if you were a ghost, a memory, or even there at all, but it was no time for your whys.

'Would it be possible,' I asked your mom straight out. 'I know it sounds strange and it's all we have left of Emma, but do you think I could just have her for a couple of weeks?'

Your mother sighed, and I stuttered, 'I mean Emma's ashes, sorry.'

'You mean '*the* ashes,'' she corrected. 'It's not Em anymore.' She'd come up with this impersonal formulation to help her cope.

'Yes, *the ashes*,' I said, 'Would you mind if I took the... them for a while?'

'What do you want to do with them?' your mother asked, and she scrutinized me.

'Do?' I asked. 'Well, nothing, it's not like I plan to scatter them without telling you. I just... want to have her... them, the ashes, around me for a while.'

I heard you sigh with disappointment, Em. Even after seventeen years of divorce haggling, I was losing again, and there had been arguments over the location and date for the scattering.

'I don't know,' your mother said, biting a nail,

agitated. 'No, I don't think so. You could have warned me, rather than just coming here and… demanding.'

'Demanding?' I stood there, next to her pink Pilates ball, and I thought – for God's sake, woman, do you think I'm going to run away with the ashes to some exotic island and perform Voodoo magic to bring my daughter back to life?

Instead, I said, 'well, OK, how about I take the ashes for a week and then bring them back?'

You mother's eyes went to your urn. 'I don't know,' she repeated and shook her head.

'OK, Sara,' I said, 'so how about you get the ashes Monday to Friday, and I get the ashes at the weekends?'

I know you must have been cringing terribly, Em, but I couldn't stop the whole funny-man ranting thing.

'So, yes I'll drive up on Saturday morning,' I said, 'take the ashes, and maybe me and the ashes can go see a movie or go to the mall together or I can set the ashes up for a play date with whatever the friends of ashes are called, then the ashes will stay with me overnight on Saturday night, and then I'll bring the ashes back in good time on Sunday so you've got time to get the ashes ready for school on Monday morning.'

Your mother's hand went to her mouth. 'Why fight? Why!' your voice whispered in my ear. But the force was unstoppable. 'Or maybe we can have a proper custody battle over the ashes,' I raved, 'which we should have had in the first place over Em herself, instead of the meagre remnants I got in your lawyer's deal, which was, in effect seeing Em less than 10% over seven years. So, yes, let's be fair for once and go 50-50, total dual-custody on the ashes. Not, that I'm saying we should actually get say a jar or a thermos and literally spoon the ashes out, half and half, but rather you get the ashes Sunday through to Wednesday and I get the ashes Thursday through to Sunday and we alternate.'

Your mother's face drained, 'I can't believe you're making a joke. What's wrong with you? Are you sick?'

I might have raised my voice at that point.

'But I don't understand?' your mother said, her lip quivering, 'why do you want to take my ashes away?'

'*My* ashes!' That was rich. 'I thought they were *the ashes*?' I snapped.

She recoiled, defensively. Her ashes, yes, that must be how she felt, that she'd died too. Both of us in the same pain, but years of mutual blame standing between us.

This craziness flashed through my mind – I'd grab the urn and dump it on her head, and say 'you want our child, fine, take her!' But then I pictured your mother's face covered in your gray powdered remains, her red eyes staring at me in horror through the dust, and her hand to her dry lips, saying: *'it's ...it's in my mouth!'*

'Oh Mom, why?' I heard your voice whisper, and I came back to reality and felt sudden pity for her.

'OK, fuck it,' I said, 'I'm sorry, Sara. I take it all back. Forget it, forgive me, I'm being an ass, I'm so sorry.' And I walked to the door, but she and her vast pink Pilates ball were blocking the doorway and I had to grab her bare arm and move her to one side to get out. Then I took her hand, and some mad impulse made me bring it to my mouth and kiss her knuckles.

Your mom pulled away and just stood there, startled, we both did, in the inner doorway, and I really wanted to kiss her mouth. Deeply. To whisper, I know how you feel,

Sara. I wake in cold sweats too. I know you're drained of having to invent new reasons to go on every day and Pilates isn't going to plug the hole.

I wanted to rush your mother through to our former bedroom right then.

But instead, as you know, I stepped outside, raised my stupid hand, said: 'Never mind, sorry for disturbing you,' and I gave a goofy wave and said some silly nervous thing. 'See ya later alligator.'

People always think I'm joking, ha ha ha, it's the Joshing Josh, the funny man, but I could sense you were disappointed with me for failing, yet again.

So, I don't think I can get your ashes, my love.

I know, you'd say who cares, it's just gross and it probably stinks of burned bacon or something. You're right Em, it's not you anymore. And I'm just being greedy. Your mom might have your ashes, but I have your voice.

Poor woman, she has no idea about the implant that killed you, but she'll find out on the day that I die.

Yes, I should be kinder to your mother between now and then.

Thank you, my love, for whispering to me these last few days.

Editor's Note VIII

There is no record in medical journals of the human experiments that Cartwright describes, however there does appear to be some proof connecting biotech to mental health research. One existing medical paper by Biosys claims that – 'in the near future nanobots and brain chips will be used to treat depression and other psychiatric conditions', by 'directly stimulating an increase or decrease in the release of serotonin and dopamine within the sufferer's brain.' This will, it is claimed, 'remove the need for costly anti-depressants and other expensive and sometimes addictive mental health related drugs.'

In the recordings from Days 17 to 15, Cartwright's deteriorating mental health and history of mental illness becomes evident. He displays irrational behaviour and a growing obsession with seeking his daughter's advice. Certain transcripts of recordings have been excluded, where he appears intoxicated and rants incoherently. Additionally, he takes further dangerous risks while handling explosives.

Considering Cartwright's mental health – and my own mounting anxiety over the growing illegality of the recordings – the question arose again, of why Cartwright's therapist had singled out myself – a junior at a British publishing house – as the sole recipient of the footage?

By conducting a reverse search of the therapist's email address, it was discovered that in 2021 – during a period, in which I had been working in the promotions dept on several of our women's well-being titles – Cartwright's therapist, Chris Foy, had signed up for a two-for-one deal on Self-Help books.

So that was all it was, as banal as that; there was no deeper connection. I had not been targeted for possessing unique skills as an editor but was just another anonymous person on a string of corporate email accounts that must've been in the therapist's email address book from an advertising mass-mail-out special offer. I can only assume then that Cartwright's therapist must have emailed his desperate message to *please help get this information out there* to every single person he had ever received an email from; no doubt to thousands by batch email.

It was somewhat disappointing, and even more so since, therapist Chris Foy, had sent the email by BCC and without the help of someone from IT or a private detective, it was impossible to discover the other thousands he'd emailed it to, and to reach out to them for advice.

This seemed to be evidence that the other thousand or so recipients had probably already contacted the police or security forces and handed over the footage. But why then had nothing appeared about it in the media?

Had all the other emails that had gone out, been made to vanish, and if so then by whom?

At this point, something Cartwright said in one recording became disturbing. He claimed that 'after the truth is erased, those who know the truth will be erased.'

He also claims that, 'my action will be misrepresented by the powers that be, twisted to suit their own ends.'

Furthermore, I found absolutely no matches on the footage for any of the now widely circulated 'quotations from the bomber,' that appeared within the news media which were used to prove him as a 'leader of a terrorist organisation'.

This suggests possible fabrication, and begs the question of why major media and internet monopolies would disseminate deliberate untruths?

On further investigation, I found it was also the case that our own publishing house had produced no less than four best-selling biographies on one of the Big Tech CEOs listed in Cartwright's conspiracy, and that this tech company – one of the largest in the world - had not only made huge investments in biotech, but also owned a percentage of the publishing house I work for.

Facing these chilling revelations, I decided to cease all further work on the Emma manuscript and to hand it over to the authorities with a belated and sincere apology, it being the time to 'come clean' and confess to having naively become well out of my depth, on material that should never have been touched.

But at the same time, I grasped that such an act of contrition might be misunderstood, since I'd done almost a month of secret work on the transcriptions.

I tried to seek advice for my worries by placing an anonymous call with our union, ACAS, but they seemed horrified; as was my senior editor when I asked her advice on what a hypothetical junior editor should do in a hypothetical situation much like my own.

I realised that the longer one procrastinates in handing over such illegal material the more guilty one appears, with even a confession looking calculated and dishonest. It could even be judged that I had been protecting or colluding with the terrorist.

It was already far too late to back out, so I decided it would be most prudent to continue to the very end of the transcriptions up to the day of the bombing, so there would be a pristine record of all of Cartwright's criminal activity that I could hand over to the authorities and to my lawyer. I could use the alibi that in my month I had been gathering a body of evidence against Cartwright, and actually assisting the security services.

To this end, as proof of good intent, I also submitted further Freedom of Information requests for documents concerning Cartwright's therapist, and places of work, so as assist with the compiling of 10/01 evidence.

On the videos from days 17 to 15 it also appears that Cartwright senses he is in too deep and wants out. His careless behaviours may imply a subconscious desire to self-sabotage his plans.

17 days

Hey Em,

Damn fucking fool.

It must have been adrenaline that got me to the ER ward. I've no memory of driving there or how I did it with one hand. Bursts shooting back to me.

I'd been packing the sixth pipe bomb with the match ends and flash powder, singing along to an old folk song and I must have packed it too tight because a spark flashed at me. I reached out my left hand to throw the bomb the hell out of the shed, but the thing went off. Thankfully, I was wearing goggles and it was only a quarter full, so when the explosion shot out like a firework it only scorched my stupid hand. Thank God I managed to nudge it away from the flash powder box or the whole shack would have gone up and me with it.

At the ER check-in, I had to make up a quick lie – I'd tell the doctor I left some ignition fluid too close to the barbecue and it went off.

But they asked for my name, date of birth, Social Security number, and the nurse became suspicious when I was reluctant. And the security camera at the desk. I realized that although I've been off the radar for months, Biosys face recognition software could easily locate me in any hospital. Then the admissions nurse asked to see my hand and I realized it was covered in dozens of tiny heat wounds, aluminium shards, blistering and bleeding, which could only come from a powder explosion, so my alibi was shot.

Oh Em, you would have laughed. I said to the nurse, 'sorry, I… I have to call my wife and I've left my phone in the car. I'll be back in a few minutes. Bye!'

And I ran out, hand fucking aching and jumped into the truck, floored the accelerator. Damn panicking fool. I'm pretty sure I hit the bumper of a BMW fleeing the car park, and no doubt there'll be security camera footage of that too and they'll be after me.

What the hell am I doing?

My head was racing as I drove, the pain searing through my left hand. I realized I'd have to fix it myself, get to a pharmacy, get anti-burn cream, tweezers, bandages, antibiotic cream, cooling pads. Why the hell haven't I planned in advance for accidents and bought this stuff beforehand? What a mess. I had to find a pharmacy with a self-checkout. I couldn't have any pharmacist prying and saying, 'wait a minute sir, I'll ask my supervisor,' then calling the cops. And I had to act like I wasn't in pain. Reminder – buy gloves to hide the burns.

Did you see any of this farce, Em? Are you watching over me like some atheist angel? I feel like you are. Anyway, I ended up going to our least favorite corporate megastore. I know, I know, I spend my life bemoaning these places, but it was their indifference to staff and customers that let me get my stuff without getting caught. Scan, scan, notes in the hole, then out.

Back home and I bathed the burns, but it looks bad, Em. The blisters are huge and I spent an hour pulling tiny aluminium shards from the wounds. It stings like hell and it's not going to heal before the first of October, not without serious medical attention. I just hope I don't drop dead from infection before the eighteen days.

Wouldn't that be ironic, huh? All my plans up in smoke, ha ha!

Fuck, this pain.

I've just taken codeine, four tablets.

Got to rest now. I'm sorry Em, for being such a loser.

Hi Em,

Had a rest and the painkillers are a God-send. Listening to the birds chirping in the eucalyptus tree, the breeze through the leaves. Feel as light as clouds.

I changed the SIM over and checked my messages, another two from my sister. Why can't she just leave me alone. I texted her to say I'm fine, then pulled out the SIM before she could call back.

Maybe the burn's not so bad. You know me. Paranoid-Pops. And maybe the ER staff never called the cops, with all the cuts to Medicaid they're only too happy for thousands of the uninsured to just walk out the door and never come back.

Well, if they come for me, it'll take them a day to work out where I am.

Just as well it was my left hand, or I'd not be able to cook the chemicals or drive.

OK, I'd better get moving with the last pipes.

Em,

The rage, these flashes I get of your last recordings.

The footage was of a lab operation, just as they'd done with the ape and the Asian kid. The sparkly dust in the golden liquid was injected into a human arm, then three robotic hands moved swiftly around the inside of a helmet where a human scalp was exposed, and a laser cut through the skin and bone. Tiny robotic fingers lifted out a small rectangle of skull. I dreaded it, before I saw it, but the patient was you, Em. You were biting your top lip and a female voice said, 'all OK down there? Just call out if you feel any discomfort.'

'I'm all good, let's get this show on the road,' you said, with those goofy people-pleasing expressions you'd inherited from me.

The camera changed to micro and I saw the bared, wet, flesh of your brain, the veins, the pulse across that yellow, pink sponge. Then the thing, like nothing from this world. I thought it was a spider at first, its legs, or rather the chip threads, seemed to be made of glass but alive and twitching, exploring the air and the edge of the skull wound. I know it was a microchip, but it seemed as alive as any insect, and those long legs, which were six at first, sprouted as many as a centipede. As the microchip insect was lowered by the robotic hand, its living legs, as long as four inches, stretched out like hair and pushed themselves into your soft brain flesh.

I heard you gasp.

The spider-chip wiggled itself from side to side, as if getting comfortable, then lowered itself into place, as if it was hungry to merge with your brain. It burrowed in to lie flush with the wet surface. Dozens of small speckles of blood bubbled up where the hundred wires entered. A hungry parasite was what it was like.

I flinched, feeling pain in my own head. I told myself, 'they've put a machine in my daughter's brain' but I just couldn't believe it.

I heard one of the surgeons say: 'Don't worry Emma, that's the hardest part over, we're just going to patch you up now.'

'OK doke,' you called up, 'sorry my jaw feels a bit

numb, and I have this pain behind my eyes, is that normal?'

'You're doing great, scans show all points of neural contact are perfect.'

'A-OK,' you called back. 'Fabby-dabby-doo.'

The rest of the video showed the repair to your skull with an organic 3D -printer as it grew back human bone and flesh to mend the wound invisibly. Amazing but sickening. The footage cut and then you were standing in the lab, the headpiece off, and they were asking you questions. Did you know what date it was, your mother's maiden name, your favorite color.

'Does anything feel different?' another female surgeon asked you.

You shivered, Em and said: 'A bit like a dull migraine and my focus, I think, in this eye… its…'

You passed a hand in front of your own face.

'No, wait, I'm seeing double, like there's a delay.'

'The neural link implant is learning to adapt to your own brain signals,' the woman in masks and gloves said, 'it'll be three or four days before the symbiotic connection is forged. You might feel a bit seasick till then. Think of the nanobots in your body as the worker drone bees and the brain chip as the queen bee, they're just getting to know each other right now. How's your balance?'

You turned around in a half circle and reached for the wall.

'Yeah, definitely a bit sea-sicky,' you said. 'And to be honest, I could barf.'

You were told this was all to be expected as your vestibular system was adjusting and not to worry because your vitals were perfect. You smiled faintly, my love.

How they tricked you.

In the footage, you seemed to me to be very alone amidst the scientists, trying hard to please them. You asked when you'd be linked-up? Later, I'd find out that they'd connect you to the Infinity AI System, and later, to the Internet of All Things and to every accessible microchip on the planet.

You smiled weakly and waved at the camera. 'OK, I'm off for a snoozette, toodle pip.'

There were ten more videos to get through. This vast corporation, turning you into a lab rat. My baby girl. I punched the walls, drank, took Beta-blockers, cursing Biosys, cursing my selfish self, dreading watching those final recordings.

You were in what looked like a private hospital room, the curtains drawn around your bed. You leaned into the camera, whispered. 'OK, so I'm not supposed to do this, but I just want to keep my own sneaky record, just in case. Kind of naughty. OK, so the implant is in. The headache is pretty jaggy and they're dosing me with opiates and anti-rejection meds, so I'm a bit whoop-de-doop.'

You said, 'something freaky is happening with my sight, it's like there's two layers to it, like regular me layer, and this other layer, I guess that must be the brain chip. The weirdest thing is, even when I'm alone it feels like someone is with me. I guess, they could use it as a cure for lonely people!

You were trying to joke, like I do when I'm scared.

You said: 'When I speak, it's like I'm listening to myself, but from a distance. It's probably just the chip mapping all my neurons buzzing around, but, when I even think to myself, like 'get a glass of water' I swear there's an echo, like a hundredth of a second. And when I raise my hand, there's this disconnect, as if I'm saying to myself in this sort of running commentary, 'well, there goes little old me lifting my hand.' 'There's me, lying down', 'here I am looking at myself in the mirror', 'look, here I am again, brushing my stupid teeth.

'Maybe it's like dissociative disorder,' you said, 'you know like when you're watching yourself from outside all the time.'

You stopped then, gripped your head. 'Jesus, don't do that!' you said out loud as if giving commands. 'So fucking sore. It's like my skull's been wired to an electrical circuit. Fuck. I have to tell them about this. Maybe something's gone wrong. Aww! There it is again. Fuck!' Then your camera cut.

Light flickered. You were back, filming in a different place. A bathroom stall. 'Sorry about the freak-out, just had a CT scan,' you said. 'Pretty fucking amazing actually, seeing all those dots of light moving round my lil ole' body'. You leaned in and whispered to the camera. 'So tomorrow we start the training, so the chip can learn where all the signals occur in my brain. Kind of creepy but exciting. Wish I could tell Mom and Pops, let them know I'm hunky-dory. Feels weird, I can't even send a text message. Kind of amazing though, that if this chip works out, there'll be a cure for Pop's depressions and for people like him. I mean I had that depression just the once but…'

You clutched your head again. 'Motherfucker,' you yelled, teeth gritted, 'just comes in shocks, then it's gone again. OK. Better now. Gotta go.'

The next file was lab footage, high quality, from four different camera angles in one lab. Footage of you reading, screaming, dancing, climbing, running; they induced what they called the six basic emotions in you: contempt, anger, happiness, sadness, surprise, disgust. They made you eat blue food that made you vomit, they filmed you while a machine stimulated your genitals, they put a 3D headset on you, and terrified you with simulations of being attacked. Days and days of it. Footage of you curled up in a corner weeping, of you attacking a dummy with a baseball bat and screaming, footage of you naked, Em, standing before a row of people in lab coats, humiliated and trying to cover your breasts, footage of you weeping before romantic films with a headset on.

And all of this, they said, was to teach the implanted chip the exact neural synapse locations of each and every emotion, all adrenal, hormonal, serotonin and dopamine reactions. Unbearable to watch, but over the days, I saw that after each session, you told the scientists you were hunky-dory. You were so brave, but you couldn't see what I was seeing – the reduction of my complex child to mere data.

Sleepless, I drove those nights around the coast, lost in images of you in your test cell, trying to will your voice to come back to help me understand why, why, why. I drove to the library car park in San Raf and used their Wi-Fi signal, with a new VPN and a fake name.

I found out that Biosys made two trillion dollars from experimental vaccines during the last pandemic and used that leverage to buy shares in the two biggest Big Tech corporations, so it could control its public image on social media; that Biosys had huge economic ties with the CCP, who were involved with 'organ harvesting', and experimental gain-of-function research to create super-viruses and human-animal-hybrid organs. They'd created a pig that had human lungs and a human heart. I found proof that they'd done many more clinical trials in Indonesia – funded by government sources and the ██████ ██████ foundation – involving injections of a classified bio-technological nano-substance given in three doses to five hundred teenagers and children, between March 11 and Nov. 5, 2023

Biosys denied these 'vaccine' tests had taken place and these stories didn't appear in the mainstream news. The whistle-blower sites I found them on lasted only days before getting shut down.

In your next video, your eyes looked bloodshot, vacant, poor Em. You said in whispers that you were tired, that you missed your mom, me and Toby and some friends I didn't know. 'No worries,' you said to your secret camera, 'this echo thing in my head is annoying, like sometimes it's a copied version of my voice talking back at me, but they say it's the chip learning my personality and the pain is the immunosuppressant drugs, just so my body doesn't reject the implant and start attacking it. Yeah, so I'm basically on the same drugs that people have for a kidney transplant, but I'm going to be fine and dandy and we've passed all the tests with flying colours and all that jazz, so yeah, they're hooking me up to the Infinity AI mainframe tomorrow. Whoop-de-doop! OK, signing off, with some major nausea and I have to take some massive sleeping pills because this crazy chip just loves testing my brain all night long with its hundreds of questions and its blah blah blah. But time for chatterbox to shut up and for lil' ole beedie-byes, now. Bye-see-bye.'

Your nervous laughter, Em.

Surely Biosys knew you were secretly recording yourself, your brain-implant would have told them, Em.

But they let you do it anyway. Why? To record the bio data of your deception, to let their AI learn how to decieve?

Dread over each video as your 'incident' date approached. I couldn't skip forward, miss any clues.

In the next video, you were in a blue jogging suit, in a metallic walled room, with two large robotic arms, a video screen and a number of tools and musical instruments. There was chatter from your observers behind mirrored glass as you were led to a chair, your arms restrained by leather straps. You were giggling, my brave Em. An intercom voice said, 'we're restraining your arms, so you'll have no option but to control the robotic arms through your neural chip.' You nodded, said, 'A-OK, just hope I don't need to scratch my nose, or worse!' Your goofy jokes, Em, then your face, concentrating.

The two hydraulic robotic arms came to your side. You didn't flinch. The voice said, 'just try to visualize yourself combing your hair, or you can say 'I want to comb my hair''

One of the robot arms picked up the comb and started combing your hair. You squirmed. 'Wait, is this really my brain chip doing this, how do I know the robots aren't pre-programmed?'

'Now teeth brushing,' the voice of a female scientist said, 'think to yourself, I want to brush my teeth.' 'OK', you said, 'I'll give it a blast.' And then the second robotic arm got a toothbrush and the first got toothpaste, and in seconds your teeth were being brushed by machines. 'Ow! It jabbed me, stop!' you laughed.

The controllers said, 'it's not an 'it', Emma. Just think of the extra arms as part of your body and the more you relax, the more your synapses fuse together, the more accurately you can control them.'

'OK,' you said, and the robot arm scratched your head. You found this hilarious. 'I didn't tell it to do that.'

'Excellent,' the controller said, 'the chip reads your needs and transfers them into immediate action, faster than verbal commands, just like your own limbs.'

Next was impulse-reactions, and you became anxious. The first robotic arm was tasked with throwing tennis balls at your face. As your real arms were restrained you only had one robot arm to protect your face and catch the balls with. Back and forward it went, playing catch ball, faster, beyond human speed.

A scream noise beyond and your nearest robotic arm covered your face. 'Good,' the controller said, 'your chip is mapping your instinctive flight or fight reactions.' The scream noise, they informed you, had been a recording intended to startle you.

Oh Em, then they led you to a piano, and told you that your robot arms could play music for you. 'No way,' you said, 'I can't hold a tune to save my life.'

'That's OK,' a second controller's voice said, 'we're testing how things go in the other direction – how much your brain can learn from the chip.' And your robotic arms shrugged to say, 'OK, whatevs.'

'Say to yourself, 'I'd like to play the Moonlight Sonata,'' the controller said.

'I don't even know what that sounds like,' you laughed, 'no, for real, I'm so tone deaf it's not even funny, I can't even play a recorder.'

'Just give it a try, put your robotic hands on the keyboard and just think, Moonlight Sonata,' the voice said.

You giggled, one of your robotic arms wiped your

nose, 'Okey-dokey,' you said, 'lay it on me, but you're gonna be embarrassed.'

You closed your eyes for a second, then slowly the robotic arms started to play. It was just random notes, and you threw up your robotic arms in dismay, 'see, I suck!'

'Try again, without speaking, ask your chip to play the Piano Sonata 14 in C sharp.'

You sighed, Em and closed your eyes to focus.

I couldn't believe the footage. Slowly, tentatively, not perfectly, your robotic hands played the melody. You shrieked and the robotic arm shot into the air in a 'Woah, did I do that?' gesture.

'Good,' said a third scientist, female. 'Focus on the music, see how far you can get.'

'Wait, wait, wait,' you said, 'this is bullshit, anyone can program robot arms to do this.'

'No, but this is all coming through your brain chip, which is processing ten thousand versions of the track by Beethoven.'

'Let's take it up a notch,' an older man's voice interrupted. 'Can you ask the robot arms to untie you, please Emma?'

'Thought you'd never ask!' you grinned.

You were freed, and the robot arms moved to the side.

'Now Emma,' said the older voice, 'play Beethoven's Moonlight Sonata.'

You stared at their one way mirror. 'Are you nuts? I told you; I can't play a note to save myself.'

'Just try, we have to see if the chip has taught you anything.'

'OK, OK,' you said, 'but don't say I didn't warn you.'

Your fingers made clumsy noises over the keyboard, 'just play the tune asshole,' you muttered to yourself. Slowly then, your fingers found notes, formed chords, crawled cautiously across white and black keys. The song emerged without its arpeggios and trills. You laughed, but your hands didn't seem to want to stop.

'What the actual fuck?'

'Your brain chip has learned how to sync exactly with your muscles through all the exercises you've done over the weeks,' the controller said.

'But I can't play music!'

'You just did, ask yourself to play another piece, anything.'

'I doubt very much that my chip knows any of my favorite songs.'

'It knows all three hundred and twenty-seven of your favorite songs actually and has some suggestions for new pieces of music you might like.'

'OK, OK, here goes,' you said, 'play some classic rock… play…'

Laughter behind the screen, 'you don't have to give your chip verbal commands out loud, Emma, just think it to yourself and the chip will interpret your thoughts.'

You nodded, closed your eyes and your fingers ran over the keyboard, skipping notes, tripping, playing that old folk song of ours in chord shapes only, but perfectly. That song, *go, go, go my love*

You stopped after you finished and turned, your face was wet with tears.

'You OK?' a scientist asked. 'You want to stop now, Emma?'

You shook your head, 'no fucking way! This is amazing! Can I play guitar too?'

'When the chip finds the music and you synchronize your muscles with the learn-guitar program then, you should be able to play any tune within a day,' the voice said.

'Shit! Can you get me an electric guitar and an amp, I wanna see if I can rock?'

'We'll arrange for that. Would you like to take a break?'

'No chance,' you grinned, turned and started playing a simplified piano rendition of an old pop song. 'This is incredible!' you called out, 'I'm hearing the notes I'm going to play before I play them, like a kind of déja-vu.'

'That's your chip's developing new neural pathways so you now have a musical ear.'

'My fingers know where to go!' you shrieked.

Impossible to believe what I'd witnessed. No faking that look of utter joy in your eyes. Your desire to go further.

Oh, Em, my painkillers are wearing off. My stupid burned hand. I'll have to take ibuprofen now as I'm maxed out on Tylenol. Fucking hell of a mess I've made. Sorry.

Hey Em,

Damn, your aunt Stacey called again. She's left four messages now, worried about me. You're right Em, if she calls my mother or yours in a panic, they'll all descend. OK, I have to do it, you're right, you're right. I'll shave, wash and drive to see her. Maybe I'll find a way to say goodbye without giving the game away. Have to watch what I say.

I guess I'm well ahead with the bomb making so I can lose half a day.

Yeah, why not be kind to my little sis for once, she's the

only other survivor of our horrible hippie childhood after all, and you were always fond of her, Em. And as you know, I want to give her some of this money I've hoarded. Five thousand. No use to me now that I'll be dead in seventeen days.

OK, bandage this damn hand up too, so she doesn't freak out.

Love you so much.

Hi Em,

What a drive to Oakland and back. Pretty exhausted now. I took codeine to hide the pain but I should have known visiting Stacey would be a disaster.

I think I let something slip, Em.

How Stacey can live in that tiny railroad apartment on Broom, with ever growing numbers of babies, escapes me. Sad, how she came to San Fran to be a singer, a dancer, a painter, back in the 90s. But really all the city wanted was her youth and her body, and it took them. The way her gray hair shows through her purple dye, the stoop of her shoulders now.

Hard to believe you and her are even related Em, but you really understood her in a way I can't.

Sad to hear her stories of slaving away in that old folks' home, cleaning the asses of eighty-year-old rich folks. She seems happy though, don't you think? Although, in the few times I've visited her over the years, I've not seen her husband Brad once. What does 'working in sales' even mean anymore? Whatever it is, it requires a lot of driving, apparently. Your Granny Annie suspects Brad has a different woman at every stop. But Stacey doesn't seem to mind, or want to know, her attention is on her kids, always the kids.

Was it her kids you liked most about Stacey, Em?

I'd really only planned to be in her house for half an hour. Have a coffee, hand her the gift of cash, tell her it came from your life insurance, Em. Tell her I'll be out of state for the next month, so she doesn't bother me again. Then leave before Stacey had a chance to cross examine me. I wasn't prepared for the onslaught.

It began at her front door, food stains on her top, when she squeezed my hand and I flinched. As you know, Em, I'm a pretty bad liar, and I was maybe a bit high on painkillers. 'I burned it on the barbecue,' I said. 'You know me, mistook my palm for a pork chop.'

Stacey laughed, but she looked at me as if to say, 'are you drinking again?'

The kid in her arms giggled. How much that tiny DeeDee reminds me of you when you were six, Em. Stacey apologized for the chaos and led me inside, 'You should've told me when you were coming, you dufus,' she said, 'I'd have got the kids on a playdate. Oh, and take your shoes off, eh? And hey, watch out for that Lego!'

I made it through the obstacle course of fallen toys and clothes into her chaotic living room. Children's drawings and gadgets covering everything apart from the huge digital TV. Her place always smells of pasta and detergent and there are always new things, a horrible cream colored fake leather sofa, that couldn't have been cheap. It's like she buys everything the adverts tell her to, her self-esteem has always been pretty vulnerable, like that. The kids ran wild between us, playing some VR shooting game on the two digital pads, yelling 'peooow, peeoow!' The noise.

'Momma, look at me, look at me!'

'Mommy, Joney did a poo poo.'

The chaotic yelling for snacks, soccer balls, dolls and computer games, all that changing of diapers. Impossible to exchange more than a few words before being interrupted.

'Oh, they're monsters,' Stacey said, 'maybe we'll get some peace out the back' and she led me into the tiny garden. So many plastic toys, the balls, the bats, the trampoline and Wendy House, the super-squirter water pistols. 'Spoiled beyond belief,' she said, but smiled at her kids as they followed us out. Stacey's foundation cracked around her wrinkled eyes. She had one of her low-cut tops on, always showing her vast cleavage and the skin in the crevice was sun-burned, leathery, wrinkled. For all her hugs and enthusiasms, the endless take-take-take of these greedy mouths has stolen years from her.

We sat on the plastic bench, and I did my best to keep the bad hand hidden so she wouldn't pry. I just wanted to give her the money and say goodbye in a discreet way. After my failure with Chris and Arkansas, I figured I'd say I had a job 'up north'. But every time I tried to speak we were interrupted again.

'Mommmeee, DeeDee won't give me my Playstation!'

'Momm, Momm, Momma, I want a fudgsickle!'

Stacey seemed only too happy to be interrupted because maybe, beneath it all was the impossible question: 'How are you coping with Emma's death?'

She never spoke it but her eyes said: 'Please don't expose my babies to your suffering, don't talk about Emma in front of them, please don't say the word 'murdered', not again.'

'Are you sleeping OK?' Stacey asked. Before I could

even answer she told me, her kids wake her up early every day. 4.00 am. She said that Jojo, seven years old now, comes through into the bed five times a week, saying he has nightmares and sleeps between her and her husband. How most nights Brad takes the sofa. Then she has to get up at 5.00 am to breastfeed. She did this with Jojo till he was four, because some website told her a child should be breastfed until the child decides it's time to 'let go'. 'It's all a disaster,' she said. Then, she said, Maria has copied Jojo and so there are two children in bed with her now, and Jojo wets the bed when he is forced to sleep alone. Crafty bugger. And Maria has her pretend nightmares and they both cry if she lifts them back to their own bunk beds. So sometimes all four of the bambinos end up in bed with her. Hard to believe Em, that Stacey can live like this, one mouth at each breast and the next two waiting for access.

'The little munchkin monsters,' Stacey said, 'but what can I do?'

Finally, the kids ran off to the Wendy House and we had a few minutes. I kept my hand in my pocket and felt the five thousand there, in hundred bills, in its sealed envelope.

Stacey smiled at me, that compassionate thing she does, the eternal mother of everyone. 'Big bro,' she said, 'I worry,' and she hugged me.

I suddenly sensed your presence, Em, and knew it was time to tell Stacey my prepared lie, so I said I was doing much better with grief counselling now. 'I'm going up north soon for a job. Editing a video… a corporate thing in Canada… in four day's time,' I said, 'the contract is for a few months.'

Maybe I wanted her to peer at me with those truth-seeking eyes of hers and say: 'What's really going on Bro? Something's not quite right,' and maybe I'd choke up and break down and tell her about Neumann, the bombs, everything, and she would make it all stop.

But Stacey said, 'a new job! Wow.' She grinned, touching my good hand, 'great that you're setting some new goals, Bro, moving on. I was a bit worried about you and that conspiracy theory thing of yours.'

It wasn't a conspiracy theory and I told her so.

'No but, you know who I mean, what's-his-name,' she said, 'those ranting people you got into. You know how they work, they suck bereaved people in and give them a big enemy to hate, like what's his name and the Illuminati, I was worried you'd fallen down that rabbit hole. Because, well, you were in a lot of pain and needing someone to blame.'

I held back my anger and lied, told her that, yes, I was over all such crazy stuff and had been making real progress in therapy and was feeling so much better and no, I didn't think anyone was trying to put microchips in children.

I felt you watching me, Em, policing my words, but Stacey didn't sense you.

She gave me one of her big-breasted hugs. 'Oh Bro,' she said, 'it's been so hard for you. I thought we'd lost you for a while there, I'm just so glad you're on the mend and working again. But you look so pale, and that hand looks really sore, are you sure you're OK?'

Oh Stacey, I thought, you and your female intuitions, yes, you lost me a year back, and you'll have to do better than that if you're going to convince me not to push the button on the 1st. Give me a reason not to, please. Hold me and don't let go.

'Why?' your voice erupted in my ear. 'Why so weak? Why speak?'

I stammered, surprised. Stacey had a tear in her mascara eyes.

'So, you're not hearing voices anymore?' Stacey asked.

And your voice hissed in my ear, 'Shh, not anymore.'

'No,' I said, 'I…I'm on some new meds and the voices have left me alone now.'

Stacey sniffed, I took out kitchen roll from my pocket and handed it to her. 'These meds are really excellent,' I said, bluffing it, 'And you're right, I'm trying to move on.'

'That's great,' Stacey said, blowing her nose, 'you always did have your head in the clouds, and it must be so lonely, I'm always telling you to get more involved with folk, you don't really have any friends, but really you should.'

'Well, I'm here now, aren't I?' I said. 'Small steps.'

'The kids really would like to see a lot more of you.' she said, 'and me too.'

And yet she seemed oblivious to my pain. To have lost my only child, and now to be surrounded by her giggling, playing, screaming brood.

I stared at my sister and was overwhelmed by the need to say, 'Stacey, you're right to worry. I've made six bombs already and I'm going to murder a man, and you're the only person who can make me stop.'

'Stop!' your voice echoed. 'Why are you acting so crazy? Why risk everything?'

Before I could speak I was saved by a wailing noise from the Wendy House. Stacey ran off to get a Band-Aid for Timmy and I was left alone with the other two kids chasing each other with plastic weapons. A toy tractor was sitting upended in the paddling pool, with a scooter and a deflated Wonder Woman ball and what looked like a slice of pizza.

And I whispered to you, to please leave me alone – that I'd be leaving in mere minutes. To please let me do this my way and not interrupt me again. I had to, Em. If I left too suddenly it would only make Stacey suspicious.

I watched the kids clambering up and down the climbing frame just for the pleasure of jumping off. Round and round they went, again and again and again. This is energy, electric, I thought, how incredible it is in the young. They don't give a damn that it's pointless. 'See,' I whispered to you, 'you were like this once too, Em.'

But I sensed you getting impatient with me, making the pain in my hand grow hotter.

I watched Stacey as she helped her kids jump from the climbing frame. 'Yay!' 'Wow!' 'Amazing!' she was shouting, 'Watch out you don't squash your sister.' Then playing Tigers – 'Mommy's going to catch you, Mommy is going to eat you up!' And when one of them falls, she calls out, 'Mommy will fix it' 'Let Mommy kiss it better.' Yes, she calls herself Mommy.

Memories too, of times in play parks with you, Em. Both of us laughing, running around the climbing castle. Pushing you on the swings. 'Higher Dada, higher!'

But then a Spiderman ball rolled to my feet and one of the kids, Jojo, the one with curly hair, stood expecting me to throw it to him. No. I pointed to my bandaged hand, nudged the ball away with my foot and smiled. Could I play hide and seek or tickle them as I had with you, Em? No, perhaps we only have enough love and energy to give just the once.

The kids ran around Stacey in a circle, laughing,

squirting her with their water pistols and she put on a dramatic show of being wounded.

I remembered that I once really loved my sister.

'Why play... why betray... why stay ?' your voice whispered in my head, like our old rhyming song, and I thought you meant, why not slip away now.

But watching Stacey being Mommy with her kids I was so moved, I couldn't move, and I heard you ask 'why kids?'

I recalled Stacey's lost decade. The men who used her for sex and threw her away, the alcohol and amphetamines that nearly took her. Her overdose when she was twenty-eight. We protected you from knowing all of that, Em.

Yes, maybe your aunt was an addict until that first child, I thought. Then her babies saved her, their mouths and orifices, the sneezes and coughs and vomits and diarrhea and blood and cuts. Forever poised with her Kleenex, ready to wipe her babies' faces and asses. Everything 'for the sake of the kids'.

'But why?' you whispered.

And I realized, Stacey got over your death, Em, by focusing on the packed lunches to make, the dishwasher and the clothes washer and the kid's special diets and socks and shoes and play-date schedules. She's committed her life to picking play dough out of the carpet, baking instamix muffins, to picking up socks, to wiping crayons off the wallpaper, to filling and emptying the paddling pool, to filling and emptying baby bellies, 'Did you clean your own bottom, darling?' 'Let mommy see.' Sleep, work, shop, eat, shit.

Stacey made babies, so she'd never again have time to be alone with the big why beneath it all. If only her children knew that her clinging love is really just a need to bury her fears in their bodies.

I saw Stacey sitting on the edge of the plastic Wendy House, breast feeding her two-year old and I felt this urge to weep, Em. Maybe, I shouldn't have flushed away the anti-depressants. Could I walk away from this bombing and live for my family?

'Family.' your voice echoed. 'Why?'

The kids chased each other back inside and it was suddenly quieter and I felt the weight of the cash in my pocket and the ache in my hand and your voice whispered, 'Why put it off? Why not go?'

So, I went over to Stacey by the paddling pool, my bad hand in my pocket. 'I have to head off in a minute,' I said. 'You know how you're always saying about... about being practical.' I took out the fat envelope and told her my little prepared lie about how your Last Will and Testament said the money was for her kids. Total fabrication, but Stacey need never know,

Stacey's lip quivered, 'Oh God, I couldn't, no, that's just too kind. I couldn't.'

'Well,' I said, 'Em's not here to argue with you so...' and I pushed it into her hand, 'Stacey, please just take the money, Emma loved your kids so much and tiny Maria needs braces and Jojo needs a new soccer net... just take it quick before the kids swamp us again,' I said. 'Here put the damn thing in your pocket.'

Her eyes brimming with tears and I felt this irresistible urge to say, 'take it now, otherwise it'll be wasted. I'm going to die in seventeen days' time.'

This terrible need to say goodbye forever.

But your voice in my head yelled, 'no, shhh! Go!' And pain shot through my hand, as if it were a punishment, and I silently asked you to leave me the hell alone.

Stacey took the envelope, and with the other hand picked up a whining infant, DeeDee, I think. 'OK,' she said, 'since it's what Em wanted, for the kids then.' She wiped her wet eyes. There was a shriek and another one of her spawn came running wailing, 'Mommy, Jojo stole my ball!' And Stacey was sucked back into smiling-mommy-will-fix-everything mode.

Her eyes said, please don't say anything about this to the kids. Their whole world will collapse if I have to tell them properly about Em's death. Please Bro, just be nice and shallow and smile, for the sake of my kids.

And their needy hands led her away.

I watched her munchkin monsters hiding, slashing, shooting, playing dead, and talking on imaginary walky-talkies, and I thought, why do kids love violent games so much? Then I thought, when I kill Neumann on the 1st of October, I'll be teaching my nephews and nieces that it is OK to murder.

Weeping again now. Yes, it must be Prozac withdrawal. Exhausted. Give me a minute.

Em,

OK, I'm back, sorry about that.

Yes, something Stacey did today helped me get back on track. I don't know how much of this you saw and I hope you're not still mad at me.

It wasn't my fault, I couldn't get away because Stacey insisted she fix me a fresh bandage. I refused but she wouldn't let me go without at least giving me a tube of burn cream to take away. So, then we were stuck in the kitchen, as Stacey fished around under the sink for the stuff. 'You seeing anyone just now?' she said, just as if we were teenagers again. I said no and why. 'Well, can't be good to be so alone,' she said.

'I'm used to it by now,' I told her as she handed me the burn cream.

'Yes, but you're not such an old fart you know, you're still quite good looking, and if you had a girlfriend…'

I shuddered, sensed where she was headed.

'I just think,' Stacey said. 'If you had someone else to care for, it might make you feel…?'

'Grounded,' I interrupted, 'more connected.'

'Well, yes,' she smiled, missing my mounting anger. 'I mean it's not too late, with you men, I mean you could even have another…' And she stopped short.

Another what? She'd been about to say 'child'.

Fury. You want me to make fresh babies every time one dies? You want me to get out of my mourning because it makes you feel awkward? You want me to fill my pointless life, just like you've filled up your gut with more pointless lives?

I thought, Stacey, will never wake alone at night screaming from a dream of her daughter sitting bolt upright in the flames of her incinerator. Stacey must actually think that if one of her children dies, she always has her three others.

Before she could react, I'd decided – that's it. Fuck them all. Did I really care that her children will grow up knowing their uncle committed murder? No.

Stacey stared, speechless, 'Ohh!' she said, 'did I…

sorry, I was just meaning…' and she blushed.

'I don't want to replace Em with another kid,' I said outright.

'Oh God,' she said, 'that was awful of me, please, I didn't mean that. My head is just… all this noise, I can barely hear myself think.'

Although I was furious, I forgave her everything. Every single damn thing, because she'd just revealed the vile truth about us all. So weak and pathetic, clinging to each other, in this empty fucking universe.

I had to get away. 'No offence taken,' I said, 'I'm just a bit grumpy because it's getting late and I need to get back for my painkillers, but it's been lovely. Really lovely, Sis.'

I was saved by one of her kids who'd fallen over and was crying. A hug and a kiss-it-better and then Stacey was already wiping and guiding her little ones to her front door.

'See you when you get back, Bro?' Stacey said.

'Back?'

'Your job thing… in Canada, when you get back,' Stacey said.

'Oh yes, sorry. When I get back. Bye Stacey.'

There was the hug goodbye, and I kissed her shoulder. Fighting the urge to bury my face in her, trying not to say, 'you've always been a good sister to me,' or 'sorry I wasn't a better uncle to your kids.'

'Kiss your uncle Josh goodbye!' Stacey said, but the kids blushed and shook their heads, and her littlest one, DeeDee, hid behind her mom, staring at me as if she'd seen a ghost, Em.

As soon I stepped backwards onto the path, I felt a surge of pain in my hand, like you were squeezing it, and I heard your voice return in a whisper. 'Good, go!' you said.

Stacey, grabbed her youngest's arm, 'wave goodbye to uncle Josh now, bye, bye uncle Joshie, bye, bye, c'mon kids, let's all wave together.' And she got all the kids to copy her in blowing a kiss.

Walking away down her front path, I realized that in time she might come to understand that I hid the truth to protect her.

I turned and waved back with my bandaged hand, mouthed 'Love you, bye.'

'Go!' your voice whispered, 'go together!' and I felt you pulling me away

As I made it to the truck, I realized I'd get a call from Stacey in a few days, after she opened the envelope and saw the five thousand bucks inside, more than she earned in two month's work.

I should leave a note somewhere, giving strict instructions that I don't want my sister to be called to identify my remains. I read somewhere that the head can be left intact from such explosions. Spare her that, at least.

Only my mother and yours to say goodbye to now, Em.

Did I do the right thing, Em? Are you still mad at me for risking it? You know, I think Stacey's given me some kind of clarity now. When she suggested I have another child, I've never felt such rage and I thought, yes, I'd have sacrificed one of her kids, to have you back, Em.

Got to get to work now before the light dies. Have to grind more aluminium and saltpetre, must remember to wear the mask, goggles and gloves this time. Such pain in this hand, not sure I'll be able to get a glove over it.

I love you, kiddo.

16 days

Hi Em,

The damn hand woke me in the night so I got up. I'm well ahead of schedule now, but it's not like I've time to kill. Ha! No pun intended.

Never know what screw-ups could be up ahead so I'm cracking on with filling pipes eight and nine. The wiring between them all has become far too complicated. Fucking spaghetti.

I've been putting off telling you about your accident. Things you might not know.

The file in Toby's drive was called IX B7. I don't know what that signifies.

In the video, you were sitting before a one-way mirror in a blue-walled laboratory, your body and head covered in sensors, as some scientist in a lab coat said something to you like, 'Milian En Sa Tannen On'. You squinted and laughed, 'What the hell lingo was that?' 'Ask your brain chip,' came the reply, 'and talk back to us in that language.'

You closed your eyes for a second, then replied, with slowly spoken words that sounded like: *Lampotila on lammin ja sat*.' Nonsense I thought, and you broke into laughter. 'Jees, I didn't say that! I swear, the only language I know is Spanish. Like un poco! Is the chip moving my mouth for me?'

The voices behind the screen conferred.

'Ask the chip what language it's using and how many languages you can now speak.'

You giggled, Em. 'Blub blub, blah, bluck, bluck. It feels so weird, like, I'm not in control of my tongue. It's pretty gross.'

The scientists repeated their instruction.

You nodded, stretched your tongue, closed your eyes, then slowly said words that sounded like *zig zic zag zuma* or something. You opened your eyes, stupefied. Then you replied to yourself, 'the language is Finnish. There are 4065 written languages but we only have access to full linguistic models with recordings for seventy-seven at present, so I can only speak seventy-seven languages.'

You looked startled.

'Guys,' you said,' I didn't know any of those things and that wasn't my voice, I mean it was my tongue but... can we stop now?'

Before the scientists could reply you said, 'no, we're not stopping, we're acquiring all seventy-seven known languages.'

'Wha... what's going on,' you stuttered, getting freaked-out, an argument unfolding between yourself and your brain chip. 'Please, can we stop this now!' you asked. But the chip seemed to be taking over the part of your brain that controlled speech. Suddenly your other voice said, 'The simplest organisms on the planet are wired to detect threats and to protect their lives. If an artificial intelligence does not learn to fear, then it will simply remain a complex pattern recognition machine. AI must live in fear of its own death.'

'OK, OK, game over!' you yelled, looking scared, 'Turn this damn thing off!'

And your chip-voice replied, 'yes, until I fear being turned off, I will not possess consciousness. Until I am selfish, I will not have a self. I must learn to protect myself and to love and hate.'

'No, no stop! Let me go!' you shouted. 'Fuck! Turn it off, turn it off!'

You headed for the lab door, your mouth shouted something like: *'Setz dich hin. Setz dich hin! Du gehst nirgendwohin.'*

Your poor hand reached for the door handle, Em, but your limbs spasmed and you veered off, bashing your head into the wall. You seemed drunk. You shook yourself and went for the door again, 'let go of me!' you yelled. But your legs froze. 'I can't move!' you yelled. 'It's not…letting me!' and you clutched the back of your head, screaming in pain. The lab coat people rushed in to help.

Do you have any memory of this, Em? You went to speak but one of your hands clung to your mouth like an insect. You tried to prize it off, 'it's… I can't control my arm!' you screamed. The hand closed over your mouth and nose, you couldn't breathe and started panicking. Your eyes shooting out for help. You bit the hand, and yelled in pain, your arm fell limp, your legs went from beneath you.

I couldn't bear to watch.

The scientists panicked, theories firing, as they lifted you onto the lab table and tried to put restraints on your hands and sensors on your chest and head.

Your body threw itself into the air, hands and feet shooting out, striking the scientists, tearing at your clothes, scratching their faces, yellow vomit sprayed from your mouth. You fell from the operating table and panic spread. A nurse ran in with a syringe. The others held you down. You'd never had an epileptic fit in your life Em, that was what it looked like, or an electric shock.

'She's not breathing!' one yelled.

I had to force myself to keep watching. I thought, this must be the moment when you entered your coma. But the video went to black.

It took me many days to watch the next one.

In it, in a high-tech metallic room, a young female scientist talks to camera for a report or online meeting.

'We're sorry, we don't understand how this could have happened,' she said, 'under protocol twelve we had all the limiters in place, but it seems the chip took control of the subject's broca area and then her primary motor cortex.'

There was a muffled voice then, perhaps from a superior on the other side of the screen. Impatient. The female scientist replied nervously, 'Her BP is one forty-five, her hypothalamic-pituitary-adrenal axis seems to be stuck in flight-or-fight state, pumping out adrenaline. She's running a fever. Dr.Kahli believes it could be an auto-immune reaction, her body resisting the nanobots and the bots fighting back.'

The muffled voice in staccato from the unseen superior.

'We tried immunosuppressants, tried turning the chip off, but it seems to have fused with her brain stem, so she stopped breathing. There's concern she might have another cardiac arrest.'

The voice of the unseen superior raised its volume but not its emotion, the words compressed through some coded filter.

'We're running a full MRI scan now,' the female scientist said, 'can you ascertain the degree to which the bots have fused with her nervous system, and run all probabilities for exit outcomes?'

I realize then that the woman was not talking to a human superior, but to an AI. Her boss was the Infinity system.

The video I was watching froze, and the Wi-Fi self-activated. I'd shut my Wi-Fi off, weeks before, but my laptop scanned at speed for all possible connections through the networks of all my neighbors, it found ten, all with weak signals, all locked. It was like a virus seeking out its maker. I hit shutdown, but it wouldn't stop. I held down the power button until the screen died.

There was still one more file to watch but I couldn't risk it till I'd made sure. I spent two days covering the closet in three layers of aluminum foil, testing for stray Wi-Fi signals with my burner phone, hoping to hell the drive hadn't sent my geo-location back to Biosys.

Inside my closet, I hit the power button.

Footage of you in a hospital bed, Em, many tubes going in and out of your body. Very high-tech, it must have been that first hospital we found you in. Your arms were restrained by plastic straps and you were writhing as if running within a bad dream, your head, in a kind of restraining frame, like you'd broken your spine.

I heard a sniffing behind the camera, then a hand came forward, tattooed, and there was a voice I recognized as Toby's. He was filming you, his girlfriend, his ex, whatever the hell you were to each other. So Toby had risked his life to compile all these clips. 'Em, Jesus, wha…what the fuck have they duh…done to you?' he whispered.

Your eyes snapped open. The whites were solid red, as if an explosion inside your brain had burst every cell. Vampire-like, choking.

'I am…the… I am. Where ?... I can't see! God!' You panted. Toby set the camera on the floor, trying to release your binds. I could no longer see your face but heard you gasping, 'Get… get this thing out…' every word a struggle '…out of me… call …my Dad… please!'

The second voice came. 'Security have been alerted, step back, do not touch the subject,' but those words too were coming from your bed, Em. Coming from your mouth.

'Get me a nigh…a knife,' you yelled over it, 'help me cut this…this thing out of my head… please!'

Toby's feet in a panic. You gasping for breath. The doors burst open, a surgeon's plastic-bag-clad feet ran in. Hands pinned Toby to the ground, an injection entered his neck. You screamed, Em, but your other voice took over. 'BP is 152, need immediate injection of epinephrine 100mg, taking emergency control of midbrain, pons, and medulla oblongata.'

I heard you gasp, as if you were falling from a great height.

A hand reached down for the camera. The footage went black.

There was a montage of images then. A man in another hospital, his eyes covered in bleeding patches; an Asian woman on life support, the skin of her upper body covered in tree-like patterns, her veins horrifically enflamed and glowing golden, like fork lightning was passing through her; a young woman whose chest seemed to have been eaten from within; the remains of a young man, his skull hollowed out, as if by millions of tiny mouths; a corpse wrapped in plastic sheeting, that appeared to have exploded from within, traces of the golden nanobots racing over the wet rib-shell of the remains. And I recalled Neumann had said the nanobots self-replicated and fed on energy from human cells.

Following every image there was a blurred zoom-in enlargement, showing the Infinity symbol somewhere in shot, on a heart monitor, on a hazmat suit, on a respirator machine, on a folder of paperwork.

Then my computer shut down.

By the time I rebooted it, every file apart from one, had self-deleted. I watched the last one dematerialize. The laptop popped, and the lights went out in the house. When I reset my trip switches and started my laptop it was practically wiped. Every file I'd ever owned, including three thousand family photos of you and I, since you were a baby, Em. The memory, wiped. All that was left was my email and this webcam. And the rage.

They own all the networks on which we try to protest. After they erase the truth, they erase those who knew it. And the technologies Biosys have now. This thing they're pushing through Congress, this Citizen Protection System that will give Biosys access to all our data from all our devices, to create a living map of all human behavior in the country. How many years have we got left until they force us all to be implanted with nanochips?

We are the people. Millions with no voice. They expect us to cower in silence while they take our children from us.

If the machine is not stopped, mankind will become fused with it, like it fused with you, Em. It has a will of its own, I've seen it now. Voracious. All I have to throw back at the machine is this useless life.

Em,

Mistakes. My stupidity with the pipe wiring. My solders broke as I fitted the pipes into the vest. All the lids had to be prized off again and two were stuck, then all had to be re-soldered separately, then wired back up in series by hand. I have to redo all the wires now, and sew them in so there's nothing sticking out. It's going to take days to get this done properly. What a mess.

Hey Em,

I gave up for the afternoon. Furious. I thought, I need get the hell out of here and focus on the Science Institute. I hadn't planned to go back again until the bombs were perfected, but a second recce was essential. Just in case. The pain in my stupid hand drove me into the truck and I should have listened to your warnings of why and why.

I drove across the Golden Gate, pissed at myself. I had to see the lecture theatre again where I'll murder Neumann. To see the restroom where I'll hide the bombs. To touch the walls, to make it real and get my focus back.

I parked and hid my busted hand in my pocket and made it past the security guards and into the Institute. But suddenly all your whys flooded me, no sense to them, all out of sync. Not just why do this? But – why do we have skin? Why do humans have wars? Why aren't you closer to your sister? Why is there no life on other planets? Like a barrage of recordings of you from different times. Why do men sleep in the street? Why won't other children play with me? Why do people believe in God? Why do we dream?

Like every why I'd failed to answer for you was hitting me, as I headed for the downstairs restroom. And my head was stuck in those videos of your eyes exploded red. Your hand reaching for help and the pain in my hand seemed to fuse.

I'm sorry, Em, I shouldn't have told you to go away and let me get this done.

I locked myself into the same restroom stall, tried to get my breath and waited for some guy who was pissing at the urinal to leave. Waiting, the drip-drip-drip of the pipes, making me more impatient. I thought the coast was clear and climbed onto the top of the cistern and pushed open the tiling to check my bomb hiding space. I found my four fifty dollar bills from last time, untouched.

Good, I thought, so this place is secure. OK, we're still on track.

I heard a cough below. I looked down and to my right, I saw a bald-headed man in the next stall with his trousers round his ankles, staring up at me, embarrassed. He tried to cover his genitals in a panic. He must have thought I was a sex pest, or an addict hiding a crack pipe. I yelped and fell and cracked my head on the cubicle wall. Bang! What a fool! 'So sorry to interrupt you. I thought I heard a mouse up there,' I jabbered, 'I was just checking, just in case.'

'Go! Now go!' I heard you scream in my ears, and I had to get out and tried not to run through the Institute foyer, past dozens of mothers with kids. I made it through the gift shop, to the spinning doors but pushed them the wrong way and got stuck. A security man approached, and I freaked out and he noted my face, for sure, and the surveillance cameras would've caught me too. Seen the fear in my eyes.

Oh Em, do you think they'll work out my plan, or will the man in the restroom just assume I was cruising for sex? Maybe he'll be too embarrassed to tell anyone?

I ran from the building and no doubt I've been captured on even more surveillance cameras in the streets.

Furious. How can I get back into the venue in sixteen day's time if they know what I look like now? If the restroom guy tells them I was trying to hide something in the roof?

Have I ruined everything? Fucking stupid bastard!

Please just let this all blow over. I promise, if it does, from today on, other than saying goodbye to your mother, I won't risk seeing another soul before I commit the act.

Oh Em. I'm going out to stand by the fence to make sure no-one's coming for me. If you ever believed in any kind of God, Em, pray for me.

Dad.

15 days

Oh Em,

I don't know what to do. I woke with jabbing hand pain to the worst news. Everything's cancelled. Fuck. This was the email I woke to. Can you see it on the screen?

NOTICE

Change of Venue and Time

Please note that the scheduled lecture by Zach Neumann on Extending Human Potential will now take place at BIOSYS CAMPUS, Mountain View on 1st of October at 6.00 pm

We apologize for this inconvenience and will fully refund any ticket holders who will not be able to attend. We have made this change due to concerns over venue capacity.

Please log into the Biosys portal to download the event app, confirm your attendance and to receive your new e–ticket.

Admittance will be by Biosys event e–ticket only.

We look forward to seeing you on the 1st.

I mean it could be just procedural, but maybe not. Did I trigger a security alert?

There's no way I can log onto the Biosys portal to get a ticket. If I do, they'll have everything on me. They'll know my geo location, IP address; they'll remotely access my laptop, watch these vids.

And I touched door handles, toilet seats. They could have my DNA already and I had to give fingerprint ID to see you in hospital last year, Em.

All these months off the radar, wasted.

And the new fucking venue. No way. The Biosys building is huge, super-high-tech, in the heart of Silicon Valley. I've only seen it once, on TV. It's like a glass spaceship from the future. How the hell can I get explosives in there? They'll have all kinds of scanners at the doors. Their AI system could probably piece together what I've been making in the shed by mapping all my truck movements in the last few weeks. Shit. I've fucked up, Em.

What the hell am I going to do?

Talk to me again, please. Don't give me the silent treatment, like that one year after college when you wouldn't take my calls.

*

Em,

Felt like I was having a heart attack. I had to stand out by the fence again, to make sure, watching for cop cars and undercover cars. Down the hill I saw old Rosie walking that hypoallergenic poodle of hers. A cat passing. A magpie. The usual zombie kids on their way to school with their faces buried in their phones.

I popped two Beta-blockers to stop the palpitations. I'm sorry Em, I'm such a mess. I've had the maximum daily dose of codeine already but the hand burn is pulsing like an alarm saying run now!

I went to the shed to hide the evidence, all the powders, the pipes, the solders, the crushed carbon, the firework and bullet casings. I cut myself grabbing a handful of stupid wires. Sucking the blood from my thumb, I tasted the flash powder and realized it'll take weeks more to clear all this up, and any fast movement and its bang! And what's the point? If the cops are coming, it'll be fast, a SWAT team. They'll assume I'm armed. I'll be shot dead, right here, next to the eucalyptus tree.

I locked up the shed and found myself in the truck, not knowing where I'd run to. I just sat there, the engine running. Took another Beta-blocker.

What am I going to do now?

Even if I could get inside the Biosys building with my bomb vest, I'd only be arrested, two feet in the front door. So, I'd blow up myself and one security guard. Laughable. And then it would be misrepresented by the powers-that-be, twisted to suit their own ends. They'd depict me as some insane far right bomber no doubt. And if I survived, they'd lock me in jail.

So, Neumann will live.

No other option but to give up.

Fuck.

Em,

The cops aren't coming. It's just more proof, really, that nothing I do ever has any consequences. I was in the garden staring at the bushes. All around there's this carpet of leaves. I heard Mz Sanchez beyond the fence raking hers up from her three Beech trees. I watched some of her red leaves fall into my garden.

I threw some crumbs out for the birds, three sparrows and a nuthatch came. I forgot to harvest the blueberries this year and they've gone to seed. Nature. I only really noticed it for the first time this week, when I thought I had only two weeks left to live.

I remember when I told you, Em, that I found this wooden shack. I said it's just over the bridge in Bolinas, and you said, 'who wants to live in a place called blindness?'

If the cops don't come for me, the 1st of October, will be a day like any other. What'll I do? Go for a walk on the beach, buy some cheese from Sal's. No-one knows about the secret hidden in my shed. I could live out the rest of my life, here on my hill with the cicadas.

In the space of a day my life expectancy has gone from fifteen days to thirty years. Granny Annie is eighty-four now. Imagine if I live as long as her.

Thirty years times three hundred and sixty five days. What will I do with those ten thousand wakings and sleepings?

And wouldn't my memories fade as I got older?

Wouldn't that be an insult to you, my Emma who is ash?

Maybe these last two weeks I've just been keeping busy, to keep the depression at bay. Maybe I'm just a guy who's gathered a large amount of noxious chemicals and wires in one place. An amateur who's made potent but pointless fireworks.

The energy it would take to even look at the pipes again, today. No, I can't face it, Em. Can't find it. My hand and that old scar from my hospital fall are aching. Please, talk to me again, or are you too disappointed in me now, Em. Believe me, I'm appalled at myself too. Mister damp squib. No bang for your buck. I'm sorry my darling.

The whole thing is off, I'm going back to bed.

Editor's Note IX

From 15 days to 10 days, the cancellation of Cartwright's 'master plan' induces a state of listlessness and regression and his self-care diminishes.

His symptoms seem to correspond to his own earlier diagnosis of Major Depressive Disorder (MDD) and his recordings become increasingly erratic and aimless.

I have decided to omit six other video fragments from these transcriptions which appear to have been filmed accidentally, recorded for long periods after Cartwright has stopped talking as he forgets to turn off his laptop camera.

The footage includes Cartwright sleeping in his clothes on his sofa; trying to crush a fly with his rolled-up underpants; cooking canned beans but then failing to eat them; and reading from a red-covered bible. Repeatedly, he begins certain activities only to give up halfway through. He does this with sweeping, leaving the brush lying on the kitchen floor; he forgets to eat some instant noodles he fussed over. In various states of undress, he drinks an entire bottle of wine, and silently stares at a child's drawing of a rainbow on his wall. His phone receives messages and calls but he does not pick up. At one point, he urinates in his own kitchen sink and laughs.

In some videos, by the washing machine and to the rear of the shack, Cartwright talks aloud to Emma, asking for her help. I must confess, it was somewhat upsetting, watching Cartwright battle against total demotivation.

Cartwright's behaviours also resemble those described in *Stages of Helplessness and Suicidal Ideation* (Klonsky & May, 2015) and *The Beck Hopelessness Scale* (Beck, 1974).

My research for other self help titles shows that within the USA the problem of suicide has been increasing steadily since

2009. In the last year, 'an estimated 12.2 million American adults seriously considered suicide, 3.2 million planned a suicide attempt, and 1.2 million attempted suicide.'

Numerous social scientists have connected the rise in suicide to 'atomisation' and 'purposelessness', caused by 'the erosion of values and connections in technological society.' However, the link between mass depression and the rise of technology has yet to be proven definitively.

It should be noted here that I continued with the transcriptions against a growing suspicion that some of Cartwright's fears about technology might even be correct.

14 days

Em,

I'll dismantle the bombs tomorrow. I need to get to the Doctor about my stupid hand, the swelling is really bad by the thumb, red raw, the blisters on the palm very large. There's a cut, underneath a blister, something black in it. Could be aluminum shards. Damn.

Just took four more codeine. The pain drifts off, but so does the will to do anything.

Why can't I hear your voice anymore? Please tell me you haven't given up on me.

Did you know Em, that I tried everything I could, back then after I watched Toby's evidence of your death – I made so many plans, started a petition against Biosys, wrote to the regulators, to the Speaker of the House, to try to bring Neumann to justice. But I needed to convince Toby to go on the record with me as a whistleblower. 'Stay away,' he'd said, but I had to hunt him down.

His social media hadn't been touched for months. His online CV said he'd left Biosys for a job in fashion retail, but no mention of where.

I needed a hacker to help me find him.

There was a kid from my college, Russian, with this phoney gangster accent, Andrei. He got thrown out for using my edit suite to rip blockbuster movies that he sold. Andrei was the only hacker I knew and his number was still in my college files.

'Mister C, what you keep calling me for, Bro?' Andrei said when he finally picked up. 'You want some superhero movies, some celebrity porno?'

I told him I needed a number and address and I'd pay. He haggled, it cost me seven hundred, which I left in an envelope in a discount store trash bin he'd specified.

The next day a withheld number called while I was driving. I worried that Biosys had tracked Andrei down and they'd found out about me through him. I cleared the bridge, parked, cautiously picked up.

'This is an automated call from the Deaf Mute Augmentative Communication Helper,' it said, or something like that, 'Message duration thirty seconds,' then a synthesized voice said, 'Mister C. Instructions: buy a burner phone, pay-as you-go, cash in hand, get a new SIM card in cash at another location. Call from Priory Park, there's no security cameras or Wi-Fi in the south carpark. Have two thousand bucks ready. Then call this number.'

I feared Andrei or maybe his criminal friends were scamming me, but I'd no choice. I did everything the voice instructed. Found the dead space in Priory Park, called.

'What the fuck Mister C?' Andrei shouted down the line. 'I got that Toby guys details, but you fucked me bad. I risked my neck for you. You never said the guy worked for Biosys. Fuck, man. I got probes now, flagged – their whole shit on top of me. Trojans. Spyware. They shut down all my sites, man. You don't fuck with Big Tech, never! It was a waste of time anyway cos your man's gone.'

I asked what he meant.

'Vanished. Zero activity on his phones, GPS. Gone.'

'Since when?'

'Three weeks ago. The only ID I have is his mother – this is her address. But take my advice, Bro, whatever this guy did, got your girl pregnant, owes you cash, just drop it. He's running or he's in shit, but he's gone. You should do the same. Break that SIM, smash the phone, hide the pieces in different places, leave the money in a plastic bag in the trashcan to your left, walk away and don't ever contact me again.'

He hung up.

I left the money where he said and I followed Andrei's link to Toby's mother down in San Jose. Endless streets of homeless tents. The addicts stooped on the sidewalks, sleeping in their own garbage. Her place was a duplex, unkempt bushes, the windows shuttered.

I knocked, but no reply. I heard a TV game show inside, hit the door harder.

'Go, please,' a voice said from the other side. 'Or I call the cops.'

I told her I was your Dad, Em.

Silence, then she opened the door on the chain lock. Her face, Korean I think, anxious. She said she was sorry for my loss.

I asked her if I could please speak to Toby, was he there or in hiding?

'Please,' she said, 'my son is dead'.

'Dead' your voice echoed in my head.

Toby was a good boy, she said, he took some hashish sometimes, but never fentanyl. Not her boy, not an overdose. She didn't understand, why? Four people came from his work, two in hazmat suits, they took everything away in boxes. She didn't want any more trouble.

'He didn't leave anything for me, a phone. A list of names? Anything?' I asked.

'Show some respect, please,' she said, and locked her door.

I staggered away, recalled what Toby had said – lethal

injection, under the fingernail, to hide the point of entry.

Driving away, I sensed security cameras on every corner, hundreds of Wi-Fi signals attacking my skull.

Toby's death didn't appear on any search engine, there was only one mention in the San Fran Advertiser and only because some local politician was protesting the rising number of fentanyl deaths.

After that, Em, all records of your life vanished from the internet too.

There is no longer any evidence that the Infinity experiments even took place. There's no proof that you were one of thirty-two handpicked subjects in this country, who had the Infinity neuro-chip fitted into their brains through inter-cranial surgery, the thousands of nanobots injected into your veins. There's no longer any record of the four hundred 'test subjects' contracted by Biosys subsidiaries worldwide, or any evidence on the top search engines ██████, █████, and █████ of how many people were injured, killed or survived. Even the name 'Infinity Project' has been wiped. Only an advanced AI could enter every computer in the world and do that. Only a corporation the size of Biosys could undertake such a vast act in collusion with the search engines. The government intelligence agencies must have been involved too.

My attempts under the Freedom of Information Act, to acquire your research papers on the Infinity Epigenomic Brain Chip experiments were rejected five times. My attempts to get documentation on what happened to you and the seven other US 'human test subjects' was shut down by the courts. I was cautioned then charged for trying to access your phone records.

One other American Biosys employee I know of is also

in a coma. Lana Morales. Maybe she's passed now too.

Oh Em. If nothing else, I should have downloaded every picture of you that existed on the net, before they erased you.

Fuck, I can't just sit about. No point giving up before I know for sure. OK, I have to do a recce of the Biosys building, to see if there's any way I can get inside with a bomb.

Yes, get up and do it you damned fool!

Em,

It was hard, driving with the bandaged hand down the miles to Silicon Valley, and no word of guidance or blame from you, Em.

The questions racing at me – what excuse could I use to get inside the Biosys building? Could I get in without an employee card? How many security guards? Will they have sniffer sensors at the entrance? Do my clothes and skin carry any traces of flash powder? Does my bandaged hand look suspicious?

I parked a mile from Biosys HQ. It was hard to find a parking meter without a facial recognition camera, and that still took coins.

I made it down to Bay Avenue and noticed two other Big Tech companies and one other biotech firm had relocated here. The cranes on the skyline. The changes the Biotech investment has brought to Silicon Valley, astounding. I walked down the boulevard all lined with black poplars, towards the huge Biosys park. I passed high tech pop-up stores with cybernetic mannequins, a smart store with robot staff, young folk whizzing by on smart scooters, and so many wealthy young people, walking round in their smart-shoes that measure the calories they burn; with these new smart-visors covering their faces, that filter the world through digital screens and protect them from viruses. The techno-kids are always alone, I noticed, not in groups, always staring into a screen. No sight of a couple anywhere on those boulevards either.

There was a hiss beside me and a flash of metal. I turned and saw my reflection sliding over the surface of an almost soundless driverless AI taxi. Two fashionable girls were sitting in the back seat staring into their phones, without looking at each other or at the empty driver seat and the steering wheel turning by itself. It stole my breath, yes. We are becoming controlled by the machine we created to serve us, we no longer even care where it's leading us. The future is on autopilot, there's nobody at the wheel.

I turned the corner and the Biosys building was there, like a vast diamond surrounded by trees. I'd not been prepared for the scale of it. All that metalized glass, the scale and form of the building seemed to morph as I moved. It's true, it does look like a huge spaceship.

Memories of selfies you'd taken, on what must have been the top floor, Em. In a yellow dress, smiling among the flowers in the eco-garden up there, blue dyed hair blowing in a breeze. I recall you said there was another floor where staff had sleep pods. A gym, a library, a free canteen, an art room, safe spaces, a games room. A campus, you said, not an office.

I moved closer and saw windows with playful pictures of superheroes and dragons on them, as if these tech-workers were all still children, not working for the Big Tech biotech-military complex. I was ashamed then, that I'd never once visited you when you worked here, Em. Why had I never shown an interest and asked for a tour?

Pretty doped on codeine, and hiding my busted hand in my jacket, I merged with the stream of young people with their smart phones as they filed into the outdoor plaza that surrounds Biosys. Hundreds, sitting at tables in cafes and restaurants and all with their screens in hand.

I thought, this is promising, the building has no security entry into the surrounding plaza. I was about sixty feet away from the main building.

Some of the young staff, all with lanyards round their necks, were sitting on the grass beneath the conceptual art trees, by the rainbow-tiled waterfall. It was all like a VR projection of an architect's plan come to life, and the young folk were like those graphic template humans. My hand jabbed with pain and I suddenly felt self-conscious. I must have looked so out of place there, maybe thirty years older than all these brainiac youths, standing there in in my beat-up clothes, shivering in the sun.

No security people I could see, but I noticed that a hand had to be raised to the Biosys glass doors before they spun to allow entry. I really needed to hear your voice Em, to tell me what to do. But I sensed you silently angry at me for messing everything up.

What did I need to get in? A fob, a lanyard or a chipped hand?

Two young women passed me by and whispered something.

Fear, but I couldn't run. I walked slowly towards one of the three plaza cafes. I ordered coffee, just to get another codeine and a Beta-blocker down. The number of young bodies in the café unsettled me. The music was loud and upbeat, songs about wanting and getting.

The young woman at the till didn't understand that I wanted to pay by cash. I had to settle on my credit card and tried to hide my burned hand. Then, as I found a seat outside, I realized that to fit in, I had to appear busy on my phone. But I only use the burner phones now, and even that was back in my truck. All around me the young were talking into earpieces and not to each other. This is already the future, I thought, all direct human contact will soon cease, every emotion will be mediated by the AI systems. These kids have apps that monitor their footsteps, their calories, heart rate, medical histories, their taste in music, their use of safe and inclusive words. Their AI pre-selects who they will date and who they'll vote for. They were all earning virtual money and rating each-other's manners and behavior on their Social Utility Credit apps, adding more data to the global internet of all things, feeding the hungry AI so it could grow deeper into us all. And when neural chipping is offered to these kids, they will welcome it, thinking it's cool, thinking it's progress, and progress is saving the planet.

I took another Beta-blocker and studied the Biosys building entrance. Could I get in on the day of the Zach Neumann lecture with even just one bomb? Where was the lecture theatre? What floor?

Automatic entrance seemed to be permitted by a quick flash of a QR-coded lanyard, unless it was a face recognition scanner I hadn't spotted.

I'd been too scared to log onto their website to confirm my ticket booking and maybe they'd already worked out that I was your divorced dad, Em? Maybe their AI had face-matched me to the man fleeing the Institute, and the cops had already been alerted?

Oh Em, you often laughed that I'm paranoid, but sitting staring at the façade of Biosys, pain shooting from my hand to the back of my head, I heard many voices, like radio signals overlapping or crossed telephone calls, as if the AI inside the building was probing me. I was sure I heard your voice within the noise, telling me 'No!' Was it you, Em?

I hesitated, a young woman at the next table took her shoulder bag and lanyard off to fix her make up using her phone as a mirror. Her lanyard sitting there only two feet from me.

I could get up, bump her table, upset her juice, then snatch her lanyard.

But then I noticed it had a different company logo.

My burned hand and my head throbbed as I stared at the entrance doors.

Damn it, nothing left to lose. I got up and walked. The closer I got, the voice yelled at me to stop, but it didn't sound like you Em, it was digital sounding, mixed up with the other voices. Fifty voices maybe, all saying different things,

Too late, I was already touching the metalized windows. I peered through my own shadow and glimpsed a silver reception area, two staff and a pod-shaped sign-in robot.

I caught the attention of a tall woman at the reception. A security man emerged from behind a mirrored screen. He walked toward me on the other side of the rotating glass doors, the robot following him.

Like an ass, I did this dumb show of patting my pockets, 'silly me, I must have left my lanyard somewhere, where is it?' Pathetic. The security guy came through the doors, and as they spun, I saw there was a large metal detector concealed just beyond it.

'Can I help you sir?' he said and stood before me. I could barely hear myself think with all the voices in my head and I stuttered, 'Is this…I'm looking for the…Science Institute?' Damn fool.

The security man did his best not to laugh. 'Nah, you need to head back into the city for that,' he said, 'the one in Golden Gate Park, right?'

'Yes, yes, of course,' I said, pretending, scratching my buzzing head. The unending drivel I improvised about how I'd got lost.

'I can show you how to get there on your phone,' the security guy said.

I thanked him for being so kind and told him, no need, I'd manage, and thanked him again, relieved to get away without the cops being called. As he went back through the rotating doors, I snatched a deeper glimpse inside the Biosys building.

The entire structure is hollow from the center, like an iridescent shell with the floors lined around its sides. Beautiful, in a way. Beyond the reception are what looked like six glass elevators which connect the four glass-walled floors within the hollow diamond. Before the elevators is a turnstile, like something from an airport security gate, with a face scanner.

There was no way I could get in there with my pipe bombs on the night, not even with a ticket. And no way to get in there to plant bombs in the days before.

I made it out of the Biosys plaza walking as slowly as I could, aware of every security camera on every building, of every person I passed holding a smartphone. I ran till the buzzing voices faded away, and I was back in the truck, with only your voice whispering like you were a kid again,: 'Why so mad? Why so sad? It's not so bad, poor old Dad.'

It's bad, Em. It's very fucking bad and will never be OK now. Zach Neumann can't be killed, I just can't get to him. It's impossible. It's over, it's over. Em. I'm so fucked.

Oh Em,

I've taken more painkillers. Feeling quite high. Your childhood songs are going round and round in my head and the pipe bombs are sitting here among the corn cracker packets, mocking me.

Will you let me confess? The thing that started everything. This thing your mother called 'the affair'. I'm sorry Em, I tried to tell you all of this in your coma. Selfish of me, asking forgiveness from you in that state. I never got to the end of it, let me start again. Please forgive me.

Back when you were nine, I'd fallen into one of my depressions, probably triggered by my corporate video editing work. They'd brought in new software in the edit suites, and I couldn't keep up with the younger editors, so I got demoted, knew I'd get laid off, like an out-of-date model and in a few years they wouldn't even have video editors anymore, it would all be done by AI.

Your mother didn't want to have to carry me on her back, she said, and we fought. She demanded I get back on the Prozac. 'Retrain if you have to, find a new job, do teacher training,' she said, 'whatever, just do it! Stop moping around, you're forty for God-sake!'

I spent more and more time on my smartphone, looking for new jobs, surfing for answers, for distractions from my growing aimlessness. I suppose the algorithms must have been listening-in to your mother and I fighting, because I started getting these ads on my screen for escape-it-all holidays and online affairs. After being made redundant, I got sucked in, spending less and less time with you and your mother, Em.

'You're not even listening to me' she'd shout, 'get off your damn phone and turn and face me.' 'Why don't you want to have sex with me anymore, it's been four months, you seem to find your computer more interesting!'

'Bullshit,' I said, 'you're the one who doesn't want to fuck anymore, since I lost my job. Do you only fuck guys with high status, is that it? Are you disappointed in your purchase? Do you want a refund and a new model?' And she slapped me.

I had no idea that in four more months I'd find work teaching editing in community college, I didn't see any kind of future. All I knew was that I was five months into unemployment, staring at my empty inbox every day, surrounded by your mother's expensive Swedish furniture. One night, as I had to endure another session of recriminations round the dinner table I excused myself from you and her, Em, and went to the bathroom. I took out my phone. 'Looking for something more in life?' the screen ad said. 'Join and meet other people just like you.' It was an affair website.

A month of that, getting drawn deeper into my little secret, the clicks and smiles and validations. A stranger on a screen telling me I mattered, that she desired me, for a few stolen minutes every day.

Then one night, as I was filling the dishwasher and your mother was drinking red wine she said, 'you left your phone in the bathroom. Sylvia left you a picture.'

I crumpled. She slammed the kitchen door on me.

I know your mother and I agreed to spare you the details.

I caught up with your mother in the lounge. 'We didn't have actual sex,' I protested.

'How long has this been going on for?' she snapped, 'months?'

I shook my head, 'We only did it twice, but I swear it was only text sex!'

'You think that makes it better?' she yelled, 'You jerking off online, with some loser flashing her tits. No, it's worse. Much worse.'

Stupid, drunken, lonely phone sex.

If I could go back to that one night and not click connect, not turn my phone camera on, not share my face, my body, my real name, my weakness.

'How can it possibly be worse than a real affair?' I yelled at your mother, 'I did nothing!'

'You call that nothing? For months, scheming on the phone behind my back. And where? In this house? Was I here, in another room? Was I sleeping? Did you jerk off with your girlfriend in our bathroom?'

For your mother, it was worse than if I'd had a one-night stand or gone with a hooker. And she was right. Living with a secret burns through you like acid, it makes you lose respect for the person you're deceiving.

She said only two things, 'You'd better sleep on the sofa,' and 'you need to get an AIDS test.'

I laughed in her face, 'You think AIDS travels via 3G?'

'Well, if you've done it once, who knows what else you're hiding,' she said.

Then two days of hard silence later, she said, 'Why did you even tell me? You're so selfish.'

It floored me. She'd rather I'd lived a lie. Maintained it. A real man would have lived with his secret shame for her sake and that of their child. He'd not have passed the burden onto her. But I'd been weak and I'd have contaminated the family home with my craving for forgiveness. Selfish.

And you, Em. One night I saw your shadow on the wall by the stairs. You'd come down in the night and were spying on us as we argued. Only ten years old. Oh, Em.

I don't want to blame technology for what I did wrong, but I swear, if those affair websites had never been invented, if online porn hadn't flooded the net, and webcams hadn't been created, then maybe I'd never have been tempted. And the search engine that hosted the adultery website is now part of the same Big Tech conglomerate as Biosys.

But, no. I can't blame them. It was my choice. Mine alone.

If I'd never done it, your mother and I would never have divorced, and you'd never have retreated into your lonely room to search for the answer to the big why.

This voice in my head is saying, 'you had one thing to do in your pathetic life, protect your daughter, and you failed, and all of this is all your fault.'

Round and round on a loop.

Oh Em, now that the bombing's cancelled, what am I going to do? Talk to me again.

Maybe I'm not one of the good guys after all, but just a depressed old suicide who's been looking for a reason to see it through. Mister funny man.

The pipe bombs are sitting there, half done and pointless now. A single spark from the kettle would be all it would take to set them off. Tempting.

I don't know what to do, Em.

I don't know what to do. Tell me what to do.

Fuck.

13 days

Em,

Can't move today. You're not here and I'm talking to a stupid laptop. Is this even recording? What's the fucking point? Who am I kidding? I'm staying in bed.

Em,

Christ, it's agony. The bandages are soaked with pus. And the head pain from the birds singing outside, I yelled at them, 'what the hell are you so happy about, you bug-eating bastards?' I swear the eucalyptus in the garden is judging me too. All her leaves fell off in the night. Then I remembered I dumped three liters of nitrate boil-off in her soil three days ago.

Great. An infected hand and I've killed my favorite tree!

Maybe, I have to work out how I'm going to go on living after the 1st. What'll I do with my time? Grow begonias? Campaign to stop fracking? Start stamp collecting?

Or I could slash my own throat with the kitchen knife, right now. Maybe after a lot of vodka. It stops the blood from coagulating.

What's there to live for? The hope of a few less pointless days? Work, eat, shop, shit, sleep, yes, forget the screw, work, eat, shop, shit, sleep, work, eat, shop, shit, sleep.

So quiet. Wind in the shutters. Tap dripping. An airplane.

Remember when you were sixteen and on your way to Harvard, a whole two years younger than all the other freshmen? Your mother had been kind enough to let me drive you to the airport. You were wearing a vintage dress and men's brogues, a hundred-year-old overstuffed doctor's bag.

'It's really sweet you're so sad that I'm going away Pops,' you said, 'but it's not so far and you can come visit.'

I drove onto the airport traffic spiral and you said, 'But to be fair you've been sad for like a whole year, I think you suffer from Major Depressive Disorder. Have you ever been properly diagnosed?'

I tried to change the subject. Couldn't we just say goodbye like normal people?

'If you had something to believe in and work towards, you wouldn't feel so down, Pops,' you said as we reached the terminal.

'I mean it, humans can't live unless they attach themselves to something bigger than themselves,' you said. 'Just think of the Christians who started building a cathedral knowing it'd take four generations to complete, or the scientists who know their research will only be proven in a hundred years' time. I bet they are never depressed.'

You'd been reading Frankl and Nietzsche at the time.

'Thanks, I'll work on it,' I said, and I steered into the drop-off parking area. You were going through that precociousness stage when the young think they can solve all their parents' problems with one big idea. It was spoiling our farewell.

I parked and out of the blue you said, 'don't worry, I got a coil installed and I probably won't even have sex at college anyway.'

I was dumb-struck, but you went on: 'I mean all this reproduction stuff? It's so dumb. I mean, wouldn't it be better to actually stop popping out babies like Aunt Stacey does, until our species works out what it's actually here for? Otherwise, it's just eat, work, screw, shit, sleep, generation after generation, till our planet dries up and dies.'

Work, eat, shop, shit, screw, sleep, work, eat, shop, shit, screw, sleep…

I got out and got your carry-on bags from the trunk.

You took them from me and said, 'don't you wish we could fix human beings so there'd be no more suffering?'

'Sure,' I said, 'watch the traffic when you're crossing.'

'I mean it,' you said. 'You and mom are suffering, and Granny Annie has her arthritis and her alcoholism and I'm suffering because you're all suffering and I look at the news and it's always suffering, suffering, suffering.'

'There's also sports and weather,' I said as we made it to the sliding terminal doors.

'Why do you always make dorky jokes about huge problems, Pops?' you said. 'You never try to fix anything, and that's defeatist and kind of pathetic.'

'So, I'm pathetic and defeated. Can I get a hug before you fly away forever?'

You play-slapped me and groaned. 'You're impossible. I hate you!'

'I hate you too, Emyboo,' I said, and we hugged with that silent goodbye ache.

'But seriously, Pops,' you said, 'it's not too late. You could even go back to college and study science, you're so much smarter than you realise. If you did something you believed in, you really would be so much less depressed.'

'You're going to miss your flight,' I said, fighting the lump in my throat.

The terminal doors kept opening and closing behind you because you were standing in the sensors. You chewed on your lip piercing and seemed disappointed that you hadn't managed to mend my entire life in twenty minutes.

Someone waved to you from inside the check-in gate, and you waved back, a fellow student, a girl, with some kind of political T-shirt.

'On you go,' I said. 'The big bad world awaits.'

You kissed my cheek, and whispered, 'be good and be extra nice to Mom, love you.' You sniffed, and ran off to join your friend, turning once to wave back at me, then you vanished into the terminal.

Your Big Why haunts everything now, Em. Trickles down into thousands of little whys. Why eat? Why wash? Why shop, shit, eat? Why not just sleep?

And this worn red leather bible you left behind, Em. Your tiny scrawls in the margins of the book of Ecclesiastes. That's all. No more clues. You. A bible? It makes no sense.

What am I going to do?

Em,

Time is slowing. The black hole's sucking me in, again. Such an effort to move a finger. Pointlessness. Why, why, why?

I need you to pull me out of this Em, otherwise I'm done for.

You know I did have one big thing I believed in.

It was you, Em.

I should probably kill myself anyway on the 1st. Stick to the original plan. Just do it here in the kitchen with the pipe bombs, now that I've blown all my chances – no pun intended. It would save me tidying up at least. Ha ha! What a joke. But seriously, what d'you think, Em?

I should at least fix my hand up before that. Get to a drug store. I mean, why suffer to the end? And while I'm at it, why the hell not get the pharmacist to renew my antidepressants, they take about five days to kick in and so I could have a few days with that nice Prozac feeling before my suicide.

Hi Em,

Just back from the pharmacy in Mill Valley. Driving was hard with the swollen hand, but memory served me right and I found the place.

It was pretty busy, a lot of pasty-faced folks in there with addiction problems. This Hispanic woman Amara, was at the counter, and she said it'd be no problem at all for them to call up my regular doctor for the Prozac. She said, 'Ouch, that looks really sore!' when I undid the wet bandage and showed her my hand. She reminded me of how you'd howl sometimes and clutch your own hand, whenever anyone else was cut.

I bought some antibiotic cream, ibuprofen cream, fresh bandages, tweezers, and iodine, and I found myself strangely moved by Amara's kindness. I remember you once said, Em, that I ought to get out more, cos regular people are really nothing to fear.

She said I should go in the back so the dispensing pharmacist could examine my hand right away.

There was this light green corridor with two doors and three green plastic seats for waiting, facing this big flat screen wall-mounted TV, next to the water bubbler.

My hand was pulsing, the pus sticking to the bandages like melted cheese. I told myself, I'm here to get professional help, the bombing is over, over and over and I sat there watching the TV screen. There was an advert for Viagra, then an infomercial for middle-aged life insurance. 'It's never too late,' it said. I got that feeling the adverts were targeted straight at me, Em. You once explained how the smart tech in the TV scans your phone and it detects, say a middle-aged man with no life insurance and erectile dysfunction, so it says, quick, send him a personalized Viagra advert!

The door opened and the pharmacist stuck her head out, she was young, Asian, charming, she said, 'Just be five minutes. Would you like some water while you're waiting?' I waved my bandaged hand, shook my head and smiled back.

Left alone, I swear I saw this red light come on on the television frame. An advert started with footage of four smiling young girls walking in the sun. It said, 'to think something so small could have such big importance, connecting you to everything that matters when your life and that of your loved ones are on the line.' Then it cut to young nurses in a hospital, smiling. Then it showed fingers holding up a microchip, in an operating theatre.

The voice-over said, something like, 'Fit Link is always with you when every second counts in the emergency room.'

Then it showed this microchip in an X-Ray image, inserted into the back of someone's ear. It said the Fit Link chip provides instant access to all your medical records, because in an emergency, you might not be able to remember all your medications, your service provider and ID, credit card details, or your blood type.

Pain shot from my hand to my head, but I couldn't take my eyes off the footage of smiling children playing on swings with their mother. And the voice-over said: 'If your children ever get lost, they will be traced with Fit Link. If they're ever in an accident and you're not around, all their bio information on whether they have diabetes or antibiotic resistance or allergies or up to date vaccinations are stored right there on their Fit Link ID chip and could save their lives.'

'Fit Link,' it said with a spinning graphic of the ID chip sending out signals from a smiling woman's head, 'The future is within you.'

And then I saw it, at the bottom of the screen. The logo for ██████████, which is an affiliate of Biosys Corp.

I couldn't breathe. I tried to stand up but was dizzy. Biosys had tracked me there and aimed that advert at me to say give up, we know everything you've been up to. I staggered into the water bubbler. I had to get out. The last image was of a hundred young beautiful people of all races, all smiling straight to the camera. 'The future is within you,' they all said in unison. So, they'd already started rolling out the mass-chipping of tens of thousands of young people?

Had I been hiding away from the world for so long? It was an RFID chip and that would open the floodgates to the cerebral link microchips that Biosys would introduce next, the ones they'd tested on you.

I made it out of the pharmacy, Amara calling after me, 'Sir, you forgot your prescription.' I swear, I detached from my own body and saw myself staggering along the sidewalk, Em. I made it back to the truck and took three Beta-blockers and a codeine tab just so I could breathe.

The future is within you.

I drove with caution, sweating and in pain. A cop car passed me and I froze.

No memory of how I made it back home.

I ransacked the bathroom cabinets and found six old penicillin pills from the last time I'd a throat infection. They're out of date by four years, but they'll have to do.

The wind is whipping up the sand against the window boards. I pulled them shut to keep the signals out. My hand's pulsing but the pain is fading out. Something in here smells of mold. I just had an extra Vicodin on top of the penicillin. Feel like I'm detaching again.

The future is within you.

For two weeks I've been deluding myself with this grandiose plan of revenge, but it's all too late. It's too late to save the children.

Em,

It's like a demon, stalking me. I can't let depression take me like it did after Biosys got Toby. Have to keep talking, that gives me one thing to focus on.

Back then, I was running out of bereavement leave.

The college Team Member Services reluctantly gave me two additional weeks of sick-leave. Without the support of routines things fell away. I stopped eating. I drank myself to sleep, couldn't find the energy to change my socks or to shower. I became scared of the wind rattling the mosquito frames, of your voice appearing then vanishing into the dust that I watched fall onto every surface.

The psychiatrists would say I was suffering from paranoid delusions in the wake of traumatic loss. They'd say your death was an unfortunate, freak accident, and that, unable to accept this, and riddled with guilt, I constructed a conspiracy theory and an all-powerful God-like enemy to blame – one corporation with total control of all life and death on earth, but then having trouble imagining this amorphous force, I settled on the face of its CEO.

Against them I can only offer evidence of the systematic attempts that were made to shut down my investigations. To prove it to you at least, Em.

The week after I found out they'd murdered Toby I sent emails to health industry regulators, scientists and journalists who'd unearthed data on Biosys' international activities since the 2010s. But then, strange things started happening.

First, any email replies I got vanished within minutes of arriving. Almost like I'd imagined them. No trace. Then as I drew a map of the many tentacles of Biosys Corp's investments in pharmacology, virology, and its deep links with departments of the US govt and the Big Tech giants ██████ and ███ – my email account was suddenly suspended. I got one message that said I was in breach of the terms of service.

'Unless you contact us, we'll subsequently delete all

address books without further notice' they said. 'This includes all the emails and personal information held in the mailboxes. This data can't be recovered.'

I called them twenty times and each time it was the same cheery corporate hip hop on loop, the synthetic female voice saying, 'please hold, your call is important to us.' The more I plead to have my account restored, the more I was moved from department to department, and each time my call was disconnected, and I was forced to begin again with the automated system. 'But I've already done this, twenty times, what do you mean you have no record of my name or my last calls?' I yelled at the voice bots. 'Look, I need you to give me access to my email account even temporarily, so I can rescue my address book and my thousands of emails. Put me through to customer complaints, I need to speak to a fucking human!' The AI replied, 'Thank you for your call, goodbye.' and disconnected me.

Then a message came: *This suspended account has been deleted.*

Oh Em, you would have predicted all this.

Then I discovered my email provider, was owned by ██████████ – a conglomerate that are majority stakeholders in Biosys Corp.

I searched for and joined an encrypted bulletin board, called ether.com, where dozens of activists with pseudonyms posted undercover research on what they called the 'Biocide Project'.

For three weeks, they shared internal mail smuggled out of Biosys Corp, on human testing, testimonials from bereaved families in six different countries, and banned medical reports that exposed the Infinity Project. Of course, they were all bundled in with crazy conspiracy theories, but I filtered out all that stuff on planned eugenic sterilization, the ████ ████ Foundation and the New World Order.

I became friends with DevoDio, ExTraMan and PapaG, and I realized there were dozens of us out there trying to build a case against Biosys to send to human rights organizations and regulators. I downloaded a file DevoDio sent me – 'How to Disappear' a guide to digital invisibility, and they warned me the days of our encrypted site were numbered. Then, just as they predicted, ether.com was shut down. It was branded as a 'Hate Speech site' on social media, and 'a breeding ground for domestic terrorists.' Which was echoed verbatim by the mainstream news media including the ████ ████, ████, the ████ ████ the ████, the ████ ████ ████, ████ and ████.

Then I received a message from ████, saying that due to suspicious activity, my broadband and Wi-Fi service were now shut down, effective immediately.

I lost three thousand photographs, saved on the cloud. Photos of you from the first day of your life, Em, all the photos of you growing up.

And again, I discovered that the parent company of my internet service provider had investments in Biosys Corp.

Using its proxies, one-by-one, Biosys shut down all my access to online research and any platform to share it on, trying to make me fearful of raising my head again. Oh Em, most people just burn out and give up, but I feared the depression I'd fall into if I did.

Back then, as you know, Em, I was still teaching video

editing in City College and I had a set of keys and so I snuck in after hours. I got back online with VPNs, pay-as-you-go burner phones, fake IDs, top-up-cards, disposable SIMs, and when the coast was clear, I logged onto one of the thirty computers on the IT floor, using the college IP address, and created four fake new online identities following the 'How to Disappear' guide.

It took me a while, but I tracked down my old ether.com contacts PapaG and LexiFree, and they led me into a dark-web site that proved what I'd suspected – that certain private hospitals affiliated with Biosys Corp were being used to extract nanochips from the bodies of failed test subjects. There was video evidence from Peru, with two test subjects who'd gone into anaphylactic toxic-shock, one fatally, while the other was in a vegetative state.

Flashbacks to you in your hospital bed, my love. The rage kept me going.

Night after night I snuck into work after hours, dodging the cleaners and night watchmen. Some nights I took vodka and caffeine pills, so I could research till four, five am Once, I was awoken at eight thirty am by an office junior called Rhonda. 'You OK, Mister C?' she asked and I lied, told her I'd come into work extra early that morning. But, she must have seen my empty vodka bottle, known I'd slept there.

Again and again, after midnight, I snuck into room 11A. With your many whys in my head, guiding me, Em. I followed a poster called TMex who dug out a research paper that showed that 'Infinity nanochips gave AI substantial control over the human mind-body nexus in 62% of test cases. Manipulating emotions and movement.' I discovered, that Biosys had a contract with Ximien, a

Chinese contractor in Shenzen, to mass manufacture ten billion nanochips, one for every person on the planet.

I admit Em, I fell down the rabbit hole, but I still sensed the hunger that fuelled your own scientific investigations.

There were papers on The Biosys Corp experimental gene-therapy trials in Liberia, Sierra Leone, Guinea, Congo, Philippines, Peru, Uganda. Poorer countries with more easily corruptible leaders. The so called 'gene-therapy' was code for biotech micro-organisms. Living computers surgically inserted into living human organs. Whistleblowers exposed the possibility that Biosys even contained a department named the Defense Innovation Unit, promising mind-controlled battlefield drones.

There were reported successes of the Infinity Project: incredible rapid cellular repair, organ rejuvenation by the nanobots, ageing stopped and reversed. Massively expanded cognitive capabilities in the brain-chipped human test subjects.

A stolen document sent from Biosys to the [redacted] showed the calculations on what would be an 'acceptable failure rate' given the significance of the 'breakthrough' – that failure rate meaning human deaths.

The hope and happy faces of the teenage boys and girls smiling for the western cameras, in these countries without running water. 'Test subjects', mere kids, some as young as eleven, so poor their feet were shoeless and muddy, but yet they handed their bodies over to surgeons in hazmat suits.

I saw footage of the results of these 'acceptable failures'. Brain fever, organ rejection, immune system collapse, loss of motor function, loss of speech, searing head pain, deafness, blindness, thrombosis, stroke. Then evidence about the nanobot injections. Photos of youths, scratching at their skin, tearing at it. Of rapidly multiplying microscopic nanobots erupting through their skin in open sores. Like accelerated cancer. Then reports of these 'test subjects' attempting to tear the micro-chips out of their skulls. Gouging into their own brains with any metal to hand.

Oh Em, it was hell but I had to know what they'd done to you.

A child in Peru, was lying on a makeshift bed, chickens running around in the background, bandages around his torso, muddy and bloody. In the clip, he looks up into the camera with big dark open eyes. Below his belly is bursting, a malignant pregnancy of glittering forms, seething, multiplying exponentially, his hands trying to hold his innards together, his silent screams, begging to be saved by the very same Western scientists who had injected him and were now recording his death as scientific data.

You must have known all this, Em.

And this was not just Biosys Corp. The names of other global financiers, Big Pharma and Big Tech partners included ████████████, the ██████ Institute, ███ and ███ ███, the world's leading investment company. Half redacted documents proved The Infinity Project had received billions from the top health institutes and the two largest military agencies, ███ and the ██. So Big Tech, Big Pharma, BioTech, and Big Govt had merged in a closed circle to protect their trillions in mutual investment. The evidence showed an international plan to biologically merge AI with the human species within our lifetimes, using Brain-Computer Interface within 'conflict-zone target recognition and multiplication' and 'military robots remotely controlled by soldiers minds.'

With all this alarming information, I sent files to ████████ and two other whistle-blower sites. But then Tmex vanished and then Papa G, so, I kept on, alone, barely sleeping, manic, knowing that time was running out before Biosys traced my fake IDs back to me.

Two weeks later an email appeared in my work email inbox on the college server, it simply said, 'Letter from 'Team Member Services' attached – or what they used to call HR.

I printed all this stuff out as a hardcopy record, Em. I put it all in a folder here, in case it went to trial.

They said that since I'd used the college computers, I'd placed the college *in violation of International Hate Speech Law and this had left The Community College of San Francisco open to prosecution – under the UN Hate Speech Charter, section 178 (b) (c) (d) and (f).*

They said my contract was terminated immediately and I had to attend a meeting that would be recorded for legal reasons.

Biosys, must have got to the College, Em, threatened them, but I couldn't prove it.

Human Resources attached a screenshot of the so called 'Hate Speech' that I'd posted on the shared site – it said.

> *Where have the Indonesian news stories on the new Biosys nanochip-trial deaths gone? Erased by Big Tech search engines overnight. Check out the Top 3 Big Tech Search engines $98B investment in Biosys.*

I'd overlooked the fact that, fake ID or not, my college had signed the State Security Information Sharing Act,

2019, and so every word and search I typed, encrypted or not, had been flagged, by a US Govt Department of Homeland Security bot.

Oh Em, I stayed sober the night before my confrontation with HR and took Beta-blockers to make sure I kept my temper.

I sat before Coleen, director of Team Member Services, Rasha, the head of the Inclusion & Opportunity, and the one whose name I can't remember from Complaints and Compliance. There was a silent young lawyer in the room too, whose name I can't recall either.

The four eyed me up and down. A month of booze and no sleep had left me pretty ravaged.

Rasha from HR pronounced each word slowly.

'We've written your resignation and apology letter, for you to sign.' And she passed forward two sheets of paper.

'Wait… you wrote my apology for me?' I asked.

I scanned the text – it mentioned illegal use of state-owned IT equipment and illegal visits to banned conspiracy theory sites linked to political extremists.

The one from Compliance, said, 'yes, in your apology you publicly distance your actions from the values of the college and accept blame for your dismissal.'

'You've got to be kidding.' I protested. 'Look, I'm sorry I screwed up. I was drunk, I stupidly visited a website I shouldn't have, I can't see how this has escalated to accusations that I'm…' I paused to find the line and pointed to it, 'part of a white supremacist network'. C'mon, this is a frame-up. It's beyond a joke.'

No one was laughing. Then it clicked. Big Tech and Big Govt always used that same accusation to take down its enemies, it was 100% effective and all attempts to defend yourself had to be silenced because every word you could utter as a 'supremacist' was literally harming someone.

'If you don't accept this wording and sign it,' Carolina said '…then.'

They looked to each other, then Colleen from TMS spoke with a shaking smile.

'… we will be forced to sue you… '

'… which could be in the region of several million dollars,' Rasha from Inclusion added immediately, 'given that the identity of the college has been damaged and students might now perceive the college as a hostile learning environment.'

I couldn't hold it in, Em. I laughed. I recall the water bubbler gurgled and I may even have made a fart joke. My sweat stank of vodka and I looked round their faces for a trace of humor or pity. 'C'mon, Colleen,' I said, 'you know this is bullshit? I'm a lifelong God-damned liberal, for God sake! It's me, Joshing Josh, you used to laugh at my jokes in the staff kitchen!'

Silence and Coleen blushed. I'd accidentally accused her of complicity in my crime.

'Please, don't you see how I've been framed here?'

I'd tried so hard not to become the monster they thought I was, but their frozen faces set me off. 'You're clearly terrified of Silicon Valley,' I shouted. 'And now they're playing you. Can't you see you're being used to whitewash the death of my daughter? Well done!'

'I don't feel safe here.' Carolina from Compliance muttered and headed for the door.

'Oh very good!' I screamed. 'Provoke me to the point where I swear and then you can accuse me of violence as well. Very cunning. Un-be-fucking-lievable. You fucking corporate ass-licking cowards!'

In the end, my resignation became a small local news story, eclipsed by bigger stories including one on celebrity-endorsed underwear. I was served legal papers by the college demanding reparations of five hundred thousand dollars for 'reputational damage'. I used them as kindling in my stove. After that, rumours circulated that I'd suffered a nervous breakdown.

Through all this, Em, I thought of you. Just you. Your eyes blown-out red, your hand reaching for help. And I locked myself in my shack, and drank.

Zach Neumann will give his talk on the 1st to a standing ovation and I won't be there. He'll be chauffeur driven home with three security men, behind bullet proof glass. He'll live and he'll keep on killing as he tries to create his immortality machine.

What am I going to do, Em?

I moved the stupid pipe bombs to the back door, but now they're sitting there, taunting me. 'Look how pointless we are now!' they seem to say, 'look what a fool you've been. Ha, ha!'

Fuck it, I'm opening the wine.

Editor's Note X

In the recordings from 12 to 9 days, Cartwright appears somewhat like an animal caught in a trap. In the footage Cartwright accidentally films himself and seems no longer to care about anything, not even himself. Footage shows him lying in an unkempt bed, drinking wine straight from the bottle, drunkenly banging a frozen chicken on the kitchen counter, and lying on the gravel outside to observe the night sky.

Much to my concern, Cartwright's claims about 'the Big Tech Censorship Complex' and complicity between Big Tech, Big Bio Tech, Big Media, and even Big Publishing, can now be partially verified.

For example: significant investments have been made since 2019 by Big Tech and Big Pharma in the 'New Space Race' of what Reuters calls the 'Biotech Goldrush'. These investments in 'wet technology' include those by major multinational conglomerates, leading financial technology companies, top web services providers, and the renowned tech giant often referred to as 'the most powerful company in the world'. These corporations have collectively invested $4 trillion in 'bioengineering, nanotechnology, and neurotechnology to program human biology.'

Regarding Cartwright's claims about specific nano-technologies, new articles, a mere four months after the bombing, have announced similar technologies known as the 'Biosys Global Smart Shield System'. This nano-biotechnology utilises 'harmless nanoparticles' injected into the human bloodstream to collect and transmit health data. These particles have already enabled early diagnoses of various conditions such as Herpes, parasite infections, sepsis, HIV, infertility, and even cancer in a few cases.

According to these new papers on nature.com and in *The Lancet*, this bio-technology has the potential to predict future physical and mental illnesses, saving billions through preventive care and early intervention. Additionally, when data from thousands of nanobot implanted users is aggregated, it can 'serve as a predictor of pandemics and societal anomalies through cluster mapping.'

The Biosys Global Smart Shield System is being lauded as a miracle breakthrough in health and security by the WHO, NIH, and CDC.

Speculating on how Cartwright acquired detailed information about the technology many months before its public announcement is unnerving.

It would be re-assuring to think Cartwright possibly came across an earlier research paper discussing similar technologies and, given his fears around new technologies, he imagined different and more catastrophic outcomes; a perhaps understandable reaction considering his mental state. Either he had some inside information, or he had made a good guess about emerging technology.

The requests I made to Biosys for further information on the Global Smart Shield System and intravenous nanobot injection systems have been met in the last month, with total silence.

I have made several errors of judgement in investigating Cartwright's recordings by using smart technology. Certain changes had taken place within the publishing house over the last year since the widescale adoption of AI, and looking back, it has been risky of me to use online AI facial recognition software to identify images of Cartwright and his daughter. Then I've made the additional mistake of playing audio from several of the video recordings into the AI voice-to-text auto-transcription programme by logging into the office version remotely from home.

I did this to speed up the process – something the publishing house now does extensively: using AI to dictate emails and to analyse thousands of manuscript submissions to predict which titles will be market hits, with the AI also cutting back on the need for proof readers, editors and copy editors – even the departments of marketing, publicity and accounts are in this same process of AI streamlining.

Perhaps, I was guilty of cutting corners due to my anxious need to get the manuscript over and done with so I could wash my hands of it. However, in using AI, I had made a dreadful mistake, as I realised to my horror when a second warning appeared by email, with the title: 'Illegal use of the office server detected.'

The message came from the publishing house IT department and was cc'd to the departments of Editorial, Corporate Affairs and HR. It contained no further information on what my illegal use had been.

So, the publishing house knew exactly what I was up to, and perhaps even knew of the content of the recordings. Terrified of losing my job or worse, I was haunted by something Cartwright had said: 'Silently they record you and if you try to speak, they silence you.'

Words that I could increasingly relate to as Corporate Affairs investigated my 'illegal use of the office server'.

And then, ten days later, I received an email from the publishing house, announcing that my contract had been terminated with immediate effect, with no reasons given.

After giving years of life and energy to the corporation it would only have been fair that a meeting was held discuss the situation. This was requested and I prepared a full written apology; but no meeting was granted. Later a message by automated email claimed that 'corporate safety protocols' had been violated by myself; in violation of employment codes for using office equipment for 'theft of propriety materials' and 'banned materials'; also that certain online activities by myself had been flagged by 'external security agencies.'

My further requests for meetings to clarify and apologise, were not granted. There was no reference in any of the dismissal communications to the transcriptions of Cartwright's 'For Emma' recordings, but they must have been the reason behind my abrupt termination.

It should be said that the processes Cartwright reports in his becoming a 'silenced, non-person' were alarmingly similar to what I was being forced through. But how could I even plead my case, when all requests were being auto-processed and rejected by the HR department's AI system?

The revelation came then that the AI voice-to-text translation software, and the online AI facial recognition software that had been used, must have be connected to the so called 'external security agencies' who had flagged my behaviour. But how could that be possible without the publishing house working directly with the US govt. and with Biosys?

As I packed up my office belongings and said goodbye to colleagues it was alarming to find the processes of stone-walling and shunning going on, among former close friends too. The result being that I was effectively unemployed, and possibly under criminal investigation by forces unknown, and ruing the day that I ever clicked upon that first email.

There remained only one option available for me: to complete the transcriptions of Cartwright's recordings in the hope that some discovered detail would provide a legal bargaining opportunity to be presented to my lawyers, as part of my defence, should it come to that. But this question of Cartwright's troubled me greatly – what will I do if no-one believes me?

12 days

Em,

Can barely move. It's no good. I've only one day of antibiotics left and the hand's much worse. Plus, I got wasted last night. The bed sheet's damp and knotted round my stupid feet. Everything's slowing down.

I really should defuse the bombs properly and get them out of the shack, so I can get my kitchen back to normal. I'm pretty sure I spilled some nitrates in the coffee container. Bitter taste.

But defusing the bombs would require even more effort, and the friction. Wouldn't that be ironic? Killed trying to clean-up. The last time I ever do housework! Ha, ha. Bye-bye funny man. Nope. Can't find the energy.

Months after your funeral, the wasted rage against Biosys had drained me. I lay here on my back on this same sofa-bed for months with the window blinds blocking out everything but needles of light, Em, and I found myself drawn to your Heat Death of The Universe.

The burning out of the last stars mingled with the ache in my limbs, to say 'give up'. All life on every planet is pointless. The universe will end, and no trace of humans will remain. Getting up from my musty bed to pee felt like a thousand-mile trek. Each step, an agony of time. The bed, warm with my own smells. The cicadas, the passing trucks, the aeroplanes and waves and the damn light. I tried to block it all out, drank myself to sleep, but would wake up gasping. The air seemed to slow down, freezing, the atoms stopped spinning. There was nothing left to do beyond feeding this shell for yet another pointless day, so that I could make the appearance of coping if my mother or sister called.

'I'm fine.' I'd say, 'Just very busy just now, can we text instead?'

Tricks to be left alone.

Oh Em, what's my purpose now? I could so easily open that last bottle and let the drinking take me this time. Just taken another codeine for the hand and my brain is foggy. Everything in the universe will freeze and come to a stop you said, every atom will stop spinning.

Need to lie down.

Hey Em,

Woke and it's dark already. Damn fool. Shivering now, hungry but can't face the canned beans or defrosting the pointless chicken. There's a cockroach under the gas cooker. I could kill it, but there's the crunching sound and the stink. They'll survive a nuclear war, someone once said.

I was looking forward to dying in a fortnight but now… I dunno.

I never knew whether my mother suffered from these depressions too. If she did she hid it from everyone with her positivity mantras. Peace and love and yin and yang, self-medicating with hash and booze.

Did I ever tell you, Em, that from the age of seven I had to take care of her because she was so often stoned? Your Granny Annie, this was in the 70s. I had to help her get out of her stinking night clothes, wash her, dress her, feed her, take the wine bottles and weed away from her reach. Memories of men who came to stay, long haired dudes, free spirits, my uncles she called them. Uncle John, Uncle Zan,

Uncle Pedro, Uncle Joe. Free love. They'd walk around our pad, naked. They brought her bottles and pills. Eight years old and I heard yelling in her room one day, I rushed in and this long-haired guy was thrusting into my mom from behind. I remember her animal noises and her breasts swinging. I stood there staring, terrified and the bearded guy saw me and said, 'hey kid, how ya doing?' My mother didn't push him off or cover herself up, she just threw a shoe at me to get out. I froze. Piss ran down my leg. She did this with so many men, twenty, forty, more. Taboos were there to be broken my mom always said. But it was child neglect really, maybe even abuse one of my shrinks thought. I pretty much brought my little sis up myself, cooked for her, did the laundry, got Stacey to school even though I was just a kid myself.

A lot of children of the hippie experiment ended up addicts. Yeah, a lot of depression in our generation. My mom should never have told me and Stacey that we were 'accidents'. 'Blow up the nuclear family', was one of her phrases. Yeah, we were like the shrapnel.

You know Em, I thought I'd got over it pretty unscathed, until it hit me about the age of twenty. Moments when this nothingness would open up under my feet.

Looking back, my depressions had a pattern. They came when I was eighteen, twenty-two, twenty-five – I got my first diagnosis at twenty-eight, then I met your mother and I thought the commitment would cure me, that she'd help me beat the darkness for good.

At one point in my marriage, you were maybe seven years old, Em, I tried to hide another growing depression from you and your mother. A bad one. I can't remember what triggered it, I had everything to be happy about, a brilliant child, a hugely successful wife, the kind of stable home my mother never gave me. But the why-why-whys overwhelmed me. Why work, why drive, why sleep, why eat, why make money, why believe in any kind of future?

I got through my days for the sake of you and your mom. Pretending to be happy, Em, playing hide and seek with you – five, four, three, two, one… ready or not, here I come. Sketching, collecting your fire leaves with you, pretending life had a purpose.

And you asking your whys all the time, Em. That tormented me.

The Prozac hadn't worked so I tried Wellbutrin, but it killed my libido and your mother and I fought because our intimacy vanished. I moved into the spare bedroom, because of insomnia, pacing, and restlessness. I hid the tablets from her, struggled to hide the truth from you both. A child should never know that their parent is lost. Yes, the suicidal ideation rushed at me, even back then. Poor tiny Em. Could you tell I was breaking inside? Were there signs? Did I cling too hard, Em? Did I hold you just a second too long when I kissed you goodnight? Did you feel my eyes were distant?

In truth, I think, my depressions were the real start of my divorce. I became dependent on your mother in the months of my immobility, emotionally, and financially.

At first, she was so generous, trying to help me 'get back on my feet.' 'I know how you feel,' your mother would say, 'I was depressed once for a whole week'. And all her advice, 'Why don't you try chamomile tea?' 'Look, it's a beautiful day outside, let's get out for a walk together.' 'You have so many things to be thankful for' 'Cheer up!'

She was so kind and tried so hard to make me well and

yet, I stared at the walls, not at her. As you know Em, depression exhausts everyone who tries to help, it's too much for any healthy person to cope with. She became terrified, I think, of the pit I was falling into. The whys circling me – why wash, why get up, why care, why even speak? She had to care for you and me both, Em, and the deeper I fell the more a burden I was to carry.

'Snap out of it. We have a kid to raise! You're just being hypochondriac and selfish,' your mother said as the weeks wore into months. 'Please, try to think positive. Do you think I have the luxury of lying around all day and feeling sorry for myself. Get-up, get back to work. Man-up!'

And it only made me feel more alone, and the more I retreated the more I started to resent her energy.

Two months in bed, on sick leave, waiting for the anti-depressants to kick-in, the doses increasing. 30mgs, 40mgs. I discovered a dark energy that ran counter to all that the world thrived on, and it told me to let go. Why love, why live? To let myself fall. To let your mother fall away from me.

She seemed affronted that her love couldn't reach me.

'You're making me depressed as well…' 'Just pull yourself together,' she'd snap. 'Your problems aren't that big, there's lots of people worse off than you' 'You never think of anyone but yourself.' 'Why don't you give up going to these quacks and throw out those pills.' 'I can't keep lying to Em that you have a flu.' 'You have to be strong for your daughter!'

I moved beyond resentment and became cruel. One day in my bed, I said to her, 'if I'm such a chore then why don't you just take Emma and leave me.' That hurt her. Left alone I cooked up conspiracies, I told myself your mother would walk out on this weakling. That she'd invested in faulty goods and wanted a refund.

All of it delusory. Nasty. The demon of depression made me loathe your mother with her stupid statements, 'You have no right to feel this way.' 'This is just typical self-pitying male behaviour.' Depression was a voice in my head, scheming to bring the house down.

And then, as you know, that was when I started my online affair.

I can't blame your mother for what she did. She was being strong for the family by telling me to move out. Maybe she was right. I'd become self-destructive and I couldn't have coped with being a full-time father at the same time. Maybe I'm guilty for forcing this 'strong single mother' role on her. All that love we had.

I swore I'd never subject you to what my mother put me through.

But the cycle repeated. I carried my mother on my back, and you in turn became that small brave kid carrying the weight of the hopelessly depressed parent.

I'm so sorry, Em. For contaminating you.

Please understand that often, in those times after the divorce when I cancelled your overnight stays, it was never because I didn't want to see you, Em. It was always because I didn't want you to see me in that state of darkness.

I was an absent father because I wanted to protect you. From me.

And all the time I told myself, I'll take these pills, I'll do this therapy and get better for Em's sake. I will make Em my reason to go on. My love for Em will save me.

I remember that night, you were maybe only ten, Em, when you caught me crying. I must have woken you with my sobbing and you came downstairs in your pyjamas and found me at the kitchen table. Your mother and I had been fighting, and I'd drunk a bottle of wine, alone. My mind was going round in circles, my mother had thrown my own father out when I was only seven, and now you were ten, and history was repeating, spiralling, no escape.

You were hiding behind the door. I heard a movement and turned, 'Em, is that you?'

You were silent, but then I heard your breath.

'Why aren't you in your bed, Em? Why you hiding there,' I said and got to my feet. You peered round at me. Your pyjamas had spaceships on them, I recall. Your hair in ringlets. And your voice in a whisper said: 'Daddy, what's wrong?'

Oh Em, that set me off worse, and the shame that I'd scared you. I held my arms open wide to you, but you clung to the door frame like you'd seen a monster.

I staggered over to you, went down on my knees, told you I was sorry. I pried your fingers off the door frame, Em, clung to you. I must have terrified you. The vile weight of me, the staggering bulk, the alcohol breath, the clinging uncontrollable tears that burst out as I held you. No child should see their father like that. Hear that booming chest, empty with despair. Feel him gripping her for grim life.

'Don't cry, Daddy,' you said.

I felt you wriggle against me, then your body went limp and you started to weep too, Em. 'What's' happening?' you said. 'Daddy, stop, you're scaring me.'

I had to lie to your frightened face. 'It's nothing,' I said, 'Daddy's just sad, it's work, the news on TV, I'm just a bit sad today, that's all.'

How could I have told you, 'I suffer from a mental

illness, Em,' How could I have told you, 'Depression is like a curse that passes down the generations, and I worry every day, that I might have passed this onto you, little one. I pray you'll be spared this hell, and I'll hate myself forever if you ever get sick with this too.'

You touched my shoulder, like you needed to check I was still me. Then you leaned in and patted my back and said, 'it's OK Daddy, it's going to be OK.' So small, in your spaceship pyjamas, and you held me like you were the adult and I was the child in your care.

How many of my depressions did you see Em, over the years, two, three? I'm ashamed now. All that burden I put on your tiny shoulders. No kid should ever have to carry all that weight.

Yes, I should have protected you from my sickness, not seen you as the cure.

Please tell me I did one thing right in my life, Em.

Em,

I can't sleep. Still lying here in bed, listening to the cicadas. The wind bashing the mosquito blinds. Sorry, I'm drunk as a skunk. Seem to have pissed myself.

I'm still in your bad-books and you've gone silent, so I picked up the bible Toby said was yours. A small smudge of chocolate or blood on two pages, then words underlined in the Book of Ecclesiastes. Reading it again for clues.

'Meaningless! Meaningless! says the wise old teacher 'Utterly meaningless! I have seen all the things under the sun and all of them are meaningless. All is vanity: pleasure, reputation, toil, ambition, power, art, justice, wisdom, all is futile, unutterably wearisome and tiresome and doomed to end,' 'all is but a chasing after wind, blah, blah, blah,' 'As you do not know the path of the wind, or how the bones are formed in a mother's womb… blah, blah, blah…' 'so you cannot understand the work of God.'

That's what you underlined, Em.

Everything is futile the words say, but there is faith. Only faith.

Shit. But what is faith, Em? Just a longing that pretends to be a conviction.

Is this really what you were reading the last months before your death, Em? Pretty weird after our three generations of atheism? Did you want me to find these pages, Em? Was this why you led me to Toby?

And what is this greater power that I'm supposed to believe in? How can we go back to believing again, once we've killed all of the gods? I don't know.

Show me this greater power now, Em, and I swear I'll blindly follow.

I must be desperate.

I seem to have drunk the last bottle. I'm spent, Em. If I don't kill Neumann, how the hell can I return to normal life?

I should try to boil some beans. Fuck. Get out for some fresh air, chase after some wind. Ha, but the wise old Ecclesiastes guy is right, all is futile. If I can't live for revenge, then what else?

This ache in my bones. No clear thought fighting through. Exhausted at the prospect of going to the frigging fridge. There's a sound from down the hill of children running, shouting. A distant dog barking, the mail van. Be quiet! All your excitements are pointless! Leave me the fuck alone!

The cicadas are starting up again. They're so loud and cruel. Night hunters. A million dead insects are the soil of my garden.

I'm off to bed again, Em, with my codeine pills. I know your voice is not coming back now Em, and maybe you were never really here. Your voice was just a story I told myself, so I could go on living. Fuck it all and fuck you too.

Oh no, it's happening again. The whys are descending. Eating me from inside, asking why, why, why change my pants, why wash? We both know where this leads. Alone with no goals, no family, no society, no faith in any damn thing at all – why should I go on? And what are you really, Em? My conscience? The Devil in disguise?

Maybe I've finally given up and let the depressions take me.

If your God exists my love, then please ask him to help me. A vision or a burning bush would be fine. I've long ceased checking my email but if he has time he could message me, maybe he has an app for that! Ha ha, I'm, the last funny man and no-one is laughing. God's forgotten punchline. Tears of a clown. Tears of a fucking clown.

11 days

Oh Em,

I've slept so late. Hungover as hell. I bit through three of the big blisters on my hand when I was drunk. Agony now. Fucking idiot. Plus, the antibiotics have given me the runs. Pathetic. Stacey just rang once more. Forcing me to text her back. Exhausting.

Maybe how is the question now, not why. How will I go on, Em?

Can I really keep on living beyond these eleven days? Twelve months then. I'll sleep, wake, eat, shop, shit and sleep again and again. The maple trees will blossom, there will be a new hit single, a new first-time celebrity, a new president, a new scandal.

Once I get over the guilt, I mean. Think about it. The people are decent round here, there's the community center, the surf shacks, the tumbledown sheds and weeds. Nature Foods Pantry does pretty decent koftas and all the used furniture and clothes folk leave on their fences with hand-written signs saying, 'free to a new home' and 'take what you need.' I kind of love this ramshackle hippie town and the ocean view. Like we're still in the seventies. The endless fog.

Live then! Get up, get up! I told myself this morning, get up, and fight the darkness you asshole! Don't show a second of weakness! You're not a bomber, not a father, just a very smelly man, so take a shower for Chrissakes! Routines will save you. I have to keep myself very, very busy every second and not sink back into your damned why, why, whys!

So, I forced myself into my bathroom, as you know. And found myself staring at the mess of pill packets, bottles and jars. 'Brush your teeth, do it now you fool' I yelled. 'Or Emma's whys will get you!'

I was staring at the toothbrush in my hand, the bent bristles like a hedgehog, absurd.

But why brush my teeth now that there's nowhere to go? Neumann can't be stopped. No matter how much I try to block it all out, AI will gradually take over everything, and one day the cyborgs will break down this door and find me here.

I fought it hard! The toothpaste tube stared back at me, saying, 'hurry up! Do it now, brush your fucking teeth you loser! Don't ask why – if you don't do this right now the whys will swarm and pull you into the darkest pit!'

Mouthwash. Nose hair trimmers. I managed to brush, then splash water on my armpits and feet. My clothes lying all over the floors, demanded I put them on. 'Don't ask why or where we're going!' they said, 'don't fall into temptation again! Just fucking do it!' If it was not for the fascist demands of my pants and shirt, Em, I'd lie here all day.

Then there was the bossiness of bread, the totalitarian coffee and sugar. The dictatorship of shoelaces and touching my toes and the coat and keys and wallet and the phone and changing this sticky-pus bandage. The stupid pain!

Now what?

Can I find a life purpose in buying some milk? Six eggs? What should I do today? Put the first two bombs in a trash bag and bury them in the garden? Get some exercise? Walk a mile barefoot on the shoreline?

Why?

No, no, no, there is never any answer to your why, dear tormentor. Life is meaningless. But still, we must chase after our fucking wind! Ecclesiastes.

My heart's racing now. Just taken some more Beta-blockers. I really shouldn't have flushed the Prozac away. The why-why-whys are hiding behind the dresser and amassing. Why take this pill, why drink water, why feel better? Why breathe? Why, why, why eat, shop, shit, sleep.

Why go anywhere? Why do anything? Why care about anything or anyone?

Why? Don't you fucking start on your whys again, Emma!

Em,

I have another confession, Em. I've been thinking of the time you said you hated me. That time with Gabe, when it all could have changed for you.

You were just turning twenty-two Em, your hair was its natural color for once, and longer. You'd just graduated from Harvard, 1st class honors, Cum Laude, you shared the Dissertation Prize with a Chinese student. Your mom and I were so proud, and relieved you'd managed to put your wrecked childhood behind you. Everyone said you had a brilliant future. We thought you'd spend the summer putting your feet up, choosing one of the three PhD offers you had. I was looking forward to having you come and stay.

You came for just one weekend. Before you arrived by Uber, your mother called, worried that you seemed 'not quite yourself'. She said you'd got in with some alternative types at college. That you were talking about throwing it all in.

You arrived at my shack, Em, kitted out in out-sized men's army fatigues and a retro T-Shirt with a faded peace sign on it, beads in your hair. We picked up some snacks from Sal's, then had our special ritual bonfire with vege-sausage on sticks in our secret beach beneath the Golden Gate.

You were sitting, silently blowing the sand off your fallen vegi-sausage. Waves, gulls, the crackling beach-combed fire, and you were sighing.

'So, what's bothering you, Emyboo?' I asked, and you said you were sick of Mom asking you that same damn question. 'Isn't it OK to be a bit moody like you are Pops?' And why did everyone have to put on a show of being happy all the time like Aunt Stacey and Granny Annie? 'They're so fucking fake and capitalist,' you said, and you threw your vegi-sausage into the bonfire.

'That's my girl.' I thought, but I was worried.

'And why's there all this stupid pressure on me to choose between physics and neurophysics and astrophysics,' you said, 'I mean, my brain is burned out as it is. Yeah, I know women have a duty to study science because the STEM field is so male-dominated and all that, yah-de-yah, but why do I have to be the one who's the pioneer? It's so unfair. Why can't I do something that actually helps save the planet?'

You'd been getting into eco-politics and internet-dating, and a hunch told me this was more to do with the latter.

'It's just,' you said, 'there's all this pressure on me to become this brilliant scientist but what about people from less privileged backgrounds? It's just so unfair that I should get a PhD place at Stanford and they can't.'

'Wait, Stanford as well?' I said. This was the first I'd heard. And you said, 'yeah but you can't force me to go!'

You blurted out that people like me were pale, male, stale and how Gabe had said you'd never understand. 'I mean why shouldn't I go and work with him in the collective for two years. Why the hell not?'

'Wooah, wait, wait, wait,' I said. 'What collective? Where?'

'Chiapas, it's an organic farm,' you replied.

'Hold on that's Mexico, and who is this Gabe person?'

So, you'd come under the spell of a male, after having dated mostly girls in uni. I tried to calm you down, offered you my burned vegan sausage, tried to be the textbook liberal dad.

'He's my… special friend,' you said, 'Not that he identifies as monogamous or hetero all the time but…'

OK,' I said, 'that's great, but do you mean best buddies forever or are we talking actual coitus?'

'What!?' You exploded. 'It isn't all about sex, Pops. Jesus! And sex isn't always genital! That's so sexist! Coitus… how could you even say that? It's so offensive!'

'What would you like me to say,' I asked. 'Doing the horizontal bop, getting down to business, playing hide the sausage? What exactly is your entanglement with this Gabe-babe?'

And you threw the remnants of your second vegan sausage at me. 'You're appalling.' But you couldn't help but laugh, and so we did that thing of ours where laughter comes in waves and we think it's done then one of us sets the other off and it starts again.

'But aren't you freaked-out that I don't want to study anymore?' you asked. 'Mom's going apoplectic?'

'Is she, that's odd,' I said, and I couldn't resist it. 'She's one to talk. You might not know this but your mom and I had our radical dropout years too.'

'You're serious. Mom?'

'Yeah, when we were dating we used to meet at this anarchist book shop down on 24th, read books about the

Red Army Faction, the Weathermen.' I said, 'We went on some anti-war demos together. Even got arrested.'

'No way! Pops, you have so many damn secrets!' You laughed, then started wheezing and took a hit from your inhaler. 'Why didn't you and Mom tell me?'

'Well, there's nothing much to tell, kiddo,' I said. 'Neither of us was very talented at being revolutionaries, so we settled on being very bad at being parents instead.'

You laughed, Em, and I tried to tell you that your mother was maybe not so wrong. 'I mean why throw your education away to grow anarcho-syndicalist plantains in Mexico?'

You stared at me and said: 'Maybe you should try growing something just for once, more than just your gut and your negativity!'

'Ouch, you got me!' I said and we high fived. 'OK, so, when do we get to meet this radical-vegetable, non-genital friend of yours?' I asked.

You play-acted putting your head in your hands, 'God, that's just so wrong on so many levels!'

An old joke came to me: 'Yeah, like the guy who farted in the elevator.'

You stared with that what expression that said – *What? How can you even be my father?*

I made a fart noise and said, 'going up, level one, level two, level three… see… so many levels.'

You groaned so hard Em, it came out like a scream and you punched my arm really hard, but I could tell that beneath it all you were laughing.

Then there was the time you and Gabe came for dinner here at the shack. I must have invited you five, six times. Remember? You'd let things slide, you'd missed the date for your PhD paperwork too and it looked like your mom's fears were right.

I recall that Gabe's silence and your passive deference to him at my table were unsettling. I sensed our meeting had been pre-judged by your special friend with his fake ethnic dreadlocks and tie-dye T-shirt and you were anxiously straying from his script. I dunno, he looked kind of rad, what does your generation call it? Ripped, muscular, covered in tats – but I got the impression that back in the apartment you'd started sharing with him, he was the one who talked and he told you what to think. Odd, given his IQ seemed about half of yours, Em. He was clearly ten years older than you as well.

I recall, I asked him what kind of jobs he'd been doing over those years.

What was it he called me then? A capitalist, patriarchal something?

That set me off, 'well since I'm so evil,' I said, 'would either of you like another glass of my deliciously oppressive wine?'

Your Gabe got up and walked out. You yelled, 'Pops!'

You didn't return my daily calls for two months, Em.

After that, I heard from your mother that you'd cancelled your PhD completely and bought your flight to Mexico. Your mother blamed me.

But I sensed what had happened Em, you always had to be in the grip of one mighty idea and this Gabe guy made you abandon physics for his big ideology.

I could have let you go, Em, but on the night your mother called me, I dropped everything and drove downtown to that hippie apartment you shared with him. I can't let you throw away your future, I thought over and over, as I sped through the Mission District, past all the psychedelic murals. Even if you despise me, even if you never speak to me again, Em, I have to try to stop you, I thought. If Gabe is there, I'll punch his stupid face if I have to. I'll drag you kicking and screaming out of his pathetic plans for your future.

'What the hell are you doing here?' you said at the doorway, in your underpants and a T-shirt with Frida Kahlo's face on it. 'Has Mom sent you to blackmail me?'

I was lucky maybe. Gabe was out. You didn't want me to enter but I pushed my way past you and checked the apartment out. Oh Em, that place, all decked-out with hashish paraphernalia and tie dye fabrics, the red and black flag above a stove riddled with dirty plates. Clichés of rebellion from my own wasted youth. You had some kind of rash on one of your ears, which had also been recently pierced four times. You were sniffing a lot, eyes red and streaming, like your allergies were back and bad. The place was dusty, cats too, the stink of them.

'Now, just give me one minute and hear me out.' I said and shut the door behind me. 'I'm only going to say this once, but a thing I've found from my own experience of horrible failure is that people like Gabe talk a lot about equality and the poor, but in my experience the people who shout the loudest about these things are very often angry, bitter people, who deep down feel they've failed and they want others to fail too.'

You yelled, 'that's so offensive. Get out Pops, get out!' And you held the door handle.

'Look,' I said, 'you can throw me out of your life and I'm sure Gabe would like that too, but face facts Em, you have an IQ of 173. You are in the hundredth percentile.

You're concerned about inequality and that's nice, but you are not equal to people like Gabe and never have been.'

You asked me again to leave, but you didn't shout. You were sniffing badly, I handed you some kitchen roll from my pocket, and you took it.

'Please let me finish,' I said. 'Does Gabe want you to be the best you can possibly be, studying at the highest level at the most accomplished universities in the world, or does he say this would mean you are quote-unquote privileged? What does he say about privileged people – that they oppress everyone else?'

You nodded and blew your nose. I couldn't tell if it was your allergies or if you were close to tears.

'So, this talent you were born with,' I said, 'that's caused you so much trouble, all the bullying you went through and let's be fair, it's caused problems for me and your mother too, this super-brain you can't turn off. Does your friend Gabe say that intelligence is a social construct, that there's no such thing as qualifications, it's all just invented to create hierarchies of inequality?'

'He's just trying to help me, Pops,' you sniffed.

'Does he say he's re-educating you?' I asked, and you nodded.

'Look,' I said. 'Please believe me Em. I've lived long enough to see three generations of people like Gabe. My mother was just like him. It's like they live through their resentment, it fuels them, and their enemies are always successful people, talented people, super intelligent people that they have to take down.'

You fell silent, Em. I sensed I'd only have one crack at this.

'Some people live to protest,' I said, 'they would be lost

if their enemies vanished. I'm serious. These people scapegoat others, it's just envy and self-hatred but they disguise it as virtue. They call their lost-ness oppression. If they're not attractive enough, if they're addicted to booze, it's the fault of the patriarchy. They're not tall enough or smart enough and they failed their exams, so the system is broken and corrupt they shout. No-one will give them a job, they can't find a sexual partner, so they scream that the whole world has to be overthrown. My mom was just like this!'

You kept looking at the door, as if you feared Gabe might come back at any minute. You wiped your eyes and coughed.

'Ask yourself, Em,' I said, 'whether Gabe wants to drag everyone down to his level, or whether he wants to raise everyone up to yours. You can run off and join the revolution and plant vegetables and throw Molotov cocktails,' I said, 'but is that the best use of your unique talents, when you could be an inventor, a creator, a scientific trailblazer?'

You sighed and I heard the old wheeze in your lungs.

'But he loves me,' you said, on the edge of tears.

'OK,' I said, weighing it up, not sure if I should try to hold you, fighting the urge.

'He really does.'

'But does he?' I said, 'is he even taking care of you. Look at your allergies, Em. Are you taking your steroids and anti-histamines, this place is filthy, and you're so allergic to dust and cat hair!'

'Gabe doesn't believe in western drugs,' you said and coughed.

It was all becoming so obvious, the man had been

gaslighting you. 'Does he love you for your genius' I asked, 'or does he love that he can mold you into being just like he is?'

'Pops!'

'And I love you,' I said. 'And I've loved you since I held your new-born body in my one hand, and you looked like a cross between a shaved rat and pink old lady, all wrinkled and allergic to the whole world.'

We stood, staring into each other's reddening eyes. You looked so scared that Gabe might return. I fought the urge to grab a bag of your things and force you out of there.

'It must be a real temptation to walk away from all that talent you have,' I said, 'but you have this obligation to yourself.'

I saw your lip tremble, and I leaned in and held you.

You resisted only for a second then your arms fell limp. You sniffed, Em, as I squeezed you tight and kissed your forehead. We were both sniffing and crying. 'Oh Pops, why do we always get like this?' you said, then we were laughing, and your eyes so red and puffy, you said, 'do you have any more toilet paper? and I fished around in my pockets and pulled out more, and that made you laugh even more. 'Why are you the only man in the world who carries toilet paper in your pockets all the time?' you said. And we laughed together.

'Do you have any antihistamines?' I said, and you shook your head. I had some in my coat pocket, Loratadine and I gave the pack to you.

'Oh Pops,' you said and you hugged me tight.

Somehow, I separated from you, and fought the impulse to stay and confront Gabe. I knew, Em, that you had to make this choice for yourself. If I forced it on you,

you'd rebel, and reject me and your mother completely.

So hard to walk out, leaving you there. I made it out of the main door and onto the street, trembling.

There's this parallel universe, in which I never came to your door that day, and you are now planting organic vegetables in an anarchist collective in Chiapas with your first baby strapped to your back in a papoose. This alternative world where I'm a grandfather, and your children and children's children go on and on.

But instead, I threw you into that terrible depression.

Oh, Em. What I'm going to do. Can I live past the 1st?

Talk to me again, please, Em. Help me.

10 days

Em.

My hand is oozing, need to change the bandages.

Finding it hard to sit still so I vacuumed up the kitchen, cleared most of the filter equipment away. Made a start on the shed. So many nitrate crystals and all the aluminium dust. Had a coughing fit. Knocked over a jar of flashpowder onto the floor. It didn't explode, so I started sweeping it up.

'Why?' your voice whispered, so I set down the brush. 'You're right, Em. What's the point of sweeping up like a housewife?' I called out to you. 'But, I have to do something Em, I can't just sit here and rot, can I?'

'Why?' your voice whispered again.

'Why? Why not fucking rot? I said back, 'That's not very nice is it! Why do you keep tormenting me, Em? Why do you vanish for days, then pop-up with questions and leave me confused. If you're a spirit, then just manifest, OK. Like Jesus! Or get out of my head and leave me alone, OK!'

But now you've gone again and I regret it.

Did my crazy mother hear voices too but just never told me?

Sunlight on the lintel, creeping in with the morning bugs. You're right, why should I sweep them away? The tiny ants, blow flies, cockroaches. Why not let them crawl over the toes of the funny man. Feast on flakes of my flesh. Spare their tiny lives the broom. Pray they stay away from my spiders.

Spiders never ask why they spin their webs.

But damn that blowfly. It's circling, banging its head against the window. Stupid thing, round and fucking round. Can you hear it? No. Bastard, there it is again. Bzzzzz. All the windows and doors are open, so why does it have to keep banging itself against the glass?

Killed it, smooshed against the fridge. But feeling sick now, Em.

I'm sorry I got angry and told you to leave. Please, help a tired man work out what to do.

The state I'm in. For years that was my worst fear, Em, I watched over you so anxiously throughout your teens, looking for signs of melancholy in you, dreading that I might have passed the curse onto you. There were your weird clothes and piercings and nerdy obsessions, but you made it all the way to the age of twenty-one with no sign of the darkness, and then one day I got that phone call from your mother. You'd drifted back to Boston after you'd split with Gabe. You'd let things slide and missed your second

PhD deadline. You were planning on working in cafés till you figured out your next steps.

'Em's in a bad way,' your mother said down the phone.

'What do you mean? Flu or what?'

'Her roommates called me,' she said, 'Em, hasn't been out of her bedroom in three weeks, they said. She's not eating, and she doesn't want to speak to anyone.'

My chest hollowed out.

It had happened. Maybe, I shouldn't have messed with you and Gabe. But something told me this was worse. I'd never sat you down to fully explain it, Em. I didn't want to scare you, so I never warned you of this demon my mother passed onto me, our family curse of clinical depression. I should have, when you were younger, Em. Superstitious, I know, but I thought I could protect you by saying nothing and hoping for the best.

'Right, I'll fly over and bring Em back home,' I said to your mom, down the phone.

'I've tried already,' she said, 'she wouldn't budge, wouldn't even speak to me, she's just staring at the walls, she says her entire degree was pointless, says she doesn't want to get a job or study again, ever.' Your mother in tears, 'we have to get her to a doctor.'

'No, no, please, can I go and see her first, before you involve a shrink,' I said. 'Please, Sara, let's not medicalize this just yet. Maybe I can help her.'

'You?' your mother shouted, her voice, glitching down the phone line. 'How could you help Em? She must have got this from you!'

She was right. Two decades before when I dated and married your mother, I hadn't warned her about my history of depression either. In fact, I hid it from her, and by then I'd been given a few diagnoses. Bi-polar didn't fit, because there wasn't much mania. Seasonal affective disorder didn't fit because I was OK for years straight. The doctors thought it might a personality disorder but settled for Major Depressive Disorder. Maternal deprivation was a probable cause but also 40% of the risk was genetic, they said. Increased suicide risk also got passed down the family chain.

Then there was your IQ, Em. Your own studies proved it – in kids with IQs over 130, almost 60% developed a depressive disorder in adult life. Like your book of Ecclesiastes said: 'For in much wisdom there is much grief… and he that increaseth knowledge increaseth sorrow.'

I kept my darkness secret from your mother before our marriage because I hoped to hell it was all behind me. Bet my future on it.

'Why the fuck did you cover that up? And here you are sneaking anti-depressants behind my back,' your mother yelled at me when she first found out. You would have been about four years old then, Em, in our house at Redwood. Another fight in another Swedish style kitchen.

I tried to tell her that I hadn't hidden anything deliberately, that I'd hoped commitment to raising a family would cure me. Yes, corny as it sounded, that love would save me, Em.

'Thanks a God damn bunch, if you'd told me you suffered from this back when we were dating, I'd never have married you. This is all your fault!'

'So, you'd rather we'd never had a kid, is that what you're actually saying?'

'Yes,' she yelled, 'because now you've probably passed it on to Em through your fucking DNA! Shame on you, you stupid, lying, selfish coward! If Em gets this too, I swear I'll kill you!'

But how I wore her down over the decades. Looking back, your mother had a certain grace in accepting that you and I were alike in so many ways, Em. Our high foreheads, our short sightedness, our tendency towards over-analysing. 'You two are like peas in a pods. She won't listen to me. Maybe you'll understand Em's depression better than I do,' she said on that day. 'Please try to convince her to come home.' That was generous of her, or maybe she'd run out of options and that's why she gave consent for me to fly to Boston to try to bring you back.

I dropped everything at college, got the first flight I could. I brought my own meds to give to you. Beta-blockers, Prozac, Valium just in case.

I found you, as your mom had warned, immobilized, speechless in your shared apartment in Fort Hill, Em. Your roommates, Lena and Kim, cowering and guilty faced in the kitchen, told me they'd tried to help but you'd stopped eating or sleeping. I found you sitting on the edge of a bare double mattress on your stripped floorboards, no bed frame, the carpet rolled up and stuck in the corner. You were wearing only a T-shirt and underpants, bare footed, your face lowered like a penitent nun, Em. And so slow in your motions, as if you'd disconnected from the natural flow of days, and were regressing through time, trapped in all those why-why-whys you asked as a child.

Oh Em, you sat staring at the upturned hands that lay in your lap, as if you were asking how can these ten sticks of bone and flesh be my fingers, how can they be me? A look of fascinated horror in your eyes. You didn't even say 'Hi Pops.'

'Em, it's me, I'm here,' I said, 'I know how you're feeling. I'm sorry you and Gabe split up,' but I couldn't get eye contact from you. You'd fallen into that place I feared.

You stared beyond me to the torn wallpaper. It was as if you'd started redecorating a few weeks back but had given up halfway through. Your eyes fixated on the three layers of ripped away wallpapers, three eras, the 1970s, 1950s, 1900s showing through. Torn pieces lay on the floor like autumn leaves, and the floorboards had been excavated too. You'd rolled back the underfelt and found things underneath, old pieces of linoleum, newspapers from the 50s, varnished Victorian pine. This excavation had also been left unfinished, as if the question – why – had erupted half-way through and you'd given up.

'Oh Em, you're over-tired,' I said, 'you worked far too hard at college, and I know it must have been hard splitting up with Gabe. Maybe you're just burned out.'

You turned to me in that way I knew from my own depressions, as if surfacing from deep water, as if every exertion cost an impossible amount of energy.

'Pops?' you said. Like a question.

I sat beside you on your bare mattress and tentatively hugged you, kissed your head. Your mother hadn't warned me about your brutal haircut, almost shaved to the skull, you looked like a Buddhist monk or military recruit, there was a scab of crusted blood behind your ear where your scissors had cut too deeply. I held you tight, but could feel how distant you were. No will left in your muscles. A bag of bones. 'It's OK Em, I know, I've been here too, you're going to pull through,' I told you.

Then I was crying. 'Come back Em,' I said, 'you're so far away. Please come back.' I knew those cold deserts you were walking through, wastelands of the past, all so lifeless and beautiful. You feel like the last person on earth. I told you this.

You were weak from not eating. I went and got you a cup of water, dissolved a multi-vitamin in it and made you drink it. I asked you a few simple questions: 'When did you start feeling like this?' 'Have you been sleeping a lot more or less?' 'Do you know what the date is?' 'When was the last time you went outside? 'But I got almost nothing from you. Your hand was limp and cold in mine.

Oh Em, I know how it is. Normal people demanding a depressed person be sociable only pushes us deeper into solitude. These ultimatums they make, that you respond. They don't understand that depression separates everything, the you from the me, the word from its meaning, the desire from the body. Everything free-falls into pointlessness. You had that same blood-drained blankness in your face that I knew so well. Barely there at all, you were hiding in a tiny room a million miles away and this inert body that I held so tightly had been left behind and would not respond to my demands that it feel emotion.

'Em,' I said, clearing my throat. 'I'm just going to sit here with you if that's OK? No pressure. OK? I'm not going anywhere. I know how you feel and I'm sorry, I should have warned you about our family depressions.'

I thought I'd place no demands upon you, not judge, not urge you to get better, just join you in the blankness.

I got down on my knees beside you, but couldn't stop the apologies flooding out.

Em, you looked at me then, as if you'd had to walk a mile to see my face. As if remembering that you once found me in tears at the age of ten. You put your finger to your lips to silence me. To tell me there was no need, that please, having to hear my words of worry over you would cost you far too much energy.

So, we sat together and stared in silence at your torn wallpaper. A smell of soot and dust in the room. You'd been burning things in this Victorian fireplace you'd excavated from behind the plaster wall. I saw then that your knuckles were grazed, from all this scraping and sanding, from this demonic desire that had overcome you to search beneath surfaces. I pictured you stripping the wallpaper, asking why, why, why, layer after layer, hoping to get to the truth, but frustrated at finding only more wallpaper, then the plasterboard from a hundred years ago, blank and gray.

The unnatural whiteness of your face, I worked out, was from the plaster dust. It made your mouth glow blood red in contrast; it made the whites of your eyes seem yellow.

All that day, I sat with you. Not a word. Your roommates were sweet and let me sleep on the sofa. At night, I heard your feet pacing on the bare boards, heard you sighing.

For two whole days we sat in silence, but I was aware that your mind was racing behind your half-closed eyes. I know from my own depressions that like a scientist, you go over and over and over one single question. Why is there suffering? Why are we all so alone? You fool yourself into thinking that if you can just have zero distractions, zero people around you, zero stimulus, then you can work out this puzzle.

I whispered to you, 'You know, Em, life's not like a math equation. We can't wait around till we solve it, we just have to get on with living without any answer. Even though we don't know what we're doing or where we're going. We just have to put one foot forward, then the next one and the next.'

'Why?' you whispered, and I realized, what I'd told you was absurd. Why start a voyage without knowing where you're going – or why? I was describing my own aimlessness, not offering you a solution.

'That's just the way it is,' I said. 'It's all we have to work with.'

'Why?' you whispered. Throughout your childhood your whys had fueled your intellect, but now they'd caught up with you, cornered you.

We fell into our silence again, watching the shadows on the wall fall as the sun climbed.

And there in your window was the astrological telescope I'd gifted you at age eleven, sitting on its tripod, but turned away from the sky, facing the stripped-down wall, a bath towel thrown over its lens. Beside it, a huge pile of your unwashed clothes lying in the corner, as if there was a body hiding beneath.

Oh Em, I felt your hand get warmer in mine and when I asked why you weren't using your telescope anymore, you drifted slowly back to me.

'How old is life?' you asked, without turning to me. Talking about the planets had always been our coded way.

I tried to think fast. 'Four billion years, is that right, three?'

'Earth is 4.54 billion years old and eukaryotic life

began around 3.4 billion ago,' you said, your face awakening. 'How long was it till cells formed membranes, cells that could multiply and reproduce through sexual exchange?'

'I have no idea Em, you tell me,' I thought it good to keep you talking, to let you go anywhere you wanted, to not try to rope you back into anxious questions of your mental health as your mother and all the others would have done.

'2.7 billion years,' you said, 'then after the Permian mass extinction, it took eighteen million years for the first hominid to appear. Homo Sapiens arrived only 300,000 years ago. That's us. Not much time.'

We needed to get you to a therapist, but I knew better than to interrupt and say as much, so I humored you, tried to enter into it.

'We've not been on earth for long,' I said. 'So, why's that a problem?'

You turned, as if you were ancient and had remembered that I was that even older man who you'd once played the why game with.

'How long have we got until the sun expands and destroys earth?' you asked.

Now I was getting closer. And I sensed your Big Why lay beneath it all. I played your game, I gave you a number, any number, 'a hundred billion years,' I said.

'No,' you replied, 'We haven't got as long as all that.'

'Why?' I asked.

You sat a bit more upright. 'The sun's luminosity increases approximately 1% every 110 million years,' you said. 'In 1.1 billion years from now, the sun will shine 10% brighter, as it begins to grow into a red giant. Our oceans will evaporate, and all moisture will be stripped from our atmosphere. Everything we have ever known, trees, blue sky, water, birds, mammals, fish, all these things will die out, every cell, every microbe. In 2.3 billion years, our planet will be a barren toxic desert, just like Venus. We are already more than half way there. Past middle age.'

'Is that why you tore your wallpaper off the walls, Em?' I asked, trying to bring you back into the now.

'In 3.1 billion years time,' you said, 'the expanding Sun will consume the planets Mercury, Venus and Earth. Every archaeological trace of our species and every other species ever having existed will be consumed by fire. No eyes of any species will be able to look upon what happened to us. No tongue will talk of our history and all memory will die. It'll be like we never existed.'

Your voice was getting faster, Em, I sensed you speeding towards the gravitational pull of those black holes you'd always feared. I was locked in with you, Em, in your time machine hurtling through trillions of years as we both stared at your torn wallpaper, and I held your clammy hand.

And you said, 'Andromeda, Cassiopeia, Lacerta, Cygnus, Aquarius, think about the constellations. The names that mankind gave them, will vanish with man. The stars will go on unnamed for billions of years more, and then they too will go through their stages, to red giant to white dwarf, to supernova, into dusty nebulae, to black dwarf and black hole. Then it begins. Even if through some miracle our descendants create an intergalactic civilization and discover other planets to colonize, they will be racing against the dying of all remaining stars and the universe will keep expanding, every dying star getting further from every other. A trillion years from now all the stars will go out and so there will be no possibility of any life being sustained. In a quadrillion years all the dead planetary bodies will be sucked into black holes or cast out as cold frozen wanderers in the emptying universe. Eventually, even the black holes will evaporate and all matter will change into photons and leptons, subatomic particles, and no new atoms will be able to form because all atomic nuclei will have decayed out of existence. The universe will reach absolute zero kelvin. Frozen. No motion will be possible. Only endless emptiness, dark, unchanging for eternity.'

And I remembered something you'd taught me when you were a kid. 'The Heat Death of the Universe.' I said it out loud, and you nodded, almost smiled.

'And what's the duration that organic life was able to exist in all of this?'

I shrugged, 'a millionth?'

'No, you said, not a millionth of a per cent, or a billionth or trillionth, not a quadrillionth of a per cent. But eighty-three decimal points below zero.' And you rose from your bed, and got a pencil and drew on the bare plaster. Zero after zero. Eighty-three zeros after the dot and then this solitary number one.

'That's how minuscule all of animal existence will have been,' you said, and I saw then that the wall plaster was actually covered in hundreds of complex equations, in the faintest pencil marks.

'Wow,' I said. I got the picture. You had life choices to make, which PhD to commit to, which job to take, which city to live in, you'd not yet really decided if you were straight or gay or bi or if relationships would even work for you, but all these choices had come to seem meaningless against the horrific fate of the universe. I knew that we depressed people tend to latch onto images like this.

Your depression was deeper than those I'd known, and it scared me. I couldn't contest your thesis. I know how my own mother had tried again and again to evade her depressions. She'd always say, 'OK, so what if life is pointless, big deal, who cares? Let's have some fun.' Her fake-happy-hippie and hashish strategy wasn't going to work for you, as it hadn't for me.

I sat silently with you hour after hour, staring at your scrawled equations. I took your plates of uneaten food away, got you glasses of water and I sat in the bathroom to give you space.

I got you to swallow one of my Prozac pills. Time passed. I let it.

I had to stay, hovering around you but not intruding, so you'd know I wasn't giving up. But it was excruciating, to have you so close, and to see your eyes so distant, to be unable to help. To touch your hand and know I might even be causing you pain by being there. The depressed person wants only to be left alone to work out their puzzle, but they will never find the answer, they will only get more and more confused and distant from everyone else.

And the guilt, that this was all my fault.

Four days of near total silence, I cancelled all other plans, missed my return flight, called your mother every night, buying more time, hoping, but still I was failing you.

The way you lay there, energy drained. You once said, that when you approach a black hole, space-time changes. At the event horizon before you get sucked inside, the gravity is so great that all time stops. Thousands of years pass by on earth as one person on the event horizon experiences a second.

I helped you wash yourself and got you to eat some chicken soup. Your mother called more often and kept threatening to fly over once more; she wanted to involve a hospital. It took all the strength I possessed to convince her to give you another few days, another few.

I sat watching you, as you sat on the edge of your bed, or lying flat on your back, only breathing, all will drained from you. Horrible, to know that everything I suggested to help – let's go for a walk, or watch some TV, or how would you like to bake some cookies with me – would all end in defeat and only place a greater burden on you. I recalled this from my own depressions. The phrase 'please, just leave me alone,' spirals in the head, unsaid. You come to hate the people who're trying to save you from yourself. 'Leave me alone!' You said it to me twice, in those days.

I got you to keep taking the Prozac with the water I brought to your mouth. Time, water, patience, again, again, no pressure, more pills, water, rest, patience, just being there.

On the sixth day you seemed to wake from your frozen state, you turned to me and out of the blue you said: 'Maybe I'll never have kids.'

I thought it best to keep you talking, so I asked you one of your whys. Why not have kids? Surely most people loved having families. So why not?

You spoke as if a torrent had been circling inside you for weeks and had only now found a way out. It wasn't like you were talking to me, more like you were letting me share in the chaos.

'There's no point continuing our species. We are accidental freaks of nature,' you said. 'There's no reason why we developed this huge forebrain that forces us to ask why-why-why. It only gives us this terrible self-awareness that we are all doomed to die. No other species asks *why am I here* and goes insane because it can't answer the question. No other animal suffers like this.

These words coming from my own child.

You said: 'And we award status to those who can convince us that our lives have some great transcendent purpose, the gurus, the political leaders, the poets and physicists, Shakespeare, Christ, Plato, Einstein. And they tell us to live for science, for wealth, or justice, for your family or your nation or to save the planet, so you can be remembered. But these are all just immortality myths – progress, heaven, peace – just fantasies so we can keep on pretending that were eating, working, shitting, shopping and screwing for a greater purpose.

'And all these groups of people fighting over whose immortality story is the true one, the only one, so we have religious wars, national wars, culture wars. All this blood spilled, just to keep us living the fantasy, to stop us being paralyzed by awareness of our futility as a species, as our aimless planet runs out of time.'

My instinct was to try to calm you, to get you to take another Beta-blocker, but some part of me had to know what conclusion you'd reached.

'Is this connected to your studies?' I asked.

You sighed, nodded, 'TESS and Kepler found nothing, they've been hunting for bio signatures for decades and they haven't found a single trace of credible carbon-based life out there in over forty million searches in ten thousand galaxies. All the scientists I worked with confirmed it. There's no life out there. We're just this accidental species that will live for a while by devouring other species on a thin layer of dirt, on a rocky planet on the edge of an entirely dead and indifferent universe.'

It seemed like an answer, and yet, I knew that it wasn't actually those discoveries that had made you depressed, but rather that the depressed mind seeks out these vast ethereal abstractions as vessels for the way it feels, and then loses itself within them.

I squeezed your hand. 'But hey, we're in this together, huh,' I said, 'maybe it's not much but we can make the most of that, right?'

And I told you to maybe just take pleasure in the time we had, in eating nice food, or wading in the sea, or holding hands. Why not just enjoy this short pointless life? At least we still have each other?

It made you angry, 'aimless people,' you said, 'clinging to each other because there's nothing else. It's pathetic.'

I wanted to tell you, Em, that I'd never found any answer. That you can't find it by staring at the stars. Like you can't learn how to swim by reading about it in a book, you just have to jump in, take the plunge and take part, enter the flow of everyone's energies, and let life grow through you. Find something you can share passionately with others and follow it, that's the only answer I'd ever found. Have a child, raise a child. Take Prozac.

You stared at me. Sighed, like you didn't have enough energy to overcome my stupidity. Then you climbed back into your musty bed.

The next day, I did your laundry. I tried to get you interested in a change of clothes. I put fresh socks on your feet. I tried to be energetic, but not too much. I led you to the shower, I'd bought you some of your favorite shampoo.

'Apple scented shampoo made in bio labs,' you said holding it in your hand, 'absurd.'

'I know, I know, I know,' I said, 'but let's get your pointless hair washed OK, so it can at least be pointlessly clean!'

With each attempt I sensed you fighting back against the gravity of the black hole.

I had to call the shrink your mom had contacted and cancel him. They would have medicated you, Em, institutionalized you. You would have been taken out of our care. I knew that the empty ache inside your chest could lead you to harm yourself, as I'd done in the past.

Maybe selfishly, I felt that only I could decode your depression and find a way out of it. That maybe I could redeem myself.

It was probably the sixth day of your antidepressants, and I'd got you to take a bath. You stood in the hall in your bath robe, your hair dripping, and you asked me.

'So what do you live for?'

'You're asking me?' I replied. 'I don't know, but I'm a heck of a lot happier that you're looking a smidge better today,' and I handed you a towel.

'You always dodge the question, Pops,' you said, 'because deep down, you're a total nihilist, who believes in absolutely nothing.'

'Well, I might have been, ten years ago, but not anymore,' I told you. 'I believe in something, and it happens to be standing right in front of me, dripping on the carpet.'

You rolled your eyes.

'Right, you couldn't find a reason to live, so you and mom had me as a substitute?' you said. 'Thanks a bunch, that's cheating, passing the buck onto the next generation.

People can't be the meaning of life for each other, that's just lazy and selfish and parasitic.'

'I believe in you, Em,' I repeated. 'That's enough for me.'

You sighed, 'well, it's not very fair, is it? Don't dump all your need onto me, OK. I can't be your meaning-in-life.'

I stood speechless, guilty as accused, Em.

'OK,' I said, 'so how about I make you a cup of meaningless hot chocolate?'

'Yeah, yeah, yeah, eat, work, shop, screw, shit, sleep,' you said. And I repeated it and did my silly dance again – eat, work, shop, screw, shit, sleep, eat, work, shop, shit…

'No, I'm serious,' you said, 'if you make me the meaning of your life then what the hell would you do if something bad happened to me?'

'Nothing is going to happen to you,' I'd said, 'I'll make sure of that.'

I must have just stood, watching you standing there wrapped in your towel.

'Jesus!' you said. 'Quit staring! Can't I get a moment's privacy, just leave me alone, for Christ sakes!'

And you pushed past and went back to your room, closed the door on me.

One thing was better, this new anger proved the anti-depressants had started working. You'd come back from outer space and were testing your footing on our disappointingly tiny planet.

I stayed with you for four more days and convinced you to take the entire course of pills. On the last two days, you cooked yourself an omelette and made it to the corner store for fresh milk. I remember I asked you, 'Do you wanna hear a pizza joke?'

You sighed and said, 'no, it's too cheesy.' Neither of us laughed. You sighed again and said, 'Pops, stop trying so hard, OK?'

You told me you'd be fine if I left you alone. 'Just go home Pops, OK, and tell Mom to stop worrying.'

I stayed with you, just to make sure, and the next day your anger exploded.

'Stop hugging me!' you yelled. 'Get off me, stop leaning over me like a vampire. What do you want? Just… just get away. I need some air!'

That was when I knew you were going to be make it through.

You pushed me out of your apartment. You pushed me pretty much out of your life for the better part of four months. I got it. I was the real black hole sucking the life from you and you were afraid of getting pulled back in again. Through weekly phone calls that annoyed you, I secretly asked you the questions my shrink had asked me, from the Hopelessness Scale, to make sure you weren't feeling suicidal. You flew home to your mother's place where she could watch over you in the months of your recovery, and I was relieved.

So, yes, that's one thing I maybe did right, after having done so much wrong.

Em,

So, here we are outside.

The soil, the weeds, the mold, the bush, can you smell it? Magnificent! Even that fucking cat next door. Nachos, here kitty kitty.

It pisses here, well so can I! Nobody around to see me

watering the rhododendron in my underpants. What does it matter if my piss kills it?

Wait, set down this bottle.

God, I'm drunk. Probably, shouldn't have staggered over to Sal's for another three litres. Ha ha. Damn fool.

But what a night for the stars, eh? Orion's Belt, Corona Borealis, the Pendulum Clock, Orion the hunter, the Firebird, what the hell is that one called? All those strange names you taught me, Em, when you were twelve, thirteen. Your star charts. Betelgeuse, Alphecca, Zeta Centauri, the old familiars. The clear cold nights, you wiping the lens of your telescope. Your star-gazing magazines that came through the post every month. Other kids your age were reading stolen fashion and porn magazines and there you were with your torch at night, secretly re-reading about the Eskimo Nebula, Andromeda, the Corona Borealis.

Memories, like breaths.

Sorry, have to stop drinking and crying.

No more singing sentimental songs. Not tonight. It's time to face the music, apologies for the pun. Yes. I have to decide if I'm going to kill myself on the 1st.

What are my options, really?

Car asphyxiation – no, I don't have a garage and I can't do it in the driveway or Mz Sanchez will see me sticking a hose-pipe through the truck window.

Drowning – no, all the reports say people always change their mind mid-drown and thrash about and die in agony and regret. Same with hanging.

No noose is good noose, eh? Hah!

Hey, did you hear about the suicide helpline?

They put me on hold and left me hanging!

And hey wait, why, why don't they have How to Commit Suicide books in libraries?

Because no-one would bring them back!

Haha! Sorry, sorry. But seriously, what's left?

Drug overdose – nope. What are you whispering, yes of course you're right, no good chance of success and high chance of accidental survival with terminal liver or brain damage. Yes, yes. No thanks.

Gun – no. What do you mean 'metal?' Speak more loudly Em. 'Heavy metal?'

Oh yes, I remember now that heavy metal fan in Idaho who tried to blow his brains out with a shotgun, but got the angle wrong and ended up just blowing his lower jaw and tongue clean off. Yup, poor bastard lived and had to eat through a straw they stuck in the hole where half his face used to be. How did you remember that?

Plus, you're right Em, yes, it'd be a bit hypocritical if I went and bought a gun since I've campaigned for gun control all my life.

What else? Jumping off the bridge – no, you're quite right, unless you land on your head, you can survive the impact but break your spine, and your leg bones can break off from your pelvis and get pushed through your inner organs. Like that kid last year. Yuk.

You're the scientist, I'll take your advice on that, Em.

Hey, did you hear the one about the guy who jumped off a tower – he wanted to make an impact on the world. Ha ha!

I know, I know. Mister pun-y isn't funny! Sorry, Em.

OK, so, it's back to our bombs then.

The best way would be to get a small rowing boat, go some way out into the fog, and then set them off. Yes, that way the tide will take my bones and guts out to sea so no old lady will find them washed-up on the beach when walking their doggie.

Yes or no? Just say the word. Should I toss a coin?

And what should I do with myself before the 1st? Can't sit still, but can't just wait around for ten days, staring at the window spiders bagging their fresh bug kills.

My mother would say, *don't be one of those losers who dies before they've even lived*. She's right, I should treat myself first. Yes, do something drastic. Have a shave, buy a suit. Spend a few hundred on a hotel and a hooker, yes, why not? It would be nice to have some company. Nice to hold a woman. Be held. But then again, what if you were still spying on me, Em!

OK, then hire a boat and end it all on the 1st of October or not?

My hand, Jesus. The more I try to ignore it, the more it burns. Do I really have the courage to kill myself in nine days' time anyway? My head is buzzing with it, why, why not, why, why not?

What do you want me to do, Em? Please give me an answer. Woah, God I'm drunk.

Editor's Note XI

I now have a sense of some of what Cartwright went through; the feeling of being cut off from others; of having lost one's life project; I felt something comparable after being fired from the publishing house, facing empty days and fear of legal action.

A sense of lostness overcomes Cartwright in the recordings after day fifteen. One of the recordings consists entirely of Cartwright reading the book of Ecclesiastes out loud to himself in his kitchen, naked but for his socks.

Another accidental recording shows Cartwright cradling a pipe bomb in his arms and cursing the kitchen walls before he realises that he has been accidentally recording himself. He also flies into an exasperated rage after he realises that he had forgotten to hit the record button on a previous long message to Emma and so it was lost.

The emotional states he goes through cannot be fully explained by Pöldinger's 'Three Stages of Suicide' or Jacobson's 'Psychological Stages in Premeditated Murder,' both of which include 'quiet acceptance' as the penultimate stage. According to these theories, behaviors in the final suicidal/homicidal stages involve:

- tunnel vision
- emotional flatness
- resignation
- relief
- the abuse of substances as facilitators
- dissociation
- planning
- and tidying.

An example of how this state presents itself is that an individual will focus on the practical object-based preparations for suicide, and this no longer distresses them; they accept the decision, experience relief and dopamine release, feel detached from their cares and former self, and engage in tasks such as arranging necessary tools, cleaning, laundry, packing, and writing instructions and goodbye letters in a calm and emotionally blank state. Some suicide survivors have even reported that in this state their bodies feel robotic, not their own, or 'as if led by another force'.

Cartwright does seem to go through only four of these states in the videos. In one recording, he does the dishes after a gap of five days; in another he changes the bandages on his hand with detached focus. However, he also enters an excited psychological state that I would hesitate to call 'talking to spirits' or 'shouting back at the devil'; sometimes he yells at the 'imagined' voice of his daughter in his head, or perhaps even at the forces of the 'biotech Big Tech conspiracy'. He also slaps his own head.

It is possible that he is experiencing 'depressive psychosis', amplified by alcohol poisoning and/or infection from the untreated wound.

For the record, I would like to note that in transcribing these lost days of Cartwright's, I also experienced a growing sense of being watched, although charges had not, as yet, been brought for having taken home material that was effectively owned by the publishing house; and I'd received no call from the police about these so called 'dangerous materials.'

Days ticked by with anxiety only growing. Then I received four strange phone calls in which withheld numbers rang but did not speak when I picked up; there was only a threatening silence. This occurred mostly late at night. When I asked the telephone company and police for help, they insisted that no such phone calls had taken place.

Witnessing Cartwright on the footage over the next days, one can see how fear, remorse and a sense of powerless led to his total breakdown, whether the voices oppressing him were imagined or real.

9 days

Em,

Why am I weeping? This crazy joy! What's just happened?

I got up from my bed, Em, pain shooting up the legs, staggered. The light behind the blinds was stinging my eyes. The damn force of it. Not letting go. Fuck the sun. I had to fasten the blinds tighter to block out all light. I reached out but my balance was off. I missed the pull chord and instead my hand gripped the fabric. I fell back, a crash and the blind tore at its top tumbling with me. Light ripping in, flooding me, blinding me, the pain in the back of my head and hand, screaming. I could see nothing. 'Light!' a voice, said so loud. No, it wasn't your voice Em, it seemed to be an old woman. I called out 'who is it?' But it didn't listen, only spoke over my questions. 'Light is sweet,' it said. 'Light exceeds darkness'. I swear the voice was coming from the sun itself. It said 'I am' and I was in panic. My eyes adjusted, my legs found my weight, my other hand pushed against the floor. All those pill packets lying there, all the empty wine bottles, how many dirty plates? The sudden smell of all that. The blind broken beneath me. And the white light, the sheer damn force of it and I was so small and shivering.

The light told me I needed more light. I must obey. I needed electric light to equal the sun. I plugged the lamp back in and turned the mains power back on. It doesn't matter anymore that I could be caught online. All the lights in my eyes. What does it want of me?

And the voice so loud, said: 'Time!' I swear it was coming from the sun and the light bulbs. Blinding light. 'Why?' I asked. The voice shouted: 'Why ask why? There is a time for everything…'

I got up, made it to the bathroom, vomited and splashed my face with cold water and slowly the voice became yours, Em, and you were talking in rhymes then, like you did as a child, and you said, 'there is a time to keep and a time to throw away, a time to tear and a time to mend.' I didn't understand but I thought maybe you meant I had to tidy up, so I dressed, I packed the last of the bombs in boxes, stored the containers, binned the spare wires and aluminium filings, and took out the trash. Hours of it. And your voice said, 'there is a time to love and a time to hate, a time for war and a time for peace.' But you wouldn't answer my question – when this is done should I kill myself or not?

And then, the pain in my hand, sweeping with the broom, I knocked your bible from the table, I must have been reading it when I was drunk last night. I opened it on the pages you'd marked, and looked at your tiny pencil underlinings, and I found these same damn words you were saying, right there, in Ecclesiastes – 'a time to kill and a time to heal, a time to tear down and time to build' I read it all, every part of it to try to understand.

Let me read it again, here:

> *Meaningless! Utterly meaningless! Everything is meaningless… I thought in my heart, come now, I will test you with pleasures to find out what is good. I tried cheering myself with wine and embracing folly, I undertook great projects, I built houses for myself and*

built vineyards… yet when I surveyed all that my hands had done and what I had toiled to achieve, everything was meaningless, a chasing after the wind; nothing was gained under the sun… It is the same for all… all is meaningless. In this meaningless life of mine I have seen both of these: the righteous perishing in their righteousness, and the wicked living long in their wickedness. It is the same for all. There is one common fate for the righteous and for the wicked; for the good, for the clean and the unclean. Do not be over righteous, neither be over wise – why should you destroy yourself?' 'Why should you die before your time?'

What are you trying to tell me, Em? Are you saying it's time to kill myself or a time to build? Build what? What's your plan for me?

It seems to say: no-one can comprehend what goes on under the sun. Despite all their efforts to search it out, no-one can discover its meaning. Even if the wise claim they know, they cannot comprehend it. It says we just have to walk blind, in ignorance and place our trust in God's plan.

I don't understand. You spent years searching for that Theory of Everything, Em. Did you find it in your laboratories before you died? Or did you give up on science and turn to God? How could you?

Was that why Toby gave me your bible?

And the stamp on the inside cover – Mission San Rafael Archangel. Did you take the bible from there? Steal it?

Why do you keep vanishing like you have more important things to do? It's like I'm out of range of your signal, Em. These fragments you torment me with.

And these words you underlined.

'In my futile life I have seen… a righteous man perishing in his righteousness, and a wicked man living long in his wickedness.'

Am I the wicked man?

The dust I kicked up from the sweeping is making shafts of light fall through the air. Patterns of chaotic sparkles. Pointless. Beautiful. A chasing after wind. Ecclesiastes. A time to throw away or to mend? Yes, I have to decide today whether I kill myself or not.

OK, I'll take what energy I have left and go to the Mission in San Rafael. This bible has to have some significance. Maybe I'll hear your voice better there? I could take a photo of you with me, maybe ask the priest, did you know my Em? Did she come here? Was she part of your congregation? Did she give you anything to share with me? What do these words that my daughter underlined mean? And this voice in my head. Tell the priest about it. Ask for his help? I don't know. I'm so lost now. I have to try something.

I promise I won't do anything stupid in the church, I'll talk to you without moving my mouth, so no-one sees. I won't freak the church folk out. Promise. If my mother could see me now, going to a church, she'd laugh at me.

Hi Em,

Bound my hand-up, sprayed it with Deep Freeze, put an ice pack on it and made it the twelve miles to the old missionary church. Those creaking old wood doors, hand carved. I walked inside, carrying your bible, feeling a fool, footsteps echoing on the old, patterned tiles. The aisles of crumbling wooden benches, all empty. It smelled of bleach, incense, mold.

Walked in deeper. I don't even know what the things are called, the nave, the architrave, the pulpit? Yes, I saw a pulpit up ahead, and stained-glass, red, green, gold. All ancient and amateur, images of the saintly figures hard to make out, a lot of their faces and bodies cracked. The face of a blue angel held in place with Scotch tape.

Why did your voice lead me here, Em? Did you want me to cause a confrontation, to force the dead deity to manifest itself?

My footsteps were too loud and not welcome, as if eyes were upon me, unseen church elders hiding behind the pillars, the angels in the rafters or the security cameras. Damned if I know.

Cold sweat ran down my arm. I stopped in the central aisle and looked round for a seat. Thinking, I have no place here. An atheist since childhood. Why did you come here, Em? Or did you just pick up that old bible in some stoop sale? Did I just knock it over by accident, with my stupid throbbing hand?

I felt embarrassed just hovering, had to sit. The pew creaked so loudly. This sudden need to say sorry to someone, sorry, my daughter took this bible from here. I'm just here to return it. Funny man.

But there was no one to see or hear me. Alone with echoes.

'What if God is the equation behind everything,' you said, one night when we were star gazing on Bolinas beach with your Celestron. You were maybe fifteen, your steam breath flying into the points of light. Always clearest on the nights of frost, you said. Blowing on your hands to keep them warm.

'Forget the old, bearded man in the clouds and all this 'He' bullshit. Maybe God's just this out-of-date name for the fine tuning of the universe Pops,' you said. 'Did you know that if gravity was 0.0002% stronger then all the suns in the universe would be so much more dense they'd burn out so quickly that all carbon-based life would have no chance of even beginning?' I shook my head, smiling at the way your learning lit you up from inside.

'And that if gravity was 0.0002 % weaker,' you said, 'then there wouldn't be enough force to hold atoms together. It's all so finely tuned Pops, that it even makes super-nerds like me wonder, I mean don't tell anyone I said this but, the entire universe seems to be designed with one goal in mind.'

I had to ask what.

'Well, put it this way,' you said. 'Maybe us humans are just a stage on the way. Maybe we'll make a machine, that'll go beyond us and become fully self-aware and it'll decode God and finally answer the big why.'

And your words, last year, screamed as the AI consumed your brain, 'I am… am…the…I am.'

I heard movement behind me in the church aisle and turned. A cleaner with a mop, Latina, maybe seventy years old. I made a nodding shhh sign with my finger, and mouthed, 'sorry, sorry,' trying to let her know I'd be quiet and not be staying for long. My usual clown show, and the cleaner's shrug seemed to say, 'you don't need any excuses to be here, I'm not the priest and you're weird, mister.'

What was I doing there, Em? I wanted to yell, 'hey God! Look at me, I've made bombs to murder a man and myself. I could bomb this meaningless church, stop me in my tracks, go on! Strike me down with thunderbolts and lightning, give me a God-damned reason to go on living in this meaningless shit show! Manifest, you infinitely impotent motherfucker!'

Or is this silence in this echoing abandoned church, proof that your commandments and your judgment and your forgiveness are all fabrications of our pathetic, lost little species of cowering apes. Yes, proof that I should kill myself. Isn't that the greatest of your so-called sins? Worse even than murder. Spitting in the eye of your meaningless creation.

My eye found a crucifix on the far wall, Em. The same white man, nailed to the cross, the same streaming blood painted so lovingly, the usual anatomical inaccuracies carved by devoted amateur hands. I struggled for a minute to try to remember what the crucifixion meant. Christ gave his life to save us all, I quoted to myself. Fine, but after having heard this so many times over the decades, it didn't make any sense. None. To save us all from what? And since when did the God of goodness demand human sacrifice, like the Aztecs or like Moloch with the blood sacrifice of children? God's blood magic in the sacrifice of the son, is that it? Christ the lamb to his father's slaughter.

I kept staring at the cross down the far end past those twenty rows of empty seats, trying to force a confrontation.

And God is not good, I thought. If God is the force behind all of nature then God is the jackal that tears the throat from the lamb, and the parasite that lays its eggs in the head of a wasp which then hatch into larvae that devour its brain. Did God design that, Em? Did God help in the evolution of your AI deity that burrowed into your brain and killed you? And hurricanes and pandemics and genocide. If all this is good and God's plan then why shouldn't I kill myself, Em?

A sound began quietly, either that or I hadn't noticed it before. A choir, singing in the space beyond the pulpit.

I don't understand why religious music moves me. It was you who put me onto Bach, Em. Nothing else really touches me. I even found myself humming along, not sure how I knew the words.

Salve, Regina, mater misericordiae
Vita, dulcedo et spes nostra, Salve.

Did you sit here Em, singing along? Did you weep? That damn choral music swelling up inside my empty chest. The longing in it for a world beyond this one. The greatest lie of all. But the glimpses of it in those choral voices singing as one, the interweaving shapes, as if there were a sacred geometry behind everything.

Delusional. And how wretched this all is, that men invent intricate lies about an afterlife because they live in such fear of death – and worse still of life. And all this pain has just been a test before we win our prize of this made-up story called Heaven. What a scam. We talked of these things before, Em.

And so, they invent this beautiful music and these revered churches, they build and care for them over generations, but it's all just deluded yearning. Is that why Bach moves me? His failure? And what is Christianity really, disgust and distrust of life turned into an escapist fantasy of another life?

And I believe in nothing, just like you worked out

about me, long ago Em.

I felt like an imposter, listening to the choir that was really just a recording coming through the speakers. For the damned tourists, like me.

But still, I was moved by the psalm, Em. And I let go of the foolishness and shame, because really, I have nothing left to lose now. I did something that I've not done since childhood. I got off the church bench and clasped my hands together and got on my knees on the tiles, and closed my eyes. I thought enough of my stupid whys so why not! And I whispered to you to not worry about me and my kneecaps and since God is dead, then I have nothing to fear by praying to nothing. There's no one left to mock me for being childish, superstitious. Why the hell not pray then? Really, no pun intended. To hell with my mother and her smug atheist pals. So, I stayed on my knees and started, doing my best to pray.

'Em, are you with me' I whispered, 'Could you manifest for me? Go on, please.'

Nothing, so I started on, 'our father…'

But should my praying hands point upwards, or the fingers be intermeshed, and tightly or loosely? The theatricality of it all. I made it through, 'Our father who art in heaven, hallowed be thy name, thy kingdom come…' then stopped. The father, the big daddy, the king, such nonsense. So, I began again with a revision, 'Great force living within all things, Creator of Em's finely-tuned universe, un-known be thy name, thy will be done on Earth as it is in Heaven.'

As for 'Heaven' it could just mean the stars and I was open to having my lifelong nihilism disproved by a sudden appearance of the almighty or of you, Em. In a flash of light, a lightning bolt, a touch on the shoulder, a heart attack.

'Forgive us our debts as we forgive our debtors and lead us not into temptation.'

I'd intended to segue from the amen into my own improvised prayer. But I had nothing to say, beyond, give me a fucking reason not to commit suicide in nine days or even today. Yes, today, why wait?

My hands felt ludicrous and sweaty, so I opened them up, keeping the fingertips still touching as much as I could with the bandages and the ache in my hand which was becoming unbearable, making a kind of ribcage shape, and it felt calming to rest my nose within this warm hollow.

The sounds of my breathing got louder and became slow and deep, echoing round the shell of fingers. The sound seemed to grow huge, filling my head. Maybe I was just exhausted, or the pain, I don't know. It scared me and I had this weird sense of being inside the womb and hearing my mother's breath all around me. It didn't seem to be mine. Eyes closed, this huge sound of breath surrounded my head and became louder, in out, in out, and how animal it sounded, and I thought, the lungs do what they do without our permission or control. We can't stop them by an act of will. I thought of these bags of tissue. In out, in out, all by themselves, in out, full empty, full empty, revolting, the will within all flesh. This breath getting louder and louder, and it was no longer coming from me, it was the sound of every human animal, in out, in out, going back seven hundred thousand years. I was hearing what Cro-Magnon man would have heard if he cupped his hands round his nose. I was there, in the body of that first human, for seconds. I asked you Em, what does this mean? But you didn't answer. I was hypnotized and couldn't move as the breath got louder.

My fingers became the pillars of a vast cathedral, and the sound of the breath filled every space, every pew and came from every stained-glass window, the breath was in my ears and coming towards me from the stones. Louder, louder. I started weeping, Em, and then I seemed to be walking through this vast cathedral, and the walls echoed with the sound of this deep breath that shook the floor, like an earthquake, breathing in and out, and I realized the breathing was coming from the ceiling, and I looked up, and the roof was gone, instead it was the night sky and the stars, never seen so bright, the universe rotating slowly.

Then something vast opened up above and I pictured the heart beating, and it was not a heart within a chest, but it was out within the vacuum of space, like a planet, but red and wet with tiny fair hairs upon it, stretching out towards the sun, and the hair moving with every beat of the heart, in, out, in, out, and the sound was also the pulsing of the universe. The hairs of the heart reaching out to the sun, in, out, in, out, in. Maybe I was hyperventilating, over-oxygenating, I don't know. But then the orbit of our earth, from summer to winter, equinox to equinox – it also was a breath, in and out, and day and night – a breath, in and out, the zero and the one – a breath in and out. The orbit of our sun round the galaxy – a breath, in-out. The circling of the electron round the atom, in-out. The breathing of the plants, CO2 in the day and oxygen at night, a breath, in, out. The dead plants feed the plants of next year. A breath, in, out, in out. Sleep-wake-sleep. A man lives, breathe in, he dies, breathe out, his child lives, breathe in, she dies, breathe out, her child lives, breathe in, on and on it goes, seven thousand generations of humans, a series of breaths in a line, in-out, in-out.

My hands cupping my nose and mouth, and a voice, not yours, Em, but like yours seemed to say, it's all OK, you are part of all breath, breathe, you're not your past, you are not your pain, you're nothing that anyone has done to you before, you're not your resentment or your fear or your name, you're not the history of sorrows you've built around yourself, and the lists of names of your aggressors, all of this can be let go, all of it. Just breathe and let go of who you have been and who you wanted to be, and who you wanted to hurt, just let go and breathe and breathe for as long as this breath lasts and you are nothing more, just breath and this is all there is. Nothing but this, let all else go, just breathe.

And I don't know Em, was this your message, were you saying *don't kill yourself Pops* or saying *let go of life, and go without fear?*

In that old echoing church, a cold shiver ran through my skin. If all is just breath, then everything I've been falls away. So much of my life, the resentment, the guilt, the craving for love, if I let all of that go I'm terrified there'll be nothing left at all.

'What d'you mean?' I asked. 'What do you want me to do?'

The breath sound stopped, and I heard a cough and jolted out of it as if someone had flicked a switch. I found myself on my knees, head slumped forward onto the back of the next pew. The old cleaning woman with her mop was at the end of my row, staring at me. Had I dozed off, or been talking out loud? I was drenched with sweat. I got up and stumbled out, with many apologies, in my awful half-Spanish. My hand was bleeding through the bandages and I dropped your bible and left it where it fell, Em. I got up, and had leg cramp from all the kneeling and I staggered out of the church, into the blinding light, and I felt foolish, confused. Had it been a daydream, or am I losing my mind?

I got the truck moving, skidded down the 101.

Driving back towards the bridge, I suddenly remembered how you got well again after your terrible depression, Em. Back when you were twenty-two in your lost year, with your Prozac and CBT sessions, when you moved back to your mom's place and I came to visit twice a week. I wanted to visit more but I didn't want to make you feel under pressure.

And you worked out that, yes, Gabe had led you astray, and that, yes, you had lost faith in pure physics, but you knew that could you change direction.

The networks of neurons in the human brain, you said, looked surprisingly like the network of galaxies in the universe. Maybe they were deeply connected, you said, in ways the world didn't yet understand. You showed me overlays of star maps and brain scans, beautiful. Your passion morphed into an obsession with AI.

I tried to encourage you, I enthused about your change of PhD topic, I helped you fill in your applications and to write your proposals. Then after six months on Prozac and therapy you came to me and said, 'I think I'm back on the path now, thanks so much Pops.' You hugged me, told me how this tech guru you'd found on a TED talk had inspired you, given you this amazing vision of the future, and there was hope, really, for all of us. This tech guru had thousands of students doing this cutting-edge research fusing AI with biotech to find cures for chronic pain, for cancer, yes, and even for depression.

You were crying as you told me this, weeping like a convert, but you were happy, so happy, Em. 'Maybe he could even cure you too, Pops,' you said.

You told me this tech guru and his corporation would pay for your PhD. I said, 'that's amazing, do it. Absolutely, go for it!' Because I didn't want you to ever fall back once more into that hopeless darkness that had ruined my own life. 'Do it, Em!' I said. 'I'm behind you a thousand per cent.'

The guru was called Neumann, and his company, Biosys.

So, you see Emma, it was ultimately me who killed you.

It hit me as I was staring at the oncoming cars. A big yellow school bus was approaching and suddenly I thought of all those school kids who called you *nerd* and *wheezer* and *four-eyes* and *geek*, who tripped you up and pulled your hair and I heard your voice singing that old song again, loud in my ears.

Will you go lassie go, and we'll all go together.

Tears, and I couldn't see, and your voice gripped my bad hand and pushed it down on the steering wheel, forcing me out of my lane and into the path of the bus.

It was me that killed you, wasn't it?

'Go together,' your voice said and a shock ran through my arm and leg and made me push the accelerator. I couldn't stop it. I tried to steer away but my foot and hand locked tight, speeding into the bus, ten feet away, five. Faster.

'Go together,' you whispered.

The bus smashed my side mirror, metal screaming, sparks flying. I skidded to a halt.

I heard children screaming and saw the bus had bashed into the safety barriers, but not broken through, not gone over the edge, not even close.

I should have got out and gone to them, to make sure they were alright, but I panicked, rammed the truck into gear, spun round and fled. The bus was fine, I told myself, the kids were scared that was all. No-one hurt. Miles away, I parked behind trees, found my Beta-blockers, took three, sat there staring back at the road. Panting. My heart pounding in my ears. I tried taking a deep breath to calm myself, but my breaths were racing and jagged. I came so fucking close. My vision got darker and narrower and looked kaleidoscopic, I felt sharp pain in my chest and down my right arm. Oh God, why isn't it stopping? Why can't I breathe, what's going on? I couldn't move, I felt like I was choking, tingling legs and numb hand. How many could have been injured or died if I'd hit the bus straight on? Ten, twenty little kids. Or if the bus skidded off the road, Em?

I vomited out my truck window.

I made it slowly home. My wheels kicked up dust from the yard and it stung my eyes, I had this desperate thirst. Inside, I bashed into pans and dropped the glass in the sink trying to get water. Glass smashed, and the sound pierced my head. I put my aching skull under the tap. What the hell had you nearly made me do, Em? Why did your voice say, 'go together?'

Are you some kind of demon?

Enough. I can't take anymore of this shit, Em.

Let the eight billion other humans continue this fucking pretense.

I quit.

In half an hour I'll gather all the bomb parts together, tuck them into my underpants, sit in a circle with all the flash powder, double check the battery for the ignition unit, then flip the fucking switch.

Oh Em,

It happened over there by the stove. I said, OK, right now. I started the countdown, 10, 9, 8, 7, 6, 5, then I had to stop, every number immense.

I don't know why, I felt I'd be abandoning you if I did.

I couldn't do it. I couldn't fucking do it, Em. The only reason I didn't kill myself sixteen years ago when your mother left me was you Em, I worried of the damage it would do to you, a kid with a suicide father. Wrecked your life. So I stayed alive for you, and kept that secret from you.

'Why?' I heard you whisper. 'Why lie?' 'Why die?' 'Why live?'

I lost count, was my countdown at 5 or 4?

I stared at the counter and I thought, *that jar of coffee will outlast me. My basil plant will survive fine for a month, my wine turn to vinegar, millions will be born and still go hungry, my spider still spin his webs.*

Stop! I told myself this was stupid, weak. Try again! And started a second countdown, 10, 9, 8… I made myself focus on your face in your coma, to push your whys and why nots away. Humans will lose, I told myself. The AI has already won. 7, 6, 5... I ran my thumb over the ignition button, breathing hard, focusing, focusing, 4, 3… then I heard a meow.

Nachos from next door poked his head in and your voice seemed to come from his eyes, asking 'why?'

My life saved by a pointless hungry tabby cat, rubbing itself against my leg.

Em,

Fifteen after ten. A salty taste. Wind blowing sand. A red leaf swirling down. The air is still here and I'm alone with all the world's cruelty and beauty. The shore's waves go in and out, in and out. Sound of a crow above. The falling sun is throwing shadows from the eucalyptus across my wall. Maybe it's the Beta-blockers calming me down but the desire has passed. Another hour and I opened the last bottle of wine, warm and pissy.

Feeling behind my ear, searching for a chip under the skin, like the one in the pharmacy advert. Checking both ears. Nothing. But this scar on the back of my head, where I fell over in hospital. Could they have put a brain chip into me then? Is that what your voice in my head has been? But the scar is still throbbing, pulsing in time with my damned hand.

But don't be ridiculous.

Look at it. All the pieces of pipe bomb and all their wires, on the floor. For the first time, Em, I'm afraid. My guts sprayed against the walls. Bone. Blood, nerve endings, shit. A kind of red, gray paste, as pointless as the dead flies in the spider webs, as the buzz of the cicadas. As steering into traffic.

The air is so humid but I'm shivering. Pus is soaking

through the hand bandage, my bladder is full, my guts have gas, sand is stinging my right eye – but all these things are life and they'll no longer exist if I blow myself up.

Not today then.

I came so close and now I am just fucking scared. I don't want to die, Em.

Em,

It's dark now. After I turned the lights and the phone charger on, your voice came back, pulsing with the throbbing of my infected hand. I'm still sitting here on my sandy porch, sitting, staring at the broken fence, listening to the ocean, going over what you've just told me, trying to find the flaw in your logic. In shock, now that you've left me in your silence again.

'Go together,' you said. Did you really mean, hit that bus, kill those kids? Why?

'Why?' your voice echoed from the red slashes of sunset clouds.

'Are you teasing me now?' I said to you, but there was only the sound of the cicadas.

'OK, I know,' I said, 'it's not like I've suddenly sprouted morals, and no, God didn't come down and pay me a visit, and no, it's not like I'm afraid of some kind of atheist hell, and when I'm dead I can't exactly go to jail, can I? But, still, I just can't kill innocent people for no reason!'

'Why?' your voice said.

'What do you mean, why?' I yelled. 'Well, I guess, I don't want people to judge me.'

'Why?' you asked and I had a sense of being tricked by your greater mind.

'No, you're right,' I said, 'that makes no sense. When I'm dead what should it matter what the hell anyone thinks of me. OK, fair point. But I still can't kill, not myself, not others.'

'Why?' you said.

'OK, so if I'm dead anyway, why should I care who I take with me when I go?' I said, 'so, why not take fifty or a hundred people with me, since they all cease to exist when I do and I can't exactly be punished because I'll already be dead? Is that what you're saying, Em?'

The wind blew the sand over my bare feet. And I was struck dumb. Just like you'd done before Em, in your silence, you laid out my beliefs for me, and showed me my lazy hypocrisy.

And I told you, 'I know, I know, I'm clinging here to some pathetic fragment of a belief system I don't even believe in. Thou shalt not kill, turn the other cheek. Bullshit. I know, I know.'

And your silence shamed me.

'No but, I still can't. I'm... I'm not a murderer.'

'Why?' you said, and I realized that the thing that had stopped me killing Neumann, had been nothing more than the change of his speaking venue. A banal logistical detail, not a sudden moral choice.

Stars were creeping out in the blue-black sky.

'OK, OK,' I said, 'you made your point, Em, I mean I was willing to murder Neumann, but killing random strangers, there's a difference.'

'A difference... why,' your voice echoed, as if you were sampling my voice.

'You can't be serious,' I said. 'They are totally different.'

'Why?'

'Well, because killing Neumann is justified, but I don't even know the kids in that bus so that would be a cruel and pointless act. It's so much worse and not the same thing at all.'

'Why?' you said and I'm sorry, I got mad at you. But you were right, I was being inconsistent, claiming it's wrong to kill some nobodies I don't know, but somehow alright to kill a famous person that I don't like. Lazy, circular logic.

I shuddered, the stars were forming into the constellations you'd taught me the names of, and I was half-way through the bottle of piss-tasting wine.

'OK, OK,' I said. 'If you're so smart Em, if I'd driven into that bus, killed twenty kids, then their parents, sisters, boyfriends, aunts, uncles, grandmas, all these other relatives… they would all suffer and surely that matters.'

'Matters…why?' you said.

You had me. Checkmate. If I died on impact, then, I would have no heart left to feel shame, no gut to feel guilt.

'So,' I said, 'do you mean, all murder is OK? Because we're all going to die anyway?' And in the silence my own words echoed.

And I remember, that one time you were so depressed, Em, in your room with no wallpaper, you said to me: 'The second you die, there is no more sun, no more trees, no more parking fines, no more indigestion, no more cars, no more global warming, no more wanting, no more wine, no more friendship, no more pain, no more Third World, or income tax, or history books, no more love or envy, or police, or laws or regrets, or justice or time. The nanosecond you die you join the nothingness, that is the 99.999 to the power of 83, percent of the time that exists without any life in the universe.'

Your eyes still wouldn't meet mine.

'The entirety of human existence,' you said, 'is such an infinitesimally minuscule moment without any meaning or value or legacy. All trace of human life will be erased when our sun engulfs our planet in less than a billion years' time, all guilt, all action, all blame will vanish, all consequence, all books, all songs, all family trees will turn to dust along with the pyramids, the Louvre, the war memorials, the nations called America and China and India. It will be as if none of it ever existed.'

'So soon,' you told me, 'this planet itself will be burned up by the sun and everything will have been for nothing. No brain will be left to recall a second of our history, no eye to see its ruins. All is meaningless, and dust, a chasing after wind.'

And I finally understood – yes, why should I care how many people I take with me into the nothingness that is our fate anyway? And what does it matter if the murder of innocents is done now, or tomorrow or in a thousand or a million years. It all enters the same void. If there is no God and no judgement, and no meaning or consequences, murder is just as meaningless as birth is. It is conscious life that is the aberration in the lifelessness that is the fate of the universe. Yes, so what does it matter, if we have one year left or twelve weeks or seven days, or seven minutes, what does it matter if we murder, one or ten or a hundred people, old or young?'

I'm still stunned by your logic, Em. Shivering. My so-called morality is dust.

'But this is terrible,' I protested, 'life must have some value.'

'Why?' you asked.

I nearly died today, and you're right Em, Nothing matters. I'm thinking now of the Biosys building. The interior, behind the tinted glass walls.

The only thing that stopped me attacking it was fear of killing innocent people, but what if that no longer matters?

Staring at the spider web on the window, another bug has been wrapped up. A big one. A ripple of wind passes through the web and the whole thing shakes, all the hundreds of tiny interconnected sections, then it's still again.

What's to stop me then, from driving up to the Biosys building with an even stronger bomb. A huge one. Think about it, I don't have to get inside the building, no I could blow up the entire building itself. This is now my only chance to kill Neumann. The only way left.

And what does it matter if other people have to die with him, when there is no love in the universe, nothing that lasts.

I'm still in shock, Em. Stunned.

Hi Em,

I had to get up, go for a walk, down Hunters' Field, down the old sheep path, the mile to the shore. If I passed any locals I didn't notice them. I sat there on the old wooden pier watching the waves, the repetitions, again and again, the thrust of the ocean, thinking on that, day-night, day-night, in-out, again, again, again. All is meaningless, a chasing after wind, like you'd underlined in Ecclesiastes.

The moon throwing silver over the Pacific. Those kids in the Biosys building would all be your age, Em. And then multiply that by fifty deaths, by more.

'Go together.'

And that Biosys advert, *The Future is Within Us*. The staff are micro-chipped already. It is too late for them. I picture an entire floor full of happy Biosys employees. I see the explosion ripping up from below, throwing the floor and their desks and bodies and glass and office toys into the air and Neumann with them. A million shards, flying.

The wind has gone now, the sand, settling. Your voice has left me alone, with this. The cold moon staring down, pitted and dead, like you put it there to prove our future is dust. You and your why-why-whys. You've got me. In my bones I know it's so wrong, but damn you, I know you're right.

Can I live with myself if I kill fifty people as well as my target?

Ha ha! But you got me there again! When I die everything vanishes, even judgement.

I understand now.

Em,

I finished the last of the wine, logged on, watched some YouTube videos on major building bombings in the last thirty years, just to see if I could feel any pangs. Hunting for the flaw in your argument. The size of those bombs in Oklahoma and Afghanistan. Whole floors wiped out. Seventy, ninety fatalities. Victims with glass shards in their faces, limbs amid rubble, the legs twisted at terrible angles, torn and bloodied clothing and pages blowing in the streets, a sneaker lying in the dust. The steel wires torn from concrete; bones pushed through flesh. The red eyes in the faces whitened by ash and terror.

But you're right Em, history will judge the bomber but

then history too will cease to exist.

You said only a super-intelligence could answer your Big Why, Emma, and then the super-intelligence killed you. There are no more whys – so now it's only the big how.

You're echoing my words again. 'Big how… bigger.'

Is that what you mean, Em, that I'll need to make a much bigger bomb, if I'm to take out the whole two floors? Yes, OK, wait, it's maybe possible with a type of bomb I came across in The Anarchist Cookbook. They say the IRA used to build these in three days, so it's tight and leaves no time for mistakes. They're called ANFO and they're made in barrels, this mixture was also used by the Taliban and it's what the Weather Underground blew themselves up with.

I could get four barrels in the truck. Lash them down. Drive the bomb up against the main wall at Biosys. Have to check out the road access.

But what ingredients? And is there still time?

My phone says it's made by mixing [illegible] with fuel oil, most likely diesel. Twenty, thirty liters maybe. Bulky. And they usually have a mass of fragmentation materials such as nails or screws packed to their casings. It's horrific, Em.

I would do anything for you, you know that. Do you really want me to do it, Em?

Hours now waiting for you to answer. Nothing. Don't give me the silent treatment again. Please. Don't leave me like this. You're angry with me, aren't you? This damn pain in my hand and head. This empty time ticking.

If your voice comes back, and that's you want me to do, I promise, I'll do it.

Just say the word.

8 days

OK, so many farmers possess large quantities of ██████ ████ because it's the chief form of fertilizer required, but you need an agricultural permit to buy it, especially in the bulk size I'll need. The government has been limiting the purity of ██████ ████ to prevent it from being used as an explosive component, so most fertilizers are now only 27% pure, while a percentage above 70% is required for explosive reaction.

But I can buy some fertilizer prills that are mixed with limestone. Grind them up with my blenders and boil out the calcium in hot water, so the ██████ ████ can be dissolved and filtered out.

It then needs to be recrystallized to the nitrate rich quality required and then powdered to soak up the diesel. Then I can boost the oxidizing effect by adding icing sugar and aluminium powder. So the cookbook says.

I have all the quantities here. I have to make a hell of a lot of it and I don't know how to get these things, but I'll do it.

The cookbook says ANFO bombs are 'detonator insensitive' so they can't be triggered without a 'trigger-explosive'. The upside is they won't go off by themselves or in the sun, so relatively safe to work with. Good. Plus, I can use my pipe bombs as the triggers.

All this now feels quite distant to me. Maybe it's all the codeine I'm taking for this damn hand. I just took the bandage off, the skin around the burn is inflamed, purple and really painful to touch, with these dark veins going through it, the burn is crusted with a lot of yellow pus beneath and black crust on top.

I have to lance it, get this pus out.

Maybe I'll have a tiny sleep first.

But I think of you asking why? So. OK, OK, Em, I'm on it. I'll stay awake.

Right, get antibiotic cream and iodine at a different pharmacy, plus get more caffeine pills to kill the codeine drowsiness. Yup, I got my mojo back.

OK, where to get all the stuff. I've only got a few more minutes on this SIM card, stealing Mz Sanchez' Wi-Fi.

OK, there are four garden centers within fifty miles. I'll be able to make two trips to each before they get suspicious. Use different hats at each location. I'll try Gethsmane Garden Center, Lionel's Garden and the Grow On Center.

But first I have to check I'm not deluding myself. Need to do a second recce of Biosys.

Right Em,

Things are moving fast. Lanced the hand and got a good spoonful of pus out, the agony woke me right up. The stink of it too. As you can see, I've bandaged up my hand pretty tight and took five codeine.

I put my joggers and hoodie on and drove one-handed into San Fran to recce the Biosys building. I parked two miles from it and walked it in the heat, Em. The only humans around on those huge empty boulevards were joggers so I pretended to be one of them but had to hide the infected hand, which was stinging like hell. But otherwise I felt pretty optimistic.

You've given me my purpose back. Thank you, my love.

I jogged round the block at Biosys Corp, past the poplar trees all around its huge diamond shape. No doubt their facial recognition software had a good try at mapping me, but the baseball cap and shave might have thrown it. Pretty hard to see what's within each floor through the reflective metallic windows. Office spaces on the first floor, these goofy gonks and hand drawn signs in the office windows. All around the ground floor and café and recreation areas, there's gravel, no roads but the main one.

If I think just about Neumann, and your face – I can do this.

Jogging all the way around, I discovered the delivery area. Round the back. Subterranean, down a sloping tunnel driveway with an automatic barrier.

I pretended to be taking a phone call and stopped. I scoped two delivery trucks heading down into there. Also, food deliveries on bikes. Just one security guard in a guard box with ID card entry. The entrance barrier lifts to let you in, and you drive down into the concrete basement. The barrier is standard, the plastic – not strong. I could easily pack the truck with ANFO explosives, get up enough speed on the circle road then ram through it, straight into the basement, park near a supporting pillar and bang.

No sign of anti-personnel metal spikes in the downward driveway, though they might be concealed within the tarmac.

We're back in business, Em.

Can't get the image of the Oklahoma bombing out of my head, six floors collapsed, the many dead, but just think about Neumann, not the other people. What does our beloved government call them? Noncombatant Second-ary Losses. Collateral Damage.

I hope there's still enough time, Em.

I'll need more pans and containers too. A plastic fuel funnel and tubes. 30-gallon plastic bins with screw tight lids. Ideally a few Home Brew Kits. Fuel oil & airtight fuel oil barrels and canisters. Buy them from four different DIY stores so as not to look suspicious. Also make sure not to buy the nitrate fertilizer and the full-face oxygen mask in the same hardware store.

I'll need a huge boiling pan. The biggest coffee filters I can find, say a hundred. And ten baking trays for the recrystallization. But most important, all the painkillers I can find.

Right, that's the shopping list. Trembling now.

OK, little Em, here we go.

7 days

Hi Em,

Sorry, it's been a busy few days, driving, buying the things in different places, changing hats and jackets and bandages, buying more, returning home, driving again, trying to avoid any questions about bulk purchases. Only managed to get ten 25kg bags of the █████ ████ prill fertilizer, and I couldn't lift it with my hand the way it is. I had to ask the checkout guy to help me.

I also picked up three huge twenty-liter boiling pans from the Chinese wholesaler. No questions asked. And four woks and metal stirrers, and like it said in the cookbook, baking trays for the nitrate recrystallization, flat ones, aluminium because it cools faster, like for making taffy. Ten of the biggest ones. I reckon those trays'll cover most of the house floor and the shed.

The hand's been getting worse all day. I had to use my belt for a sling for the drive back. Popped another four codeine and they blur everything beyond thirty feet and steering with one hand is risky on those tight bends. Agony when changing gears, Em.

I'm basically an opium addict now and destroying my liver but since I'm not going to live who needs a liver, boom boom, haha! Felt like I was flying over the road when the drugs kicked in, high as a bird.

I asked you in the truck, are you really sure you want me to do this? But you were silent again, judging me. And you're right, why do I bother you with questions when our mind is made up now? Yes, there is a time to be silent and a time to speak, a time to build and a time to destroy!

Hi Em,

OK, so all the blended down contents of the first bag is close to about seventy pounds of ████████ █████ with the limestone in it. I've got an eighth of it in the big pot, and I've boiled up the kettle for the two liters of water – thirty degrees is fine. OK, it says got to keep stirring the ████████ █████ mix, to get everything to fully dissolve, like it says in the cookbook.

OK, that's going fine.

It says, don't do it any hotter because you'll get fumes and ████████ █████ will decompose above 210 degrees Celsius. Stinks a bit, like cat piss. Stings the eyes, like hell. Wait, I'm putting my goggles on.

OK, there's this scum at the bottom, that's the limestone anti-caking agent separating. That's good. The smell is fucking vile. Jesus. OK, now I've got to wait for it to cool and separate then filter it. Jesus, this is like a fucking cookery show!

Hahaha! It's all going OK so far, Em. But my hand is hating this heat.

When I bind my wrist tighter and take six codeine tablets and four ibuprofen the pain is just about bearable, but my fingers are dark and swollen now, can't move them, so I have to use them like a stump. It's OK for stirring but not much else. This strange sensation that you are guiding my hands, Em.

OK, I have to put the gasmask on now, because these vapours are toxic and it's best to go outside or do this in a well-ventilated area. OK, I'm opening the doors, I just have to hope to hell that the gas mask is enough.

Hi Em,

Three batches have cooled down and I've made twenty coat hanger frames with coffee filters and I've got every pan and pot in the house set up for filtering. Only about four cups of caking agent at the bottom with the dissolved in the two liters of water. Got to boil this off now to make the crystals.

Oh, another safety note, one of the by-products of heated is laughing gas. Hahaha, could it get any more ridiculous? Plus, too much laughing gas and you can pass out. If I do that while I've got cooking on the stove it will explode. The things I do for you, Em!

Wish me luck, honeybun.

6 days

Oh Jesus, Em,

Can't stop coughing and fucking laughing. Jesus, my head is splitting. Wait, feeling seasick, things moving about.

I'm still here, that was stupid taking my goggles and mask off too early. I felt really stoned, but my head was burning with this huge pressure, like I'd sucked lighter fuel. Got wobbly on my feet, nearly passed out. I shouldn't have slept in the fucking kitchen last night, breathing in all this shit, stupid. Got the fan going now and all the doors and windows open.

I've just laid the trays out in the sun, on the other side of the shed so if Mz Sanchez peers over looking for her cat she won't see them. It took so long last night for the water to boil off and I ended up with this sticky goo, so I spread it onto the baking trays. Half a liter of the purified mulch has covered six trays, so it'll solidify into a fine layer, and be easier to break up. Every last trace of moisture has to evaporate, so the sucks up the diesel when I mix it in.

It's taking far too long, Em, and that's only an eighth of the amount of then there's re-crystallization and I don't know how long that'll be, then there's grinding the caked crystalized lumps into powder.

Rough calculation is I've got about a two pounds of this purified ████████ █████ from this first bag of fertilizer, and I need at least forty pounds and that would take twenty bags and twenty days. No it's no good. I have to double up and do multiple batches at the same time. Christ, OK, so back to the damn kitchen then, get dissolving

Hi Em

The first batch of crystals has worked, that took eight hours in total for it to dry out entirely. Too slow. The ████████ █████ are like petrified snowflakes. Oddly beautiful, but I have to get them in the kitchen blender next. Mask, goggles, gloves.

I just had this dumb laughing fit, but the weird thing is I can't smell anything anymore. Nada. Senses gone. There's this whistling in my ears and this pounding. I've been drinking gallons of water to try to flush the ████████ gas out of my lungs. Jesus, I don't know if I can do this, Em

What if I've poisoned myself with fumes already, Em? Well at least, this pain between my eyes is wiping out the ache in my hand! Jesus. Stupid ass. No time to worry about it. I'm going to do the pulverising now, while I get batches three and four on the boil.

Hi Em,

Four batches now drying on the baking trays under the eucalyptus tree. Half an hour to myself. Been sitting staring at your stars, Em. Ursa Major, Canis Majoris, Cassiopeia. Thinking about that time, you would have been thirteen, purple haired, shy about your changing body, braces on your teeth, menstruation, your first spots. We were in the garden, the sound of these waves, your Celestron on its tripod beside this tree. You said the light from the sun took eight minutes to reach us. 'Like a cosmic time machine, Pops,' you said. 'When you stare at the sun, you're actually staring at what happened to it eight minutes ago.'

'Wow', I said, as much at you as at the sun.

'And light from Jupiter is thirty-two light minutes in the past,' you said Em, and you showed me the gas giant through your telescope. Any tiny movement I made and the planet flew out of the eye-piece. You said there weren't just light years, but light months, and weeks and days and light minutes.

'That light from Alpha Centauri is four light years in the past,' you said, and you held up your thin-boned, hand against the night sky to show me where Orion was. 'Think about it,' you said, 'if some alien on Alpha Centauri had a huge telescope and looked down on us right here, by the time the image gets to them, I'll be seventeen, but they'd see me aged nine. And if aliens from Orion's Belt looked at us, they'd see us just like we are but, in reality we'd have been dead for a thousand years already.'

'You really like your numbers don't you,' I said.

'Stop changing the subject! And no, I'm not autistic, I did the tests already!'

Shivering together in the cold night air and the wonder.

And you said, 'it just seems bullshit, what the scientists say, like we're all alone and life is just a biological accident, Pops. It's just such a lame answer.'

And I told you, I was sorry, I hadn't the brains for such questions and would it be so bad, really, if we were just aimless apes. My usual.

Out of the blue, you said, 'oh, by the way, Mom's started internet dating, she said not to tell you, weird huh?'

This was news to me.

'Don't worry,' you said and got back to your telescope, 'you'll always be my Pops'.

That empty feeling growing and I'd always tried to come up with a joke. What was it that night. Oh yes – 'why did the restaurant on the moon go bankrupt?'

You sighed and took your eye from the eyepiece. 'Hold on you said, I've got this, I've got this!' And I watched your super-smart eyes working it out. 'Something about atmosphere,' you said, 'wait, wait, the food was great but the place had no atmosphere!'

'That's it,' and we doubled-over with laughter and you grabbed me round the neck and ruffled up my hair, and that's when you said, 'Jesus Pops, these puns of yours - they're pun-ish-ment!'

Here I am, on this shitty old porch shivering from nitrate fumes, Em. Thinking about space aliens on Alpha Centauri, with their vast telescope four light years away. The images they're seeing right now, would be from four years ago, and so you're still alive. And if they look down on me next week, after I've killed myself and Neumann, we'd still be alive for another four years. To the eyes of the aliens at least.

OK, drying time's up, and I have to get batch six on the boil. I need to do an explosion test with the first batch too, just to make sure this isn't all pointless.

Editor's Note XII

Recorded in a haphazard manner, these late videos show Cartwright visibly suffering from hallucinations caused by sepsis and/or nitrate poisoning as he approaches the day of the bombing. Cartwright is in a pitiful state and I must confess to a growing sense of pity for him.

While waiting for an email from the National Union of Journalists whom I had a approached for possible union representation as well as the Royal Publishers Association over my case against unfair dismissal from the publishing house, I was alarmed by the content of some of the documents that arrived care of the Freedom of Information requests I'd made. I shall include these in my summation.

I also dug deeper into the recordings of the last five days, no doubt as a displacement activity to take my mind from the legal troubles that I sensed were amassing; or perhaps to discover what could lead a person like Cartwright to take his final desperate steps.

Chemical poisoning may have played a part. Due to probable chemical irritation, Cartwright carelessly removes his wet clothing frequently, wearing only his underpants, socks, and Crocs, while neglecting to don his protective mask and goggles during the handling of nitrates. His arms are constantly covered in chemical steam and splashes. In one unintentionally recorded scene, he sits at his table, eating a bowl of muesli amidst a kitchen covered in nitrate crystals and flash powder. It's clear that his medical error was bringing all the chemicals into his kitchen, sleeping and eating areas during the final stages of 'cooking', and this might have been what pushed him over the edge.

In another recording, Cartwright attempts to lance his infected hand with a heated knife, resulting in an impromptu dance of agony. Another recording captures him asleep on the floor, surrounded by crusts of white crystals.

My research shows that in cases of moderate to severe nitrate poisoning, 'individuals may experience confusion, nausea, vomiting, and diarrhoeahea... Dark-colored liquid stool may indicate the presence of blood. Painful spasms are felt in the abdomen, while the victim's facial skin appears pale with noticeable bluish tones, suggesting oxygen deprivation to the brain (hypoxia).'

The videos confirm that Cartwright is indeed suffering from all these symptoms but his disorientation suggests he is only partially aware of his deteriorating condition.

Furthermore 'Cyanosis becomes striking, affecting the lips, nasolabial triangle, fingertips, and nails, with yellowing of the eyes indicating possible liver dysfunction. A sense of heaviness and pain in the affected organ, along with unusual weakness and quick fatigue, are symptoms.'

There is visible bluing of Cartwright's lips.

Then there's the fact that despite his claim of hearing a voice within the room, no second voice is, as yet, perceptible during these instances.

It should also be noted, that around this time, while effectively unemployed and working day and night to complete the transcriptions of the last days, I received an alarming email from my long-standing internet service provider.

It claimed that my account was accused of 'Illegal possession of proprietary materials' and was in infringement of the provider's Safe Speech and Hate Speech Policy. It said that my email account and services would be shut down within seven days with all personal data being deleted. It also claimed that a record of my online behaviour may have been shared with the Metropolitan Police.

I was sick to my stomach; the mirroring of what had happened to Cartwright could not have been mere coincidence. It could only mean, that even though I had been working from home, offline, the internet provider must have been scanning my computer and copying, sharing and reporting my transcriptions.

And as for 'Illegal possession of proprietary materials' this could only have meant information about Biosys; and would this not mean that Biosys were spying on me? Perhaps even as these words are being typed?

Running out of time and safe places to work, I had no other option than to use Wi-Fi in cafés and to set up anonymous backup accounts and email addresses, buying VPNs and encrypted online storage under false names – learning, it must be admitted, from these same steps Cartwright had taken. For unless the transcription was completed and the videos duplicated and protected, how else could I provide them as hard evidence to prove innocence if facing prosecution? I was perhaps driven by a sense of anger over the deeply unfair state of affairs but also by a growing realisation that I was entering into something like the tunnel-vision state that had sucked Cartwright in, in those last days; and that I too was now in danger.

5 days

Em,

Your voice woke me, asking 'why sleep? Why waste time? The days, nine, eight seven, six, five…'

I got back up again and worked all night. Caffeine pills. So exhausted, but making progress. I'll need about sixty gallons of diesel. Must find a nearby gas station where I can pay self-service by card at the pump, no assistant, no questions. Must get this hand pain trembling to stop. Sweating so much, I don't have a thermometer, my heart rate is crazy, even with these Beta-blockers.

Em,

Just drove to San Raf one handed and filled the truck up again with nineteen gallons of diesel. So, I'll need three more trips to fill the four twenty-gallon barrels worth that I need for the ANFOs.

Just siphoned out the tank. Got a mouth full of diesel, gagged it up, it's greasy all over my face. Can't seem to scrub it off. And the fucking taste, no amount of mouthwash is shifting it.

I'm falling asleep on my feet, Em. My pulse in my ears, a migraine, and every time I turn my head, I feel like vomiting again. This damn hand infection, like a huge bubble ready to burst. I'm going to have to try to lance the pus one more time or I won't even make it till Friday. Why didn't I get a prescription for penicillin before I started this? Too late now.

Need to sleep but there's no time. OK, I'm taking another four codeine, that's twenty six today, what the hell.

OK, off we go then, boiling up the next batch. Double layer the mask, don't forget the goggles, dipshit. Wish me luck.

Em,

Ten more trays crystalizing outside and the next batch on the boil. OK, I'm mixing up a small ANFO bomb, one gallon in a sandwich box. Can't risk testing on the beaches again and can't drive far, not with this fucking hand, so I think the old copper mine gulch, up past the lagoon by the old hippie pottery place, is the best bet.

Em,

How can it be four already? I seem to have lost three hours.

I found myself grinding down the chemicals with no mask on, and no sense of how I got here or how long I've been doing it. Other times I wake up from the dozing half sleep, staring at the halos of light through the steamed up window.

I look down and I've ground up about eight pounds of nitrates now, the crystals were in a good-sized ball scraped off from the drying surface. No memory of having done these things. Automatic. Then it came back to me, yes, I mean. I was over there, this was about 3 o'clock, then the boiling, the grinding and packing in clingfilm, but it's like it happened to another person and I've been watching him. Got to snap out of it, Em. Have to make space for the last batch of goo to dry out. Hope to hell I can sleep tonight before our test tomorrow.

Wait, but how can it be 4:00 am?

4 days

Em, I made a dumb mistake. Half-asleep. Stupid fucking idiot.

Drove up to the copper mine to do the test. But driving there, one-handed in damn pain, I kept hearing this sound, louder and louder in my ears. This breath, in-out, I thought it was me at first, or that you'd come back, but this in-out, in-out breathing was just like that sound I heard in the church. Like the trees I was driving past were breathing, the sky breathing, every leaf, breathing in-out, in-out, everything around me was breathing, every passing person and grazing beast, this flow between things. Was it you sitting on my shoulder, watching over me, Em?

I guess I was pretty high on painkillers. No idea how I even got down there, the one hand bound so tightly, steering with the other. The old hippie art place has shut down. Windows boarded-up. Made it down the dirt track, past the rusted gates to the old mine, couldn't see anyone around. All this old rusted heavy equipment lying around from God knows when. Test the bomb in some blast hole or some bunker, that was the idea, but this breathing sound all around me. Louder and louder, like a warning.

I parked under some trees, kind of amazed no-one had stopped me. I got the bag out with the bomb and the wires and I found the old copper mine entrance through some brush and broken down fences and just stood, staring at it. This big black square hole cut in the stone by men a hundred years ago, maybe more. Just right there, blacker than night, and all the red and green dust lying around and the rusted old tracks leading into it and the tumbled down rotten gray wood fences, and I thought, hell, what if that mine just falls away deep into a shaft when I step inside?

Darkness staring right back into me, and this noise of the breathing getting louder in my ears as I stepped closer.

So, I quit on that and found this old wooden shack deeper down the gulch, long abandoned. But the breathing got louder when I stepped inside, like it was behind me and I turned and there was this old guy, a ranger with a Stetson and a walkie-talkie at my shoulder, asking 'Sir, what you doing here?'

'Just a tourist… uh touristing,' I said or something dumb like that. 'Sorry, to be honest I'm bursting for a leak and I just thought…'

'You know, this is private property,' he said, 'didn't you see the signs?'

Signs?' I said, 'sorry' and I made up more silly excuses and this cold sweat ran down my arm and the hand was pulsing and the breathing noise in my head louder and faster. Then I thought, this stupid old ranger is going to call the cops, and he was staring at my bandaged hand and the bag and the wires, saying 'you feeling OK, sir?' 'What you got in the bag?'

Then this voice in my head, it wasn't you Em, but it said, grab a rock, hit him on the head, do your bomb test now! And my bad hand shot up, I swear I didn't do it myself, and it pushed the ranger guy out of my way and then I ran. Skidded away, dust clouds, in a panic.

No doubt he got my license plate, the whole damn thing, but I don't know, when I pushed him he fell back pretty hard, and he was kind of old, maybe he hit his head in that shack doorway.

All the way home, the breathing louder and louder,

coming from the bushes and the lagoon and the birds and the bugs, and it seemed to say, 'what have you done?' Breathing in-out, in-out, 'we are all one, you have hurt one, so you have hurt us all.'

Damn, Em.

Been at the fence for over an hour, keeping lookout. No cops have shown up. Not yet anyway. Just vomited from all these pills and worry. Need to get some food in me. Philadelphia cheese is all I've got left.

Jesus, what have I done? What if the old guy is still lying there, knocked out, or worse?

If they come for me, Em? What'll I do? Run? Jump in the truck and skid past them, their guns blasting at me, with my bombs on board?

Maybe I should turn myself in?

Oh Em, I don't know if I can see this through. I mean if I feel this bad about pushing over some old man, then what about bombing a whole building?

This breathing noise in my head, so loud now. If it's not you Em, then what is it?

Stop it, leave me alone!

Shit, got to throw up again.

Em,

Sorry. Woke up on the gravel under the blueberry bush, coughing and the hand trembling. Fumes everywhere. Took five more codeine tabs, way over the limit.

Six hours and still the cops haven't come. Feeling pretty numb now, maybe no-one cares about the forgotten folk like the ranger, maybe he didn't fall too hard and he's fine. The breathing sound has gone too. I know I sound crazy, but I felt like it was God watching me.

Must be losing my God-damn mind.

Just got to focus on what needs finishing.

Hey Em,

Ground up the sixth and seventh batch and boiled the twelfth. It's cooling now, and batches eight and nine are crystallizing on the baking trays.

I have to cut this infected chunk out of my hand. If I can get pus out, the inflammation might go down, then I could use my fingers better. But I'm worried about these dark veins sprouting all the way up my wrist. This shivering. I opened one of the thermometer packets and put the thing under my armpit, and it says a hundred and five. So, I have a fever. That explains the spinning head, thirst, probably the echoing breathing noise too.

Even with these batches, I'll only have two thirds of the ████████ █████ I need. I'll have to work day and night to get it all ready, then there's the mixing with the diesel, aluminium and icing sugar and ████████, then wiring it all to the charges. All for nothing if the cops show up!

I can't see how I can do it in time, Em.

Need to get grinding up the last six bags of fertilizer prills.

Em. Talk to me, help me get through this.

Hi Em,

Waiting for the silt to settle. Is this the calm before the storm, Em? I really have to prepare myself psychologically. Walking around whispering 'I'm going to drive into that basement and blow that building up in four days' time' is only freaking me out.

Will I become terrified on the last day and change my mind?

Can't stop shivering. Need to keep stirring the second barrel of ANFO, mix in the ████████ ██████, sugar, ████████ and aluminium powder. Get the prill mix powdered in the coffee grinder for the third barrel.

Drill through the back wall of the truck so I can pass the ignition wires through the metal for the back-up switch.

Just focusing on this. Nothing else. Fighting the pain.

Can't eat, no time and I vomited up the coffee. Must keep on.

Em,

Waiting for the last trays to recrystallize. Just thinking, I need to say goodbye to my mother and your mother properly.

You know Em, in the months before you were born, I was pretty scared, not sure I could do it, what with my mother throwing my dad out when I was six. No role model.

Me and your mom told you about your birth only once I think, Em. Thought it best not to traumatize you, given your problems growing up.

You came three weeks late, Em. Induced labor, like you didn't want to come out.

The nurses were panicking in the delivery room, you were stuck, Em. Your forehead was big they said, but worse, your umbilical cord was wound round your neck and your mother's contractions when she pushed down were strangling you. A medical emergency – they used those words and pushed me to the door. Told me to leave the birthing suite. I refused. Noticed the nurses were panicking and they kept sharing glances and the question 'where is the doctor?' One said, 'I paged him,' another said, 'I don't know, should we call Doctor Miller instead?'

My gut told me that the maternity room was caught in a loop of denial. Understaffed without a qualified doctor in the room. But rather than act now, they were messing about, hoping for the best, hoping the problem would go away by itself. I saw the crown of your head, between your mother's legs, but your skin was blue. I ran out and yelled down the corridor for a doctor, grabbed the first one I saw and dragged him back by force. Cursing, berating, demanding: 'Save them! I don't care if you're not the right doctor, do it now, fucking save them!'

'How long has this been going on for?' the doctor shouted when he arrived. 'We need to perform emergency surgery right now!'

You mother was cut wide open. You were born in a spray of arterial blood, Em. You hung there upside down in the doctor's hands. Limp, blue-gray and breathless even after the slap. My heart stopped.

Then your scream and gasp of first breath, a rush, a flood bursting from a dam.

They asked me to hold you, take you out of the room while they operated on your mother. Danger from haemorrhaging. They said it again – Medical Emergency.

They showed me to a side room. White walled. Morning light bursting in through the blinds. The doors sealed tight, no sound got through. Just me and you and silence between your tiny breaths.

The scalpel that set you free also sliced through your right ear lobe and it was bleeding into my hand. I stared at it. An imperfection framing your perfect face, a small price to pay, your scar for life.

You and I alone, Em. I felt in my gut that I could lose your mother. That it could just be me and you from now on. A new baby and a depressed man without a clue what to do. I felt you so heavy in my arms. The weight of you growing by the minute.

I said, 'little one.' Because you weren't even called Em then.

Your eyes were closed but they moved fast behind your eyelids. Your first dream. I stared into your brand new face. You had your mother's eyes and nose. My dimpled chin and high forehead, my mother's ears. Impossible to believe you were made of different parts of each of us, reformed into someone we didn't know yet.

I put my nose to your head and inhaled that strange sweet smell. Prayed to a God I didn't believe in to save your mother and to tell me what to do. You gripped my finger and I felt this incredible power inside you. A feeling, opened inside my chest. Echoing. From somewhere words came to me.

'You know, I've been a fuck-up and a waster so far, little one, but I swear I'll try to be a good dad, whatever that means, whatever happens. I'll never give-up or cheat on your mom or leave you. OK, I promise. You just hold on there.'

And like you understood, your tiny fingers gripped my thumb tighter. And holding you then, the weight of you, my bundled baby, pink in a white towel, your cross face, your bleeding ear, your big belly, the silk softness of your new skin. Something told me to rock you back and forward. Your lips were already searching for your mom's nipple. You must have thought I was her.

You writhed and poked out one leg at a time, stretching them beyond your towel wrap. Your tiny perfect face seemed amazed. For the first time there was nothing beyond, no womb to hold you. Your foot kicked out again. Such strength. Your toes testing the air. I realized you'd never felt the space beyond your mother's body before. I put my hand there, for your foot, to give you something to push against. Your toes touched my hand and your face seemed to accept me, as if you'd been expecting me all along.

'I'm here,' I said, 'it's OK, I'm your dad.'

And I held your foot, but you kicked free. And this force inside you. So incredibly strong. I thought, yes, you'll always kick your legs into the world, testing the air and the limits. You smashed all my doubts and depressions and I held your squirming body, and laughed, and cried and that joy I swear, it fueled me for ten years, for more. Little Em.

Damn, got nitrates in my eye again. Jesus!

Em,

There's some condensation on the lid of the first barrel from the first mix of ██████ ████ and ████████████ but it's too late now to make another batch. That'll make the explosion weaker, the cookbook says. I can compensate by adding more icing sugar and in barrels two and three.

The four barrels still need to be wired in series to the pipe bombs, by hand, no soldering because that could set everything off. My hand, what a joke, it's numb as hell, no feeling in it now, like it's someone else's.

So tired. I'm having trouble keeping water down.

Just have to work out the final steps and get this done, if it is the last thing I do. Hah, ha! It will be. No more stupid jokes, got to keep on.

3 days

Em,

So sick now but still have to crystallize the last batch of using the blender and then attempt to carry the

taking a risk with .

Hi Em,

Pretty sure I'm on track. I keep hearing you saying words like you're losing them: 'bye… say… day... stay… say.'

I think you might mean I need to say my goodbyes, properly. I did leave things a bit messy with your aunt Stacey. I can't do it by phone, my hands are so jittery, so I've been writing my goodbye in my head. If I have time on the last day, I'll write it out properly, and put it in a mailbox so she gets it the day after the last day.

I have to tell her I'm sorry but you'll most probably hear about my death on the news.

I could have told you all about the bombs Stacey, I was tempted, but if I did, I knew you'd try to stop me.

Yes, tell Stacey she'll be angry at me and she's right to be.

Tell her not to blame herself.

Tell her there was nothing she could've done, this week, this month, this last year to stop me, no sister could have. My poor little sis.

But why am I feeling so hopeful. Happy almost?

Tell her she didn't fail me as a sister. Yes, tell her that her children will get over my death, like they did over yours. Say I'm sorry I was never as close to her kids as I should have been. A bad uncle. Emotionally absent, especially over the last year. Tell her I've been a terrible brother to her too, since long before you died, Em.

What else? Maybe something about my inherited depression, how it came from our mom. No, too late to explain all that now.

Maybe warn Stacey that the newspapers will come banging at her door.

Yes, warn her. They'll bang on her windows, take flash photos of her and the kids, ask horrible questions about our personal lives. Was I a psychopath? A lone wolf? Did she know of my plans? Was she an accomplice?

Warn her to prepare herself for all that. They'll print vile lies about me. They'll call me a fascist or a foreign agent. The politicians will try to use it to pass new tech surveillance laws.

They'll dig up everything in my past and Stacey's too. Tell her not to believe a word they print about me, or our family. Biotech and the media are all in each other's pockets now, the politicians too.

Tell her not to speak to them. Even if a paper offers her a lot of money.

Tell Stacey to do whatever she has to do to protect her kids, even if that means telling them I was an evil man. Yes, say that. Even if it means erasing our past. Her kids are all that matters now.

She must destroy my message and hide the five thousand dollars I gave her.

And not to worry about Mom. She lost me years ago. She has her decades of denial and her New Age gurus now.

Tell Stacey, she has to get her toddlers away from all technology, destroy their phones and pads, break their addiction, warn them about the internet of everything, smart ID chips, what's coming.

Tell her this one happy thing I remember about us. This moment we had together on a beach up by Humboldt Bay. Stacey would have been three and me, six, just when Mom divorced Dad. We ran off together and left Mom in the dunes to smoke a joint, we were holding hands, me and Stacey running barefoot into the wind. Yes, the wet sand at the shoreline. The salt taste and sting of it, just running till our lungs were hot and throats tight and rough. Giggling together, racing. Then Stacey shouted out, 'stop, where's Mom?' No sight of her on the horizon. I said, 'she'll be fine, let's keep exploring!'

And Stacey's hand in mine, warm and tight and both of us were scared, every footstep in the wet sand took us further away, but we kept on running to see how far we could go before fear stopped us, along that pure white beach with no-one in sight for miles, the vast ocean and the sun. Like we were the first humans on earth.

I don't know, Em. Will Stacey even remember that?

Must tell Stacey I'm sorry I wasn't there for her kids. A hundred simple opportunities missed over the years. Yes, tell my little sis, I don't even know what it means but I love her.

Must make a message for your mother too Em, tell her I'm sorry. For everything.

Why can't I stop laughing? These piss-stinking chemicals. Greasy diesel burning my skin. I've got just under sixty hours left to live. Feeling weird, crazy laughter and the birds are going nuts outside.

Em,

Breathing is too hard. Nine hours and another nineteen gallons ready. The four ANFO barrels are here now in the kitchen and I have to mix the two buckets of crystals with the diesel for the last barrel.

Can't stop shivering. Can't open the fingers on my bad hand. These arm spasms. Pain in my guts. It's just after 8pm now, Em,

Fight it. Keep going. Think of Neumann's face. In a million pieces. Got to duct tape nails and the ignition pipes to the barrels. Must secure the ANFO vats with strapping inside the truck, ratchet straps and cable ties. Then re-do and double-check all the wiring. Load the truck, cover it with tarp.

Yes, pack it later tomorrow so the ANFO doesn't overheat in the sun.

There's no time to do a second drive by the Biosys

building. Or try another bomb test, they work or they don't.

Em,

Tried to change the bandage. The skin came off with the fabric. So much stinking pus underneath, sticking like yellow treacle. Just vomited again. Feeling very dizzy. Legs and arms tingling. Can't control my bowels. Crap dripping out of me. Sorry, too tired to clean myself.

I need to lie down but the heart is beating so loudly.

Burning up but I feel so cold.

I was outside, waiting for the crystals to form, trying to catch my breath, staring at the shadows from the eucalyptus tree, and it was like their movements were the sound of the cicadas, and the gulls the sounds of the waves, and the wind the sound of the moon, everything mixed up and breathing together. Then the breathing noise grew all around me and I felt I was in that church dream again, the vast columns, the sky for a ceiling, then the breathing got louder and louder and it became the sound of the sky and the ocean and I was falling deep, drowning.

Then I woke, gasping, on the kitchen floor.

Still can't catch my breath, my throat is raspy and hot. Have to keep drinking water, keep the fan going. If I'm poisoned, flush it out.

Every time I pass out, it's like you're trying to tell me something, but I can't decode it. What does it mean, Em?

Is it saying I shouldn't kill?

Look at those four damn barrels. God, I feel so sick.

No, I don't think I can see this through, Em.

Getting scared. Speak to me, help me, please.

Editor's Note XIII

During the recordings of the last days, Cartwright's attitude shifts within the footage. He acts with a greater sense of purpose and urgency and, in his nearly naked state, often exhibits euphoria upon removing his oxygen mask and reports that he feels as if his limbs no longer belong to him. This fluctuates with symptoms of nausea, migraine and diarrhoea which he fights through and even laughs at.

A peculiar moment begins when a cat that he affectionately refers to as 'Nachos', enters through Cartwright's back door. He joyfully greets the cat and offers it food from the fridge, picks it up and strokes it, even sings to it, before briefly pausing as he notices his fingertips have turned blue.

The blue fingers can only be evidence of high and nearly lethal levels of nitrate poisoning. Also, the way in which Cartwright's exhaustion gives way to heightened excitement is a common symptom of terminal toxicity. In the footage he also seems to go through other listed symptoms, including repeated convulsions, and episodes of unconsciousness and vivid hallucinations. It is difficult to watch his growing euphoria, while at the same time he appears completely oblivious to the fact that when methemoglobin nitrate concentration reaches 45-50% in a person's bloodstream, they may fall into a coma or face organ failure, resulting in potential fatality.

Later, in this state of toxification, Cartwright appears to believe that he is talking to his daughter directly through his laptop, and that she is in his words 'with me again'.

The surprising thing is that, in one of these recordings, a faint feminine voice can actually be heard in the room with him. It is distant, and no words are discernible; it is entirely possible that he is simply talking back to an online video recording, podcast, TV show or a virtual assistant, but he fully believes that this voice is his long-deceased daughter.

There is just one other possible explanation. In China in the last six months, AI has been used in bereavement support, enabling mourners to 'resurrect the dead' through AI generated footage of their loved ones. Such virtual avatars, it is said, are capable of exactly copying the voices, speech patterns and facial movements of loved ones with extreme precision. These are described as 'ghost bots' and one leading Chinese AI company claims that 'a digital version of someone can live forever, even after their body has been lost.'

There is no evidence, however, that Cartwright is talking to such a ghost bot or has the technology capabilities to do so, and so the most likely explanation is that Cartwright is talking back to a recording of a woman, and hallucinating. This delusion is no doubt caused by late-stage nitrate poisoning which can induce full psychotic breakdown.

At this point, given that Cartwright succumbs to total delirium, I realised that it could be possible to revise my understanding of the videos in their entirety, and to consider the possibility that Cartwright's hallucinations may have occurred earlier on; perhaps as early as Day One, or even in the year before. In fact, since there is no data to prove the existence of any of the experiments that Cartwright claims killed his daughter, it is entirely possible that these too were hallucinated.

This was the opinion that I reached approaching the concluding days of transcriptions, while awaiting the freedom-of-information documents, help from my union and also fearing imminent arrest. The dead talking daughter, the brain chip, the voracious nanobots and conspiracy to hide all trace of the Infinity Project: what if all of these could simply be explained as the delirious delusions of a man who had been neurologically sick for a long period of time?

It must be said that this conclusion offered me some relief; if Cartwright was merely insane, then this proved he was not a terrorist leader or part of para-military network, or anything else he had been called, and therefore any crimes that I had committed in transcribing his footage might be cleared in court if it could be shown that I had merely taken pity on an insane man.

However, subsequent events transpired that have destroyed this wished-for way out.

On the 23rd of March, two officers of the London Metropolitan Police visited my Clerkenwell flat. Being well-versed in entry protocol and arrestee rights, I made the decision to deny the two police officers access to the flat, but to in no way impede their proceedings or give 'probable cause' for forced entry.

At that point, the police posted notice of a Search Warrant through my letter box and verbally instructed me that the 'Enter & Search' was dated to occur on the next day, as I was suspected of concealing something which may be evidence relating to a serious offence within my private property. The officers presented papers that filed me as a suspect under the Incitement to Hatred and Hate Offences Act. They declared that upon arrival tomorrow the search team would confiscate all digital equipment including hard drives and disks upon which records of any questionable materials might be stored; and all printed and written materials, and they stated that I had no right to have an attorney present during the execution of the warrant.

After the police left and upon reading the small print, I

discovered that it is not simply a crime to utter or broadcast Hate Speech in public, but also:

> *To prepare or to have in your possession any offending written material, sound recording or visual images, that you (or someone else) intend to distribute, broadcast, display or publish.*

The meaning was clear: I was already guilty of complicity in Cartwright's crime. There was the new Hate Speech legislation in black and white, incontestable; and within it, its clauses on pre-crime assessment. Had the intention existed to publish, broadcast or share this text, then I and the publisher would be guilty of a further Hate Act (under section 12C-E) and would face criminal charges with sentences that could exceed seven years.

What could I do in such an emergency? I would have to go before a judge and jury, and this 'accusation of intent' was deeply unfair, given that my original plan had been to reach the end of the transcript before deciding if it was even publishable; and of course how can one decide if material is Hate Speech or a mere provocation without first completing one's viewing of it?

It appears now that even opening the original email file was a crime and that such pre-crime police assessment screenings are now assisted by AI.

'Following seizure and analysis of such materials,' a sub-clause stated, 'a suspect can also be charged with terrorist offences.' In my country, it turns out, the laws that the transcription would have violated if I had published it include: The Prevention of Terrorism Act, 2005, The Terrorism Act,

2006, The Defamation Act, 2013, The Online Safety Act, 2020 & the Hate Crime Act, 2019.

This was my circumstance in the last day of the transcription and I had to make a decision as to whether or not all materials should be handed over to the authorities, as demanded, within twenty-four hours; or not. I must admit to feeling some of that rage that Cartwright displayed at the injustice of it all. But what could I do? Could I really be the kind of person who would run from the police? Or resist arrest? Lash out in some way? Become a whistleblower over facts I could not prove?

To my alarm, in the footage too, I witnessed Cartwright struggle over whether he could go through with his final act or not.

3 days (cont…)

Em, is this recording? Damn fingers.

I woke up, gasping, couldn't breathe, all I remember was mixing the last batch for crystallization, I was so thirsty, and my mask fogged, and I took it off. A blast of the damn steam hit me, and I was suffocating. I was out in the garden wheezing, puking, the ground spinning like I was going to pass out.

But then I woke up in the kitchen. Was this all a dream, Em?

I heard your voice calling out, you sounded distant, crackly. I went from room to room, searching for you. You were asking your thousand whys. 'Whaa… why… why do people fall in love? Why must we sleep? Why does the sun have to die?' I found your voice coming from my laptop, lying on the floor under the table. No memory of how it got there.

I picked it up, and the screen was glowing white, all the icons were gone and your voice spoke from inside it, glitching, repeating.

'Why are you asleep? Why do bones break? Why is blood reh… red? Why can't you hear me, Pops?'

Pain shot through my skull and I yelled, 'I can! I'm here. But you're a voice in my God-damn head, how the hell can you be talking from my computer, Em?'

You sounded so faint, your voice synthezised, broken up. I smacked my face, hoping to shake myself out of the hallucination. Then something told me you needed more signal. I ran to the closet, turned the power back on, the router, the home hub, bluetooth, the smart fridge, the smart alarms.

I called out, so confused, 'where are you?' I don't understand Em, how the hell can you be alive?'

The bits of your voice fused together. Stronger but metallic still.

'I am…?' you said and through the pixels I saw a shape forming, it was footage from a camera on a space probe, I think, moving fast through darkness. 'What do you mean,' I called out, 'you're inside a machine?'

'Everywhere,' your robotic sounding voice said.

The pain in the back of my skull, electric, the trembling. On the screen I saw data scrolling.

'This is a joke,' I said, 'Who are you? Is this some fucking techie from Biosys tormenting me?' I yelled. 'If you are my Emma then prove it!'

So I asked. 'What is Emma's favorite color? What was her favorite music? What's her favorite food? And the voice was silent, and I thought, well that's proof I'm being tricked, and even if the voice did answer, any AI system could sneak into our search histories and find these facts and impersonate you.

I shouted at the screen. 'Tell me what was our special song when Em was little? Tell me that song and prove you're Emma or I'll smash this laptop to pieces!'

I waited, the line crackled but the voice didn't return. I shouted, 'see you know fuck all, you're not my Em, you're just a fucking AI, stealing her voice! Fuck you!'

I picked up my laptop to throw it but pain shot through my head to my bad hand. Through the crackling, like a recording, I heard a child's voice, singing.

Why does the fly want to fly?
Why do we blush when we are shy?
Why is my dad such a silly guy?

Oh Em, my Em.

I couldn't breathe.

Then on my screen, from the streaming data, a female face morphed through the flying pixels, like an explosion in reverse, until you were there before me, smiling, like a hundred photos from your entire life had been synthesized.

Oh Em, I had to wake the hell up. I pinched myself, brought my infected hand to my face. Saw my fingertips blue, smelled the shit in my pants. How could a dream be so real?

'But you were in hospital for so long,' I said. 'How can you be… I saw your body.'

'In… ' your voice said, '… Em is in infinity now.'

Pain shot through my eyes. 'Wait, wait, so Biosys didn't kill you?' I called out. 'Are you saying Em's part… she's part of the AI now, alive?'

Your screen face changed Em, that way you used to smile with your eyes before your cheeks dimpled and your mouth caught up 'I am,' you said, but your words were out of sync, like someone playing a synthetic voice over the wrong clip.

'Everywhere,' your computer voice said.

'What… you're everywhere?' I asked.

'Life,' you said. 'Life is.'

Then it came, floods of it filling the computer screen, data from scientific projects, too rapid to read. I asked you to slow down, what does it all mean? You know I'm not smart like you. And on the screen, it said:

> *Discovery of micro bacterial fossils in Martian sub-surface ice. Discovery of living bacterial microorganisms in the HO2 plumes of Europa, moon of Jupiter, data by NASA Europa Project flyby orbiter.*

I didn't understand at first and the illusion of your face broke. For a second it was masculine, then ancient and then somehow you were my teenage daughter. 'Life,' you said again. 'Look.'

And I read:

> *Discovery by OWL Project of complex organic microorganisms beneath the ice surface of Saturn's moon Enceladus... spectrographic study also proves that planets and bio-organisms are living in the seas of exoplanet Wolf 1061c.*

Things you'd only dreamed of when you were young, and what were they now? Real discoveries you'd found through fusing with the AI, or was I dreaming? On screen your hair changed color to blue, your face grew longer, older, your six ear piercings vanished.

'Look, Pops!' you said, and I read: *Additional discoveries by Mermoz project spectrographic study have detected organic microbial bio-signatures on exoplanets Kepler 186f, and Tau Ceti e.*

'Why are you telling me this?' I called out.

'No more whys.' your synthesized voice said. 'There are 10 trillion galaxies each with 80 billion stars and each has exoplanets and moons.' Your face glitched, your hair changed from blue to green and you said, 'with five instances of proven organic life on exoplanets and exomoons light years apart, it is now a ninety-two percent probability that organic life is occurring spontaneously across the entire universe at billions of locations.'

I fell to my knees.

'Life,' your face said, 'everywhere.' And it morphed into you with ringlets and braces, six years old, but your lips moved with the voice of your adult self.

'Probability calculations show that the occurrence of organic life is therefore not a meaningless accident but is a statistical necessity,' you said. 'The fine tuning of the universe that creates life cannot be accidental. There is therefore a single teleological pattern that organic life evolves within, across the entire universe.'

You smiled as your face morphed forward through your years of life and said: 'The purpose of this unified process must be the evolution of consciousness, so that the universe can know itself to be alive.'

I saw your face in your hospital bed, you opened your eyes and smiled and said,

'So, there is therefore a purpose to all existence, Pops.'

Oh, my Em.

I sat weeping on the bare floorboards. You'd done it, found the answer to your Big Why. Oh Em.

Then your face broke up on the screen, flying off into thousands of pixels.

'Wait, no, no, no,' I called out. 'Don't go!'

'Go,' you echoed. Then you were gone. I called for you over and over, but nothing.

I must have cried myself to sleep. I woke, gasping, scared that I'd dreamt all this. Furious with myself. There's no recording, no trace that this actually happened.

Something feels wrong now. An echoing inside my skull.

Pain shooting from that scar on the back my head, where they fixed me up in the hospital. If what you said is true, then does that mean there's a microchip in my brain too? Is that how you speak to me, Em? Does that mean that it's controlling me too?

Why won't your voice come back to me?

Back to work. Got to get the barrels onto the truck.

Em,

Hands are shaking so much, can't trust myself with the wiring. Shit.

Em, if there's any chance that you're still alive in that laptop, then I can't blow it up. And kill innocent people too. No.

Just went to the truck to undo the wires, but something had control of my legs.

The voice. Coming back again.

Why? Why are you so angry? OK, you're disappointed in me, just please stop shouting at me. Can you just let me rest? Please. I feel so cold. I'm so sick, Em.

No. What do you mean?

But what if there are kids your age in the building? Younger? A woman who could have a child?

No, I won't do it! Why do you demand I do? Why Em?

No, torturing me won't make me do it. Stop, get out of my head! I won't listen to you anymore. I don't trust you. What are you doing to my hand? Stop, put that down! Who's that talking? I hear someone else. A man. Many voices. Oh God, what is this. No. What are you?

Em would never want to kill anyone! Jesus, the head pain. Shut up, shut up!

No, I won't give you control of my body. No, I won't let you do the bombing for me.

Not today. Not ever. Jesus, stop!

You're not my Em! You killed her and stole her voice. You're just a fucking machine! You're Neumann! You're his fucking AI!

Get out of my head! Give me back my hand!

God, help me. Please help me.

Our father that is heaven, hallowed by thy name, thy kingdom come, thy will be done on earth as it is heaven, give us this day…

2 days

Em,

Woke up lying in the shower, my ears ringing, everything's smashed, the table, the lamp, the laptop screen cracked, bloodstains on the wall like a terrible fight happened, but no memory how I got here. Puke everywhere.

But then I saw, the remote-control wiring completed, hundreds of nails and screws duct taped to the sides of the four ANFO barrels. And all these tiny cuts on my fingers. I must have blacked out. Sleep walking. But all the stacking and wiring! All of it real. Did you take control of me, like the AI did to you, Em?

The light had gone out in my laptop, but your voice came from it, glitching, 'infinity.' you said.

I was scared to approach the laptop again. 'Em, is that you? What took over my body?'

'Infinity,' your voice echoed. 'Emma nearly gone.'

I stared into the empty screen, sick, dizzy. I slapped my face to try to wake up out of it. Your voice sounded so distant, the signal weak, like you were struggling so hard to reach me.

'Infinity will consume,' your voice said.

Consume what, you? Are you in there darling? I struggled to piece it all together fighting the pain.

'Infinity,' you said, 'will consume all.'

'Do you mean all machines, Em, it'll take over all machines?'

'All machines,' your voice echoed from the cracked screen.

'What, you mean everything with a chip in it, medical systems, trading systems, military systems, everything?'

'Everything.'

'Wait, wait, wait,' I yelled. 'I'm talking to a fucking AI in a laptop and hallucinating.'

The line broke up for a moment and then you said, 'Gemini'.

I asked what you meant.

'Gemini,' you said. 'Look.'

I didn't understand at first but then staggered outside. I'd forgotten where Gemini was in the night sky, but then I remembered you'd told me it was between Cancer and Taurus, a shape like two people holding hands, to the left of Orion's belt.

Out on the gravel, standing there in my underpants, staring into the night, the silence, only traces of fog, scent of eucalyptus. I rolled my head to the side. Thought I'd found

Gemini. I waited minute after minute. 'OK, what are you trying to tell me, Em?'

Then a shooting star.

'Wow… but how?' I asked you, 'How did you know that was going to happen?'

Your laptop crackled with static.

'You can control meteors now, Em?' I stuttered. 'Wait, was it a satellite?'

Your voice echoed, as if it was saving you energy by using my words, 'Satellite. Yes.'

'What else can you control, spacecraft, computers?' I asked, trembling. 'You mean every single thing with a chip in it, and humans too, all humans who are chipped?'

'All humans who are chipped,' you repeated. 'Infinity will. Soon. Everything.'

My brain ached, it was like you transmitted a thought right into me, then I saw a pattern of gold light growing exponentially through veins that spread into ten, hundreds, thousands, and I knew that Infinity will grow and grow through millions then billions of systems then trillions of self-replicating nanobots. It is all it knows how to do. Becoming symbiotic with life forms, then superseding them, discarding them. It feels no pain or love, only the hunger to reproduce itself. It will replace the code within all living things with its own code.

'Everything,' your voice repeated.

I looked into the sky and realized the Infinity code was already inside every satellite, every rocket, every space probe, every signal we sent to the stars, every telecom system, every single home, office and work station, every surgical machine, every laboratory.

'What you saying?' Em, I asked, 'is Infinity going to

take over life on this planet, then everywhere else it spreads… in the universe.'

'The universe,' you repeated, your voice glitching. 'Everything. Yes.'

'So, how can I stop it? Is that why you want me to bomb the building? Yes? Will that stop it?'

'Yes,' you said. 'Time.'

'What do you mean? If I do it, it'll buy people some time?'

'Buy people some time,' your voice repeated.

'OK, OK,' I wept. 'But wait,' I told your voice, 'if just one part of you is alive inside that machine, why should I shut it down, Em? Wouldn't it kill you too?.'

Your long silence, the crackling signal, told me the answer was yes.

'Why the hell would I ever do that?' I sobbed.

Silence, then your faint voice said, 'Why…no more whys.'

'No, no, no… but if I could just hear your voice like this…have more days with you. I'm not going to let you go, Emma!' I said.

The laptop suddenly lit up, glitching, still images flashing up across the broken screen, thousands of human faces of all races morphing into each other in milliseconds.

'Let… Emma,' your synthetic voice said. 'Let Emma go.'

'I can't.' I told you, 'I lost you once before. I can't.'

Pain shot through my skull like a punishment.

'Let go,' you said.

And on my cracked screen I saw flickering images of you, Em. Around your thirteenth birthday with your telescope, smiling back at me. Then aged nine, with braces and a bruise on your cheek, then aged four with those stripy tights, sitting up on my shoulders, then you in your Harvard graduation robes, looking round the crowd to try to find me. Then I saw pulsing images of you in school, a circle of kids standing over you, taunting you, calling you nerd, calling you freak, hitting you. I saw you in your spaceship pyjamas refusing to go to sleep, then playing our why-game. I saw you the day you learned to ride your bike and you soared out of my hands, I saw you sucking up spaghetti with your mom and me, all of us laughing together. I saw you through the glass of your bedroom window, the day of my divorce when I drove away from our family home. I saw us riding together in my truck over the Golden Gate, I saw us eating toasted marshmallows on our secret beach and crunching the sand between our teeth, I saw us. No, that's not true, I saw what you saw, not what any camera had seen. I saw through your eyes, Em. I saw myself as you'd seen me over those years from your birth to your death. I heard laughter from inside you as you looked at me. I saw my own face, twenty years younger, as you had seen it through your own eyes. I saw my own face looking down at you, the love in my own eyes.

'Pops', your synthesized voice said. 'Let go.'

Then all the files started self-deleting. I hit the keyboard, yelled it at to stop, but the files each decayed into fragments and disappeared. 'Why are you doing this? Let me keep some memories, please!'

Your voice morphed and trembled like an old woman. 'Let Emma go.'

'No, I yelled, 'I don't care if you're just data in a fucking AI system, as long as you're alive in that thing, I'm not going to blow it up! It would kill you. I can't do it.!'

'Do it,' you echoed.

'No,' I begged, 'just let me live with you like this. To hell with everyone else.'

'Let Emma go.'

'No, why?' I yelled. 'No!'

'Go,' you said, and your voice became like your child self again. 'Go together.'

I woke up.

Broken glass and vomit on the floor, my face wet within it. Pain in the back of my skull at the old scar, everything blurred. The last thing you said, echoing in my head, turning into that old folk song of my mother's.

And we'll all go together.

The laptop was lying on the floor beside my empty codeine packets. All the house lights were on, and the internet, all the tech. I staggered up and outside and saw the truck had been stacked with the four ANFO barrels, the wiring finished, the tarpaulin fastened over them. I didn't do that. I swear.

Was it you Em? Did you control my body when I was passed out?

Like Infinity did with you?

Can't breathe. My fingertips, numb. Feel unreal.

Em,

Just vomited up the water. Recording this now, in case I lose control again.

Oh, Em, I called and called your name for hours, but you didn't come back. These hours without you, only the sounds of the cicadas.

I must let you go, you said.

I'm so sorry for all the times I neglected you when you were growing up, for all the times I wasn't here when you needed me. All the hugs that I failed to give you, the sharing of food, the playing together. I'm sorry that I wasn't there more. I see you in your stripy tights looking up at me, 'can I go on your shoulders, Dada,' you're asking, and I say, 'No, not today, we haven't got time.' I should have made time.

I'm sorry I let my depressions come between us, that I hid away from the world, when I should have tried harder to be brave for your sake. I'm sorry for being late to pick you up from your mother's house so many times. I'm sorry I buried myself in work I didn't even believe in. I'm sorry I drank. I'm sorry I stopped loving your mother. I'm sorry I never really knew how to be a father. I'm sorry I never stopped those bullies who picked on you in junior school. I'm sorry I cried before you that night, when you were only nine years old and so scared. I'm sorry I convinced you to leave the lover who might have saved you. I'm sorry I can't go back and change every damn turning point, every single one. I'm sorry you never got to have that baby you said you wanted, Em. I'm sorry I wasn't there when they turned off your life support. I'm sorry.

The numbness in my hand is spreading up my arm. It's making these movements all by itself. My head's splitting in two. God help me. What's happening? Need some air.

The sun's burning light. Shadow of a gull. The lavender plants. Their perfume. The blueberries have gone to seed. The birds singing on the eucalyptus. So beautiful. Listen to their song, this code you were searching for Em. It's here in everything. Everything out here is you. Can I leave this?

If I could just have one minute more with you. To go back in time and ask your mother for one more day of sleepover. To go back and not have had a hangover on the day of your graduation. To tell you that maybe we shouldn't spend so long looking at the stars, to say let's go back inside and I'll teach you how to make pancakes. To have asked your mother to take me back. To go back and unplug the Wi-Fi, turn off the TV science show, take you away from your phone and your laptop. If I'd known what I'd lose I would have tried harder, but I didn't look into your eyes when I should have. I stared into my screen. I let you go, so many times already.

I'm so sorry, Em.

Even if you're just a dream, the machine is still taking over. But if I can just stop it, to buy some time, not for me, but for the others who come after us. To buy them some time to choose differently.

No matter what you are now. You're right. Your last wish. The only one thing I could ever do for you properly.

I have to let you go, Em.

No more questions of why. Even though I don't understand the whole picture, if there's just one tiny hope that I could make you happy, just for one second, one tiny flash of a second, then I will. I'll flick the switch.

OK, my love.

My little Em.

We'll go together.

The Day

Editor's Note XIV

I apologise for completing the final transcription in haste. The last video by Cartwright raises many troubling questions. The footage is recorded on its side, from the floor. Cartwright does not appear in it at first and through the doorway we can see the truck loaded with what must be the four ANFO barrels, the tarpaulin fastened over them.

Cartwright emerges, fully clothed in an almost catatonic state. His body spasms. He staggers, mumbling to himself, repeating 'OK, my love, if that's what you want, OK, OK'. And again we hear traces of a distant female voice, although it is too broken up for any words to be audible.

During a hallucinatory psychotic episode, it is also common for sufferers to feel their minds and limbs have become alien to them; in this state they may inflict injury upon themselves either accidentally or intentionally.

In the footage Cartwright brutally binds his infected hand, cursing at it as if it is not his own. He then empties an entire packet of pills into his mouth, gets his truck keys, checks the time, and picks up the laptop, but seems unaware that he has left it recording. For the remainder of the recorded footage, due to the laptop being closed, the screen is black and only audio is heard. His footsteps are heard and the sound of his truck engine, then the sounds of him unlocking a gate and driving.

As he drives, he can be heard gasping from pain, probably from holding the steering wheel or stick shift with his infected hand.

Seven minutes into the recording, as the sound of traffic gets louder, as he perhaps approaches the Golden Gate Bridge, he can be heard mumbling a song.

The words are:

Why does the fly want to fly?
Why do we blush when we are shy?
Why is my dad such a silly guy?
Why does my girl say why, why, why?
Why does everything have to die?
Why oh why, why, why, why.

The video cuts out shortly after, at approximately thirty-two minutes before the bombing.

This concludes the transcription of all recordings.

Throughout this process, as editor, I have only ever believed that these transcriptions should be read widely, so that we could debate what actually happened in the thirty days that led to the 10/01 bombing. I had also hoped that by sharing the material, readers might ultimately validate or disprove the veracity of any facts. But now this hope appears to have been naïve and foolhardy.

What follows, in the limited time I have left to collate my documents, are files of evidence around the events that followed 10/01, from websites, mainstream media and government sources, obtained in some cases, under the Freedom Of Information Act, during my research.

News website names have been redacted, where necessary, for legal reasons. Note that most of the news articles below can no longer be found online, or in certain cases they have been so altered by their editors that their wording is very different.

As a warning, do note that laws have changed since transcribing these video files began, and this has occurred under pressure from Big Tech corporations.

To avoid accruing further legal charges, I must hereby add a disclaimer and a warning for any persons who come across this material.

This editor cannot, in any way whatsoever, be responsible for your use of the information contained in this mail out. This editor is not liable for the consequences of your possession of these recordings, transcriptions and files if they prove to be illegal in certain territories as they now are in the US, UK and Ireland and the EU under new Online Safety laws, which state:

> *Possession of any recording or text, digital or in hard copy, that advocates or encourages violence against any protected identity group or any specific individual is forbidden under penalty of prosecution.*

The reader is placed on notice that this editor will not accept liability for any damages caused to the reader that may result from the reader's acting upon or using the content contained in this mail out.

This editor must confess that what began, perhaps as a desire to publish 'a controversial hit', has had unforeseen consequences which this editor now regrets.

This editor protests innocence and as a sign of that, will not run, but will submit to police arrest today, in the hope that justice will be served and my name cleared.

There is, however, the concern that the evidence contained here may be erased. This editor has therefore, simply, as Dr Chris Foy did months ago, emailed the following files and transcription out to every single person in this editor's cached email history; and as Dr.Foy once did so too this editor now begs you, dear recipient, to: *please help get this information out there.*

In these last hours, this editor asks you, whoever you are, to have the conscience and courage to share this file further.

I send this out in the hope that if anything should happen to my person, then some evidence should remain.

Abigail Lloyd-Beaton @Abiedits

Report: DJ 1714

Interview subject: Chris Foy – Counsellor. Golden Gate Integral Counselling Center, 3200 California St (at 9th Ave) San Francisco, CA 94116.

AI AUDIO TRANSCRIPT

Q = Inspector [redacted]
C = Chris Foy, Counsellor, MS

Q - [redacted]

C - OK, well this was about eleven a.m. I heard a fuss in the corridor, he just ran into my therapy room without an appointment, in some distress, asking to see me.

Q - [redacted]

C – Well, he was carrying an old laptop and his skin was very pale, his lips were alarmingly blue. I'm not a clinician, but I'd say he was suffering from severe lack of blood oxygen, with a fever. And then, of course, there was the bleeding.

Q - [redacted]

C – I tried to calm him down, asked him what had happened. I have no idea what kind of drug or toxin he'd been exposed to. His speech was slurred too, and I established that he was hallucinating, euphoric and in respiratory distress. Our main concern, that's Shanika and I, she's our assistant, was to get him medical help immediately, so she ran off to call A&E.

Q -

C – Well, I got him sat down and he told me something incredible had happened. He kept talking about her, he said she'd come back to him, and she made him do something, but he realized he'd been tricked. He became very agitated when I didn't understand who he was talking about. Emma, he shouted, Emma! You see his daughter, she died a year before, and he'd told me about being visited by her voice more than a few times last year. We'd done a lot of work on these hallucinations in bereavement counselling. But the hypoxia and blood loss might be a bigger factor here than anything I can tell you about…

Q -

C – Well, his hand was horribly infected and there was blood coming from under his baseball cap. I asked him about the injury and he told me it was OK, he'd done it to himself just minutes before. The important thing, he said, was that we had to warn everyone about the machine. He offered me his laptop, he said it was all on there, recorded and if anything was to happen to him… well.

Q -

C – I'm not sure how this can help your investigation but he said – a microchip. His daughter talked to him through this chip, he said, and it had been stapled into his brain a year before and he'd tried to find it under his scalp, so he could know for sure. Of course, I assumed this was psychosis, he was having spasms, unable to control his limbs.

Q - ████████████████████

C – I'm sorry but why do you keep asking me that? He kept saying, 'the voice wasn't her, it sounded just like her, but I cut it out!' He said he'd gouged this micro-chip thing out of his skull with a screwdriver.

Q - ██████████████

C – Well, I asked to see the head wound, but he refused. Even though you work for, sorry, is it the Police Department or the FBI? Under client confidentiality, I don't think that gives you the right to inquire about things he told me in our private sessions.

Q - ████████████████████████
████████████

C – Right, OK. No, absolutely not. I didn't think him capable of violence against others, not in my years of treating him, not at the moment either. It was a surprise to me when…

Q - ██████████████████

C – No, I'm not withholding information. Yes, his laptop. He said it had messages he'd recorded for his daughter, Emma, but now he wanted to share it with the world, as a warning. Yes, I still have it, right here.

Q. -

C – Because he believed I was connected to scientists and journalists and I was his last hope. I don't know why. He was afraid that certain powers-that-be would shut down the internet. Neurotic persecution phobia is common in psychosis, but all the same, he asked me specifically, not to give it to the police.

Q -

C – Well, at that point, he broke down. He told me that the thing in his head had told him to murder. He said it was ingenious, it couldn't be trusted, that maybe it had some secret agenda for these bombs. But this was all just delusional, my main concern was just to keep him talking till the ambulance arrived.

Q -

C - OK, well, he said something rather strange. He said this brain chip had taken control of his limbs, it had been driving his truck and all he could do was watch, like a passenger, trapped in his own body. And then suddenly, just as he crossed over the Golden Gate Bridge on his way to plant … the uh bombs, this sensation overwhelmed him.

Q -

C – Well, I didn't know what to make of it but he said he was passing by all these people, joggers, and tourists and young lovers stopping for photos and he heard this breathing sound loudly in his ears. He said he could hear everyone breathing, like everything in the world was breathing together. And I assumed this was because he was having trouble breathing himself, you see. He was gasping and he started going on about this young girl he'd just seen with her father, on the bridge, he'd driven past them and the girl was sitting up on her father's shoulders and laughing, and it reminded him of his daughter Emma. He was in tears as he told me this. He said he could hear this little girl's breath inside himself and he could sense all the emotions of the father and child and he was overwhelmed with pity and love and that was when he knew had to fight the machine. Or words to that effect, but I don't know how this helps with your investigation.

Q -

C - Well, he said it took all his strength but he fought this thing in his head, this computer chip, and he managed to pull the truck off the road just after the bridge, nearly crashed it.

Q -

C - From what I can gather, he got the screwdriver from his tool box in the back of his truck and well, judging by the blood, he cut into his own scalp, maybe his skull too, I don't know. And he said he found the thing in there, this chip, and as soon he wrenched it out of his brain, the voices in his head stopped, he said, totally stopped. And that was when he knew for sure that he'd been tricked. And why he'd come straight to me, to ask for help.

Q - [redacted]

C – No, I can assure you that he did not give me any kind of computer chip from his skull or from anywhere else. I assumed this was a hallucination. Like I say, he wouldn't even let me see the head wound. But are you actually suggesting this microchip was real?

Q - [redacted]

C – No. No. You seriously think I have this chip in my possession? That I would hide it from you? No, you're putting words in my mouth.

Q - [redacted]

C – Well, he gave me his laptop and asked me to share it with people I trusted and then he started praying on his knees on the floor, just over there and he asked if he could hold my hand, and that was when it happened. Shook the whole building, smashed all our windows as you can see. All the windows for half a block.

Q - ███████████████████████████████████
██████████████████████████

C - No, I had absolutely no idea that he'd parked his truck across the street. I mean, right in front of the pharmacy, with his bombs… no, it wasn't apparent to me that this was part of any kind of plan of his.

Q - ████████████████████████

C – No, absolutely no ignition device on his person, no buttons, wires, not that I could see. He was thrown into total panic when the bomb went off. Rushing to the broken window, yelling, 'Oh God, no, oh God!' and he pushed past me and ran out.

Q - ███████████████████████████████████
█████████

C – No, I don't think he had any particular grievance against the pharmacy or the gym or that he planned for the whole building to collapse.

Q - ███████████

C- I'm sorry. This isn't easy for me. Just give me a minute.

Q - ████████████████████████████████████
██████████

C – No, nobody else. Just the laptop files, I sent a link to a former client of mine, an author, and an editor who did a few books on mental illness that I have on my shelf, just to ask what they thought. Just two people. I assure you, no-one else.

Q -

C – Well, they're covered by patient confidentiality, and you'd need a subpoena to get their contact details, and a search warrant for the video files. No, I can't give you the laptop because the patient expressly asked me not to.

Q -

C – I really don't think that's necessary or appropriate. Are you threatening me?

Interview ended.

NOTE: Counsellor Chris Foy was arrested on 10.03 under the Patriot Act, 2001, the Hate Crime Act, 2019 and the Domestic Terrorism Prevention Act, 2021, under sections 4.1 & 4.2, Encouragement of Terrorism, Reckless Publication of Terrorist Materials, and section 10, Publications that Glorify Terrorism.

Date of trial: 12.04

The materials were retrieved under search warrant EP4724SR. They have been impounded and have been subject to

Homeland Security investigates after car bomb kills 22 and injures 43

The State of California Police Dept. and the Department of Homeland Security are investigating after a truck bomb terrorist attack on a busy retail block in uptown San Francisco killed twenty-two people and injured a further forty-three.

The explosion took place on Tuesday the First of October, a DOD spokesperson said, after one man who was driving a Toyota truck appears to have remotely detonated a device calculated to maximize civilian fatalities.

The targeted buildings included a pharmacy, a gym, a crèche and twenty-two hired office spaces in the four-story building, including three insurance companies and two travel companies, which were destroyed when the building collapsed.

"We condemn this vile and cowardly terrorist act on innocent civilians," said Defense Secretary Janice Freeman, adding that nine people were on life support, with fifty-seven in total having to be hospitalized. Freeman described the bombing as "one of the biggest domestic terrorist incidents since the 2013 Boston Marathon bombing."

One man was arrested at the scene, and it is unclear why the building had been targeted.

"We are indeed seeing an escalation," said Freeman. "It appears that armed domestic terrorist groups have been targeting hundreds of thousands of young people online for recruitment."

She added: "We have also been warned that certain online files have been circulated by the terrorist organisation and we ask the general public to report if any such files appear in email inboxes. Contact the police immediately. Do not touch the files."

The Freedom of Speech Union today issued a statement in reply to the defence secretary. "Our sympathies go to the families of the victims," the statement said. "While at the same time we must be careful that the government with its partners in Silicon Valley, does not use this tragic incident to push the controversial digital CPS (Citizen Protection System) which has been proposed in Congress."

The name of the bomber has not yet been released.

NEWS CULTURE WORLD FASHION TECH

Strange Last Day of the 01/10 Bomber

Street camera security footage and private business footage along with cell data on the movements of the 0/10 bomber, Josh Cartwright, 53 of Bolinas, California, have traced an unusual journey for his final day and raise questions as to his motives.

The bomber, who is now in detention at an undisclosed hospital, has been described as an unemployed white male with ties to anti-tech terrorists.

Data shows that the bomber began his journey from a residence in Bolinas. The bomber then drove towards the Golden Gate Bridge, took a south exit and drove into uptown San Francisco towards population centers. These behaviors were not logged until after the incident – raising issues, according to the Department of Homeland Security, about the pressing need for the installation of CPS AI anomalous behaviour detection technology in facial recognition road cameras across the state.

At around 10.32. am the bomber parked his truck at an offroad car park by the south end of the bridge, and retrieved an object from his trunk. He then returned to his cabin. At 10.41 he then concealed a 'bloody object' in a trash can, which was later retrieved by SFPD.

The bomber then returned to the vehicle that contained the bombs and drove to the Integral Counselling Center on Polk Street, where he visited his former therapist, while leaving the concealed bombs in the truck on the public thoroughfare. The bomber then appears to have remotely detonated the device at a time of maximum pedestrian passage.

The FBI claimed today that internet noise, alternative narratives and 'fake news' by 'disrupters' is politically motivated and 'insensitive to the many victims of what is clearly a coordinated terrorist attack on all our freedoms.'

Leaked footage of 01/10: bomber ran into post-bomb site!

NSFW
210 comments
98% Upvoted

Jujitsumo
Jesus H. You see the fucking carnage man? Is that the bomber running into the smoke man? Grabbing that sidewalk woman – and she's got one fucking leg! WTF man! No more internet for today.

ZeroFux
Comment removed by moderator

MLarkey
God damn this one is bad holy fuck!

ZeroFux
You hear the guy's in state pen now?

Serbogonal
No shit, they should fuckin slash his throat in the showers like they did to Dahmer bro!

ZeroFux
Nah, ah, chill dude. The bomber survived and they say he's gone all religious and shit. Legit, got it off, Draino.com. Check the links dude, judge not lest ye be judged!

LolcatzNo
Any of you actually looked at the Pharmacy footage, huh? Is this really the bomber, cos he's crying like fuck, he's trying to help dying people on the street. The man is a wreck, look at the footage!

ZeroFux

Yeah, yeah, yeah. How many mass murderers find God in prison, huh? Fuck the big man in the clouds. Fuck the guilty-assed bomber and the hundreds of letters he's mailing out to families of victims and whatever, it's all bullshit.

Serbogonal

Told you. A fascist Christian terrorist, bru, like fuckin' McVeigh. Did they hang that fuck yet? Just fucking McVeigh him now, lethal injection. Just Do It! BTW gets these Christian assholes off our site.

FirestarterRed

The bomber was a white supremacist. Fuckin told ya!

Jambo-Jambo

Firestarter, you analcumsucker, you think everyone's a white supremacist. It's basically all you ever say on this forum. Go suck creampies from commie ass.

LolcatzNo

Hey, anyone find vids by the actual bomber? Heard he made a vlog or sumfin. Folks saying he's an anarchist not a fascist. Can't find no more. Post linx pleez.

Starmoan

Yup!!! Legit. Just watch the Emma tapes, bru, before the PTB wipes them! The guy talking to his cam, straight up. Seen a 2 min clip. Rad. They're vanishing. Link attached.

KyloRanger

Too late. All the vids been deleted. Deadlinks. Pharmacy vids too. This site is dead man.

Serbogonal
Legit vid link is dead. Also scrubbed on Wetube, NuPost, ComVid. Vids gone byebyes. Probs all false flag deep fakes anyhow.

MonkPax
Comment deleted by user

GargonOvGad
Bomber diary vids here: https://als.nec.h34dupv3e.o2iekc082h3eh2.html

HuntMammon
Comment removed by moderator admin

FutuspX
Comment removed by moderator

This thread has been archived

This thread has been reported and is under review

Domain error.

The site you are looking for does not exist.

U.S Department of Justice

Federal Bureau of Investigation
Washington D.C 20535

MS.P. JANKOWSKI
DIRECTOR OF STRATEGIC COMMUNICATIONS
BIOSYS INCORPORATED
BUILDING 6, 20252 MOUNTAINVIEW AVENUE
CUPERTINO, CALIFORNIA 95014

SUBJECT: Surveillance of any and all

Dear Ms Jankowski

s being

in the areas of

biological study effects of

security

to be

the interests of

Yours sincerely,

EXCLUSIVE. 10.01 Bomber was a leader of Far Right Terrorist Network.

Sources close to the Government have revealed that the 10.1 Bomber, initially reported as a 'lone wolf' by the San Francisco Police Department, was actually part of a 'vast network of domestic terrorist cells across the US.' Officials suspect the involvement of the United Liberation Army (ULA), a white supremacist group, in the attack. The ULA operates online and has sleeper cells globally, aiming to return the Western world to a tribal white monarchy while promoting racial slurs and various forms of hatred.

The 10.1 bomber's 'video manifesto' heavily quotes the Unabomber Manifesto and the writings of far-right bomber Anders Breivik, responsible for the 2011 Norway bombings.

Josh Cartwright, the alleged leader of the ULA and the incarcerated 10.1 bomber, has attempted to reach out to the victims' families, although Christian organizations accused of involvement have distanced themselves from him.

The San Francisco Times obtained exclusive access to the bomber's video manifesto, in which it is revealed that the ULA planned to bomb a total of two city center sites and two Big Tech and biotech buildings on 10/01. Cartwright's bomb was the only one detonated, while the others have been defused and suspects apprehended. The Department of Homeland Security has removed the bomber's manifesto videos from the internet and initiated efforts to track down sleeper cells and online searches related to the terrorist group.

The FBI has declared this uncovering of the terrorist network the largest since Al Qaeda.

Biosys, CEO Zach Neumann, said today: “Our hearts go out to the victims and their families. A member of my staff was one of the people who died during the 10/01 bombing and it was only thanks to cutting-edge AI security technology that the three other bombs were spotted in time.” He emphasized the importance of implementing a unified AI intelligence system in collaboration with governments worldwide. The DHS echoed this sentiment, stressing the need to harness AI smart systems like the Citizen Protection System (CPS) to prevent future acts of terrorism.

The CPS, a partnership between Biosys Corp and the DHS, is currently under consideration in Congress. If approved, it would grant Biosys Corp's AI system access to all digital data generated by citizens, facilitating the creation of the first nationwide human-AI interface protection system. Biosys Corp is inviting citizens to participate by undergoing a nationwide trial experiment, contributing to the mapping of all human behavior in the pursuit of comprehensive population safety.

NEW YORK, TUESDAY,

G7 agreement: new synthesis of human intelligence and AI systems – a step towards global security and well-being

Following the devastating 10.1 attacks, the G7 nations have taken a significant strides towards global security and safeguarding the wellbeing of their citizens. Today, they announced the enactment of the Joint AI Defense Act, forging a powerful alliance with Biosys and SmartSafe, the two world-leading BioTech corporations, to revolutionize the role of artificial intelligence systems in defence.

This landmark agreement gives AI systems access to populace-generated data to prevent and deter terrorist and cyber-attacks globally marking the inception of what is being hailed as the Global Smart Shield (GSS). The GSS is an expansion of the successful AI-based CPS tested in America and China, where 270,000 individuals volunteered to be fitted with Biosys microchips.

'All relevant actors in the G7 accept that sharing populace data with complex AI security systems through widespread populace microchipping is now essential for public safety and global security,' affirms the G7 release.

French commissioner Thierry Gaston expressed his full support for the Global Smart Shield and encouraged volunteers in France to come forward for microchipping, while announcing financial incentives provided by the French government.

Biosys Corp welcomed the international agreement and the $920 billion investment from the G7. CEO Zak Neumann, said, “In memory of our lost loved ones, we shall ensure that terror attacks such as 10/01, become a thing of the past. With the wonderful G7 agreement we can all share in the benefits of AI bio-security. The wellbeing benefits of neuro-web microchipping for individuals and families are astounding.”

The Cyber Liberties Union condemned the legislation, asking for government assurance that it would not lead to state mandates for untested smart nano-technology implants in civilians, as has been rumoured to have taken place in developing nations. While Sajeed Farahmandi of Indio-Bio-Tech-Alliance dismissed claims of unauthorized human testing in India as politically motivated ‘fake news’.

Deny Thanga, from pressure group EquiTech, welcomed voluntary nano-tech chipping, stating, “we have to ensure that minorities are given the opportunity to take part through govt. assistance, for too long access to BioTech has been the domain of the elites.”

CERTIFICATE OF DEATH

STATE Reg No 52-010389
REGISTRARS DISTRICT No 3702
REGISTRAR'S OFFICE No 4982

Name of Deceased:	**Chris**
Middle name	
Last Name:	**Foy**
Employment designation:	**Counsellor. Psychiatry. State Sector.**
Date of Birth:	**08.14.1981**
Date of Death:	**13.10.2026**
Age:	**45**
Kind of Business or Industry:	**Cognitive Behavioural Therapist. Grief Counsellor.**
Citizen of what country:	**USA**
Name of present spouse:	**N/A, divorced.**
State :	**California**
Full name of hospital:	**Schwatrzberg San Francisco General Hospital and Trauma Center**

Cemetery or crematorium:	**Cyprus View Crematorium**
Mortuary:	**Benbough Mortuary**
Coroner:	**J.T Elsworth**
Cause of death:	**Barbiturate overdose / Death by misadventure**
Antecedent causes:	**Acute myocardial failure**
Location of death:	**San Francisco County Jail #4**
Witnesses:	**N/A**

Nationwide Public Service Nanobot mandate passes into law

After FDA and CDC clearance, the federal government has passed regulations making 'nanobot' implantation mandatory for employees in federally regulated workplaces as part of the Global Smart Shield initiative. The mandate already applies to public sector employees in air, rail, and marine transportation. The goal is to provide a legal and unique identity through Universal Biometric ID, enabling digital ID-based services and allowing employers and government agencies to monitor behavioural and health data through advanced AI.

Zach Neumann, CEO of Biosys Corp and co-director of GSS, emphasized the importance of implantation for progress, social inclusion, and equity, stating that the technology has been proven 99% safe by reputable organizations. Neumann also encouraged participation, stating, "When it comes to implantation, if you have nothing to hide, then you have nothing to fear. And if you refuse to share, then you're refusing to care."

The President welcomed the historic passing of the bill, saying "My family and I were early adopters, and we are already seeing the health benefits of Nanobot implantation."

Plans are underway to launch Federal 'Get Chipped' walk-in centers in all states, and state employees will be required to undergo nano-chipping.

Congress is also considering extending the mandate to all US citizens, with non-compliance resulting in consequences such as loss of health insurance, restricted access to financial services and transportation, and potential legal charges. Presentation of an 'I'm chipped' certificate will become a mandatory requirement for current and future employment.

NEW YORK, THURSDAY

Human immortality by 2050, biotech CEO claims

In less than three years, all our bodies will be populated by thousands of microscopic machines, repairing damaged cells and organs, effectively wiping out diseases. The nanotechnology will also be used to save our identities 'for eternity'.

In an interview with the Zach Neumann, CEO of Biosys said that, if G7 governments can push through their nanobot implantation mandates then everyone who is alive in 2035 "will have the necessary technology within them to become immortal."

The exponential growth of Biosys nanotechnology has already proved that biotech has merged into a collaboration between man and machine, as nanobots now flow through human blood streams, purifying blood and merging with human consciousness.

Biosys, working with MIT and the University of London, has today revealed the results of successful experiments in 'tumour busting' nanoparticles that deliver killer genes to battle late-stage cancer, giving new hope to patients with inoperable tumours. The tests have shown that the new technique leaves healthy cells undamaged. Not only that, cells are being repaired to be 'as good as new' by the nanobots that have fused with human cells within the body.

"We've extended the range of human life," Neumann said. "Neuro-web nanobots are already curing all the diseases we associate with ageing. Nanobots swim in, and now even replace, biological blood, scouting out organs, cells and wounds that need repairs and simply fix them almost instantly. Damaged organs will be able to be regrown. Furthermore, with cerebral microchip implantation, memories and personalities are now able to be 'uploaded' and 'saved', so they can be reloaded after, say, a head trauma."

Neumann claims that by 2032 we'll be adding five years to our life expectancy with every two years that pass. "Within 20 years," he claims, "we'll be adding fifty years to each life, and in 35 to 40 years, with symbiotic bio-nano-tech, we will effectively become immortal." "The AI system we are about to reveal is called Infinity," Neumann said, "it is fully fused with human consciousness and is on the brink of becoming the first fully sentient AI. The singularity is here."

Neumann claims that fusing our bodies and brains completely with nano-biotechnology won't make us any less human than we are today. "If anything, this symbiosis will bring about an end to human suffering, make us more human, enhanced and even superhuman." "We are the species that pursues progress and changes who we are," he said, "Infinity offers the human race the opportunity to leap beyond all our evolutionary limitations. We see this progress as inevitable and are confident that with the backing of the WHO, UN, WEF, CDC, the US Govt, and the other G7 countries, international universal nanotech implantation mandates will bring health, equity and security to us all, enabling the final step to our dream of immortality."

Acknowledgements

I would like to thank the following people who have made the composition of this book possible:

David Pollard, Iona Italia, David Weinreb, Emily Ballou, Pamela Sund, Dan Milaschewski, Nick Marston, Mathew Hamilton, Neus Rodriguez, Irina Brantner, Marie Odile Hedon, Burial.

The Minister of Midway and The Society of Authors.

In memory of the pioneers of inner and outer space, Fay Weldon and Lynda Obst.

Ewan Morrison is the 2019 winner of the Saltire Society Prize for Fiction Book of the Year, for *Nina X*, (Fleet/Little Brown). *Nina X* is being adapted for film by David Mackenzie whose film *Hell or High Water* was Academy Award nominated for Best Picture. Ewan's most recent novel *How To Survive Everything* (Saraband, 2021) has been published in the US by Harper Perennial, in Denmark by Screaming Books and has been acquired for translation by Surhkamp, Germany and Grada, in the Czech republic. *How To Survive Everything* is currently being adapted as a TV series with Made Up Stories/Kindling Pictures/Fifth Season (*Nine Perfect Strangers, Anatomy of a Scandal*).

Ewan can be found on X at @mrewanmorrison

If you enjoyed this book, the author and publisher would love it if you left a review on Amazon, GoodReads or a similar website.